PHANTOM

PHANTOM

HELEN POWER

CamCat
Books

CamCat Publishing, LLC
Ft. Collins, Colorado 80524
camcatpublishing.com

Hardcover ISBN 9780744302660
Paperback ISBN 9780744302677
Large-Print Paperback ISBN 9780744302721
eBook ISBN 9780744302769
Audiobook ISBN 9780744302776

Library of Congress Control Number: 2023932287

Book and cover design by Maryann Appel

5   3   1   2   4

FOR MY FATHER,

WHO NEVER FAILS TO GIVE A HAND

TO THOSE WHO NEED IT.

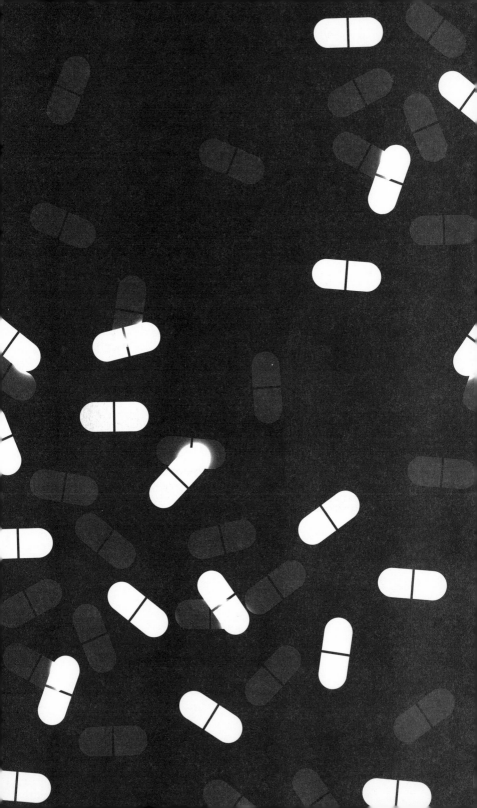

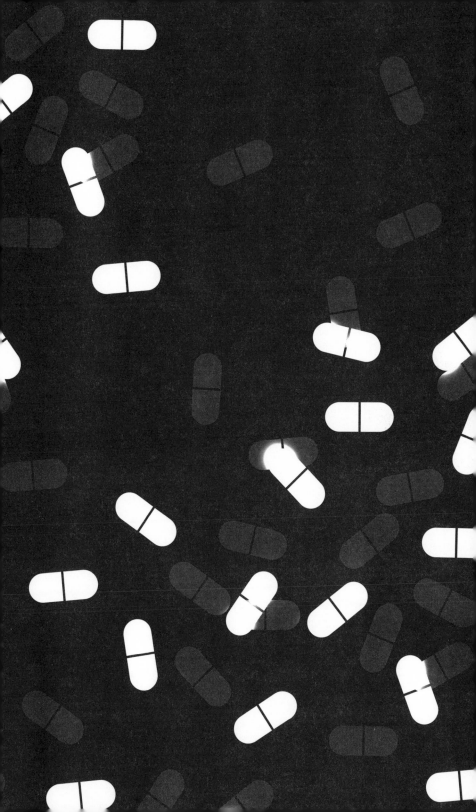

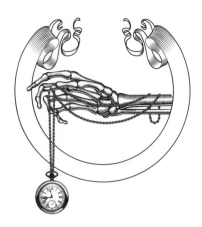

I T WON'T BE LONG NOW.

I float amid the crowd, riding the wave of the shallow and elite that swim around me like a school of fish in an aquarium. They have no idea there is a shark in their midst. Enthralled by my wit and beauty, partygoers converge upon me, eager to meet me, to be close to me, to know me. I feel like I am the honorary guest, despite the lack of invitation. Despite no one knowing who I am or why I'm really here.

I nurse my martini as I flit from conversation to conversation. They are all fools. Dullards chattering about the exhibit as if they know anything about true art. True art takes risks; it deviates from the norm, it makes people feel uncomfortable, aroused, afraid. I am a true artist, though my work will never be on display like this, at an event so pretentious and asinine. My work isn't of traditional mediums. My expertise isn't as derivative as paint on canvas or molded blocks of clay.

True creation comes from destruction.

I know that I shouldn't have come. But I couldn't resist. My gaze roams the room. I'm a predator stalking my prey. I spot her immediately. Sticking out like a sore thumb in this crowd of the sophisticated and affluent. The girl has no idea what is about to happen to her. That she has been chosen. That she is about to make the ultimate sacrifice, for art.

Envy and anticipation course through me as I watch her clutch a glass in her flawless left hand. I've been broken for too long. It's kept me from my life's purpose, from sharing my vision with the world. But soon I'll be whole again. Soon my name will return to the lips of everyone in this city, whether they're admiring my craft or simply don't understand it. Soon I can get back to my art.

It won't be much longer.

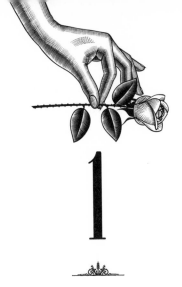

1

The event was disgustingly extravagant. Moonlight cascaded through the towering stained-glass windows and pooled on the marble floor, which gleamed a garish silver and gold. Massive crystal chandeliers strained against the chains suspending them from the vaulted ceiling. The gentle strains of a violin drifted through the hall, only to drown in the loud hum of the guests' mindless prattling. The scent of floor polish cut through the overpowering mix of expensive perfume and cologne, mingling with the unmistakable stench of narcissism and pretention. All around me, people strutted about in their decadent outfits. Draping ball gowns, blinding diamonds, and expressions laced with condescension seemed to be the required uniform of the evening.

I didn't belong here.

I shifted uncomfortably in my dress, which I'd "borrowed" from my roommate, Hanna. The Danish goddess was at least one size smaller than me, and I was starting to feel it in the bust and hip areas of the slinky red number I'd found in her closet. I placed my empty martini glass—only my third drink of the evening—on the platter of a waiter who brushed past me. I barely had the chance to grab a glass of red wine before he was gone. A splash of the liquid sloshed over the glass rim, spraying my wrist. I tensed, my eyes roving over my dress, but I hadn't spilled any on it. Hanna was quiet and I didn't know her very well, but I was pretty sure that if I borrowed her dress without permission and returned it damaged, she would kick me out of our loft apartment. She was the perfect roommate. She was hardly ever around, she let me use the main living area as my creative workspace, and she sometimes covered my part of the rent. She kept to herself and never asked prying questions—like when was I going to sell something, and why wasn't I part of any art shows, even the lousy ones like this one that featured no talent whatsoever. It was the ideal living situation, and I didn't want to screw it up.

I glanced around the hall. Satisfied that no one was looking my way, I surreptitiously bent my head and sucked the red wine off my wrist. Just at that moment, my eyes landed on a woman staring at me from over forty feet away. She looked just like everyone else here, but her arm was swathed in a sleek black sling. Flushing, I spun around and hurried in the opposite direction, humiliation hot on my heels. I had no idea who that woman was—she was too far away for me to get a good look—but it would be just my luck that someone with influence in the art world would be the one to catch me casually licking myself at a black-tie event. I pushed the embarrassment from my mind and didn't think of it again.

Another half hour and several failed attempts at networking crawled by. I glanced around the hall, but of course there were no clocks mounted on the cold stone walls. I hadn't worn a watch, because my cheap-ass timepiece would have been a dead giveaway that I didn't belong, and pulling out my phone would have had the same effect. Despite having no idea what time it was, I knew it was getting late. This reception would be winding down within an hour or two.

I shouldn't have come. I hadn't planned to. I'd gotten the invitation in the mail two weeks ago, and I'd thought about declining, despite the open bar. Amrita Tejal, one of my former classmates from college, was putting on an art exhibit. I hadn't heard from her since graduation, and part of me had assumed that she'd moved on, married, and given up the dream of being an Artist with a capital A. But no, she'd persevered and now she was displaying her work at the Grant Park Fine Art Gallery. The masochist in me decided to show up at the last minute. I needed to know what she did. I needed to see it for myself. I also couldn't pass up the free alcohol, even though it turned out to be watered down.

I'd made the rash decision to show up, and despite the appetizers and endless supply of alcohol, I was regretting it. I'd already gone through the main exhibit. I'd expected to see something intriguing, inspiring, intimidating, but instead Amrita's art was simply ... imitative. It had consisted of three narrow halls, the dull, off-white walls mounted with television screens. On them, there was a woman, the same woman on each screen, but in a different stage of undress. She was taking off her public persona—her business attire, her makeup, her facade—before retiring for the evening. The final panel, which took up an entire wall at the far end, depicted her standing by a window, stark naked. Not even a robe or a strategically placed shadow to hide her nakedness. I'd suddenly felt exposed in that moment. I was that woman, naked, mounted high for all to see, in my too-tight dress and fake Jimmy Choos.

Unable to spot another waiter, I dropped my wineglass in a potted fern. I casually approached the buffet table and selected a shrimp cocktail. I tried not to be obvious as I wolfed it down. Since Hanna was hardly ever around, she didn't keep our fridge fully stocked. I barely had enough money to cover rent from my part-time job as a dealer at the Horseshoe Hammond. I wasn't exactly pitching in for fresh produce.

My phone chirped and I glanced at the screen. It was my ex, Ben. I deleted the message without bothering to read it. He was awfully needy for a drug dealer. I'd told him I wouldn't give him the time of day after we broke up, and even though it was nighttime, I still wasn't going to respond to his texts.

"Roz! Ohmygoodness, you made it!"

I froze, jumbo shrimp half lodged in my throat. My cheeks heated up as I forced myself to swallow. I turned around.

"Amrita! It's been *so* long! How have you *been*?" My words oozed insincerity.

Amrita looked the same as I remembered. Tall and elegant, with smooth, brown skin and her hair pulled back into an elaborate twist. But her outfit was different. This one screamed wealth and success, despite this being, as far as I knew, her first art show. My attention was caught by the strange tone of one of her irises. Had she always had different-colored eyes?

"I'm doing really great. Clearly," Amrita said, gesturing around the crowded hall. She was doing better than "great." Everyone here had come to see her art. I couldn't even get so much as a form rejection letter back from the shitty little galleries around town, and she was having a show at Grant Fucking Park.

"I loved your exhibit. Very, uh, unique," I choked out the words.

Amrita smiled slightly. "Yes, the idea came to me in a dream."

Well, her dreams were more unoriginal than those of a teenage high schooler. If I'd been paid a nickel for every time I'd dreamed I was naked and on display, I'd be a millionaire. I twisted my lips into a pleasant smile. "I'm surprised you invited me."

Amrita was watching me, intently, wordlessly. She looked me up and down with her unnerving eyes. "I love the dress. It's very risqué. Who are you wearing? Abbiati?"

I smiled, though it felt more like baring my teeth. I hoped there wasn't shrimp caught in between them. "I'm not really sure. Someone else picked out the dress." That much was true. Who knew where Hanna had gotten it? Maybe it really was designer. More likely, it was Target.

I couldn't tell if she was buying what I was selling. She gave me a little smile. Aside from her initial enthusiasm at seeing me, she was very cool, calm, and collected. Nothing like the frenetic, energetic girl I knew in college. Back then, I would be tempted to douse her with a bucket of cold water just to get her to shut up. Now I was begging for her to say something, anything to end this silence and quiet the storm inside my head.

"So, is this your first art show?" I asked. I should have excused myself. What was I thinking, prolonging this torture? Jealousy reared its ugly head, and it took all my self-control not to gouge her perfect, hypnotic little eyes out.

"Yes. Yes, it is," Amrita said with a mysterious smile. "I hope you enjoy the rest of the evening. If you'll excuse me, I should be mingling. There are some important people here tonight."

Even though I'd wanted the conversation to end, her words still felt like a slap to the face. I wish I'd thought of telling her I had places to be. "As should I," I replied. I awkwardly spun around, swayed around another waiter carrying a tray, and swooped in, snatching up yet another martini.

I took a deep sip as I surreptitiously glanced back to watch Amrita dissolve into the crowd. I supposed that could have gone worse. She could have asked me about my own art.

"Are you a friend of Ms. Tejal's?" A vaguely British voice came from just behind my ear.

I tried not to flinch as hot breath tickled my neck. I turned around slowly and gave the speaker the once-over. A lazy smile clung to a remarkably unremarkable face. He wasn't tall; he only had a few inches on me. He had a receding hairline and premature wrinkles lined his forehead, but the suit he wore clung nicely to his abdominal muscles. And it was a decidedly *expensive* suit.

"We aren't friends. We went to college together," I said with a wave of my hand.

"I didn't think you looked like you'd be friends with her," he replied.

I narrowed my eyes. What did he mean by that? Could he tell that I didn't belong here? I bit back my retort when I caught sight of the Rolex on his wrist. Maybe I could get a free dinner out of him. "I'll take that as a compliment," I said instead.

He tossed me a knowing smile that was surprisingly attractive. I was suddenly glad I hadn't been rude. I was interested in getting to know him a little better.

I took a slow sip of another martini that had suddenly appeared in my hand. I casually looked away from this man, my eyes scanning the crowd, acting as if I wasn't interested in anything he had to offer.

"Are you an artist?"

"Yes," I replied. I didn't elaborate. He didn't have to know that I worked part-time and that I poured every free moment into working on my sculptures, half of which I'd burned or thrown out the window in fits of rage when they were rejected or critiqued unfairly.

"My name's Sylvain Dufour," he said primly in his British accent.

I didn't bother to respond or even glance in his direction.

He shifted slightly, as if trying to draw my attention. I finally deigned to give him a demure look. His eyes locked on mine. He was already smitten. I pushed aside any guilt I might feel at the fact that I was planning to use him. All I could afford to see were dollar signs in the form of his sparkling cufflinks and fine-tailored suit.

I gave him another once-over, my eyes lingering on his hair. At least he didn't have plugs. I much preferred a balding man over someone who was feebly battling his genetics.

"I'm Regan Osbourne," I said, keeping my tone casual as I returned my attention to the crowd.

"I haven't heard of you."

Ouch. "Well, I haven't heard of you either," I snapped without thinking. I pressed my lips together, holding my breath.

My fear that I'd turned him off was unfounded. Instead of recoiling, he sidled in a little closer. I fought the urge to roll my eyes. Men—especially the rich and self-entitled ones—never seemed to like nice girls.

"Why haven't I heard of you?" He didn't make it sound like an insult. He seemed genuinely curious.

Well, he hadn't seen my art. I swallowed, pushing aside that invasive thought. "I'm between projects. My work is more . . . private."

He nodded, and I had the dreadful feeling that he was reading between the lines. He knew I was a fraud. Untalented. Delusional.

"Ms. Tejal almost didn't have her work displayed here tonight," he said. "Sometimes you just need to know the right people."

At that, I perked up. I tried to hide my interest. "Do *you* know the right people?"

He didn't reply. Instead he gestured for a waiter to bring him another drink. I needed to learn how to do that.

"The right people?" I repeated impatiently, once he had another drink in hand.

Sylvain's cocky smirk was back. "Ms. Tejal had a benefactor. A man sponsoring her dreams. Otherwise, she wouldn't be where she is here today."

I stifled a snicker. "So, she has a sugar daddy?"

Sylvain's cerulean-blue eyes sparkled with amusement. "I'm not privy to the details of their arrangement." His eyes dropped from my face, and I waited patiently, trying not to laugh. Was he implying that he was interested in being my "benefactor?"

I finished yet another martini—my fourth? Fifth?—and Sylvain beckoned the waiter to bring me another. I giggled, then clamped my mouth shut, embarrassment flooding through me and heating my cheeks. I might not have been drunk, but I was well on my way there. "Are you trying to get me plastered or something?"

Sylvain smirked, then took a sip from his glass. I thought I heard him say, "Or something."

I blinked. "What was that?"

His lips curled into that same arrogant smile, but the alcohol infusing the blood in my veins made it seem less annoying, more beguiling. He didn't answer my question.

The rest of the night was a blur. I remembered laughing at a lot of things that seemed funny at the time. I remembered telling him he reminded me of James Bond, because of the suit and accent, but informing him that the beloved MI6 agent had a full head of thick hair. I remembered leaning heavily against him and whispering seductively in his ear. I remembered waving goodbye to a stoic-looking Amrita as I left with Sylvain, my arm linked around his waist. I remembered entering the cab, but not leaving it.

2

*S*unlight streamed through the window, its white-hot rays burning my retinas. I squeezed my eyelids shut as I swore under my breath. I felt as if I'd been hit by a bulldozer, and the pounding in my head rivaled the sound-track of a construction site. I rolled over, groaning, pulling the satin duvet over my head.

Duvet? I cracked one eye open.

"Where the hell am I?" I rubbed my temples as I sat up, taking in my sur-roundings. I was in a hotel room; that much was obvious. It was a lavish one at that, with its sturdy cherrywood furniture and ornate crown moldings. I was in a bed that was bigger than my childhood bedroom, and I didn't think I'd ever felt anything as soft as the mattress I lay on. My—I mean, Hanna's— red dress lay crumpled in a heap on the floor. A quick glance under the duvet revealed that I was naked.

Visions of Ted Bundy and Jeffrey Dahmer danced across my vision, courtesy of my mother. She'd had an inflated paranoia about serial killers and getting murdered, which made growing up in Chicago extra hard for the daughter of a single mother. If I was feeling introspective, I'd admit that that was one of the reasons why I ended up this way. Reckless and impulsive, in an effort to prove that I was nothing like my mother. But the city's most recent serial killer, the Phantom Strangler, was now inactive. For almost two years, he'd haunted the streets of Chicago, targeting young women in high-risk areas. He was known for striking at night, leaving no witnesses, no evidence, no trace. Like a ghost. No new victims had been found in the last year, so it was presumed he'd either found another hunting ground or died. Either way, he was no longer stalking the women of Chicago. Besides, if I'd been kidnapped by a serial killer, I doubted that I'd be waking up enveloped by luxury sheets in a five-star hotel.

Memories from last night trickled in along with the sound of running water from the room's adjoining bathroom. Last night's dance partner was in the shower, and I was relieved that I had some time to pull myself together before having to face him.

My phone chimed. I sighed, rolling out of bed to excavate it from where it was buried under Hanna's dress. The screen sported a brand-new zigzag crack all the way across its smudged face.

"Fan-fucking-tastic," I muttered.

The text was from Hanna. *Where are you? Rent was due yesterday. I'm not covering your half again.*

Another text chimed. *And where the hell is my red dress?*

My blood ran cold. How had she noticed it was missing so fast? I picked up the dress, groaning as my eyes snagged on the torn fabric. My new friend must have gotten a little carried away last night. Or I had. Either way, Hanna wasn't going to be happy when she discovered that not only had I ruined her good dress, but I didn't have enough money to cover even a third of my portion of the rent.

I swore, threw on the dress, and sat on the edge of the bed, thinking. This would be the third month in a row that she'd have to cover the rent—if I could manage to convince her to do it again. She wasn't going to be so forgiving this time, especially since I'd destroyed her property.

My eyes landed on a thick black wallet resting on the nightstand. Without giving myself the chance to think through what I was about to do, I grabbed it and flipped it open. The pockets were empty—no IDs, no credit cards—but that barely registered once I spotted the crisp hundred-dollar bills lining the inner fold. My agile fingers trailed over the bills as I counted. Twelve hundred dollars. I licked my lips as I stared at the money. I could do a lot with that much money.

The running water stopped.

"Regan? You awake?" A voice called from the bathroom.

I was gone before he could return for a second round.

I nearly got run over by a white sedan as I jogged in my stilettos across the street, but I was in too much of a hurry to stop to give the driver a piece of my mind. I needed to put as much distance between myself and the Ritz-Carlton as humanly possible before the man I picked up last night realized I'd stolen from him.

I was so unbelievably stupid. I shouldn't have acted so impulsively. I should have waited. I should have talked to him. I might have been able to get him to lend—or even give—me money. So much for having a sugar daddy. I was pretty sure that they frowned upon theft. And it was a theft of over five hundred dollars, which was bigger than a mere misdemeanor, if he chose to press charges. The only reason I knew this was because I'd gone to a few law classes in my sophomore year of college when I'd had the hots for the TA. After four dates, he'd professed his undying love for me. Two days later, I caught him in his office with his head between some chick's legs. A chick who was also taking that class. I'd been made to look like a fool, and after I wiped away my tears, I planned the perfect revenge. I set it up so that the prof would catch him with his pants down—quite literally—and he lost his job and his funding for grad school. I ended up dropping out of the class less than a week later.

I may have enjoyed doling out justice, but I wasn't particularly interested in the law.

I hopped on the el, ignoring the revulsion radiating from my fellow passengers. My dress was ripped along the outer side of my breast, and I distinctly remembered not having bothered with waterproof mascara last night. I smiled at an elderly woman who was wearing a pink floral jacket and Mary Jane shoes. She looked away quickly.

Once I got home, I was greeted by a royally pissed-off roommate at the door to our loft apartment. Her wild, icy blue eyes took in my appearance with unrestrained fury. She was petite, but she could be fiery, and it took a lot for her to get this worked up. I took a giant step backward.

"*Milde* Moses!" she snapped.

I didn't know what that meant, so I wordlessly handed her my share of the rent. And the previous month's rent.

Her mouth fell open as she flipped through the bills. She eyed her torn dress and my hooker heels. "How did you get the money?" Her voice was clouded with suspicious disbelief.

What she was likely thinking wasn't too far from the truth. I sighed. My head was pounding, and I couldn't conjure up enough energy to be disgusted with myself. "How do you think?"

I started to walk away, but she grabbed my arm. "My dress," she said through clenched teeth.

Blood boiling, I tore my arm away. I pulled the dress over my head and threw it at her feet. I strode past her and went to the "kitchen," which was a corner of the loft that was basically just a stove, a fridge, and a foot and a half of cracked countertop that engulfed the sink. The landlord had slapped a layer of cheap linoleum onto the cement floor before calling it a day. We had a lopsided bookcase that was our "pantry," which currently consisted of a half-empty box of cereal and a sleeve of crackers that had expired in 2021. I poured the dregs of the coffeepot into a chipped "I ♥ Chicago" mug and took a deep swallow. It was cold. It was chunky. It was bitter as hell. But it was *coffee*.

Already, my head had started to clear. I glared down at the scuffed linoleum. I sighed and turned toward Hanna, who still lingered by the front door. My best approach was diplomacy. "I'm sorry," I coughed out. "I'm a really shitty roommate."

Hanna's eyes went so large that I thought they might pop out of her head. That would have been an interesting sight. "You're not . . . shitty." Her delicate accent made the curse word sound ever so quaint.

"You don't have to be nice to me," I said. I suddenly felt so tired. Exhausted beyond my twenty-nine years. I hated thinking about how old I was. I was twenty-nine, and what did I have to show for it? I had a lousy part-time job, a dream I was no closer to attaining than I was ten years ago, and one friend—a roommate I never saw and who probably secretly hated my guts.

Hanna sighed. "Put on some clothes," she said, taking off in the direction of her "bedroom," which was actually just a corner of the loft apartment that was cordoned off with an old velvet curtain that she'd picked up at a flea market. It looked like it belonged in a fake psychic's reading room, adorning a table underneath a murky crystal ball. She hesitated. "Your *own* clothes," she added, before disappearing behind the curtain.

I went to the bathroom and took a long, hot shower, or while the hot water lasted, which wasn't very long these days. We lived in an old turn-of-the-century warehouse that had been renovated into an apartment complex. The pipes—like everything else in this place—were run down and on the brink of total collapse. Of course, our slumlord couldn't be bothered with fixing something as trivial as plumbing. Though at least today the water was relatively clear and not the rusty hue of spewed-up blood.

Afterward I slipped into my pink silk bathrobe, grabbed a bowl from the kitchen, and poured some dry cat food into it. I opened the loft door and set it on the floor.

"Hey, Little Guy, it's breakfast time!" I called out.

There was a mangy gray stray cat that spent time in and around our apartment building. I didn't know how it got into the building, let alone onto our floor, but it was in the corridor more often than not. Hanna said it only kept showing up because I fed it. But how could I resist those emerald-green eyes that looked up at me like I hung the moon? I wasn't a *total* monster. I might not have had enough money to keep myself fed, but I'd be damned if I didn't make sure I had enough kitty kibble to keep Little Guy coming back. I went back into the apartment and stood by the window, nursing another mug of coffee. A white sedan sat at the curb, and I could make out the faint outline of a man sitting behind the steering wheel. That looked like the car that nearly hit me on my way out of Sylvester—Simon?—whatever his name was's hotel.

I tried to read the license plate, but I wasn't at the right angle. Not that it mattered, since I hadn't caught the license plate of the previous car. Could it be the same one? I shook my head, turning away. I was always paranoid when I was hungover.

3

"Hit me." The high-pitched voice shot like a dagger straight through the center of my heavy, hungover skull.

I gritted my teeth. There was something about this woman that reminded me of my mother, but I wasn't sure if it was the too-tight, low-cut blouse, the lipstick that made her skin a sickly, sallow hue, or the fact that she smelled like she was dipped in gin. I wasn't unused to dealing with her type at the casino where I worked, but some days my tolerance was lower than others.

And today was one of those days.

"I'd be more than happy to hit you," I muttered. I grimaced, hoping she hadn't heard me. No such luck.

"Ex-CUSE me?" The woman shrilled.

I flipped the card, and I couldn't contain my smirk: 23. "House wins," I said sweetly.

The woman's bloodshot eyes narrowed as she glared at me indignantly. "You did that on purpose!"

Before I could respond, Al, my boss, appeared as if out of nowhere. He was always skulking around in the shadows, spying on his dealers on the floor. Waiting for us to screw up. "Now, ma'am, that's a strong allegation . . ." he began in his raspy smoker's voice.

The woman huffed. "This young lady has been very rude today. You should make it your policy to hire polite young girls, like the Rivers Casino does."

"Fill out a comment card," I grumbled.

Al shot me a derisive look. "Thank you, ma'am. I'll take that under advisement."

The woman picked up her oversized leopard-print purse and stormed off in a staged huff. She didn't make it very far, because she plopped herself down on a stool at the next table over.

Al ran a hand through his unruly copper hair. "Roz, we need to talk."

I rolled my eyes. "Uh-oh. Are you breaking up with me?"

He didn't laugh. "In a manner of speaking."

"Oh please. You're not going to fire me. How many of your dealers can do this?" I picked up the deck of cards and shuffled them with an exaggerated, professional flourish.

"Yes, Roz, you're good with your hands, but we need our dealers to be more than that."

I stiffened as the niggling suspicion that he wasn't bluffing began to sink in. "Fine. I'll be 'more than that.' I can be polite as hell to these dumbass customers."

A twitch developed beneath Al's right eye. That was never a good sign. "Roz, you will be paid until the end of this shift, but I want you to leave now."

I opened my mouth, then closed it. "W-what about second chances?"

Al rubbed the bridge of his nose with his thumb and index finger. "Roz, I've given you a dozen second chances. There are some things you just can't seem to learn, and customer service is one of them." He sighed. "Leave your vest in the staff room on your way out." He approached the woman, who glanced my way with a smirk that was so much like my mother's. He was likely sucking up to her, telling her that he'd fired me. *Bastard.*

I stomped my way to the staff room to grab my stuff from my locker. I threw my vest in the unflushed toilet in the stall at the far end—the one that my coworker, Amber, always used and which always seemed to be clogged.

I dawdled by the exit, lingering in the shadow of the statue of some ancient Greek god that I was 90 percent sure I'd memorized the name of in college. What the hell was I supposed to do now? I had no money. I'd given nearly all of it to Hanna to cover rent. I hadn't expected to lose my job. If I was being completely honest with myself, I knew I wouldn't be selling any of my artwork anytime soon. I was in between projects, and I hadn't so much as ventured into my workspace in over three weeks.

I gazed out onto the floor. The flashing lights, the chiming undertone of the slot machines, and the faint aroma of sweat and cheap beer called to me like a siren song. Today was the day. I could feel it. I would win big, and then I wouldn't even have to worry about getting another job for a while. I flipped open my wallet and ran my fingers over the last three hundred dollars I had.

I hit the blackjack table, and I lost every penny of it.

4

I woke to the sound of pounding on the front door. I peeled one eye open, then the other. The entire room swirled around me. I squeezed my eyes shut, took a deep breath, and then cracked them open again. The faded orange sheet that separated my bed from the rest of the loft glared down at me. Memories surfaced in bits and pieces. After I was fired, I'd gambled away the rest of my money, and then I'd found myself at a dive bar. At least I hadn't needed any money there. The kind of men who frequented those types of places were so predictable, and as expected, they were eager to keep me drinking. I was in my "bedroom," which meant at least I hadn't gone home with any of them. I glanced at the empty bed beside me. Thankfully, it looked like I hadn't brought home any strays either.

The furious knocking persisted.

"Hanna? Can you get it?" I mumbled. There was no response from her side of the loft. Even though I'd said it quietly, she would have heard me if she was home, because the curtain walls did little to muffle sound.

I bit my lower lip. It was rare that I blacked out and couldn't remember anything. Although I did have one vivid memory from last night. Me, standing in the street, screaming at the startled driver of a white sedan. I accused him of following me and flipped him off before I dove for the sidewalk to puke.

Maybe the visitor would go away. I lay in bed, staring up at the disturbingly large spider web that draped from the high ceiling. I didn't want to answer the door, if only because it would probably aggravate my unwanted visitor just as much as their knocking was aggravating me.

But the banging chiseled at my resolve as it continued rhythmically in time with the pounding of yet another hangover headache. Grunting, I rolled out of bed. I gave myself a quick glance in the floor-length mirror I had propped up against the exposed brick wall. I was still wearing my uniform from last night—the white blouse and black satin pants, minus the casino-issued vest, of course. I ran my fingers through my dull shoulder-length brown hair and used a finger to rub away the smudged mascara under my equally dull brown eyes. Eyes that were bloodshot and familiar. I looked so much like my mother in this moment. Disheveled, hungover, and alone.

I tore myself away from the mirror, pushing aside these troubling thoughts. "I'm coming!" I called out as I shuffled across the loft.

"What do you want?" I snapped as I swung open the door. But it wasn't Carl, the pot-bellied building manager who usually only showed up when rent was due or to act out a pathetic half attempt at a booty call. It wasn't my ex-boyfriend Ben either, who was equally likely to show up in the wee hours of the morning, begging me to take him back.

It was the man from Amrita's art show. The one I'd slept with.

The man I stole from.

"Good morning, Regan. Looks like you had another late night." His eyes roamed my body, and I felt the familiar sensation of nausea roiling in my stomach.

"Simon. I—I hadn't expected to see you again." I would not bring up the money if he didn't. If he did, I would pretend to be offended, slap him, and slam the door in his face. My plan was foolproof.

His brows knit together. "Sylvain."

"What?"

"My name is Sylvain." A flash of irritation crossed his face. He'd always seemed aloof and unaffected by everything—at least, that was the impression I'd gotten during the few hours I'd known him. Although, I'd been half drunk for most of that time, so I couldn't trust any of my initial impressions of him.

I looked him up and down. "Sorry." I didn't sound like I meant it. I gnawed at my lower lip as worry set in. Sylvain could be dangerous. He could go to the police and have charges brought against me. I probably shouldn't be pissing him off, at least not any more than I already had. I smiled tersely and tried again, infusing chagrin and self-deprecation into my tone. "I knew your name started with an *S*. I was pretty drunk that night."

"Not *that* drunk," Sylvain said. He stepped past me and entered the loft, his vibrant blue gaze always moving, roving across the surroundings and taking everything in. I could see my frumpy little double bed beyond my orange curtain and my cheeks went hot. I really didn't want him to see the shit pile I called home.

"How did you find me?" I put my hands on my hips. I refused to show how embarrassed I was.

Sylvain shot me a strange look. "You told me."

What exactly had I told him? Where I lived? Where he could find me? I didn't want to let him know that I barely remembered that night. But I did remember the morning after. I did remember stealing his money.

I frowned at that realization. I'd gotten blackout drunk last night too. That was twice in less than a week. What did that say about me? I shook away those thoughts, wiping my clammy palms on my slacks. It wasn't like me to be so nervous. Then again, it wasn't like me to steal that much money. I wasn't exactly Pippi Longstocking, but I wasn't a career criminal either. I'd broken up with Ben because I hadn't enjoyed the all-consuming guilt that accompanied courting a drug dealer.

Sylvain strolled farther into the loft, agilely sidestepping the coatrack. He continued to take in the surroundings. He glanced over the kitchen, the tidy curtain that concealed Hanna's bedroom, and the disheveled sheet that engulfed mine. He hesitated in front of my workspace and peered at one of my sculptures.

The past few years I'd been experimenting with sculpting with wire. I'd been intrigued by the female form, manipulating iron wire into the shape of a figure emerging from wire mesh. I was inspired by the way that Auguste Rodin carved women from marble. My third-grade art teacher had had a little statuette of *Danaid* on her desk, and I remembered the first time I saw it. Instantly fascinated by the smooth arch of her back erupting from the rugged marble, I couldn't help but relate to her. I wanted nothing more than for the ground to open up and swallow me whole and take me away from my life, which, at the ripe old age of eight, was just a series of disappointments, one after another.

"This yours?" Sylvain asked, catapulting me back into the present.

I nodded, suddenly feeling nervous. He continued to study the artwork, his eyes following the lines of wire that had taken months to manipulate into how I envisioned it in my mind.

"I can see why I've never heard of you."

My heart plummeted. To my horror, I felt the prickle of tears in my eyes. Why was his opinion so important to me? What did he know? He wasn't an artist. He was no one. "Well, it's still a work in progress," I lied.

Sylvain raised an eyebrow. "Don't quit your day job." He gave another exaggerated, assessing look around the apartment and glanced at his watch. It was ten in the morning on a weekday. "Assuming you have one?"

I scowled. "You were a lot nicer when you were looking to get lucky. Is there something you want?"

Sylvain's eyes narrowed. "Well, I didn't exactly 'get lucky,' now did I?"

"Well, I was walking with a limp the next day, so I beg to differ," I snapped back.

Sylvain's lip twitched. "I would say that having almost two grand in cash stolen wouldn't constitute as me being 'lucky.'"

I rolled my eyes. "It was only twelve hundred dollars."

Sylvain's eyes widened and I immediately caught my slip, but it was too late. I spoke quickly, before he had a chance to respond. "If you're here for the money, then I'll have to tell you that I've spent it all already."

"On what? The finer luxuries of life?" To emphasize his point, he looked deliberately at one of two lawn chairs and a folding table that served as our living room furniture.

I pinched my lips together. "I spent it on rent. And food." I added the last part in an attempt to garner some sympathy.

No such luck. Sylvain didn't seem to hear me. He continued to wander around my apartment. I took the opportunity to study him. He wore a suit similar to the one he'd sported at the art show, though I could tell it was less expensive. His thinning hair teased me with glimpses of his scalp from across the room, and I realized that he wasn't quite as physically fit as he'd seemed when I'd examined him through alcohol-infused glasses. My eyes lingered on the little paunch that put the buttons of his shirt to hard work. I'd been apt in my assessment that he was like a low-rent James Bond with a dad bod.

He perused more of my other sculptures, ones that I'd been unable to sell but hadn't destroyed or discarded. Some of them were made of iron or copper wire, and others were made from things I'd found in dumpsters, trash I'd repurposed, fusing them together with my handy welding torch. A lot of it was experimental, and sadly, it looked as such.

Sylvain leaned over my pile of unused items, which smelled faintly of rot and mildew. In hindsight, I was *really* lucky that Hanna let me live here.

He rummaged around the pile and picked up an old mannequin arm. The fingernails were painted with chipped red paint, and the arm had been severed just below the elbow. The plastic "flesh" was melted, as if it had been exposed to extreme heat. It had caught my eye when I found it in a dumpster, and I'd been looking for the perfect project for it. It could add a hint of the macabre to an otherwise idyllic piece. If only I could figure out how to make it work.

Sylvain glanced at me, but luckily, he didn't make any snide remarks before returning the arm to the top of the pile.

I swallowed. I wanted to say something sarcastic or cheeky to lighten the tension, but for once I couldn't think of anything. Not even something that would offend him and get him to leave. Instead, I said, "I can get the money back."

Sylvain stared at me. Those haunting blue eyes were the most notable part of him, and the intensity with which he stared at me sent a shiver scuttling down my spine.

"I mean, it will take some time. But I'll get it back."

Still no response. Still he watched me with his unreadable, captivating, piercing cerulean blues.

I licked my lips. Desperation crept into my next words. "Of course, I—I'll pay you back with interest." I was unemployed and broke. Where was I going to get the money?

Sylvain waved his hand in the air dismissively. "I have absolutely no interest in your money."

I froze. Sure, I'd slept with him that night, but I wasn't a sex worker. I wasn't that desperate. Yet.

Seeing my expression, Sylvain laughed. "I don't want you to pay me back with sex either." He sounded slightly disgusted. I tried not to be too offended, although I had looked in the mirror after rolling out of bed, and I hardly blamed him. I wasn't at my prettiest hungover, or in broad daylight. This loft had a lot of things going against it, but there was a lot of natural light, which was good for my workspace, but it wasn't exactly a pasty-white girl's best ally.

"Well, then, what is it that you want, exactly?" I allowed some bite into my words. I wouldn't be toyed with. "Spit it out."

"Remember Ms. Tejal's art show? I told you she had a benefactor—a patron of the arts, as it were."

I shrugged. "Vaguely."

"Well, I could play a similar role for you."

"Don't fuck with me. I can tell you think that my work is trash."

Sylvain smirked. "I would say it's quite literally trash." He had a point, but I still felt the sting of his words. "I don't want your artwork, but you do have something that I want."

He deliberately lifted the severed mannequin arm from the pile of garbage. He looked at me expectantly.

Despite the tension in the room, I laughed. "Have yourself at it. I just got that from the Macy's dumpster last spring. Take it, and we can call ourselves even."

Sylvain shook his head. "I believe you misunderstood me." He put down the arm and stalked toward me. He stopped only inches away and reached down, picking up my delicate yet rough hand with his soft one. He ran a well-manicured fingernail gently across my wrist, as if to mime slicing it off.

His eyes met mine. I gasped and pulled away, my hand tingling from where we'd broken contact. "What the hell?" I still didn't understand, but his unwavering eyes sent another chill down my spine. The horrifying realization dawned as I swallowed. "You want *my* hand?"

"Yes."

"My hand?" I repeated, panic edging into my voice.

"You're hardly putting it to any good use." He smirked as he glanced back at my artwork, his opinion clearly etched on his features.

I licked my lips. "Are you serious?" I laughed, but this time it sounded desperate, manic, hysterical. "Are you a cannibal or something?"

He didn't respond. He just continued to look at me with an air of faint condescension.

"What the hell do you want my hand for?"

"I will put it to better use than you would."

This brought half a dozen disturbing images to mind, none of which I ever wanted to think of again. I shoved them from my thoughts. "Get the fuck out."

Sylvain didn't seem to be surprised by my outburst. In fact, he seemed to be expecting it. "I'd be able to offer you a handsome sum of money."

"Get. The. Fuck. Out." My heart was racing. My stomach churned. I was going to be sick, and I didn't want it to be while he was still here. I needed him out—out of my apartment and out of my life.

Sylvain looked down at me, his head angled slightly. "I didn't expect you to say yes right away." He looked away and scanned the loft once again. "They rarely do," he added thoughtfully, almost to himself.

He reached into his suit's coat pocket and pulled out an embossed card. There was nothing on it other than a name, Sylvain Dufour, and a phone number. "Call me. When you change your mind. We can negotiate. I'm able to offer more than just money."

He left without another word, and I barely made it to the bathroom before I was sick all over the cracked linoleum.

5

I should have known that that bastard Al was going to blacklist me. But who would have thought that he had connections at every casino in and around Chicago? Not a single one of them was willing to even glance at my résumé, let alone give me an interview. I spent the next few weeks drifting from store to store, dropping off applications. At this point, it didn't really matter *where* I got a job. I just needed cash. Hanna expected me to replace the dress, and it turned out that it was a lot more expensive than a simple outfit from Kmart. I didn't have enough money for food, let alone to pay her back. I spent my nights drinking at bars and scrolling through Tinder, looking for guys who looked spendy enough to buy me dinner. I was even desperate enough to swipe right on any guy holding a large fish in his profile picture. While this was universally acknowledged as the sign of a douchebag, at least it meant that he might have the means to feed me.

I was sitting on my bed, sipping cold coffee and flipping through job ads on my laptop when a car alarm started blaring. I tried to ignore it at first. But it didn't stop. I jumped to my feet and glared out the window, as if the sheer hostility I was radiating would send the car's owner out to silence it. If it was in the process of being stolen, couldn't the thieves move a little quicker? I returned to my bed and tried to focus on my job hunt. I'd already dropped off résumés at most of the places that were cropping up, but something new had to appear. I needed it to. After what felt like twenty minutes of the alarm relentlessly gouging its way through my concentration, I swore and decided to go down to investigate. I would break into the car myself to turn the damn thing off.

As soon as I hit the pavement, the siren quit.

"Seriously?" I said to the deserted street. I shivered, then groaned when I looked down and realized I hadn't even put on my shoes. It was the middle of the night, and I was standing outside barefoot. A homeless person gave me the side-eye as he shuffled to the other side of the street. I must have looked pathetic. No wonder I couldn't get a job. I needed to lay off the booze. It was ruining my skin, and the bags under my eyes were carrying their own luggage. Even Hanna, who I'd only seen once since the dress incident, commented on my appearance during our fifteen-second conversation a few days ago. I still never knew where she went. She was almost always working, and I couldn't help but wonder why she didn't have a better living situation. I was too afraid to bring this topic up in conversation, because she just might realize that she could afford something a hell of a lot better than the crap show we were currently inhabiting.

I heard a loud meow, and despite my crappy mood, a broad grin spread across my face. A familiar gray form trotted up to me and rubbed against my leg.

"Hey, Little Guy. Aren't you a little cutie patootie?" I said in that embarrassing voice that people use when talking to babies and pets. If anyone I knew ever heard me, I'd have to shoot myself in the head rather than endure the well-deserved ridicule.

He gazed up at me pitifully.

"I'm sorry, I don't have any food. Aren't there any mice for you to eat? I think I saw a few on my way down the stairs." He continued to stare at me with droopy eyes that tugged on my heart strings. I bit my lip. "Do you like stale crackers?"

He gave me a look of disgust before skulking off. I sighed, self-loathing swirling in my gut. Even Little Guy wanted nothing to do with me. I turned to head back upstairs, but something on the street caught my eye. It was a white sedan, parked just a dozen feet from where I stood. I'd never noticed many white sedans on the road in Chicago, but lately they seemed to be everywhere.

I shifted from foot to foot as I stared at the car. Was it a coincidence? Or was the driver actually following me? There was only one way to find out.

Before I could give myself a chance to think it through, I strode toward the sedan and pounded on the driver's window. To my surprise, it rolled down.

The man behind the steering wheel regarded me with cold eyes. He was cloaked in shadow, but I could make out his buzz-cut scalp and the outline of tattoos that slithered up the side of his neck. *Shit.*

I couldn't back down now. "Are you following me?" I asked boldly, feeling anything but.

The man cocked his head. "Get in."

I let out a bark of laughter. "Get *in*? As in get in your car? What kind of idiot do you think I am? You're not even bothering to offer me candy!"

He pulled out a gun and pointed it at my face. "Get in."

Shit, shit, shit. I glanced down the street. No one was around. Even the homeless guy was long gone.

"Don't even think about it." His voice was calm, but there was a lethal edge to it.

"Look, I don't have any money," I said. "I'm not even wearing shoes."

"Get in the car or I'll blow your fucking head off."

My mother didn't teach me much, other than how to mix a cocktail and never to combine vodka and beer, but she did tell me not to let a psycho take you to a second location. That's how you earn a leading role in your very own episode of *20/20*. The Phantom Strangler had been officially labeled inactive by the Chicago PD, and there were currently no other known serial killers in the area. At this moment, however, I wasn't worried about being strangled by a serial killer so much as being executed by a tattooed, gun-wielding gangster.

I stood my ground, trembling on the cold pavement. I would not get into the car, but I was too chickenshit to attempt running in zigzags down the street. This guy looked like he might have an itchy trigger finger and better-than-average aim.

I jumped when the passenger door swung open and another thug stepped out. In a few quick strides he was on me, grabbing my arm and tossing me into the backseat. He climbed in after me, pulling out his own gun.

"Move and your pretty face will have another hole in it."

The thug in the front threw the car into drive and tore down the street. The thug in the back surveyed me; his dark eyes trailed over my body as a sinister smirk tugged on his lips. He gestured with his gun. "Put your seat belt on."

It took me three tries to clasp the buckle with my trembling fingers. It was a good sign that he wanted me to put on my seat belt. That meant he didn't want me hurt, right? At least, not yet. As the car sped down the street, I contemplated jumping out of the moving vehicle, but the thug kept his gun trained on me the entire time. I wouldn't so much as get my seat belt off before I had a hole in my skull. Dully, I wondered if that was why he wanted me to put the seat belt on. Not because he wanted to keep me safe, but because it was the same as being tied to my seat.

The thug grinned at me the entire ride, seeming to bask in my fear like a languid cat bathing in sunshine. He clearly had a few screws loose, and I couldn't help but wonder about the sick depravities that must have been running through his mind to have him leering like that. I'd broken out in a cold sweat by the time we reached our destination in the bad part of town. Not that I lived in a "good" part of Chicago, but there were shades of bad, and this area was darker than most. West Garfield Park.

"Get out."

I shook my head vehemently. Smiley's mouth was still twisted into a perverse grin as he grabbed my arm, fingers digging into my flesh as he yanked me out of the car. I let myself be dragged toward the nearest building. The brick exterior was crumbling, the windows were boarded up, and the front porch sagged so heavily I thought it would collapse under our weight.

I'm going to die here.

The rotting wood of the porch was squishy, reminding me that I was barefoot. I stifled a shudder as the first thug gave me a long look. He had a thick, gnarled scar that ran along the side of his face, from his eye to his lip. That lip curled at my expression as he pushed open the front door. Scarface turned, still smirking as he held the door open for me. Smiley gestured with his gun for me to enter. I licked my lips, glancing back one last time. The street was deserted, but even if there were someone out there, I doubted they'd help. They wouldn't dare call the police. Snitches get stitches, or in this case, they would get a hole in the head.

Once inside the building, Smiley tucked his gun into his pants. I glanced around the narrow entryway. Dark wallpaper curled, revealing garish yellow paint underneath. The floorboards were ancient, and something scurried across the floor, diving into the shadows.

Smiley shoved me with the palm of his hand. I looked up at him, desperation and tears pooling in my eyes. He waggled his eyebrows and nodded toward the next room.

My entire body trembled as I stood there, straining my eyes, peering into the darkened room. What lay beyond that doorway? I inched forward, slowly, trying to get hold of my surroundings. Other than a staircase that led upward, there was nowhere to run. Smiley still blocked the exit, and I would *not* be one of those idiot girls in horror movies who run *upstairs* when being chased. That's how you end up thrown out a window and splattered on the pavement. I gritted my teeth and shook away these thoughts.

A light flashed on, nearly blinding me. A familiar figure filled the doorway.

"Roz?" He seemed more confused than I was.

"*Ben?*"

6

Ben looked better than he had the last time I'd seen him. His thick black hair was neatly cropped just above the ears, and his skin was clear and blemish-free. I hadn't seen him in person since a few weeks after we'd broken up, when he'd shown up at the loft in the middle of the night to beg me to take him back. He'd looked sleep-deprived, with days' worth of stubble dusting his chin and cavernous pits all but swallowing his forest-green eyes. I'd felt a rare bout of pity for him in that moment, but I'd forced myself to shove it aside and sent him away.

Now, the exhaustion he'd been wearing like a second skin was shed, revealing a new man underneath. He radiated authority and power. His presence seemed to fill the space between us, and I fought the urge to take a step backward. He looked like he'd been working out even more than before, with thick muscles straining against the confines of his black cotton T-shirt. He'd always been tall and muscular, built like a linebacker, though he'd never played sports in school. He looked like a football player, but in reality he'd been the stoner hanging out behind the bleachers, at least before he dropped out. Ben had never been a team player.

I peered into the room beyond him. Just in my line of sight, there was a table weighed down by rows of thick wads of cash. I sucked in a breath as I glanced back at Ben, who was still watching me. My eyes were drawn to the fresh set of tattoos that crept up his neck. Tattoos that were identical to the ones on the thugs who'd kidnapped me. A nest of vipers knotted across his skin, their bodies writhing around a black skull with crimson-inked eyes.

"I see you're moving up in the underworld," I said. I clamped my mouth shut. I talked too much when I was nervous, and at this point, I was beyond nervous.

Ben grinned, a toothy grin that was slightly crooked. Seeing it, I was surprised that I felt nothing, even though that was the charmingly imperfect smile that made me fall for him. "Yeah, I'm running the show now. You impressed?"

I made a noncommittal sound, caught myself, and nodded. It was never a good idea to offend Ben. He gestured for me to follow him into the room. I did as he wordlessly asked, but I instantly regretted it. It wasn't because of the peeling paint, the shabby furniture, or the fact that the ceiling looked like it was straining to kiss the floor. It wasn't because two more thugs lounged on the tattered sofa under the window, their predatory eyes tracking my every movement. No, it was the far wall that made me question all the decisions I'd made that brought me to this point.

A black metal rack took up most of the wall, and it was filled with guns. Not just handguns, but sawed-off shotguns, machine guns, rifles, and something that looked like a bazooka. It had guns that I didn't even know the names of, ones that I'd only ever seen in Ben's video games. It was obvious that he was doing a lot more than just dealing weed. I gulped.

"You haven't been returning my calls. Or my texts," Ben said.

My eyes whipped back to him. I needed to get out of here. Ben wasn't exactly stable, which was one of the reasons why I'd dumped him in the first place. Honestly, I should have left him the minute I found out he was a drug dealer. I may not have been a saint, and I would occasionally get baked, but I wasn't a criminal. It wasn't at all appealing to me to be dating one. But Ben was a smooth talker with an irresistible grin. He told me that he was only dealing to supplement his income. "It's just weed," he'd said, that irritating smirk tilting his lips and making me feel like a stupid little girl.

He never outright told me, but I suspected when his job became more than that. He started taking me out to nicer places, restaurants that he never should have been able to afford on his mechanic's salary. He leveled up his wardrobe, which had previously consisted of stained T-shirts and tattered jeans, to include a kitschy gold chain that swung heavily from his neck. And then, on his birthday, I decided to go to the garage to surprise him with a bottle of cheap wine.

He wasn't there. His boss had said that he'd quit months earlier. I would have dumped him then and there, but I'd clung to the feeble hope that I was overthinking things.

A few weeks later, he went off on a teen who'd slapped my ass on the bus. He beat the kid to a bloody pulp while I screamed at him to stop. That was the moment I realized I'd screwed up by staying with him. That was when I'd said goodbye, packed up my toothbrush, tampons, and thongs that I'd kept in a drawer at his dingy apartment, and ignored every text and call that came from him since.

"My phone broke," I replied, unable to meet his eye.

Ben's green eyes perused my face. "Liar," he whispered.

I swallowed. "What?"

He shook his head. "For a gambler, you sure need a better poker face. It isn't the worst I've seen, but I know all your tells. I know you, Roz. Better than you know yourself. You can't bluff."

"Good thing I prefer blackjack, then," I replied. I licked my lips. "What am I doing here, Ben?"

Ben blinked, slowly, the action almost exaggerated. "What are you doing here?" he repeated, incredulity seeping into his tone. "I was going to ask *you* that."

"Your thugs brought me here at gunpoint. I—"

"Harris!" Ben bellowed.

Smiley entered the room. His beady eyes focused on me before returning to Ben. Perspiration leaked down the vipers on his neck. His sneer wavered.

"Why is she here? You're supposed to be watching her," Ben said. He seemed calm, but I knew that fury and violence were not far off. They never were.

"She spotted us. She came up to the car and confronted us. What else were we supposed to do?" Smiley—Harris—said.

Ben walked toward Harris and tapped a finger on his chest, one tap punctuating every word. "You were supposed to watch her."

"We did, but—"

"But she spotted you." Ben's eyes were alight with rage. "And why did she spot you? Do you not know how to follow someone without being *spotted*?"

I knew I shouldn't say anything, but I'd had enough of this. "Why was he following me in the first place?"

"Because I *told* him to." Ben turned and stared at me. I realized that there was something wrong with his forest-green eyes. The idiot was high. It was never a good idea to sample the merchandise, at least, that was what Ben had told me. In hindsight, I really, really should have left him a lot sooner.

"Why?" I spat out.

"You weren't returning my calls." Ben looked genuinely confused. The drugs had clearly rotted his brain. "I was worried about you. I have enemies now, Roz, and I can't have my girlfriend unprotected."

"*Girlfriend?*" I couldn't keep the shock and disgust from my voice. "Ben, I know you're high, but you can't have forgotten that I broke up with you. Two. Months. Ago."

Ben laughed. He turned back to Harris. "My girl is always playing games. She's sassy and likes to make me work for our relationship. It's one of the reasons I love her so much."

My heart jackhammered against my chest. I needed to get out of here. Ben was certifiably insane. He'd always respected my boldness. I just needed to say it like it was, but obviously holding back how I really felt about him. "I'm going home," I said. "If one of your thugs touches me again, I'm calling the police."

Ben froze.

He slowly returned his attention to me and stared at me with his enlarged pupils. "One of them touched you?"

The gun came out of nowhere. He flashed it at Harris. "Did you *touch* her?"

Harris's jaw clenched. "I had to get her in the car."

"You *had* to get her in the car? I told you to *watch* her. Why can't you follow simple instructions?"

Ben lifted the gun. He pointed it at Harris. He pulled the trigger.

I screamed.

Blood and brain matter showered the room. Harris's body fell to the ground with a sickly thud. I stood, eyes transfixed to the thick globs of Harris that dribbled down the wall. I suddenly realized I was still screaming. I clamped my mouth shut.

My heart raced. The room spun. I needed to get out of here. Now.

Ben's eyes were wild. He reached out toward me, and I jerked away.

"Are you hurt?" he asked, his tone gentle, coaxing. Calm.

I sucked in a ragged breath. "No," I gasped.

Ben's eyebrows knit together. "But you were screaming."

"You *shot* someone," I said, my voice cracking.

Ben nodded. "Because he hurt you. He won't touch you again. I promise."

Of course he wouldn't. He was dead. I glanced at the other two men on the sofa, but other than looking wary, they didn't seem ready to defend their fallen comrade.

"You sh-shot someone," I repeated. My head felt light; the room started to spin faster. The smell of metal pierced the air, and I tried not to look at the corpse that lay mere inches away from my bare feet. The blood was creeping closer and closer to my exposed flesh.

"I'm sorry. You shouldn't have had to see that," Ben said, worrying his lower lip with his teeth.

I didn't respond. I wrapped my arms around my torso, giving myself a hug. I was suddenly so cold. Ben moved toward me again, but I lurched backward. He looked hurt, but less crazed. As if the killing had satisfied some deep-seated need within him. A need for pain, for violence, for *blood*.

"You should go home." His voice cut through the haze around me. "We'll talk later."

All my strength, my resolve, my courage had dissipated with that gunshot. I wasn't going to argue with him. Not when I was one squeeze of the trigger away from joining Harris as a wall hanging.

My entire body was fraught with tension as I let Ben give me a sloppy kiss on the forehead before he sent me out the door. Scarface drove me home. I felt his accusatory eyes on me in the rearview mirror the entire drive. I didn't blame him. I'd gotten his friend killed. I could only hope this guy was afraid enough of Ben not to have his revenge on me. I held my breath every time the car slowed at a light, every time Scarface's eyes met mine in the rearview mirror. I imagined him stopping the car, ordering me out of it, and putting a bullet between my eyes. But I made it home unscathed. Physically, at least.

The sound of the gunshot echoed through my head as I trudged upstairs. The sight of the blood on the walls danced before my eyes as I unlocked the door and entered the loft. The scent of blood and brain matter clung to my nostrils as I walked like a zombie to the bathroom and turned on the shower.

I needed to get clean. I needed to wash away everything that had happened tonight. I stripped off my clothes and tossed them into the garbage. I stepped into the shower, the water scalding my skin until it turned pink. When I saw blood rinsing off my feet and circling the drain, I snapped out of my stupor. I fell to the bathtub floor and cried until long after the water turned cold.

7

I barely slept that night. Every time my eyes drifted shut, flashes of red would waltz across my vision, wrenching them open again. Every little noise from the street had me lurching out of bed to peer out the window. The white sedan was always there, parked at the curb, mocking me. I couldn't see through the windshield, but I could feel Scarface's rage and hatred suffocating me like a death shroud. I'd never felt so exposed and vulnerable.

I must have dozed off at some point, because I awoke to the sound of someone entering the apartment during the predawn hours. Shaking, I climbed out of bed and approached the hanging orange sheet that provided little protection against intruders. I hovered there, straining to listen over the sound of my uneven breaths. The front door clicked shut, the sound followed by a few mumbled Danish words. I sighed with relief.

Slipping into my robe, I bent over and grabbed my phone from where it was lying on the floor, charging. I turned it on, hoping for a voice mail or even an email from one of the dozens of places I'd applied for a job. A chill washed over me as it lit up with seven missed texts and twelve missed calls.

Every single one of them was from Ben.

I knew I shouldn't read the messages, but my thumb had a mind of its own as it tapped on the screen.

Good night XX

Then, five minutes later.

Please don't be pissed, babe.

You know I will do whatever it takes to keep you safe. Even killing every last one of my own men.

You know I love you babe, more than life itself.

Why aren't you answering me?

Don't fucking ignore me

It's YOUR fault that I killed him. He touched you, so i had to put him in the ground. I'll put anyone in the ground that touches you, babe.your MINE.

Fear surged through me. The last message was from three hours ago, and I could only hope that he was sleeping off whatever he'd been on last night. But I knew that was wishful thinking. Ben had always been possessive, and the drugs just amplified that. I'd gotten a tiny taste of who he really was when he'd beaten that teen on the bus. Last night had shown me he was capable of so much more.

What the hell was I going to do?

I stumbled out of my bedroom, my eyes landing on Hanna where she leaned against the kitchen counter, drinking tap water from a nicked glass. On the counter beside her sat a large bouquet of yellow roses.

"Secret admirer?" I asked, trying to keep my voice steady and light.

Hanna's gaze snapped over to me. "They're not for me," she said in her faint accent. "They were already here when I came in. Also, you left the door unlocked again. We don't live in a safe area, Roz. I don't want to come home to find you knifed to death in your sleep or killed by the next Phantom Strangler just because you couldn't be bothered to slide a deadbolt."

I barely registered the rest of what she said. I *had* locked the door last night. I knew this because I'd checked and double-checked it multiple times when I couldn't fall asleep.

Realization dawned on me. Ben had a key. Why hadn't I insisted he give it back to me when we broke up? Because I hadn't realized just how batshit crazy he was. The thought of him hovering over me, watching me as I tossed and turned in bed sent bile crawling up the back of my throat. Unaware of my silent mental breakdown, Hanna vanished behind her curtain. I heard the creak of the mattress as she collapsed into bed.

I eyed the roses warily. Yellow. What did yellow roses represent? Was that the universally recognized color for "I'm sorry I murdered a guy in front of you?" At least they weren't black. Or dead. The message behind those two options would be far clearer. I rooted around between the stems, reaching for a card nestled among the leaves.

"Ouch!" I gasped, sticking my cut finger in my mouth. Of course, there would be thorns.

I fetched a fork, which I used to dig out the card. Relief washed over me, immediately followed by a renewed sense of dread. The flowers weren't from Ben.

They were from Sylvain.

My offer still stands. I am prepared to give you more money than you can imagine, and I have the means to make your other problems disappear. All you need to do is negotiate.

I stared at the words, my mouth suddenly dry. Sylvain was delusional. Why was he fixated on me? There had to be hundreds of girls in town who would take him up on his offer. I looked down at my hand, *my* hand, at the pricked finger, the chipped nail polish, and the calluses from dealing cards, digging through trash, and manipulating fine wire. I was nimble fingered, which had gotten me in trouble more than a few times when I'd tried pick-pocketing as a preteen.

My phone chimed, wrenching my attention back to it. I didn't want to look. I wasn't exactly a social butterfly. There was only one person it could be.

We need to talk. I'm coming over. Be there in thirty.

Wooziness washed over me; the combination of lack of sleep and fear and dread was becoming too much. I couldn't be here when Ben showed, but I also couldn't bring myself to move. Panic held me in its icy grasp. I couldn't breathe, I needed to breathe, but the weight squeezing my chest was ruthless.

Pain cut through the fog. I blinked, staring down at my hand, which clutched Sylvain's card so tightly the corner of the cardstock had drawn blood. I watched, mesmerized, as crimson pooled in the palm of my left hand. The hand that Sylvain was willing to pay me a "handsome sum" of money for. I lifted my hand to toss the card into the garbage, but I stopped myself at the last second. He could give me money, which I did need, but could he also make my Ben problem disappear? Was I that desperate? A chill coursed through me as I realized that I was considering Sylvain's offer.

I needed a drink.

I glanced toward Hanna's curtain before quickly typing out a message to Ben, telling him I wasn't home, and not to come over. It probably wasn't a good idea to give him a heads-up that I was leaving, but I didn't want him showing up here when it was just Hanna. I couldn't intentionally put her in danger like that.

I hurried to my bedroom, threw on some clothes, and put on shoes this time before heading out. Once I was on the street, I glanced around, but there was no sign of my linebacker of an ex. I eyeballed the white sedan as I passed.

Just as I was releasing a breath of relief, the car roared to life. It inched down the street, hugging the curb, following me.

I quickened my pace, but that didn't matter. It kept up with me, maintaining less than a dozen short feet between us. I imagined Scarface behind the wheel. Holding on tightly to that grudge against me with meaty, powerful hands. I could only pray that his fear of Ben was greater than his hatred for me. It would be so easy for him to press his foot to the pedal, swerve onto the sidewalk, and take care of his problem. Permanently.

I broke out into a jog, veering into a back alley, ducking out the next street over, doubling back the way I'd come, praying that Scarface wouldn't expect that. I wrenched open the door to O'Malley's, all but tumbling across the threshold, gasping heavily and clutching the stitch in my side.

O'Malley's bar was open twenty-four seven and located a stone's throw from where I slept, making it my favorite watering hole. It was also so close to home that I hoped that Scarface—and Ben—wouldn't expect to find me here.

I nodded to Joe, the bartender, who barely gave me a second look despite my dramatic entrance. I approached the bar and settled onto my favorite stool. I ordered my usual, bottom-shelf whiskey, and told him to put it on my ever-mounting tab.

What had my life come to? I was broke and jobless. But Ben was a more pressing issue than the money I didn't have. I knew better than to go to the police, because it would wind up getting me killed. Ben had friends everywhere, something that had impressed me while we were together, but now it had much more frightening implications. Although, if he kept killing his friends, maybe they would turn on him. I knew this was wishful thinking. With that crowd, his murderous tendencies would only earn him fear and respect. The police might be able to get him thrown in jail, but for how long? What if he got out on bail? Maybe I could testify against him? The thought made my stomach churn. I'd seen him kill someone, but it was my word against his, and I was sure he'd have disposed of the body and all incriminating evidence by now. He might have even moved his operation, thinking that I would be able to tell the police where to find it. Not that I could. I barely remembered where I'd been taken last night, and I certainly hadn't been paying attention on the way back. I'd been reliving the horrifying sight of brains spraying the wall like uncorked champagne on New Year's.

Going to the police was out of the question.

Should I run? Should I leave this life behind and start somewhere else? Somewhere fresh? I'd never been outside of Chicago for longer than a weekend getaway. What would I do out there? I would have to change my name, get a new identity. That would require money, money that I didn't have.

Besides, Ben had connections. He'd find me no matter where I went.

A shrill ring shot through the air and through my head the way the bullet sliced through Harris's skull last night. I sat frozen for several long seconds before a second ring sounded out. It was my phone, not Ben. I was safe. For now.

With shaky fingers I withdrew my cracked phone out of my pocket. "Hello?"

"Is this Ms. Regan Osbourne?"

"Speaking."

"This is Sherry Denis, Acquisitions Assistant at the Morrow Gallery."

Despite everything I'd been through in the last twenty-four hours, my heart leaped into my throat. This was one of my last-ditch efforts at getting one of my pieces featured. I'd long given up hope of showcasing an entire collection—I needed either money or contacts to secure something like that—but I should be able to get a single piece into a gallery. Years ago, I'd aimed big, but at this point? I was desperate. Morrow Gallery was a safety gallery, but it was better than nothing. It was the very bottom rung on the ladder to success. Well, maybe not even the bottom rung. It was more like the rubber stopper on the bottom of the ladder leg. But still, it was something.

The uncontrollable grin that had spread across my face was immediately wiped out by her next words. "I'm sorry, but I'm calling to regretfully inform you . . ."

Buzzing in my ears drowned out the rest. I lowered the phone from my ear and clicked the "end" button without responding.

I was rejected by Morrow Gallery. *Morrow Gallery*. They'd been known to accept literal garbage. In sophomore year at college a couple of arrogant snots had pulled together crap they'd found in the cafeteria trash bins and submitted it to Morrow Gallery as a joke. And it had been accepted.

I downed the rest of my drink, embracing a burn that did nothing to distract from the sting of tears in my eyes.

I glanced around the bar, seeking out someone—anyone—who looked like they could afford to pay for my drinks. There were three homeless-looking men, all barely conscious, splayed in various sections of the dimly lit room. The weight pressed down harder on my chest. I was no better than them. Disgusting. Pathetic. Alone. I had no talent, and I'd deluded myself for years into thinking that if I just found the right gallery, the right mentor, the right inspiration, that I would break into the art world.

I drank another whiskey. Then another. It scorched its way down my throat, and I welcomed the sensation of something other than fear and self-loathing. I sought more of this bitter distraction. By the time the sun had fully risen, I was wasted.

I didn't even notice I had company until he spoke. The faintly British accent that haunted my dreams. "I'll have a club soda."

I lifted my head from where I rested it against the sticky bar top. I didn't have to look to know who it was. Sylvain.

Joe sauntered toward us, clearly in no rush to serve Sylvain. He gave him a deliberate, unimpressed look up and down, taking in his tailored suit, which was worth more than all the alcohol on the shelf behind the bar. He turned and started to pour his drink.

"Desperation doesn't look good on you," I said, without glancing over at Sylvain. I finished my drink and slammed the glass down on the bar.

Sylvain was quiet for a moment, and I resisted the impulse to glance at him. "I could say the same to you."

Touché. I gestured toward Joe. "Another," I said, despite having told myself that this was my last one. I was a little worried that my tab was creeping into the quadruple digits.

"I'll cover it," Sylvain said. I didn't know whether to slap him or to kiss him. I settled on glaring at him.

"Why are you here?" I asked.

Sylvain watched me with his exasperatingly unreadable blue eyes. "You know why I'm here. I've given you plenty of time to conclude that you are out of options."

My lips pursed. Joe handed me another whiskey, but I didn't take a drink. I thought I should probably not be completely wasted for this conversation, though, from the way that the room was tilting on its axis, I suspected it might have been too late for that. "Tell me exactly what you want."

Sylvain's thin lips curled upward into the macabre semblance of a smile. "You know *exactly* what I want. But I will spell it out for you. I want your hand."

The room began to spin a little faster. I didn't say anything.

"Your left one, to be more specific."

"But I'm left-handed," I blurted out.

Sylvain smiled. "I know."

What kind of sick game was he playing? What was the *point* of all of this? I must have spoken out loud, because he answered.

"My use for your hand is of no relevance. All you need to know is that I'm prepared to negotiate handsomely for it."

My eyes narrowed. There it was again—he was using the word *handsomely* for such an ugly trade. "You said that already. How much?"

"One million dollars."

The room began to spin with even more frenzy. A *million* dollars? I could move out of the shithole loft. I could host an art show. Hell, I could *pay* people to attend it. But I wouldn't be able to create more art without my hand—at least not easily—although the art that I'd been creating up to that point hadn't been successful. I was talentless, but with that kind of money, I could pay people not to care.

I peered down at my whiskey, which I swirled in the glass. With my *left* hand.

"Of course, I'll ensure that you're equipped with a lifelike prosthesis. It will look real. At least from a distance."

The gravity of what we were discussing hit me. My hand—my left hand—started to shake, so I lowered the glass. I wiped my clammy palm on my jeans, feeling the rough texture of the fabric under my fingers.

Sylvain's expression was curious as he watched me over his club soda. There was a gleam in his eye, something unrecognizable. Something inhuman.

I knew what I had to do. "All right, Hannibal Lecter. I have a problem that I need you to take care of."

"Your debt?" Sylvain asked.

How had he known about my student loans?

I cleared my throat. "In addition to my debt."

He angled his head. "I'm listening."

"Ben Reynell. He's my ex-boyfriend."

His eyebrows shot into his receding hairline. "You want to get back together with him? There are a lot of things I can finagle, but a love potion isn't one of them."

"No! Ew, God, no. What I mean to say is that he's a drug dealer. He's obsessed with me. I need you to get rid of him. Have him put in prison. For a *long* time. I don't want him getting out until my grandkids sprout their first gray hairs."

Sylvain nodded slowly, mulling over my terms. "I'll take care of your ex, but it will cost you. You get nine hundred thousand."

I shook my head vehemently, and a wave of nausea washed over me. I stopped moving and put a hand on the bar top to brace myself. I'd clearly drunk more than I'd thought. A passing thought flitted through my mind. Was I sober enough to be making this decision? Would I regret it once the alcohol had worn off and sobriety reared its nasty head? Then, in an instant, those concerns dissipated. "One million dollars. *And* you get rid of Ben. That's my final offer."

Sylvain smiled. "I agree to your terms. Under one condition."

I knew I wasn't going to like this. "What is it?"

"We do this today."

8

I jerked awake at the sound of banging on the loft door. I groaned and rolled over, seizing my pillow and throwing it over my head. The knocking seemed to grow even louder. Just when I thought I couldn't take it any longer, it stopped. Relieved, I removed the pillow and glanced at the clock beside my bed. It was a quarter past six. Because of the lack of sunlight in the loft, I knew it was the morning six, not the evening six.

I would have stayed in bed, but a sudden, unbearable thirst sank its claws into me. My eyes were cloudy, my thoughts muggy, and a general sense of unease was complemented by a persistent pressure across my temples that threatened to pop my skull like a grape. This wasn't my usual hangover.

I raised my hand to wipe my clammy forehead, but I was met with a fleshy lump that slapped against my face. Dread squeezed my chest as my stomach sank. My eyes flew open, but the rest of my body was paralyzed under the weight of terror that kept me pinned to my bed. I took one breath. Two. After the third, I finally found the strength to turn my head.

In place of my hand there was a stump.

"What the hell!?" My voice was raw with fear and repulsion.

I sat bolt upright. I grabbed the stump, groping the smooth and slippery scar tissue with my right hand. My hand was gone. It was missing. It was replaced with this monstrosity.

Was this a joke? A sick, cruel joke?

"No, no, no, no, no!" Memories poured through me. I'd made a deal with Sylvain. It hadn't been just a bizarre, twisted nightmare. How could I have gone through with it? How could I have given him my *hand* for money and to make my Ben problem disappear? Was I insane?

I pitched out of bed and stood there for several long moments, woozy from the sudden movement. I couldn't remember anything from after the bar. I didn't remember anything from after making the deal with Sylvain. What day was it? I looked at the stump, the smooth and shiny skin stretched tight over my wrist bones. How many weeks had I been gone? Had Hanna noticed that I was missing? How did I get back into the loft? Back into my bed?

I shouldered past the orange curtain on wobbly feet. I glanced around. Nothing seemed out of the ordinary. My sculptures and raw materials were collecting dust where I'd left them.

"Hanna?" My voice was hoarse. I was so thirsty.

I went to the kitchen. I reached for a glass on the counter, but my stump knocked it to the ground, where it shattered into a million pieces. I stifled a sob as I pressed my stump to my chest and reached for another glass with my good hand. I turned to the sink, but I couldn't twist the faucet handle when my hand was already full. I put the glass in the sink, turned on the faucet, and quickly grabbed for the glass again before it overturned from the force of the running water. I brought it to my lips, gulping the water down like it was the only thing keeping me alive. I drank another glass. Then another. Finally, halfway through the fourth, I was able to stop and take a ragged breath.

"Hanna?" I tried again. I went to the velvet curtain that concealed her living space. Her bed was tidily made. She wasn't here.

I stormed into the bathroom. Using my right hand only, I tore off my shirt, ripping the cotton at the seam. I tossed it to the floor before moving on to my pants, which were even more difficult to remove. I stumbled, reaching out to brace myself on the counter, but I couldn't support myself with just a stump. I fell, landing on my hip hard. Everything around me was blurry, and it was only then that I realized that tears were streaming down my face. I wiped at them furiously with the palm of my only hand before getting to my feet.

I needed to inspect the rest of my body. I needed to make sure nothing else was . . . missing. All I found, aside from the nasty bruise already forming on my hip, was a much smaller one on the back of my right hand. Was it from an IV? I inspected the stump carefully in the bright fluorescent light of the bathroom. It looked perfectly healed. No bruising. No scab. Smooth, glossy pink flesh, rounded out around my wrist. It reflected the faint bathroom light up at me. It was revolting.

I barely made it to the toilet before I threw up. There was nothing in my stomach but bile and the water I'd gorged on. When I finished, I leaned my feverish forehead against the cold ceramic bowl.

What had I done? I couldn't contain the sobs that racked my body. I'd been too drunk to make this life-altering decision. I had barely been coherent when Sylvain found me at that bar. He took advantage of me. He knew I was desperate, and he used that desperation to take what he wanted from me, leaving me broken.

I wished my mother were here. Or even Hanna. I wished I had a friend or a boyfriend or someone—anyone—to help me overcome this. I regretted pushing everyone away. In this moment, all I wanted was someone to hold me and tell me that everything would be okay.

Still racked with nausea by the time the sun had risen, I finally acknowledged that I needed to see a doctor. I managed to peel myself up off the bathroom floor to get ready. Taking a shower and washing my hair with one hand was a new experience—one I didn't think I'd ever get used to. I kept going to use my left hand—my dominant one—and the shock would double me over with disgust and fear and a fresh wave of nausea. It took me twice as long as usual to get dressed, even though I settled for a sweatshirt and sweatpants and didn't even attempt to put on a bra. Tying my shoelaces wasn't an option, so I slipped on my work flats.

I stood in the middle of the loft. I was feeling calmer now that I had showered and dressed, but I was a hair's breadth away from bursting into tears again. I stared at my worktable, littered with the remnants from my last few projects that had led to failure and heartache. How was I going to do my art with only one hand? My sculptures might not have been good, at least not by the fickle standards of the art world, but it was all I cared about. All I had to live for.

I took a few deep breaths, squeezing my eyes shut. I didn't have time for another breakdown. I needed to think. I vaguely remembered the deal I'd made with Sylvain. Had he followed through with his end of the bargain?

Back in my bedroom, I peered out the window. The white sedan was gone, but that didn't mean a damn thing. I found my phone, which was left on the floor, plugged into the wall. I checked the date.

Only two days had passed since my deal with Sylvain. Only two days had passed since I'd lost my hand. I stared down at the stump again. It should have taken longer than two days for this to heal so fully. How was this possible?

Struggling to tap the tiny buttons with my right thumb, I entered my bank account information after connecting to the free Wi-Fi from the restaurant across the street.

I sat down on my bed when I saw the balance: one million dollars, plus the $26.23 I'd already had in the account. Sylvain had followed through. Did that mean that he'd taken care of my other problem too? Was Ben rotting behind bars, where he belonged?

I had so many questions flitting through my mind, but there was one that was screaming louder than the rest. Was this worth it?

I took a deep breath, left my bedroom, and strode across the loft into the kitchen, sidestepping the broken glass that I didn't have the energy to clean up. The familiar routine of pouring water into a bowl did nothing to calm me, because everything was different, everything was jarring to do with just my nondominant hand. I balanced the bowlful of water on my stump and swung the front door open with my other hand.

A large cardboard box sat on the stoop. I'd forgotten about the pounding on the door that had woken me. It couldn't have been the USPS delivery guy, not just because it was far too early for him, but because the box didn't have any postage or even an address written on it.

This was hand delivered.

"Little Guy, it's breakfast time!" I called out half-heartedly as I stared down at the box. There was a little envelope taped to the top of it. I set the bowl down on the ground and gave Little Guy a few pets when he meowed up at me. "Sorry, just water for today. I'll pick up kitty kibble later." God knew I had the money for it now. Little Guy let out a little grumble as he stalked off, tail in the air.

I picked up the box with one hand and brought it into the "living room." I dumped it onto my worktable, deciding to focus on the letter first. I tore through the envelope with my teeth and wrenched out the paper with my fingers. Who would have thought something as simple as opening a letter would be so damn difficult with only one hand?

The letter was short and to the point. *"Your terms have been met. Tell no one of our arrangement—not the police, not your roommate. No one. Tell anyone and the terms are void, and there will be repercussions."*

The letter gave no indication of what was inside the box. I stared at it warily before picking up my X-Acto knife and slicing through the packing tape, going slowly so as not to slice myself open in the process. While my right hand was dexterous from dealing cards and sculpting wire, I wasn't used to relying on it for something like this. Once I'd finally completed my task, I tossed the knife onto the table and flipped open the flaps of the box.

Inside was my hand.

I gasped and jerked back, knocking over the box. My hand spilled out onto the floor, landing with a loud thud. Sharp pain shot through the ghost of my severed limb, the intensity of the pain reverberating through the rest of my body. Nausea roiling in my stomach, I inched toward my hand.

But it wasn't my hand. It was a synthetic one. I sighed with relief, leaning against the table as my heartbeat gradually returned to normal. I picked up the hand and felt the strangeness of the material and its elastic sleeve. There was an instruction booklet in the box. I studied the diagram before sliding the hand over my stump. It was snug, but comfortable. Sylvain had been right. It looked like a real hand. It just had a slight shine to it, and I obviously couldn't move the fingers, but from a distance it could fool anyone.

I may have lost my hand, but I had this expensive replacement. I didn't have a job, but I had a million dollars to blow. I'd always been a glass-half-empty kind of girl, but as long as it was whiskey, I'd never complained. I grinned, suddenly feeling a lot better.

I grabbed my phone, purse, and headed out. Going to see a doctor would have to wait.

9

It was the best day of my life. I'd never had a bank account balance in the quadruple digits before, let alone a million dollars. I couldn't wipe the goofy grin off my face, and I embraced it, my heart feeling lighter than it had felt in a long time. The first thing I did was head to my bank to make a hefty withdrawal, since the limit on my credit card was laughable. Then, I went straight to the Magnificent Mile. I didn't take the el or hop on a bus or hike it down there. I took a cab.

Butterflies fluttered in my stomach as I strode into Burberry. A sinewy store clerk with a name tag that read "Kev" glanced at me and then quickly looked away, his nose pinched with distaste. Unfazed, I strolled deeper into the store.

"You," I said to Kev in my most bored voice. "Start a room for me." I then prowled down the aisle, pointing at items randomly. "I want this one, and this one, and ooh, yes, this one will do."

He just stared at me, clearly unimpressed.

"Excuse me?" I said. "Did you hear me?"

"Ma'am." Kev was hiding a grimace. He glanced over at a few of the other patrons—mostly tourists—who were watching me curiously. "I don't think you should be trying these items on." He flipped the price tag of a pair of jeans I'd pointed at. It was over five hundred dollars.

I gasped indignantly. "How. Dare. You. Are you *discriminating* against me?" I waved my prosthesis in the air. An older lady wearing heart-shaped sunglasses and a denim fanny pack gasped almost on cue.

Kev paled. "No, I—of course not," he mumbled. He fetched the clothes I pointed out and brought them to a back room without further argument.

I was offered champagne as I changed, which I took full advantage of with my one good hand. I could tell that Kev thought I was drinking far too much alcohol for a Thursday morning, but I didn't care. I was walking on sunshine. I tried on clothes, finding out that I'd dropped a dress size since the last time I went shopping. The benefit of having a diet consisting primarily of stale crackers and alcohol, I supposed.

I selected a dress for every night of the week. I picked out a pair of jersey trousers that looked like a set I'd picked up at Goodwill a few years back but cost about thirteen hundred dollars more. I bought a new jacket and scarf that would only keep me warm for about three weeks in the fall before I'd have to swap them out for something heavier. I even picked out a gingham bikini that I knew I wouldn't have the occasion to wear, but once I'd tried it on, I had to have it. I bought far more clothes than I could carry with only one hand, but fortunately Burberry offered same-day delivery.

When I'd finished, I saw a pretty red dress clinging to a mannequin by the cashier. "I'll take that too," I said. "In a size four." Hanna's size. Maybe she wouldn't be so pissed at me if I replaced her dress with an even better one.

"And did anybody help you today?" the girl behind the counter asked as she tucked a copper curl behind her ear.

"Nope," I replied, thrilling in my *Pretty Woman* moment. I felt just like Julia Roberts, except I hadn't needed a man to achieve this. Kev shot daggers at me, but I ignored him, smiling sweetly at the girl. "If you'd like, I can say that you did, so you'll get the commission."

The girl's cheeks blotted bright pink and she smiled like I was her hero as she input her employee number. I shot Kev a condescending smile as I left. I'd done my good deed of the day. As I was exiting Burberry, I nearly tripped over an old man sitting on the stoop. He was huddled under a moth-eaten blanket. Arthritic fingers clenched an empty coffee cup. He let out a racking cough that could be heard from across the street. He looked up in my direction with cloudy eyes, and I could instantly tell that he was blind. I pursed my lips as a strange sensation washed over me. He couldn't see me, but I still felt exposed. Wordlessly, I reached into my purse, retrieved a few bills, and tucked them into his cup.

"Thank you," he said, gratitude dripping from the words.

I swallowed, but I didn't respond. Instead, I headed to the next store on the street and did my best to push this encounter from my mind, sloughing off my guilt like a snake sheds its skin. What did I have to feel guilty about? It was my money, and I could spend it however I wanted. Nevertheless, I couldn't resist the temptation to give a little money to the other homeless people I encountered on the Magnificent Mile.

What was a few hundred dollars when I was now a millionaire? The contrast of extreme wealth and poverty in the city had never been so obvious and sickening to me before. Maybe that was because I'd always hovered just above the poverty line.

After I'd purchased enough clothes to fill my side of the loft, I took a cab to the Horseshoe Hammond. I could certainly afford to go to a ritzier casino, one that had been upgraded since the nineties and didn't smell of stale beer. But I wanted to go there. I had to go there.

I strode out onto the floor, decked out in a seven-thousand-dollar black dress and a fur coat I'd bought, not because it was cold out but because it looked absolutely decadent. I headed straight for the blackjack tables.

"What are you doing here?" a familiar voice wheezed behind me.

I turned around slowly. It was Al, slightly out of breath, likely from bolting out of the security room the instant he spotted me. His red curls were plastered to his forehead with sweat.

"I'm here to play cards."

Al glanced over my outfit, his eyes nearly bugging out of his skull. "I—what—"

"Now, shoo, you're bad luck." I rolled my eyes at the couple on the other side of the table. I turned to face the dealer, Jeff. He was an asshole I'd never gotten along with.

He didn't seem thrilled to see me. I couldn't wait to win so I could rub that smug look off his arrogant face. I slapped a thick wad of hundreds on the table. His eyes widened slightly.

He cleared his throat. "What denomination?"

"Make it hundreds."

As soon as he stacked my chips, I locked eyes with him. "All in," I said, pushing my chips toward him. "Now, hit me."

Just at that moment, sharp pain cut through my missing hand. I jerked backward, staring down at my prosthesis in shock. Its artificial skin shined up at me, not at all reflecting the excruciating pain beneath its surface. The fingers of my missing hand were being torn in opposite directions, like it was strapped into some kind of twisted medieval torture device.

Tears leaked from my eyes as I hissed in pain, clutching my prosthesis to my chest, as if cradling it would make my suffering go away. Just when I thought that the pain couldn't get worse—that I couldn't bear it any longer—it shifted. Instead of a tearing sensation, my hand was lit on fire. Like I'd stuck my hand into a kiln. My skin blistered; the bones melted.

Then, in an instant—though it felt like it had been an hour—the ruthless agony dissipated, replaced by a pulsating ache. I gulped several ragged breaths as I recovered from the sudden assault. I frowned down at my stump in wary confusion. What had just happened?

Once I'd regained my bearings, my attention snapped back to the table, where the game had continued without me.

I'd lost it all.

10

My happiness was severed as suddenly as my hand had been. Once the searing pain in my stump arrived, it was clear it was here to stay. It was unbearable. Relentless. It stalked me ruthlessly, clinging to my every waking moment and smothering me even when I tried to sleep.

I didn't have to wait long in the walk-in clinic before I was ushered into one of the exam rooms. The receptionist seemed wary of me, but I wasn't sure if it was because of my appearance or the hysterical note in my voice.

I stared down at my prosthetic hand. My missing one currently felt like an amateur was enthusiastically practicing acupuncture on it with thick, rusty needles. My financial problems were gone. Ben seemed to be gone. But was this worth it? Not just the loss of such an essential part of me, but the pain? For the millionth time the past couple of days, I wondered, Why me? What if I hadn't made that drunken deal? What was Sylvain even doing with my hand?

The doctor hurried in. She looked slightly frazzled, her frizzy hair drawn back in a tight ponytail, her white lab coat wrinkled over stained baby-blue scrubs. Her name tag read "Dr. Joyce Hughes." She clutched a clipboard in her left hand. My eyes lingered on her neatly trimmed fingernails, the faint scar just below her middle knuckle. She wore no rings or bracelets, aside from a Fitbit that hugged her slim wrist.

"Have you ever been to this clinic before?" she asked. I tore my gaze away from her hand. Her tone was friendly, and I appreciated that she wasn't going to make me endure small talk about the weather or how the Cubs did this season.

I wouldn't be able to bear it if she had.

"No," I replied through pursed lips. I didn't bother to tell her I hadn't been to a doctor since high school. Aside from the occasional cold, I wasn't one to get sick.

"So you're suffering from some pain in your lost limb," Dr. Hughes said, her cavalier tone grating on my last nerve.

"More than *some*," I snapped.

Her expression softened. She gestured to my prosthesis. "Can you take it off for me, please?"

I fumbled with the sleeve, but it was too snug.

Dr. Hughes didn't seem to notice my inexperience with the thing. "How long ago did you lose your limb?"

"A couple of days ago," I answered without thinking as I wedged a thumb under the sleeve and tried to wrench it off that way.

At her sudden silence, I looked up. She was giving me a strange look.

"I mean, I've been feeling the pain for a few days," I stammered. "This obviously happened . . . a while ago."

Dr. Hughes seemed to finally realize I was having a hard time getting the damn thing off. She reached out and deftly removed it in one swift motion. She smiled kindly. "These can take a while to get used to." She set it on the table and leaned close to inspect the stump. I turned my face away. I still couldn't look at it.

"This looks like it's well healed," she noted.

I bit my lip. "How long ago does it look like it happened?"

Her eyebrows pinched together. She didn't answer.

"I mean, how long does it typically take an injury like this to heal?"

"For this level of scar tissue healing? At least a few months."

I tried not to let the surprise show on my face.

Dr. Hughes continued: "Well, the surgeon did a phenomenal job with the stitches. Who is your regular doctor? It would be better to have your regular doctor prescribe medicine for the pain."

At that moment, a dagger of pain shot through my hand. I gasped, cradling my stump against my chest. A concerned frown tugged at the corner of her lips. I evaded the question. "I—I need something right *now*."

She jotted down a note on her pad. "Please describe the pain that you're feeling for me."

"It's sharp, shooting, and then it's gone, but not for long. Never for long. It's sudden. It's unexpected. It hurts." My voice cracked on the last word.

"Where do you feel the pain? Is it in the missing hand, or in the stump?"

I blinked at the strange question. "I . . . It's in the missing hand, if that makes sense. But the hand isn't there anymore. How can it hurt?"

"What you're describing is phantom pain. It's treated differently from stump pain. Phantom pain is actually a lot more common than you'd think. Can I ask how you lost the hand?"

My mind raced, stumbling over possible lies to tell. "It was an accident. I was drunk. I shouldn't have let it happen." All true.

"Has your regular doctor prescribed you anything?"

I would have to admit the truth. "I don't have a regular doctor. I never could afford one."

Dr. Hughes stared at me. Her eyes flickered over to my prosthetic hand, which sat beside the jar of cotton swabs and a stack of pamphlets about STIs. "Can I ask who your prosthetist is?"

"My prosthe-what?"

"The person who took your measurements, worked with you, and identified the best type of prosthesis for you." Her formerly warm eyes were now narrowed with suspicion. What exactly did she suspect me of? Stealing the hand? It was pretty nice. Maybe she thought that I shouldn't be able to afford something like this, especially if I couldn't afford a doctor. I needed to be more careful about what I said, but it was hard to think straight with the pain searing through my left hand. A hand that wasn't even there anymore.

"To be honest, everything after the accident is a blur," I said when the pain finally ebbed.

Dr. Hughes nodded, but I wasn't sure if she believed me. I sat quietly as she took my blood pressure. Another wave of agony shot through me.

"Well?" I asked impatiently. "Are you going to be able to cure me?"

"Sadly there's no cure for phantom pain, but there are treatments. The exact cause of the pain is unknown. Do you have a psychiatrist?"

I didn't have a doctor or a prosthetist. What made her think I'd have a psychiatrist? "No," I said through gritted teeth.

She cleared her throat. "Well, I'm going to give you a referral for that as well. There are some therapies that are known to help resolve phantom pain."

"Therapies?" I snapped. "I need this pain gone. Now. Isn't there a pain-killer you can give me?" My voice had a desperate edge to it.

Dr. Hughes looked at me sharply. She examined my eyes, then gave me another once-over.

Wonderful. Now she thinks I'm an addict.

"I'm going to refer you to a psychiatrist," she said firmly. "If you don't have a family doctor, you'll need someone to talk to, someone to oversee your treatment. Phantom limb pain can be temporary, but it might also be something that you'll struggle with for the rest of your life."

"Great. Thanks. I would love to see a shrink. But what about now? What about the pain I'm feeling *right now*?" My voice grew louder and louder and I didn't seem to have any control over it.

Dr. Hughes retrieved a prescription pad from her lab coat and scribbled illegibly on it. "You said that you don't have a doctor, correct?"

I was getting sick and tired of the third degree. I gave her a look.

"Well, I'm your doctor now," she said. "I'm giving you a prescription for one month's worth of antidepressants—"

"*Excuse* me?" I was ready to punch her in the face with my stump.

"Antidepressants are a common treatment for phantom limb pain. I'm afraid I can't prescribe you opioids without knowing your history."

Sure, now *doctors are concerned with overprescribing opioids.* I bit my tongue. "What about my history?"

Dr. Hughes stared at me coldly. "I don't know if you're a user, trying to trick me into prescribing you meds."

"Listen, I need this pain to stop." I was nearly in tears. "Just give me the antidepressants."

I snatched the prescription from her hand, along with the referral to Dr. Josette Lavoie, a psychiatrist who Dr. Hughes said specialized in phantom limb pain treatment. Apparently, she was the best in the Chicago area. This was looking like I was already going to carve another dent into my million-dollar payday.

I grumbled all the way to the pharmacy. I didn't listen to the pharmacist as he explained how important it was to take the meds with food. Instead, I glared at him, popped open the lid, and dry-swallowed a pill.

I called the psychiatrist's office on my way out of the pharmacy, making an appointment for as soon as possible.

11

The waiting room at the office of Dr. Josette Lavoie, psychiatrist, was immaculate. The glass coffee tables sparkled. There wasn't a speck of dust in sight on the polished hardwood floors. The leisure magazines were fanned out in a way that was unusually precise. It looked like there was an exact inch and a half of each cover exposed, as if someone had gone around and checked with a ruler. Someone around here clearly had OCD.

I looked up at the receptionist, a plump girl with a Barbra Streisand nose and thin blond hair that was pulled back tightly into a perfectly smooth ponytail. My money was on it being her.

A surge of jealousy coursed through me as I glared at her perfect pair of hands as they tapped on the keyboard.

"Dr. Lavoie is ready to see you now," she chirped.

I could not deal with her cheerfulness, not when my life was falling apart. I rose from my seat and approached the door to Dr. Lavoie's office. I hesitated, reaching out and nudging the painting that hung by the door, knocking it slightly off-kilter. Maybe that would temper the receptionist's good mood.

I stepped into the office. The difference between this room and the room I'd left was quite jarring. Where the waiting area was cool and smelled faintly of disinfectant, this room was warm, and I detected a hint of lavender mixed with vanilla. The waiting area had harsh fluorescent lights, and the office itself was lit primarily by sunlight, which poured unobstructed through the large bay window. The waiting area had been decorated in cool tones; everything was shades of silver or gray. The office was all warm cherrywood, afghans strewn haphazardly, and there was a brown brick fireplace against the wall to my left. My eyes lingered on the couch centered beneath the bay window. It looked like the ideal place to curl up, overlooking the busy downtown street.

"You must be Regan Osbourne," a gentle voice with a slight French accent drew my attention to the woman standing beside a grand antique desk.

"And you must be Dr. Josette Lavoie," I parroted as I studied her. Dr. Lavoie was around my height. She was a little older than I was, no older than forty. Warm brown hair cascaded in smooth waves just past her shoulders. She wore a cream silk blouse and a chocolate-brown pencil skirt that accentuated her curves. Sensible heels that only added an inch to her height topped off a look that would seem plain on anyone else. But for her, it looked classy and elegant. Ageless and effortless. Like with every other person I'd met since losing my hand, my attention lingered on her left hand. It was elegant, like her. A gold Cartier watch rested on her delicate wristbone. Her hands were hairless, the skin smooth, the fingers slender. Her long, oval nails had gently curved nailbeds and were unpainted. She wore a tastefully thin gold wedding band on her ring finger. After I'd finished scrutinizing her, my eyes met hers. They were a piercing blue that cut straight through the bullshit I'd been planning on heaping onto her.

I shifted, suddenly uncomfortable, but unwilling to be the first to break eye contact. "Call me Roz."

Dr. Lavoie smiled, but it didn't seem to reach her eyes. "Clever nickname. Please, take a seat wherever you'd like."

Again, I scanned the office. There was the couch, which I'd noticed immediately. But there was also a pair of armchairs on either side of the exposed brick fireplace, and a straight-back chair directly across from her desk. Was this my first test?

I was exhausted from the last few sleepless nights. Every time I managed to fall asleep, I'd awoken to strange sensations in my missing hand. It had started off as excruciating pain, like someone was skewering my hand to make a shish kebab. Sometimes that pain morphed into someone trying to rip it down the center. But now, I sometimes felt blistering heat instead, or pins and needles. There seemed to be no rhyme or reason to it, and I was utterly fed up with this. I collapsed onto the sofa by the window. Dr. Lavoie followed suit, settling beside me.

"Did I pass your little test?" I grumbled.

Dr. Lavoie's expression was perfectly neutral. "I'm not sure what you mean."

I rolled my eyes. "So how does it work? How does my seat selection give you great insights into how my broken brain works?"

Dr. Lavoie smiled. This smile was more genuine, the corners of her lips curving upward and the warmth reaching her eyes, which flashed with humor. "I can't give away all my trade secrets." The disappointment must have shown on my face, because she said, "But I'll tell you just this little one. Had you chosen the chair across from the desk, you would have demonstrated hesitance for psychiatry. You would have been consciously or subconsciously putting distance between us. If you'd chosen the pair of armchairs by the fire, you would have been clearly stating boundaries, but that you were potentially willing to open up. The fact that you chose the sofa, where we would both sit together, with nothing between us, indicates that you are willing to give psychiatry a try. You're not only willing, but even hopeful that this will make a vast improvement on your life."

I looked around the room as she spoke, taking in the antique Victorian-era portrait over the fireplace. My missing hand twitched with the desire to mimic the brushstrokes. To my left, vast bookcases were filled with books and bric-a-brac, though it seemed like everything had its place. Her desk was tidy, and it crossed my mind that it might be she who had a touch of OCD. My eyes returned to hers. "Huh. I just chose the couch because it looked the most comfortable, and I haven't been sleeping well."

Dr. Lavoie didn't look fazed. "You say that, but you're already opening up. Tell me, Roz, why aren't you sleeping well?"

I clamped my jaw shut. She was easy to talk to, which meant I would have to be extra careful about what I said. I had to put some distance between us. If I revealed anything about my "arrangement" with Sylvain, the deal would be void. I didn't want to find out what Sylvain had meant by that. It's not like he could give me my hand back, but he could take the money away.

"I have what the doctor calls phantom limb pain. It's why I'm here. Not that your company isn't absolutely *delightful*." I said the last word with a little bite. "But I'm here to be cured."

"You came to the right place. I specialize in phantom limb treatment, among other syndromes." I must not have looked impressed, because she quickly got to the point. "It affects you at night?"

"It affects me all the damn time. Well, almost," I said. For some strange reason it wasn't hurting at the moment.

Dr. Lavoie nodded and made some notes with a gold fountain pen. I stared at the smooth skin of her hands. The sculpted round nails that I just now realized weren't unpainted, like I'd originally thought, but a very pale pink.

"Tell me about yourself," she said.

I cleared my throat, unsure if she noticed my staring. "Well, I lost my hand a few months ago. Basically the pain started off as simple sharp—"

"No, no. Tell me about *yourself*. Not the pain. Who is Regan Osbourne? Who is Roz?"

I stared at her. Of course I'd have to expect that if I was going to go see a shrink, I would have to do the touchy-feely crap. "Well, I'm twenty-nine years old. I'm a graduate of the University of Illinois Chicago. I used to work as a dealer at Horseshoe Hammond, but I obviously can't do that with one hand." I neglected to mention that I'd lost the job *before* I'd lost the hand. The devil was in the details.

"What about family?"

"What about it?"

"Where is your family in all this?"

I hid a grimace. I really didn't want to talk about them. Not with anyone, and especially not her. "I'd rather not."

"Why not?" Dr. Lavoie leaned forward. I wondered if she was aware of it. I shrugged but didn't answer.

"What about friends? A boyfriend? Or girlfriend?"

I was once again reminded that I didn't have anyone. I found myself inching away from her. Of course, she must have picked up on that, but thankfully she didn't comment. I grimaced as a quick pain shot through my hand. I waited, but the sharp burst subsided and was replaced with pins and needles. "I don't have many friends. An ex-boyfriend, but he's just that—ex. Cut out of my life. I have a roommate. That's about it."

"How long have you lived in the city?"

"My whole life."

"Why don't you have any friends?"

The teeth were out, and the claws were unsheathed. "Look, lady—I mean, Dr. Lavoie. I understand what you're trying to do here. And I appreciate it. I really do. But don't bother. I'm here to get fixed. I want the pain gone, and then I'm gone. Understand?"

Dr. Lavoie didn't recoil at my cutting words. To my surprise, she nodded. "All right. Tell me about the pain in your amputated limb."

I described my symptoms in excruciating detail as Dr. Lavoie took studious notes in her wire-bound notebook. I really, really hoped that there was a miracle cure for this, something that Dr. Hughes hadn't known about.

"Obviously the antidepressants haven't been working," I said. "I'm going to be needing something much stronger."

"How long have you been taking them?"

"Since Thursday."

She shook her head. "Four days is not nearly long enough for the results to be definitive. Stay on them for at least another two weeks. If there still isn't any improvement, we'll consider other drugs."

Two weeks? Was she fucking insane? "Yeah, that's not an option," I said bluntly.

Dr. Lavoie watched me with those irritatingly perceptive blue eyes. She didn't say anything, but I could feel those eyes watching me, probing me, evaluating me.

"How did you lose the hand?" she asked. Her tone was casual, but I knew better. Nothing about her was casual. Everything was intelligently calculated.

"It was a freak accident," I said vaguely. I'd come up with a whole cover story before coming here, but I was starting to question myself. Why had I thought it would be a good idea to lie to a shrink? Wouldn't my tells be like flashing red lights screaming, "I'm lying!"?

"What happened?"

She wasn't going to let me off so easily. "I'm a sculptor. I was working on a project with scrap metal. Things got a little out of hand." I winced at the unintended pun.

"Do you have a history of drug addiction?" Dr. Lavoie asked suddenly.

My eyes widened. "No!"

"A history of any other kind of substance abuse?" she shot out just as quickly as the first question.

"No."

"Alcohol?"

My eyes narrowed. Could she smell the whiskey on me? "No," I said again, but the word came out slightly hesitant. I hated how uncertain I sounded.

Dr. Lavoie didn't smile; she didn't say aha or look satisfied at my accidental slip. Instead she said, "I can prescribe you something to help you sleep, and a mild painkiller—one that is only marginally stronger than over-the-counter meds. You are not to take it until you cannot stand the pain any longer."

I must have let the relief show on my face, because she continued. "Opioid addiction is no laughing matter. Even the most disciplined can easily become dependent, ruining not only their own lives, but the lives of their loved ones as well."

Well, it's a good thing I don't have any loved ones. I glanced away from her before she could guess what I was thinking. That was a dark thought. True, but dark.

"I'll manage," I blurted out.

She wrote the prescription with a flourish. "This is *not* to be taken with alcohol," she said. I could feel her eyes drilling into my forehead, but I didn't meet her gaze.

"I want to see you twice a week. Book your next appointment for Wednesday. I have an idea for treatment that might help you. It's called mirror box therapy. It's helped plenty of my phantom limb patients in the past, and I think it might just be that magic cure you're looking for."

12

My entire life I'd made plans for what I'd do if I ever won the lottery. Even when I was dirt broke, I would manage to scrounge up the cash to buy a ticket, convincing myself that it was an investment. Whenever I gambled, I would fantasize about all the extravagant things I would do with the winnings. Buy a penthouse suite in one of those condos near Grant Park. Get that nose job that my mother always insisted I needed. Take a one-way trip to Paris to live off baguettes and fancy cheese. Buy a completely new life, become a completely new person.

But I hadn't done any of these things. I didn't have the energy for it.

I swung open the door to the loft with my right hand, barely anchoring the bag of groceries against my hip with my prosthesis.

Hanna greeted me in the kitchen. She gripped a Starbucks cup between her hands. Her fingers were pale and slim, with knobby knuckles and square nails that were bitten to the quick. I tore my gaze away before she caught the longing expression I was sure was etched into my face.

Fortunately, she hadn't seemed to notice. "What is that?" she asked, eyeing the bag suspiciously.

"It's called food. It's what humans are required to *consume* in order to stay among the *living*," I said, my tone as sarcastic as I could muster on so little sleep.

Hanna wasn't put off. She hovered as I tossed the vegetables into the fridge, which apparently wasn't running. That explained why the milk had formed floating chunks in my coffee that morning.

I took out my new iPhone (another thing I'd splurged on—a brand-spanking-new phone *without* a plan) and started browsing online for a new fridge. It was hard with my nondominant hand, but fortunately Google was able to guess what I needed.

"No, I mean, what is *that*?" She pointed at my prosthesis.

I waved it in front of her. She gasped in realization. "*Milde Moses*! What happened?"

"Sculpting accident," I replied. "Scrap metal and soft flesh don't mix, apparently."

Hanna lurched backward, her gaze flying around the living room.

I let out my first real laugh in a long time. "Don't worry, I cleaned up the copious amounts of blood. I couldn't find the hand, though. Maybe a rat took off with it."

Hanna's wide eyes stared back at me.

"Kidding!"

"Why are you in such a good mood? You're deformed now."

My lips pursed. "Hanna, I know that English isn't your first language, but calling people 'deformed' isn't polite."

"I'm so sorry. I just wish I'd known. When did this happen?"

"Months ago," I replied. I tensed as her white-blond eyebrows furrowed, but I guessed she couldn't remember seeing my left hand in that period of time, because she didn't press me further.

"You should have told me! I've been working so much, I could have taken some time off work to help out."

I was a little shaken that she would consider doing that for me. We barely knew each other, even though we'd been living together for years. But whose fault was that? I'd always kept her at an arm's distance. You can't get hurt if you don't allow yourself to care.

"Nah," I replied. "It is what it is."

She studied me for a moment. "All right. At least let me put away the groceries." She picked up the eight cans of tuna that I'd picked up as a treat for Little Guy, and she stacked them on the bookshelf that served as our pantry. Again, she gave me a hesitant look. "How did you afford all this?"

"Insurance."

"How did you afford the insurance?"

"Jesus Christ, Hanna, I bought the groceries, so you can shut up and make dinner, or you can continue giving me the third degree," I snapped.

We ended up eating tuna sandwiches in silence.

13

"You're a sculptor. That's a unique profession in this day and age. Do you sell your work?"

An innocent question, but we were only three minutes into our session, and already I wanted to slap Dr. Lavoie with my prosthetic limb. "No," I answered. "Besides, I can't make anything anymore, can I?"

Dr. Lavoie frowned. "I wouldn't say that. There are plenty of artists who have disabilities."

I scoffed and crossed my legs, leaning away from her on the couch.

"I'm being serious," she said insistently. "Have you heard of Christopher Blanzen? He was a hockey player in Canada, until an accident left him a quadriplegic. Now he is a world-renowned mouth painter."

I gaped at her. *"Mouth* painter?"

"He paints with his mouth holding the paintbrush."

The image of this man drooling on a canvas made me even more depressed.

The fact that he was *world famous* and actually sold his work, when I couldn't pay anyone to look at mine, sealed the deal.

"There's another amputee who's become a foot painter," she continued.

"A *foot* painter? Like a fetish or something?" I said. "Does he paint *on* feet or paint pictures *of* feet?"

Dr. Lavoie didn't let me get under her skin. "You know exactly what I mean, Roz. Just because you've lost your hand, doesn't mean you've lost your livelihood."

"Thank you for that," I said sweetly. "I feel all better now."

Dr. Lavoie raised a perfectly sculpted eyebrow. "I know you're hurting, but depression is one of the steps of recovery. Let me assure you, it isn't the last step. Soon, you'll be able to accept your condition and continue on with your life."

"My 'condition'? That's a nice way of putting it," I said bitterly. "Listen, Doc, I'm not here for you to make my bad feelings go away. At least, not those bad feelings. I want you to get rid of the phantom limb pain."

"Right." Dr. Lavoie stood up and set her notebook on the desk. I craned my neck, but I couldn't quite read what it said. Her penmanship was nearly perfect, large swirls and loops, but it seemed to be intentionally illegible. Probably to discourage nosy patients like myself from finding out what she really thought about us.

She went to her desk and returned with a medium-sized white box that had a mirror along its side. She placed it on the coffee table across from where I sat. There was a hole in the box facing me. She pulled the wooden coffee table so close to the couch that it brushed my knee. Dr. Lavoie sat back down beside me. I noticed that she had moved a little closer.

"Is this the mirror box therapy you mentioned on Monday?" I asked her as I stared at the box suspiciously.

"You're quite astute, Roz." My attention snapped to her, but her expression remained pleasantly blank. Was she being sarcastic? It was hard to tell. She would make a formidable poker opponent.

"How does it work?"

"Put your left arm in the box."

Again, I eyed the box. The large, cavernous hole seemed to ooze darkness. I sighed. What could it hurt? I'd already lost my hand.

I bent forward and slid my stump into the hole. I looked up at Dr. Lavoie expectantly.

"Put your other hand forward and look at it in the mirror. Position it so that both arms are about the same position and distance from your body."

I didn't see where this was going, but I did what she asked without comment.

"The idea behind this is that phantom limb pain originates in the brain. It's something called the theory of neuroplasticity. The neurons that are associated with your hand, your fingers, the wrist, do not realize that the hand is gone. With neuroplasticity, we can possibly rewire those neurons, redirect them to your other hand."

I crinkled my nose. That made no sense whatsoever.

"This has been a successful therapy in the past, and it is the least invasive option."

"What do I do?" At this point, I was almost willing to sell my right hand to make the pain stop. Almost.

"I want you to look at the reflection of your hand, and we're going to go through a series of exercises—"

"Are you fucking kidding me?"

Dr. Lavoie's eyes were ice. "I may have been wrong about you, Roz."

"What?"

"I thought you were open to therapy. That the pain was so great that you would do anything to make it better. I did not expect you to fight me every step of the way."

I opened my mouth, then thought better of saying anything, and closed it again. She had a point, and dealing with unruly patients who acted like they didn't want her help was probably not in her job description. She could probably have her pick of the patients, and according to Dr. Hughes, Dr. Lavoie was the best in phantom limb treatment.

She was my only hope.

"I'm here to help you, Roz. And you know that my services don't come cheap. If you want to waste both your time and your money, then that's your decision." Her French accent was stronger now. "And I will *not* be prescribing you any more painkillers until we've exhausted all the other options."

My heart skipped a beat at that. I was almost out of pills. "Fine. I'm sorry," I said. "I just don't like being screwed around with. Tell me what to do."

Dr. Lavoie stared at me for several long, excruciating moments. "I suspected the tough love approach would work best with you. I'll be straight with you. If you do not put in the effort, you will not get better. I hope you understand that."

I gave her a little nod.

And just like that, she was back to her usual cool, calm, collected self. "I want you to imagine that the reflection is your missing limb. Visualize that hand making these same movements. It's a way to trick your brain into rewiring these neurons to your right hand."

I looked at the mirror and balled my right hand into a fist.

"Now extend your fingers. Good. Do that another ten times."

I worked through the hand exercises as Dr. Lavoie dictated them. I didn't feel any pain in the phantom limb. Although I realized with a shock that I hadn't felt any at all since entering the room a half hour earlier.

As soon as I took my hand out of the box, it was on fire.

"Shit!" I bit my tongue and tears welled up in my eyes.

Dr. Lavoie frowned.

"Does that mean it didn't work?" Now the tears weren't just because of the fire that consumed my missing hand.

"No, not at all," Dr. Lavoie said quickly. *Is she lying to me?*

"Take the box home with you. I want you to do these exercises as often as possible. Remember to visualize that it is your left hand doing these things. And continue with the antidepressants."

"Tell me the truth," I said, my tone flat. "Will this work?"

"It can take a while for the neurons to be rewired." Dr. Lavoie ushered me out of the door, handing me a large plastic grocery bag to carry the mirror box. "The fact that you're feeling pain now might mean that it's already working."

It wasn't.

14

I was desperate. The pain was unbearable. I called Dr. Lavoie's office several times over the next few days. She wasn't any help. She simply handed me platitudes that made me want to reach through the phone and strangle her. I needed drugs, not exercises or motivational speeches. I spent my entire weekend in front of the damn mirror box. It wasn't working, but what else could I do?

It was the middle of the night, but I couldn't sleep. The burning in my hand would wash over me in waves. It would ebb just long enough for me to start to doze, before crashing back, ripping me away from peaceful slumber. I was going to go insane.

I'd taken the last painkiller Dr. Lavoie had prescribed to me early yesterday morning. I should have rationed them. I should have known that I would need some sleep, some reprieve from this living nightmare.

I paced the living room, treading as quietly as possible so I wouldn't wake Hanna. Not for the first time, I thought back to that reckless decision that ruined my life. I shouldn't have made the deal with Sylvain. This wasn't fair. This wasn't what I'd bargained for. I'd considered reaching out to him—demanding he somehow find a way to set this right—but I had no way of contacting him. I'd tossed the business card he'd given me, and with it, any chance of contacting him. Besides, I knew in my heart that if I reached out to him, it would only make things worse. What if the only way he'd help to alleviate the pain was if I sacrificed another limb? My stomach churned at the thought.

I continued to pace the loft, racking my brain for other options. Why couldn't Dr. Lavoie have prescribed me more painkillers? She'd seen how much pain I was in. She had to know I wasn't a drug addict, desperate for a fix. My pain was *real*. The pills she'd given me felt barely stronger than children's Tylenol. I needed something stronger. I couldn't wait until my appointment with Dr. Lavoie that afternoon. I needed something *now*.

Without deliberating any further, I slipped on my flats and was out of the loft. The cool air on the street was sharp and cut through my hair, brushing it away from my face. I embraced the chill. I welcomed the sensation of something—anything—other than the burning in a limb I didn't even have anymore. I glanced up and down the street. The damp pavement was the only indication that it must have rained sometime since I'd ventured out last. The parked cars lining the side of the street were dark. There was no white sedan. There wasn't a single living soul in sight.

I shivered. Where should I go? I knew I shouldn't be out alone at this hour. I hated it, but I was more vulnerable now that I had only one hand, although the prosthesis had some heft to it, and it was easier to wield than a brick, which I'd once used to fend off a would-be rapist a few years back. The guy had been sent to the hospital in critical condition, and I was almost charged with assault. That was the world I lived in.

I couldn't go back. Not until I had what I needed. I picked a direction and started walking. I was almost tempted to stop at O'Malley's, but I knew that it wasn't enough. Alcohol didn't seem to dull this pain, although it dulled my ability to think, which I was starting to appreciate more and more these days. Besides, I wasn't supposed to mix alcohol with the antidepressants. Not that the antidepressants seemed to be helping, but I was hoping that they might kick in eventually.

The regret hanging over me was so thick it was almost palpable. What had I done to myself? Of course, I couldn't have known that I would have phantom pain. According to Dr. Lavoie, it was quite common, but I'd never heard of it before it happened to me. I was never one for research, but I wish I'd at least done a quick Google search before making such a drastic decision.

I'd been drunk when Sylvain found me, but I'd had weeks to think the decision through. I'd done a lot of things I regretted in my twenty-nine years, but never anything this stupid, this reckless, this *dangerous*.

What I was about to do was dangerous as well. My weed guy—back when I could afford a weed guy—had told me he knew where I could go to "score some stronger shit." I hadn't pressed further, because even my alcohol and weed-addled brain had suspected that it wasn't a good idea to screw around with "stronger shit." Now, I couldn't care less if I became a drug addict, on the streets, craving my next fix. If I was being honest with myself, I was already at that level of desperation.

I hopped on the el, ignoring the leering looks from the two creeps sitting across the aisle from me.

"Hey lady, you look lonely."

Shit. Apparently not looking at them hadn't done me any favors.

"Hey, lady, my buddy's talkin' to you," the other guy said. His voice sounded closer.

I swallowed back my nerves. I should have taken a cab. I had the money now, but old habits die hard. I kept my eyes trained on the window. I could see the reflection of the two guys in the windowpane. One of them was skinny, reed-thin, and looked like a good gust of wind could knock him over. His friend, on the other hand, had some heft to him. Of course, that was the one who got out of his seat to approach me.

Double shit.

"Hey lady, you're not half bad lookin' in the dark," the guy breathed his onion and cigarette-laced breath on me.

I stiffened. "Not interested." I didn't look at him, in case he could read the fear in my eyes. He reeked so bad that I had to breathe out of my mouth.

"How much?" he asked.

"What?" *Shit, don't engage!*

I saw his sneer from the corner of my eye. My heart tumbled around in my chest. "How much for a night of sheer bliss?"

The other guy jumped out of his seat and whooped so loudly that I nearly jumped out of my skin.

"I'm not a hooker," I said flatly. My body was pressed against the window in a feeble attempt to put as much distance between me and this creep as humanly possible.

"Hey, man, did you hear that? Lady says she isn't a hooker!" the guy called back to his idiot friend.

"Coulda fooled me!" the other guy replied.

I'd been dressed for bed, but my outfit wasn't particularly revealing. I was wearing sweatpants and an old Halestorm T-shirt, although I was heavily regretting my choice not to wear a bra. I was regretting a lot of things these days.

Without thinking, I swung my prosthesis around and hit him on the head. He flew backward into the aisle, clutching his eye, which was streaming blood.

Despite the situation, and the unadulterated fury that the injured guy was radiating, a grin spread across my face. So my prosthesis *could* double as a weapon.

Taking advantage of the element of surprise, and the fact that the el had just stopped, I jumped out of my seat and slipped off the train before the doors slid shut. The guys didn't make it to the door before the train sped away, swallowed by the dark abyss of night.

I took a few moments to catch my breath. That was close. Too close. I inspected my prosthetic hand, which had just a little bit of blood on the thumb. I wiped it clean on my sweatpants.

As I waited for my heart rate to gradually slow, I glanced around. Fortunately, I was only a few blocks away from my weed guy's place. I stalked down the street, keeping an eye on any stranger who strayed too close. Living in Chicago, I knew only too well the dangers of being a woman outside, alone, at night. I'd seen just a tiny reminder of this danger on the el. While those guys might have been long gone, they could easily be replaced by another dozen assholes on this street alone.

I made it to my weed guy's apartment without another incident. Kris was a former classmate of mine, although he had never made it past the first semester of freshman year. He had taken the exact opposite route of Amrita. Where she was a budding artist, just beginning to develop her brand through exposure, he was a businessman, prospering in a city where everyone and their grandma wanted a little weed now and again to dull the passage of time.

I rang the buzzer for apartment 406. There was no answer, but I didn't give up that easily. I rang again. And again. Finally, a groggy voice answered in the most eloquent manner possible: "What the fuck?"

"Kris! You sound absolutely delightful at this time of night," I said, grinning. I had to admit I took some pleasure in his irritation. The guy always ripped me off.

"What the fuck?" he asked again. Like I'd said—delightful.

"This is Roz. Remember me? I used to be one of your best customers."

There was silence on the other end. "Come back during business hours." He cut off the line.

Swearing under my breath, I buzzed again. This time he picked up on the second ring. "Listen, it's the middle of the fucking night. Why can't you wait until the sun comes up, like a normal person?"

"I've never been normal. Besides, it's only two in the morning. Shouldn't that be prime work hours for you in your line of work?" I loved being antagonistic to people when they'd been antagonistic to me in the past. I'd never forget the time when he charged me twice as much because he knew he could. This was just me returning the favor.

"It's the middle of the night," he says again. "You'll have to pay me triple." There it was.

"I'm not buying what you're selling. Not tonight."

"What the fuck?"

The guy needed a broader vocabulary. "Listen, remember when you told me you knew someone who could sell me something a little stronger than your typical batch of weed?"

I could almost hear Kris nodding. "Yeah, stronger shit."

I was starting to genuinely wonder if that was what the stuff was actually called. "Can you be more specific?"

"Stronger-than-weed shit."

Yeah, this guy had smoked a few too many. I just hoped that my brain didn't end up like his. Although, maybe then the pain would stop. "Does this guy have a name? A location?"

"Why?" Kris suddenly sounded suspicious.

"Listen, I'm fucking desperate. Give me a name and I'll tell them you referred me."

"I'll be down in a second. Jesus." Kris was off the line.

Searing pain shot through my hand, and I rode it out while I waited. Finally, Kris appeared in the doorway, bare-chested, wearing sagging joggers that exposed a little too much. I averted my eyes and tried not to gag.

"The name?" I asked.

Kris looked me up and down. "Are you working with the police?"

"Do I look like I'm working with the police?" I asked. I gestured to what I was wearing.

Kris stared at my breasts. "Are you wearing a wire?" he asked them.

"You're not finding out. Give me the name, or I'm leaving."

Kris gave me a look that told me he knew that I was bluffing. I wasn't going to leave. I oozed with desperation. People who weren't desperate didn't wander Chicago in the middle of the night in their sleepwear, looking for a fix. "The guy's name is Trap. Here's his number." He slipped me a scrap of paper that looked like it had been partly chewed, but the phone number was written legibly in blue ink.

I turned to leave.

"Tell him I sent you. Unless you're with the cops. If you are, then just leave me the hell out of it."

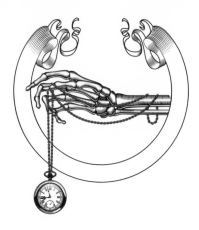

I DRIFT DOWN THE STREET, the crisp wind tousling my hair as I blend into my surroundings. I don dark colors. I cling to the shadows. No one will see me. No one will know I'm here.

Not until it's too late.

I pause for a moment, allowing the anticipation of what I am about to create to bring me to life. I lift a hand to my face, inspecting it in the crass glow of a neon liquor-store sign. The red and blue lights illuminate its perfection. Smooth skin. Long, slender fingers. Delicate, yet sinewy muscle. The scar just over the wrist bone has almost completely faded, removing any indication that this was not always mine.

It is identical to what I'd lost. What had been savagely stolen from me. My last subject had taken me by surprise and fought back. One slam of a car door, and I'd nearly lost everything. My life's work had been put on hold, my art wrenched away from a world that yearned to be sophisticated enough to appreciate it.

For nearly a year, I've been lying in wait. I never left, not like the newsmen theorized. I wasn't locked away. I didn't die, and I will never quit.

But I haven't spent this past year sulking or mourning. No, I've spent it planning. My loss became an opportunity; I see that now. My work before was good. But now, I can be great.

Some creatives are emotional and spontaneous. While my art is still instinctual, I'm a planner. I spend weeks—months, even—studying my subject, drawing upon my deep well of inspiration, envisioning how to distort it, paint it with the darkest of human emotion, and present it for the world to gaze upon with awe. I've been preparing my magnum opus for over a year. And tonight it finally begins.

I watch the building, counting down the seconds until the door swings open, right on schedule. A young brunette steps into the streetlight, pulling her jacket tight around her shoulders to protect herself from the sharp chill. She shoots a quick glance up and down the street before hurrying to the deserted alley where she foolishly parked her car.

The city has grown complacent. This is almost too easy. But tonight is the first of many, and the others will be far more challenging. Besides, this brunette isn't the one that matters. She isn't the signature piece. That girl is currently tucked away in her loft apartment, unaware of the role she has to play.

She won't be unaware much longer.

I emerge from the shadows. My stomach flutters with excitement. My fingers twitch with anticipation. I glide down the street, closing the distance between me and my fresh canvas.

The time for preparation has come to an end. Now, it's time for my renaissance.

15

Immediately after I texted him, Trap gave me concise orders to go to Lincoln Park, alone, with five hundred dollars in cash. I knew I was being swindled, because there was no way that painkillers should cost that much, but I didn't particularly care. I had the money and I needed this.

The clock crept past six as I waited on a park bench, hunched over, cradling my prosthesis to my chest. A notification from the news app I'd downloaded drew my attention away from the insufferable pain. The Phantom Strangler was back after a nearly year-long hiatus. He'd strangled an unnamed woman last night.

Wariness trickled down my spine, fear overriding my pain if only for a moment. I shouldn't have been wandering the streets alone. I could have easily been that girl.

A twig snapped and I jumped to my feet. A man who bore a striking resemblance to Ben's thug that had kidnapped me emerged from the bushes.

I spotted his neck tattoos and the ragged scar that sliced downward from temple to mouth. My entire body tensed. This *was* Ben's thug, the one I'd nicknamed Scarface. The one who'd stalked me, under Ben's orders.

I swallowed. "Y-you Trap?"

He lumbered toward me, blocking my escape. "I know you." His words were slow, deliberate. Menacing.

"I get that a lot. I'm a brunette with a plain face that looks hot with the right shade of lipstick. I'm basically every other girl in Chicago."

"You're Ben's girl."

"Ben's *ex*-girl," I said. "And I'm not here as his anything. I'm here as a customer."

Trap didn't root around in his pockets for the drugs. He didn't even glance at the wad of cash I gripped with white knuckles. "Where's Ben?"

I blinked. "What?"

"Ben's missing. Has been for weeks. Nobody's seen him since that night."

"Which night? You're going to have to be a hell of a lot more specific," I said through a clenched jaw. The pain in my phantom limb was back, and it was taking all my concentration not to slam my invisible hand against the park bench. Anything to make the pain stop.

"You know what night I'm talking about. The night I brought you in. The night you got Harris killed."

I struggled to follow his words over the fire consuming my arm. Ben was missing? Had Sylvain managed to get him arrested and thrown in prison without any of his minions finding out? "Have you checked the jails? The guy is psycho. He probably got himself arrested."

"That would be one helluva coincidence." Trap moved closer, breathing his rancid breath down on me. I held my ground, even though my feet were itching to run. "That we bring you in, and then suddenly he gets arrested."

Unfortunately for me, Trap clearly wasn't sampling his product. He'd noticed the connection between me and Ben's disappearance. Why hadn't I thought of this sooner? Why hadn't I realized that having Sylvain send Ben to prison immediately after I found out about his operation would put a target on *my* back? "I—I'm just here to buy fentanyl or oxy or whatever it is that you're s-selling."

A vein bulged on his forehead as he continued to glare at me. "Ben isn't in jail. He isn't anywhere. He's missing. He's gone, and I wanna know where."

"Why? So you can update your Christmas list?"

Trap grabbed my arm and yanked me toward him. He looked down at my prosthetic hand in surprise. "That's new."

I tilted my chin upward, defiantly. "Just give me the damn drugs."

His lips curled in disgust, as if I was the one who smelled nasty and had two rotting front teeth. "I'm not selling you jack shit. If I find out you had anything to do with why Ben's gone MIA, then you'll get your drugs." He leaned closer, breathing his fetid stink all over me. "In the form of an overdose. They'll find you lying belly up, bloated and dead, swimming in your own vomit."

I tried to pull away, but he was too strong, his grip too tight. He squeezed my arm even harder, before suddenly letting go.

I caught my balance before I fell back onto the bench. I schooled my facial features to hide the terror that coursed through my veins. "That was unnecessarily graphic, Trap, but I get the picture. I had *nothing* to do with Ben's disappearance." My heart thundered in my chest.

Trap shot me a toothy, rotted grin, and said, "You better hope not. Don't forget, I know where you live."

At that, he disappeared down the path, and I flew out of there like a bat out of hell.

16

I must have looked as terrible as I felt, because Dr. Lavoie's secretary, whose name I could never seem to remember, visibly cringed when I stalked into the office.

"Regan Osbourne. Here for my three o'clock," I barked before collapsing onto one of the metal waiting room chairs. My hand was feeling a little better now that I'd spent the better part of the morning and early afternoon at O'Malley's bar. I hoped I didn't smell too strongly of liquor. I popped a stick of spearmint gum into my mouth and began to chew, frantically.

By the time Dr. Lavoie finished with her previous patient, the pain in my hand was exchanged for the pins and needles sensation that occasionally cropped up. While I despised all the phantom limb sensations, this one was preferable over the others, because it didn't leave me curled up in the fetal position on the dirty floor. It was simply uncomfortable. I could survive uncomfortable.

I took my usual seat on the couch beneath the window. Dr. Lavoie was on the other side of the room, filing away a manila envelope in the oak cabinet.

Her serene smile wavered as she approached me. "You're not looking well."

"Well, I feel about a million times worse," I snapped.

"Have you been doing the exercises with the mirror box?"

"I've spent almost every waking moment doing the damn exercises. They're not working." I picked up the mirror box that I'd brought with me and basically threw it at her feet.

Dr. Lavoie moved her Gucci strapless heels away just in time to prevent a scuff. "I see."

"That's it? 'I see'? Listen, I'm paying *top dollar* for these bullshit sessions, and so far, the pain is *worse*, if that's even possible. How can you just take my money and not do anything to help me?" To my horror, a sob escaped my lips. I clamped my good hand down on my mouth to muffle the sobs that followed. This was the first time I'd cried since the night Ben killed someone, and it was in front of a basic stranger. Even worse, it was a stranger who looked like she did—cool, composed, elegant as hell, without a strand of hair out of place or a fleck of lint in sight.

Dr. Lavoie took a seat. She waited, patiently, until I managed to pull my shit together.

"The mirror box works for some but not all of my patients," Dr. Lavoie said, her voice saturated with pity. "There are other therapies we can—and will—try."

"I need painkillers, Doc."

"Are the sleeping pills not working?"

"Those pills wouldn't make a Chihuahua yawn. They're that fucking weak."

"I could prescribe something stronger."

"And get me addicted to sleeping pills instead of painkillers? Wow, you really seem like you know what you're doing." I couldn't control the vitriol that spilled out of my mouth.

For once she seemed uncertain. For once she seemed out of her element. I'd put her there, and I wasn't sure if I should be proud of myself or ashamed.

Dr. Lavoie suddenly stood and strode back to the oak cabinet, opened the drawer, and withdrew the manila envelope I'd seen her depositing earlier. I didn't have the energy to ask her what was inside the envelope. She didn't say, but instead she placed it on the coffee table in front of me. She took a seat beside me again, but this time a little farther away than before.

"I may have an option for you," Dr. Lavoie began, "but please bear with me. I want you to be as candid as possible during this session before I make my final decision."

That was ominous as hell. I leaned forward to pick up the envelope, but she was faster. She snatched it up and placed it on the floor beside her.

"Not yet." Her tone left no room for negotiation.

I raised my hands in surrender. "Ask away."

Dr. Lavoie nodded. She clasped her hands on her lap, her thumb worrying the wedding band that hung a little too loosely on her ring finger. Her fingers looked strong, like she could be an artist.

I wondered what she did in her free time, and if these activities required the use of her hands. Was she a painter? A pianist? Did she crochet little hats for stray kittens for charity?

Whatever hobbies she had, whatever secret passions, I hoped she appreciated her freedom to pursue them. You never knew when it all could be torn away from you in the blink of an eye.

"You said that you've spent every waking moment with the mirror box—is this true?"

I gritted my teeth. "Every moment I wasn't eating or shitting."

Dr. Lavoie gave me a look.

"What? You said to be candid."

"I'm asking because it is important for someone in your position to have a support network. You mentioned having a roommate?"

"Yes, Hanna. She's lovely. Hardly ever around. She cleans the bathroom. It's a match made in heaven."

"But are you two close? Do you talk about what you're going through? Does she know about your difficulties with the pain and sleeping?"

I shrugged. "I've been up a lot at night. She hasn't been around much, but she did comment about it the other day. I think my pacing was keeping her up. I really, really don't want to piss her off, because I don't want her to kick me out."

"And why is that?"

"Why is what?"

"Why don't you want her to kick you out?"

"Because the apartment is cheap." As I was saying it, I realized that that argument didn't stand anymore. I had money now. I could afford a better place.

Well, I could afford a better place for a while. I didn't want to blow through all my cash right away. It had turned out that I had spent more money than I'd thought on the day I got my payout, which I fondly referred to as my Day of Debauchery. But still, I didn't *need* the loft to live anymore. Yet I felt like I did need it.

Dr. Lavoie watched me as I went through this thought process. I couldn't shake the feeling that she was reading my mind. My cheeks reddened. "There's also a lot of space. For my artwork," I added.

Dr. Lavoie nodded. "Your artwork. Which you said you'd abandoned. On account of the lost limb."

"Right." She was talking me into a corner here.

"So, if you have truly given up your artwork, your passion, your zeal for your sculptures, then you wouldn't need such a big place. You could find a smaller apartment for less rent."

"Right."

"So, either you're attached to Hanna, or you're not ready to give up your passion for creation."

"Right."

"I think it might be a little bit of both," Dr. Lavoie finished. She smiled slightly, seemingly pleased with herself.

"What, exactly, am I supposed to do with this information?" I snarled.

She looked surprised by my reaction. "Roz, there is nothing wrong with having attachments. There is nothing wrong with growing to depend on someone—or something."

"Isn't there?" I tasted sourness in my next words. "Getting attached to things only leads to pain and heartbreak." I couldn't do my art. Not with only one hand and the phantom pain stalking my every moment. And I knew, I just *knew*, that the moment I came to rely on Hanna, she would let me down, just like everyone else in my life had.

Dr. Lavoie was quiet for so long that I thought she was ready to call it quits. I had no such luck. "Does this have to do with your father?"

"Never met him. Never had a chance to get attached."

She cocked her head. I realized that this was the most I'd told her about my family. I couldn't do this. "What about your mother?"

I shot her a snide smile. "That's a topic to fill an entire session, Doc."

"Very well." She leaned backward, disappointment flitting across her face. "We've covered a lot of ground today. I'm proud of you, Roz. You've come a long way in just a few short sessions."

I barely listened to her. I was eyeing the manila envelope. It was too thin to hold a bottle of pills. So what could be in it, and how could it help me?

"There is a new drug trial that is searching for participants."

"Drug trial?" I reluctantly brought my gaze back up to hers.

"Yes. Ryofen. It's a radical new drug that is about to undergo its first round of human trials. If you'd like, you could be one of the first to try it. I think you would be a perfect candidate."

My mind was whirling. "What does it do? Is it a painkiller? Is it for people with phantom limb pain?"

"It is a painkiller—yes—but it's unique in that it targets the pain receptors in the brain. It reduces the sensation of pain without—theoretically— any of the typical side effects of a painkiller. It is expected to not dull the sensations or cause brain fog. The reason I thought of you is because it is—or will be—marketed as a strong painkiller without the dangers of addiction. With your tendencies toward dependence and ... overindulging, I think you might benefit from this."

I ignored the obvious reference to my lack of impulse control, something I'd tried not to tell her about but that she'd clearly picked up on regardless.

"A painkiller with no side effects? Sign me up!" I grinned.

"Not so quickly. This is a trial run. It's been approved for human testing, but there is still potential for side effects. It has only been tested so far on *nonhuman* subjects. Meaning the doctors have no way of knowing for sure how a human would react to being on this medication. There may very well be harmful side effects." Envy engulfed me as her fingers deftly removed a document from the manila envelope. Something so simple that I'd once taken for granted and would never be able to do so easily again. I glared at her hands. Oblivious to my attention and sudden unwavering resentment, she flipped through the pages, skimming the document. "These recruitment forms don't provide details. That's information that only the scientists working on the study know. They may be worried about intellectual property theft." She frowned thoughtfully. "Nevertheless, they should have included the potential side effects."

I sighed, tearing my eyes away from her perfect hands. "I wouldn't care if the side effects made me grow a tail. Seriously, Doc, sign me up." I reached for the forms again, but still she held them out of reach, like a parent tantalizing their child with a brand-new toy. If I'd had two hands, I could have easily snatched it from her.

"I have one condition."

"No drinking while on the trial?"

Dr. Lavoie looked genuinely surprised at my remark. "You should not be drinking now. Roz, alcohol and the antidepressants you're on do not mix."

"I was kidding," I said quickly. I leaned away from her, hoping that the stench of whiskey wafting from my pores wouldn't betray me.

Dr. Lavoie eyed me warily. "As I pointed out earlier, you do not have a support network. Many who are suffering as you are have family and friends to fall back on. You have neither."

"Ouch. Why don't you tell it like it is?" I said, producing my most charming smile.

"I want you to join a support group."

My smile faltered. "What, now?"

"Many benefit from speaking to others who have suffered or are suffering from similar mental or physical duress."

"You mean, like go to a meeting and talk to complete strangers?" My lips curled in distaste.

"It is not unlike what you are doing right now," Dr. Lavoie said, hiding a smile. "There are a few local support groups for individuals who are suffering from the loss of a limb. I want you to pick one and attend meetings. Regularly." Dr. Lavoie produced a pamphlet out of nowhere and handed it to me. It listed a bunch of locations, one of which was not too far from where I lived.

"I don't know . . ."

"You will benefit from talking to others with whom you have this in common," Dr. Lavoie insisted. Not for the first time, I noticed that her accent grew stronger and her English more stilted when she was being earnest about something.

I sighed. "Will I? Won't they all be veterans? We'll have nothing in common."

"Some will be veterans, but others might be just like you."

I looked down at the pamphlet. It didn't have any pictures, which was probably because an image of a group of people missing random body parts might be a little too depressing to depict on a self-help booklet.

"Fine," I said, stifling yet another sigh. What was the worst that could happen?

Satisfied, Dr. Lavoie handed me the manila envelope that promised to change everything.

17

There was a problem with the paperwork. I bit the end of my pen nervous-ly as I glanced around the sterile waiting room. Northwestern Memorial Hospital was always busy, always bustling, but the area I found myself in was nearly dead. Designated for "Research and Development," this wing brought in the megabucks with Big Pharma grants and funding. At least, that's what the overly talkative lady who'd sat beside me had informed me. Despite her chatter, she'd finished the paperwork more quickly than I had, and she was already in the interview room talking with the research team.

I glared down at the form I was currently filling out. I was having diffi-culty with certain questions, particularly the history leading up to my ampu-tation. Who was the doctor that took care of me afterward? I'd given them Dr. Hughes's name, and I hoped that they wouldn't follow up with her. Now, I was filling out the rest of the questionnaire.

History of mental illness in the family?

Nope.

History of substance abuse in the family?

Visions of my mother dousing herself in vodka during one of her bend-ers when I was fourteen flitted through my mind. I hastily scrawled: "Nope."

My knowledge of my family's medical history was all pretty one-sided, so I got creative and said that my father had asthma. Nobody was perfect, and maybe this little tidbit would trick them into thinking I wasn't lying through my teeth about my mother's addictions and my lack of information about my father. I would not take the risk of being disqualified from this medical trial.

"You're finally done?" the receptionist asked when I presented her with the clipboard.

I could tell she didn't mean to insult me, but I still snapped at her. "Yes, I'm left-handed, so it took a while." I showed her my prosthesis.

She had the grace to blush and awkwardly busied herself with my clipboard. "Have a seat, and the team will be ready to meet with you soon."

As I was plopping back down onto the plush chair, my phone chimed with a news alert. I pulled it out of my back pocket.

The Phantom Strangler's Latest Victim Has Been Identified. I bit my lip as I swiped upward. The article had the name of the victim, Tessa Brown, and a smiling photo of her from her high school graduation. I tore my gaze away from her soft brown eyes, which were framed with laugh lines. Her body had been found mere blocks away from the loft. She'd been killed in the middle of the night, the exact same night I'd been wandering the street looking for a fix.

It was sheer luck that I hadn't been the victim. If I had died, nobody would miss me, except for perhaps Hanna, when rent was due. This girl, Tessa, had friends, a stable job, a doting boyfriend, and a loving set of parents.

The police were following so-called leads. They surmised that the killer must have been behind bars or possibly out of town for the last year. A sicko like this didn't just stop killing. He wouldn't go on hiatus by choice. Something stopped him, and the police were convinced that this "something" was what would lead to him getting caught.

I put away my phone, feeling a little better. It looked like the police were close to catching him. Hopefully, they would before he made his way down my street.

"Ms. Osbourne? The doctors will see you now," the receptionist said. "Third door on the left."

I hastily combed my fingers through my hair before entering the room. Three men and a woman wearing lab coats were seated at a round table. I was relieved to discover this wasn't an examination room but a conference room. I should have realized that this meant I was in for an interrogation.

"Good morning. I'm Dr. Ralph Bohmer, principal investigator." A tall, gangly man with salt-and-pepper hair extended a bony hand.

I noticed I was trembling as I took his hand in mine.

He looked surprised. "You have a strong handshake."

"That's what all the boys tell me," I replied.

"Right. Er, well, we've looked over your file. You come highly recommended by a Doctor"—he consulted his clipboard—"Lavoie. Tell me, in your own words: why do you want to be a part of this trial?"

My entire body tensed. I hadn't prepared for an interview. I should have washed my hair that morning and worn my lucky red lipstick.

"Dr. Lavoie gave me the sales pitch. It's very . . . enticing." Was that word appropriate?

My eyes landed on the woman at the far end of the table. She was taking copious amounts of notes, far more than my response warranted. I tried not to watch her. The three men stared at me expectantly. I didn't offer anything else. This might be the reason why I bombed most job interviews. Although it was probably safer not to say too much than to really speak my mind.

Dr. Bohmer nodded, as if what I'd said was astute. "Well, you're a perfect candidate. Ryofen is designed for pain reduction in cases where traditional therapies don't work. According to your file, you said you've already exhausted all other treatments?"

"That is what the file says," I said vaguely. We'd tried the most common therapies—antidepressants and mirror therapy. I'd known from WebMD that there were other options—anticonvulsants, acupuncture, TENS therapy—but I didn't want to miss my chance with this trial. So, I would lie through my teeth to get a coveted spot.

Dr. Bohmer nodded again, and I wondered if he was part bobblehead. "Phantom limb pain is not well understood in the medical community. It's a *fascinating* condition. I would *love* to have someone with this disorder involved in this trial."

"Well, I would *love* to be in this trial," I said with a strained smile. I would not say something sarcastic. I would not snap at him. I could be polite for a few minutes, right?

"You aren't on any medications now, correct?" Dr. Bohmer looked at my file. "It says here that you're on antidepressants."

"They were for the pain receptors in the brain. No history of mental illness. None whatsoever. I have a sparkling clean bill of mental health." I snapped my mouth shut to stop from babbling.

"Right." Dr. Bohmer frowned. "Are you on those now? If you're on antidepressants, we'll need to wait a thirty-day period before you can start the Ryofen. It's the required protocol. We definitely don't want anything contra-indicating the Ryofen."

Thirty days? I couldn't wait *thirty days*. "Oh, I haven't been on those meds in over a month," I said.

Dr. Bohmer looked at me. "Why did you list them on the paperwork?"

"I got confused. Because of the pain." I grimaced while pointing to my prosthesis. My hand was uncharacteristically pain free at the moment, but they didn't know that.

Dr. Bohmer seemed to believe me. "Right, then. You aren't on any other medications? You know that you also won't be permitted to drink caffeine or alcohol while on this trial."

No alcohol *or* caffeine? I licked my lips. "I hardly ever drink anyway." A sharp pain shot through my hand. I winced and unconsciously clutched the prosthesis with my right hand.

"Are you experiencing pain right now?" Dr. Bohmer asked. His face lit up, and the other doctors leaned forward dramatically. The woman at the far end was writing even faster now, and she was already on her third sheet of paper.

"Yeah . . ." I said. Their extreme fascination would have been amusing if I hadn't been focusing all my mental energy to keep from spewing out a long string of cuss words and slamming my head against the table to make the pain stop.

"It looks like the pain is quite extreme." He glanced back down at my intake files. "You rated it as sometimes reaching a nine out of ten, is that correct?"

"That would be correct," I said. I took a deep breath. In and out. "If you don't mind, can we wrap this up?"

"Just one more question before I send you to the examination room for your physical. I need to confirm something. On your form you say you have no history of substance abuse. I need to ask you this again, just to make sure, and so that I can sign off on this."

I pursed my lips in irritation. "Why do you need to be so sure? I thought that one of the miracles of this drug was that it's supposed to not be addictive?"

Dr. Bohmer didn't quite meet my eye. "That's one of its main benefits, yes. But it may still exhibit addictive properties in some patients."

That didn't sound ominous at all. I smiled tightly. "Nope, no history of substance abuse," I replied. "When will I know if I'm accepted for this trial?"

"Right now!" the bespectacled man sitting on Dr. Bohmer's right piped in. His cheeks were stained pink and he glanced at Dr. Bohmer, who shot him a look. Apparently, Dr. Bohmer was the only person who was allowed to speak to the patients. I hadn't even gotten the names of the others in the room.

"We want to make sure you understand the risks. This is a large cohort study, and we intend to follow you longitudinally."

I nodded, though I had no idea what that meant. "Yeah, okay."

"Here are the forms that indicate what you are agreeing to. You'll be required to come in for a physical examination weekly for the first two months, then biweekly. The forms also contain some legal jargon, with a clause stressing that you're waiving any right to pursue legal action should you experience any of the listed side effects."

Side effects?

"Also, you're signing to acknowledge that you've been informed that you may not be receiving Ryofen; you might be taking a placebo."

"What, now? A placebo? I'm not getting a fucking placebo, am I?"

Dr. Bohmer's furry eyebrows shot through the roof. "This is a double-blind study. That means that no one will know who is receiving which. However, I am fairly confident in the efficacy of Ryofen, and I'm sure we'll be able to tell who is taking it in no time."

I would hate to have jumped through all these hoops just to get a placebo. I stared down at the forms he'd so kindly placed on the table in front of me. I supposed I didn't have a choice. If I was given a placebo, or if the Ryofen just didn't work, I would back out of the study, crawl back to Dr. Lavoie, and beg her for narcotics.

I skimmed the list of possible side effects. Hallucinations were at the bottom of the list. "Hallucinations?" I looked at Dr. Bohmer, raising one eyebrow as high as it could go.

"Because of the nature of the brain, and the areas that this drug is targeting, there is some chance that mild hallucinations will be one of the much rarer side effects."

"How rare?"

"As long as you're not taking unauthorized drugs or mind-altering substances while on this pill, the risk of side effects, including dizzy spells and hallucinations, should be minimal."

My eyes narrowed. I wanted to ask what his definition of *minimal* was, but who was I kidding? If this drug took away my pain, I'd take it even if I had to spend the rest of my life jostling between dancing elephants as I shuffled my way to crazy town. I wedged the pen between the fingers of my right hand and signed.

18

My phone chirped at the foot of my bed, jolting me awake from my nap—the first peaceful sleep I'd had in a long time. I slammed my hand down on the phone to make it stop, realizing only too late that I used the arm with the prosthesis on it. I heard a loud crack. I groaned and sat up. I was on Day Two of no antidepressants, and to be honest, I didn't feel any different. But the pills were almost out of my system, which meant I could start on the Ryofen tomorrow. While I hadn't wanted to wait an entire month, I didn't want to accidentally kill myself either. I did a quick internet search and found a website that said that three days between drug trials should be good enough. I hoped that was true.

I was convinced I wouldn't be getting the placebo. Dr. Bohmer said that he didn't know who would be getting which, but I trusted him about as far as I could throw him. He'd been far too excited at the thought of a person with untreatable phantom limb pain taking his drug to let me be assigned a simple sugar pill. I was counting on him being unethical and making sure that I got the real dose. How ironic was that?

My bedroom was dark, and late-afternoon light crept in through the filthy windows. I looked at the time on the newly cracked screen of my phone. I was supposed to attend my first amputee support group meeting tonight. I sighed and rolled out of bed.

I left my bedroom and found myself pausing at the border of my make-shift workspace. An overwhelming compulsion gripped me. I stared at the raw materials, the copper wire, the junk I'd pilfered from various parts of the city.

My chisel, soldering iron, pliers, and carving knives called to me. Ideas began to take form, ethereal specters drifting, but before they could manifest, a blazing fire burned through my phantom limb, ravaging my creativity and buckling my knees with pain. My eyes welled with tears as I got back to my feet, the inspiration nothing but a distant memory.

Hanna exited the bathroom wrapped in a fuzzy green towel that barely covered her torso. "You're up early," she said with a small smile.

"It was just a nap," I snapped.

Hanna frowned. "And that was just a joke."

"Well, notice that I'm not laughing."

Hanna looked like she was about to say something, but she thought better of it and instead ducked into her bedroom.

And I'd wondered why I didn't have any friends. Sighing, I went into the kitchen to put on a pot of coffee. I poured a second cup for Hanna as a peace offering. I wedged it between my arm and my torso and slowly walked toward her bedroom. I hovered outside the curtain.

"Knock, knock," I said, realizing I had nothing to knock on and no free hand to knock with.

There was no response. I knew she could hear me.

"Hanna?"

A quiet sigh came from beyond the curtain. "Come in, Roz."

I stepped past the curtain into her private quarters. I realized that this was my first time entering it. It was spartan, but in a chic way, where less is more, and not in my cheap "I don't have any money to spend on a pot of flowers" kind of way.

"I made you some coffee," I said, presenting the mug to her.

"Thank you," she said, accepting it. She put it down on her nightstand. She returned to the floor-length mirror that was mounted on the wall and continued applying mascara to every single eyelash. I noticed that she was wearing the dress I'd bought her.

"You look nice," I said. "Someone has good taste."

She rolled her eyes. "It's not as nice as the dress you ruined, but it's a lot more expensive." She lowered the wand, watching me in the mirror. "How did you afford it?"

"I sold my hand for a million dollars."

Hanna cracked a smile. "Fine, you don't have to tell me. I'm just a little worried, I guess."

I stared at her. "You're worried about me?" I hated the sound of surprise and vulnerability in my tone. I made up for it by scowling.

"I'm not worried about you. I'm worried that whoever you stole that money from is going to show up here!" Hanna said. She shot me a grin, and then continued applying mascara.

"Hot date?" I asked.

Hanna grinned. "The hottest." She stepped back to admire her handi-work in the mirror.

"Well, I'll let you finish getting ready," I said. Without a backward glance, I left her sleeping area and headed to the kitchen. I chugged my cof-fee, welcoming the blistering hot pain as a distraction from the now pulsing sensation in my severed hand.

I looked down at my phone again. The support group was meeting in fifteen minutes. Sighing, I dropped my mug in the sink and headed out.

19

A brisk wind swept through my hair, catching itself in the tangles that I hadn't managed to comb out with one hand. I hugged my coat tighter around my shoulders. While it wasn't quite cold outside, it was the wind that whipped through the air, bringing with it an icy chill that cut through my flimsy winter coat and burrowed its way deep under my skin. Chicago wasn't called the Windy City for nothing.

I stared down at the lopsided hopscotch painted on the sidewalk. I hovered outside the recreation center, reluctant to enter. I took out my phone to check the time. The support group meeting started over five minutes ago. It was now or never. I let out a sigh and entered the building, dragging my feet all the way.

I hoped I was late enough that I would miss introductions, and that I could slip into the back of the room to observe, unnoticed.

No such luck.

The basement rec room was large, but the meeting itself wasn't. Less than a dozen people sat in chairs that were positioned in a large circle. Someone in the group was talking when I entered, but she cut off abruptly when I let the door slam shut behind me. Everyone turned to stare. Heat flooded my cheeks. This wasn't quite the inconspicuous entrance I'd been hoping to make.

"I was looking for AA, but since I'm obviously in the wrong place, have you got anything to drink?"

I was openly stared at. "Tough crowd," I muttered. I guessed they'd all lost their senses of humor along with whatever body parts they were missing. Suddenly feeling self-conscious, I waved my prosthesis in the air, so they would know that I was in the right place.

"Grab some coffee and a treat," a skinny, short guy in a red flannel shirt and dingy wool scarf said. "And then have a seat. Any of the empty chairs will do. Sharon, please continue with your story."

A woman with a single streak of white in her raven-black hair continued talking.

I made a beeline for the table that held a coffee dispenser and neatly stacked Styrofoam cups. No doughnuts, I was disappointed to note. Just muffins. I grabbed a muffin that looked like it might be chocolate chip. It was blueberry, which I discovered after taking a huge bite. I nearly gagged, but I managed to keep it down. I supposed I should get in at least one fruit or vegetable today.

I glanced around the room, dread eroding my resolve. Was it too late to leave? Or had I sealed my fate by taking a free muffin? I smiled nervously and sat down on the edge of the nearest empty chair. I took another huge bite of the muffin. It might have been blueberry, but it was dinner.

I only half listened as Skunk Hair talked about her husband. Ever since I'd lost my hand, I had to spend a lot of time focusing on tasks that usually required two hands.

At this moment, I was having trouble removing the liner from the muffin. Instead of making a spectacle of myself, I just ate the wrapper. It didn't taste much different from the dry, stale muffin itself.

Skunk Hair was saying something along the lines of how her husband *still* wouldn't do the laundry, even though she'd lost her foot to gangrene. I didn't see how having only one foot made doing laundry that much more difficult.

"Try folding your panties with one hand," I muttered.

"Yes? Do you have something to add?" the guy in the red flannel shirt asked me.

I shook my head, twisting my face into an appropriately abashed expression. The guy nodded, and everyone turned back to Skunk Hair, who had digressed and was now bemoaning her sex life. *Kill me now.*

As I wiped the crumbs from my lap, I realized I was being watched. A rugged man sitting a few seats over from me was staring at me intently. He didn't smile when I caught his eye.

He wasn't conventionally good-looking, but there was something about him that made it nearly impossible for me to look away. He had a strong jawline, smooth black skin, hard eyes. A nose that looked like it had been broken one too many times. He had a lot of muscle under his faded gray T-shirt, and I let my eyes wander.

I suddenly realized that Skunk Hair wasn't talking anymore. I looked over at the red-flannel guy, and he was watching me, expectantly. A quick glance around the room revealed that everyone was staring at me.

"What is your name?" Red Flannel enunciated. I must have missed the first time he'd asked that question, because I'd been too busy ogling T-Shirt over there.

"I'm Roz," I said with a bright smile.

I jumped as everyone chanted, "Hi, Roz." Just like at AA, which I'd only been to once because of the free doughnuts. I tried not to snicker. I couldn't help but notice that T-Shirt hadn't piped in with everyone else.

"I'm Lowell," Red Flannel said. "I'm the leader of Group." He said it like it should be capitalized. "What brings you here tonight?"

"My psychiatrist and this—" Again, I waved my prosthesis in the air for everyone to see. A few people looked confused. "This looks real from a distance, but let me assure you, it's not. My doctor says I need a support network to help me through these difficult times. So, here I am."

I glanced around the group, hardly impressed with my new best friends. Everyone looked tired, a little harried, or both. Everyone except for T-Shirt, who sat immobile on his chair, watching me with cool, calculating eyes.

Red Flannel grinned. "We're twins!" He lifted his left arm, which wore a much cruder, chunky prosthetic that was twice the size his original hand would have been. "Well, you've come to the right place. Can I ask why you picked our group? There are a few around the city."

I didn't look away from T-Shirt as I answered. "This one's the closest to where I live. It's not really worth hopping on the el for something like this." Too late, I realized I might have offended him. I glanced back at Red Flannel, but his smile hadn't slipped.

"I get where you're coming from—figuratively speaking. I was reluctant to come to these gatherings too. But look at me now—I'm leading one! Maybe after a few sessions you'll feel differently too."

If I ever offered to lead one of these meetings—that would be a sure sign that I'd lost my head as well as my hand. I smiled sweetly at Red Flannel. His grin widened.

Everyone around the room introduced themselves and supplied a brief statement about which limb they were missing, and where or how they'd lost it. It was morbid, but I didn't mind. The only person who didn't fit the mold was T-Shirt. He introduced himself curtly as Jace. He didn't elaborate. A quick glance at his body and I couldn't identify what was missing. I really, really hoped it wasn't anything *too* important.

"What about you? Do you want to tell us the story of how you lost your hand?" This came from a woman wearing a faded black Def Leppard T-shirt, whose name I hadn't bothered to try to remember.

"It was a scrap-metal accident." As I replied, my hand was starting to feel an electrical pins and needles sensation. I wasn't sure if that was an indication that pain would soon follow, or if it would simply be uncomfortable for the rest of the meeting.

I was hoping for the latter.

Everyone stared at me. They wanted me to elaborate. I didn't offer anything else.

"Scrap metal?" Def Leppard looked genuinely confused. "What do you do for a living?"

"Well, I used to be a dealer at the Horseshoe Hammond. But until they make a prosthesis that shoots playing cards at customers, I'm no longer welcome there."

That got everyone's attention. "They *fired* you because of your disability?" That was Skunk Hair, and she looked even more mortified than she'd looked when describing her husband's attempts at sorting laundry.

"Uh—no—um—they let me go, but they gave me a huge—um—severance pay." I added, "Pun intended."

At that, T-Shirt—Jace—smiled slightly. I hid my own pleased smile.

The man sitting on my left produced a business card. "I'm a small-claims court lawyer. Give me a call. There's a good chance that they didn't pay you your worth."

He slid the card between the fingers of my prosthesis, and I realized suddenly that this was the first person who hadn't been openly repulsed by it, despite how expensive and realistic it looked. It was what it represented that repelled most people.

"Um, thanks, but I signed papers," I said vaguely, hoping he couldn't tell I had no idea what I was talking about.

I took the card with my good hand and slipped it into my back jeans pocket. I might still end up needing his help somewhere down the line. I shot him a smile, which he ruined by winking and licking his lips lasciviously. *Ew.* I made a mental note to toss the card the instant I was near a garbage can.

Def Leppard wasn't finished with me yet. "Did you get injured on the job?"

I smiled at her tightly. My cheeks were starting to hurt from being so friendly. "Not unless blackjack dealers are required to weld together large sheets of metal."

Everyone stared at me blankly. "Sculpture. I was working on a sculpture. It's not my job. It's just a hobby."

More like my lifeblood, at least, up until I lost my hand, though I hadn't touched my art for almost two months before my dreams and aspirations were cut off, quite literally. But even when I wasn't working on a project, I'd always been thinking about my next piece. I was always hunting for inspiration. Always on the lookout for new materials, new elements to incorporate into some of my more experimental pieces. Always mapping out and planning my next work and dreaming that it would be what finally brought me the validation I craved with every fiber of my being. But every time another piece was rejected, every time I was told to my face that my art wasn't worth someone's time, I lost a little more of that drive. The rejections had sliced away at my passion until, even months before I lost my hand, I hadn't been able to bring myself to touch my work. You couldn't continue to fail if you stopped trying altogether.

Since I'd lost my hand, I hadn't genuinely considered going back to my art. My sculptures and raw materials were sitting in my workspace, collecting dust. Maybe Dr. Lavoie was right. Maybe that was why I was feeling so out of sorts, even before I lost my hand. I'd lost track of why I was doing what I was doing. It was for the passion—for the art—not for success or fame. But now, with an endless supply of money, I could return to my art. I could create—just for myself, for no one else.

At least I could try. It would be much more difficult with one hand—but not impossible. Especially once I was on the Ryofen—the miracle drug that would alleviate my pain. I hoped.

"How long ago?" Red Flannel asked, tearing me away from thoughts of resurrecting my dead dream.

"A couple of months." A couple of weeks.

"And how are you coping with the loss of such an integral part of your life?"

I wasn't sure if he was talking about the hand or the art. I shifted uncomfortably in my seat. "I get enough of these probing questions from my shrink." Red Flannel's face dropped. I softened my voice. "If you don't mind, I'd rather just listen? At least for tonight?"

He nodded. "I understand." He turned to the lawyer on my left. "Bai, why don't you tell us how you've been doing lately?"

I immediately relaxed as all eyes turned to Lecherous Lawyer. All eyes except for one pair. Jace was still watching me. His face was still unreadable. I fidgeted, then turned to Lecherous Lawyer and focused all my attention on pretending to listen to him.

After the session, which involved each person taking a turn describing their lives and their trivial problems, everyone lingered to socialize. I went back to the table and snatched up another muffin. Blueberry wasn't so bad. I slipped one into my purse before choosing something that looked like a lemon date square, smelled like a lemon date square, but tasted like cardboard.

"If you came here for the free food, it's not all it's cracked up to be," a quiet yet deep voice resonated from behind me.

I glanced over my shoulder. It was Jace, standing at six-foot-something, looking down at me in more ways than one.

I decided to drop the act, since it clearly hadn't worked on him. "I'm here because my shrink insisted. But the free food is a bonus. Or at least, I thought it would be." I turned and bluntly dumped the half-eaten lemon date square into the garbage.

I caught Red Flannel glancing over at me from his conversation with Skunk Hair. I gave him a sweet wave with my good hand, and he smiled.

"You're not his type," Jace said.

I turned back to him in surprise. "Who?"

"Lowell."

I assumed that was Red Flannel's name. I smirked. "I'm everybody's type."

He glared at me, and I just then realized that he wasn't flirting. He was authentically pissed off about something.

My brows furrowed. "Okay, then what's his type?"

"Genuine people. Good people. Not liars."

My heart jumped into my throat. I opened my mouth to ask what he meant, but he turned and strode out of the room so quickly that I almost didn't notice his slight limp.

Who was this guy? How did he know that I was lying? How much did he know? How did he know it?

Just then, I realized that if Sylvain had made deals with other people in the city, if he'd bought limbs off other desperate people, then an amputee support group was exactly where I'd find them.

20

I'd been on Ryofen for almost three hours when I realized something was . . . off.

At the first sign of a sharp pain in my phantom limb, I'd taken one milky-white capsule with water, just as the doctor had ordered. And it actually worked. The pain disappeared within ten minutes, which was even faster than Dr. Bohmer had said when he'd given me the long and dry explanation about how the drug worked on the pain receptors in the brain.

A weight had finally been lifted from my shoulders. While the pain had ebbed and flowed since I'd lost my hand, even when it was lying dormant, I'd been living in constant dread of its inevitable return. But now? I knew that the Ryofen would work for up to eight hours, and afterward, I could easily pop another the instant the pain resurfaced. I sat on my bed, unsure of what to do with myself. I considered going down to O'Malley's for a celebratory drink, but then I thought better of it. It was not a good idea to do the one thing I wasn't supposed to do while on this experimental drug.

I hopped up and paced my apartment. I could do anything I wanted. I still had tons of money left. The Day of Debauchery and my psychiatrist bills couldn't have put too much of a dent in my bank account.

I paused my pacing and stared at my workspace. This was my chance. There was nothing stopping me from discovering if I could still create art with just one hand. I stood, paralyzed, unable or unwilling to move forward. What if I found out that this integral part of what made me *me* was truly lost forever? Was I ready to face that harsh reality?

The door to the loft swung open, revealing Hanna carrying a briefcase I'd never seen her with before. Relieved for the distraction from my dark thoughts, I all but ran toward her. "What's with the briefcase? You going for the business-casual look?"

Hanna looked me up and down. "You seem different," she said slowly.

"Let's go out!" I said.

She didn't respond immediately.

"Let's go out to dinner," I clarified.

She dropped the briefcase on the ground by the door and crossed her arms across her chest. "I'm not paying."

I widened my eyes in mock horror. "Of course not! *I'm* inviting *you* out. *I'm* paying."

Hanna looked me over again. I could tell she wanted to ask what was different, but she was probably afraid that I'd rip her head off if she asked again. It was a believable concern, because I'd ripped her head off in the past over far less.

"You're not my type," she said.

"Why do people keep telling me that? I'm everyone's type! Besides, it isn't a date. It's two roommates going out and getting to know each other better. Now go put on something pretty." I couldn't stop grinning. Hanna gave me a cautious smile before disappearing to change out of her work clothes.

She threw on the red dress I'd gotten her, and I slipped into the little black dress that I'd gotten during my Day of Debauchery. I called her over to help me zip up—I really hadn't thought through my wardrobe options—and we were out of the loft in less than twenty minutes.

I was pleasantly surprised to discover that Hanna was fun to spend time with. Guilt nagged at me, as I realized that I hadn't bothered to pay attention to anything about her in the past. How much had I been missing?

This would have to change. And if I told Dr. Lavoie I was getting closer to my roommate, and she decided I didn't have to continue with the support group, that would just be icing on the cake. I would take Hanna's company over Skunk Hair's any day. While I wouldn't mind getting to know Jace a little better, mostly in the biblical sense, it was clear he didn't feel the same way.

We were halfway through the meal when it happened. I picked up my glass of sparkling cider (nonalcoholic, unfortunately) when I felt a strange sensation in my phantom limb. It wasn't pins and needles. It wasn't the all-consuming fire that sometimes scorched and blistered me. It wasn't the searing pain that had kept me up countless nights since the amputation.

It was something else entirely.

It felt like a refreshing stream of warm water rinsing over my hand. My hand rubbed against another hand, lathering soap, rinsing off the suds. Then I felt the distinct sensation of drying my hand on a soft cotton towel. I blinked, and the sensations vanished as quickly as they had come.

"Earth to Roz," Hanna said, waving her glass of red in my face. She was more than a little tipsy. I'd never realized she was such a lightweight before. Of course, I'd never spent longer than five minutes in her company before.

I cleared my throat. "Sorry, what did you say?"

"I said I have another hot date tomorrow night. Don't you want to know her name?"

"More than anything," I replied without any sarcasm.

"Ellie." Hanna got a faraway look in her eye.

"Ellie," I repeated. I smirked. "Is it short for Eleanor? I'll bet she's an Eleanor."

Hanna didn't seem fazed. "It's short for Elissa." She sighed.

Hanna continued on to inform me that Elissa was a twenty-two-year-old from Philadelphia who'd recently moved to the area. Apparently, Hanna worked at a law firm as an intern while she was wrapping up her law degree. Elissa's father was a wealthy client. Hanna had entertained Elissa while the father had met with his team of lawyers. I told her that I doubted that what she was doing with his daughter was what he'd had in mind, and she giggled. Her laughter wrenched an uncontrollable grin out of me.

"So, is that what was in the briefcase? Files from one of the legal cases you're working on?" I finally asked.

Hanna smirked. "That's been eating away at you all night, hasn't it?" She took another long drink of wine. "I have no idea what's in the briefcase."

That wasn't the response I was expecting. "I thought you were going to say paperwork, or maybe kittens. How do you not know what's in the briefcase?"

"It was sitting outside our loft door when I got home. I thought it might be yours, but when you asked about it, I realized it wasn't."

"And you brought it *into* our apartment? What if there's a bomb in it?"

Hanna giggled. "I love how that's the first place your mind goes."

"What other things are kept in briefcases?"

"Thick wads of cash."

I leaned forward and whispered, "Is that what's in the briefcase?"

Hanna shrugged. "I don't know. It's locked. I was going to see if I could use one of your tools to pry it open, but then you offered to take me out to this *fine* establishment *and* pay for dinner. I immediately forgot all about it because I haven't had time to sit down for a full meal in at least two weeks."

Disappointed, I leaned back and picked up my fork. Hanna changed the topic yet again, and I immediately forgot about the briefcase.

21

"Are you experiencing any side effects?" Dr. Lavoie had given me the once-over when I first walked into her office, and she seemed thrilled by what she saw. At least, she'd seemed about as thrilled as her reserved and calmly pleasant demeanor would allow.

The Ryofen was working wonders. After dinner with Hanna, I had my first full night of sleep since long before I'd lost the hand. I spent most of the weekend lounging in bed, basking in my pain-free existence. This morning, I'd taken the time to shower, shave my legs *and* wash my hair, and I'd even given myself a full blowout before dressing in a pair of jeans and a new Angora sweater I'd bought online. I looked good in it. It hugged my curves in all the right places. I hadn't had to put any makeup on, since I looked less like a corpse and more like my old self.

I smiled at Dr. Lavoie. "Thank you for putting me on the trial. The Ryofen is a miracle drug."

She looked genuinely surprised when I said the words *thank you*, and I felt a pang of guilt. I wasn't *that* bad, was I?

"So, no side effects?" she repeated.

A siren sounded on the street down below, and I turned to look out the window. A pair of fire trucks plowed down the street. I took advantage of the distraction to put on my game face. Aside from another bout of strange sensations in my hand on Sunday, everything was normal. Better than normal. I turned back to Dr. Lavoie. "None whatsoever."

She nodded and leaned backward slightly. "Good. I read through the potential side effects on the forms Dr. Bohmer released to me after you signed up. Hallucinations was on the list, as well as dizzy spells and loss of appetite. Have you been eating?"

"More than usual," I said.

Her sharp blue eyes snapped toward me.

"What I mean is, I'm not focused on the pain and I have time for some of my favorite hobbies. Like eating." I took this opening and told her in great detail about my budding friendship with Hanna. "So you see, I really don't need a support group anymore. I have a roommate to talk to and confide in. We might even have a slumber party and braid each other's hair, though we're not *quite* there yet. And I imagine my idea of a girl's night and hers are a little different." I wink.

Dr. Lavoie's expression remained impassive for several long moments. She reached out, retrieving her glass of sparkling water. She took a long sip as she studied me. "You still have to go to the support group."

I scowled. "But why?" I hated the whine in my voice. "I don't need all that bullshit. It's basically just a bunch of idiots grumbling about their depressing lives and their deformities. I don't—"

Dr. Lavoie raised a hand to stop me. "Just the fact that you call it a deformity proves my point. This is a part of who you are now. You need to accept that. Whether or not you're building a solid relationship with your roommate is beside the point. You need to engage with and acquire support from others who have suffered like you have. As much as Hanna may like you, and as much as she might sympathize with you, she has not been through what you are going through."

I could hardly find a flaw in her rock-solid logic. I must have shown the defeat in my eyes, because a flash of triumph crossed her face. "Besides," she said, "building one friendship is hardly a support network. Many of the people I see here have families, friends, coworkers . . . an entire system of those who can help reinforce their therapy. I truly believe that a support group will fill that void for you, Roz." She returned her now half-empty glass of water back to the coaster on the gleaming wood coffee table. "Of course, support groups in isolation are not the be-all and end-all," she added with a smile. "You'll still need to keep seeing me."

"Aw, shucks. And here I was thinking you were done with me." I caught myself smiling as I said it. I realized in that moment that this was my first session with Dr. Lavoie that I hadn't glared at her hands, consumed with envy and self-disgust. It was a weird sensation, being happy. I thought I might actually like it or even get used to it. Either way, it didn't last for much longer.

I showed up to Group late again tonight. This time, I used my elbow to slow the door so it wouldn't slam shut. It didn't matter anyway, because everyone still turned to look at me.

"You're back!" Red Flannel—Lowell—said. He looked a little too happy about it, but I didn't mind. In fact, I thought I might enjoy having someone so blatantly excited to see me. Someone other than Little Guy, of course.

"You can't get rid of me that easily," I replied. I glanced around the group, my eyes immediately snagging on Jace. I quickly glanced back to Lowell. I gestured to the food table and raised a brow.

Lowell nodded to me and continued what he was saying. He was talking about his girlfriend, and how after his "accident" she hadn't been able to support him emotionally. She never wanted him to talk about his missing hand or the pain it had caused him. She wanted to pretend as if nothing had changed, when for Lowell, everything had. I turned away and poured myself a cup of coffee before remembering that I was supposed to stay away from caffeine. The drug was working wonders. I didn't want to jinx it. I was demonstrating more restraint than I ever had in my life. Even when I was a kid, I would gorge on chocolate and candy in the days following Halloween, to the point where my mom had to hide the last of the treats so I wouldn't catapult myself into a diabetic coma. Unlike with caffeine, not drinking alcohol was proving more difficult than I thought it would be. To say Mom had relied on alcohol would be putting it mildly. I'd always told myself I would never depend on it as much as she had. Lately, I'd been finding it hard not to drink, even though my pain was being managed. Did this mean I was no better than she was?

I blinked, my mind returning to the present. Clearly going to a shrink was making me soft. I pushed aside these introspective thoughts. Support group wasn't exactly the best place for me to be feeling vulnerable and open.

Instead of coffee, I grabbed two—no, three—brownies from the tray. On second thought, I snatched up a napkin. I really couldn't trust myself not to make a mess when eating anymore.

I took the same seat as last time and glanced around the circle while munching on the first brownie. I'd managed to effectively tune out Lowell, but I was listening just enough to be able to notice if he said my name. I'd learned my lesson last time. Everyone was sitting in the same spots as last time, although Lecherous Lawyer, who'd sat beside me before, was gone and someone else was in his place. A skinny girl, who couldn't have been much older than twenty, shot me a dirty look under greasy bangs that were so long she could barely see. She then proceeded to glower at my brownies.

I leaned forward and whispered. "There are plenty of brownies over there. Help yourself."

She glowered at me sullenly. She raised her hands, and I realized they were both prostheses—and crude, cheap ones at that. My face went bright red. I jerked myself back upright, turning my attention back to Lowell. I felt terrible. How could she function with no hands? I looked down at my high-end prosthesis as guilt surged through at me. I might not have felt lucky during this entire experience, but there were clearly others who were way worse off than I was.

I was wolfing down my second brownie when I felt Jace watching me. I caught his eye, then deliberately licked the chocolate off my lips. His expression was unreadable. What was he thinking? I recalled what he'd told me the other night. He somehow knew that I was lying. Did that mean he knew Sylvain? Was that how he'd lost his leg or foot or whatever was causing his limp? I wasn't sure why I cared. Sylvain had bought my hand. I hadn't a clue what for, and I didn't want to think about it. But something about the thought that others here could have been in the same boat bothered me. Questions that I'd pushed away because of the phantom limb pain were resurfacing now that I had a clear head. How many limbs had Sylvain bought? What was he using them for? And was Jace another one of his . . . victims?

There was suddenly a lull in the conversation, and I seized the opening. "Hi everyone, you might remember me from last week. I'm Roz—"

"Hi Roz," the group said in unison. It was a little weird, but I would provide that unsolicited feedback later.

Sensation was returning to my hand. It wasn't sudden, like the first time I felt the cold rush of water, but slow and gradual, like a rising tide. I ignored it.

"I met almost everyone here," I began. "But I haven't met you." I turned to the girl sitting beside me. "Will you introduce yourself?"

"I'm Krista." She hardly moved, barely blinked beneath her bangs.

"And how did you lose your hands?" Someone coughed pointedly from across the circle, and I turned to them. "That's how we all introduced ourselves last week," I snapped.

"It's fine," Krista said in a quiet voice. "I was in a car accident. My parents and little sister died, but I survived."

My resolve wavered. "Okay . . . th-thanks for sharing," I said. I tore my eyes away from her. I couldn't lose track of what I needed to do. I turned to Jace. "Last week you said your name, but nothing else. Would you care to elaborate?"

In the corner of my eye, Lowell was staring at me, mouth agape. Jace seemed unfazed. "I'm Jace. I lost my foot. I was on tour in Iraq."

I blinked. Of course he would have a cover story if he'd sold his foot to Sylvain.

"Army?"

"Marines."

"How?"

"IED."

"When?"

"Two years ago."

"Two years, huh? That's a long time to be coming to this support group."

He shrugged. He was good if he was lying. His responses were immediate. His poker face was impenetrable. What else could I ask him? I wanted to make him trip up, so I could prove to myself that he was lying. But I ended up being the one who couldn't think, not with his steadfast gaze trained on me.

Just then, my phantom limb gripped something cold and metallic. My fingers wrapped around whatever it was and pulled it outward. Then, they pushed it backward.

It felt like I was opening and then closing a car door.

Lowell cleared his throat. "Um, Roz, I appreciate your . . . zeal, but this isn't the way we usually do things here."

My gaze snapped over to him. "Isn't it? I'm pretty sure you gave me the third degree when I first came here Thursday."

"Yes, right, well, no. We were expressing an interest. We don't make people share who aren't ready to share."

I turned to Jace. "Were you not ready to share?" My voice had a slight edge to it.

Jace shrugged almost imperceptibly. "I have nothing to hide."

Was that a dig at my secret? If he hadn't sold his foot to Sylvain, then why would he even suspect that I was hiding a secret? More importantly—could he know what my secret was?

I needed to play nice. If I got kicked out of Group, Dr. Lavoie would have a coronary. "Sorry," I said to Lowell. "I've just been having a rough day. I thought it might help to hear everyone's story." I turned to Krista. My voice softened. "I'm sorry."

She quietly peered up at me from under her bangs, which I supposed was as close as I would get to an acceptance of my apology. I turned to Jace, but I didn't say anything. I gave him a pointed look and turned back to Lowell. "Please continue with your regularly scheduled programming."

Lowell had just started to talk again when my phantom limb sensation overcame me unexpectedly. I gasped. It wasn't painful, but it was like I was exerting my hand. It was wrapping tightly around something.

"Are you all right?" Lowell, the gentleman hipster, jumped out of his seat.

"I—I'm fine." I was fine. Wasn't I?

My hand was wrapping around something warm and soft and squeezing with all its might. I stared down at my prosthesis. What the hell was going on?

I lurched out of my seat. I snatched up my coat and bolted for the door. Once I was out in the hall, the sensation, the exertion, the feeling of squeezing mounted, until suddenly it stopped. I felt my hand let go—dropping whatever it had been gripping so tight. I took several deep breaths, leaning heavily against the plaster wall. I felt as though I'd run a marathon. The sensation washed away, leaving behind the impression of nothingness.

What the hell was that?

22

I'd never been more tempted to drink in my entire life. Instead of breaking the cardinal rule of the Ryofen drug trial, I decided to entertain another vice—gambling. I didn't go to the Horseshoe Hammond. I didn't want to see anyone I knew. I went to a spot I'd never been to before, a little place just off the tri-state. It was small, but the amount of money I lost wasn't.

The next morning Hanna left hours before sunrise. I woke briefly when the door to the loft slammed shut behind her, but I fell back asleep immediately. I woke again a few hours later to the sunshine flowing into the loft through the drafty ceiling-high windows. I groaned and rolled out of bed. After I popped a Ryofen, I took a shower and slipped on my prosthesis, pleased that it took me under five seconds to slip it on properly.

I made myself a bowl of not-stale cereal, which I'd paid extra to have delivered on the weekend, and I plopped down on the lawn chair in the living room. We had a small TV set up that Hanna had picked up at a thrift store. It looked like something straight out of an eighties sitcom, rabbit ears and all. Because most of the channels had switched to digital and we obviously couldn't afford a cable subscription, we could only watch a couple of the local channels, which were all news focused.

I leaned back and crunched on cereal as the Ken-doll-like newscaster chattered on about a store on Michigan Avenue going bankrupt.

"The Phantom Strangler has struck yet again." This time, the Ken doll had the decency to look somber. "Early yesterday evening, the Phantom Strangler claimed another victim in an alley just off Kellingwood Avenue." I blinked. That was still close to home, but a little farther away than the first one. I supposed that this was a good sign. The serial killer was moving *away* from my home address.

"According to investigators on the scene, the victim was attacked from behind. She didn't have a chance to see what was coming, or to defend herself. Police say that women should be extra careful when traveling alone at night. They should employ the buddy system—or better yet—stay inside."

I scoffed. Typical of a man like him to be blaming the victim. Staying inside wasn't always an option.

"Now, on to a discussion by panel experts: Dr. Allard, a criminal profiler for the FBI; Detective Borgnino, the lead local investigator on the case; and Dr. Kato, a forensic psychologist from Northwestern University."

The camera frame switched to the panel of experts and a blond-haired man who sat apart from the rest. "Thank you, Greg," he said. He turned to one of the men. "Detective Borgnino, what can you tell us about the most recent murder?"

"The victim—Pauline Hobbes—was returning home from spin class when she was attacked," the detective said. "At this point, it seems safe to assume that this is a crime of convenience. None of the victims share any attributes in common other than the fact that they all live or work within the same area of Chicago, and they are all in their twenties or thirties."

Dr. Allard cut in: "There are no common denominators between the victims. They all lived, worked, and had hobbies that do not intersect. Of course, we're currently looking into the most recent victim's workplaces, hangouts, et cetera, but we're confident that there won't be any overlap."

That was a funny thing to be "confident" about.

"How many victims have there been in total?" the anchor asked.

"Ms. Hobbes is the ninth," Detective Borgnino said. "She's the second since the hiatus, however."

"And what, do you suppose, is the reason for this"—the anchor paused for dramatic effect—"'hiatus'?"

"Well, there could be a myriad of reasons," Dr. Kato replied. "The kills prior to the hiatus had been escalating. The killer would have had no reason to stop. He wouldn't have been able to. He would have kept killing until he was stopped. The fact that he didn't kill for so long—almost a year—is unprecedented. There must have been an overwhelming reason."

"What Dr. Kato here is saying is that there must have been a reason outside of his control. Either he was in prison, he moved out of the area, or he was incapacitated in some way," Dr. Allard interjected.

"It's unlikely that he moved out of the area, because he would have continued to kill, and we would have a record of this in our federal database," Detective Borgnino said. "The MO is very specific, and a killer of this sort wouldn't just change his MO. He's too proud, too attached to his reasons for using this method of killing.

"However, it's interesting to note that the killer did deviate from his MO slightly with the first victim since the hiatus. Tessa Brown. She was seen leaving an evening pastry class wearing a gold claddagh necklace her boyfriend had given her. When her body was discovered, the necklace was missing."

On the screen, the image of the first victim since the hiatus, Tessa Brown, appeared. The camera zoomed into the gold necklace that was cradled by her collarbone. The pendant bore two hands cupping a heart, with a delicate crown perched on the upper edge.

The camera returned to the anchor, who was much paler than he'd been at the beginning of the interview. A fine sheen of sweat glazed his upper lip. He stared down at his paper, and he looked like he really didn't want to ask his next questions. "What could the motive be for this type of MO?"

Dr. Allard seemed all too eager to answer this question. "Well, the intimacy of strangulation implies that the killer likes to be in control. He wants to dominate these women, show them he's in charge before ending their lives. There's something sexual in the act of strangulation, the sensation of skin on skin, the feel of life draining from the victim as you cut off blood flow to the brain." My stomach churned, and I put my bowl of cereal on the floor beside me. There was something about the sensation he was describing that didn't sit well with me. It felt unsettling—almost familiar.

Dr. Allard continued: "We've profiled this individual as a male, between thirty and forty, and—"

"How?" Ken Doll interrupted.

Dr. Allard looked annoyed at the question. "Criminal profiling is primarily based on psychology, through an analysis of what the killer does and what is left at the crime scene. There's also a fair bit of statistics involved. Similar crimes are committed by similar offenders. Serial killers are almost resoundingly white men, and the few female serial killers that have existed are more likely to commit bloodless crimes, using poison as their weapon of choice. Using the same data, we can broadly state that he is in his thirties to forties. Our offender likely comes from a lower socioeconomic background. The reason why he stole Brown's necklace was not to keep it as a trophy. He hadn't taken anything from his other victims. From this, we can deduce he likely stole it so he could pawn it for cash. Not only is he poor, but he can't get women easily. He's unsuccessful in both his career and his romantic life, and he takes it out on women he finds on the street in high-risk areas."

"Is there any advice you want to add, so that the women of Chicago can stay safe?" the anchor asked.

Detective Borgnino faced the camera directly. "This killer is patient, but he's getting bolder. He isn't just killing in the early hours of the morning anymore. The medical examiner pinpointed Hobbes's time of death as a quarter past eight last night."

I shifted uncomfortably in my seat. I was out around that time last night. I would have been at Group, if I hadn't left early because of the strange sensation in my hand. A strange sensation that was awfully familiar . . .

I stared down at my prosthesis. That feeling I'd had. It had been so peculiar, like I was exerting myself, squeezing, clenching my hand tightly around something. Around a neck. I shifted again, but the metal rod of the chair was digging into my hip, so I stood, suddenly, the rush of blood from my head leaving a wave of dizziness in its wake.

This had to be a coincidence. A strange, morbid coincidence, nothing more. I'd just started taking the Ryofen, which completely decimated the pain. Maybe what I'd felt was a new type of phantom limb sensation? Maybe it was just a psychological phenomenon—my body thinking that my hand was still there, and it was filling in the gaps in what I could be doing. Like with the mirror box therapy. Dr. Lavoie had explained to me the elasticity of the brain, though I'd barely listened to her.

I hurried into my bedroom and shuffled through the forms that Dr. Bohmer had given me. I found the list of potential side effects, which ranged from the more common mild headaches to the much rarer dizzy spells and hallucinations. If what I'd experienced hadn't been a phantom limb sensation, then it was a hallucination caused by the drug. A coincidental hallucination, one that felt like I was strangling someone—to death—with a hand that I no longer had. A hand that I'd lost less than two weeks before the Phantom Strangler struck again. And before that, he hadn't killed anyone for almost a year. This was all just a coincidence. Right?

I tore out of my bedroom and paced the long stretch of the loft. Thirty steps, then I spun on my heel, repeating the process. What did all this mean? Dr. Allard had said that the Strangler wouldn't have stopped killing if he'd had a choice in the matter. He'd said that he must have gone to prison or moved away. But what if the reason why he stopped killing was because he'd lost his hand?

I stopped pacing and stared down at my right hand, which was curled into a tight fist. Sylvain had been adamant about wanting to buy my left hand. But Sylvain had had both of his hands, so the purchase wasn't for him. My stomach churned with undigested cereal, and I tasted the bile and sugar in the back of my throat. All this time I'd been pushing Sylvain from my thoughts, not letting myself wonder what he was doing with my hand, what sick perversions he was involved in. But now there was another possibility. He'd bought the hand for someone else.

The Phantom Strangler.

The Phantom Strangler, who'd been out of commission for a year, for reasons that the police didn't know. What if the killer had lost or injured their hand beyond repair? What if they weren't locked up or dead, but biding their time until they could get a new hand? What if they had bought my hand? What if they were now using my hand . . . to kill?

At that thought, I let out a strangled laugh. That was ridiculous. This was all insane. I was going crazy. The Ryofen was manifesting some extreme side effects. I grabbed my cell phone and started to dial Dr. Bohmer's number, but then I thought better of it. I didn't want to be taken off this trial. I'd felt better the last couple of days than I had since losing my hand. Last night I'd slept the whole night through. The hallucinations—if they were that—would have to get a lot worse for me to willingly give away my saving grace.

I needed to forget about this insanity. And I knew just how to do that. I grabbed my coat and hit O'Malley's.

23

I was sitting on my usual grease-stained stool at the bar in O'Malley's when the sensations started up again. I let out an aggravated sigh, focusing my eyes on the swirling amber liquid in my glass. I took a small sip, embracing the burn of the whiskey as it slid down my throat. I decided to take it slow, just in case Dr. Bohmer wasn't exaggerating when he told me not to drink while on Ryofen. I didn't have a death wish. I just wanted to quiet my intrusive thoughts, if only for a little while. I ignored the nagging voice in the back of my mind. I'd only managed to stay sober for four days.

I was also doing my best to ignore the feeling in my phantom hand. Its fingers were pinched tightly, grasping what felt like a wooden pencil. My hand was moving in large strokes, the side of my hand brushing against coarse paper as I drew.

"Nope. Not happening," I muttered. I wasn't drawing—it just *felt* like I was drawing. I gulped down the rest of the whiskey and gestured for another.

"Haven't seen you around here in a few days," the bartender, Joe, commented. He set my drink in front of me and started to wipe down the bar with a filthy rag.

As much as I wanted to forget, to pretend that none of this had ever happened, I couldn't. I knew what I had to do. I had to get answers. I had to find out who Sylvain was, and why he really wanted my hand. "Joe," I started.

He gave no indication that he heard me. This was one of the reasons why I loved O'Malley's. Bartenders in other places liked to consider themselves amateur therapists. Joe just left his patrons to drink themselves into oblivion in peace. But this time I had a question. This time, I needed more from him. "Joe, that guy who was with me about a month ago. Do you remember him?"

Joe shot me a look. "I'm not paid enough to remember people."

"You'd remember this guy. He came in a little while after me. He sat beside me. He was wearing a real expensive suit."

Joe thought for a moment. "Right, the guy who covered your tab."

I blinked. "What do you mean by that?"

Joe sneered. "You honestly didn't think I'd let you keep drinking here with that kind of tab, did you? He paid off your tab before you'd even gotten here that night."

I frowned. "He paid it *before* I came here that night?"

He gave me another look. "That's what I just said." He started to move away.

"Wait—do you have his credit card info on file?"

"Even if I bothered to keep records for the tax man, I wouldn't just hand them over to you."

"But his name—it was Sylvain, right? Sylvain . . . something? I think it started with a *D*?"

Joe came a little closer, wiping his hands on the disgusting rag. "Sometimes I need a little green to help with the memory loss."

Groaning, I reached into my back pocket and pulled out a twenty.

"How cheap do you think I am?"

Glancing over his sullied gray T-shirt and jeans that looked like they'd walked straight out of the nineties, my answer was on the tip of my tongue, but instead I humored him and pulled out another twenty.

He reached over to grab it, but I held it back. "*After* you get the name."

He smirked, flung the rag over his shoulder where it hung limply, and said, "Be back in five."

I waited impatiently, sipping my whiskey. What was I doing? Sylvain had made it perfectly clear that I wasn't to reach out to him again. I wasn't to tell anyone about him. And if it turned out that he was *selling* body parts . . . that meant that the whole operation was bigger than just him. He likely wasn't working alone. He probably had a whole network of contacts in the black market, like jewel thieves, assassins, drug traffickers—

My heart lurched. Ben. I'd totally forgotten about him. I'd told Sylvain to have him arrested, but Trap had said he'd gone missing. Missing didn't sound like prison—where there'd be a paper trail, an indictment, cops involved. Surely the cops would have questions for the ex-girlfriend he was obsessed with. What if Sylvain hadn't gotten Ben thrown in prison? What if he'd found a more permanent way of taking care of him?

"He paid cash," Joe said when he came back. I looked up at him with blank eyes. It had finally hit me. How could I have been so stupid? Ben was dead. Because of me. Sure, he was unstable, but had he deserved to *die*? Even worse, what would happen if and when his lackeys found out that I was involved? I remembered Trap's haunting words that morning in the park: *"They'll find you lying belly up, bloated and dead, swimming in your own vomit."*

Joe was staring at me expectantly, and I realized I'd missed what he'd said. "What?"

"The name you asked for," Joe said slowly, like I was an idiot.

"Yeah, his first name was Sylvain."

Joe shook his head. "No clue what his name was, sweetheart. He paid cash."

"Check again," I said through gritted teeth.

"I don't need to. It's the only thousand-dollar payment that week."

I blinked. Of course Sylvain would pay in cash. "Thanks," I said to Joe, tossing him the second twenty.

His expression lit up. "Anytime," he replied, suddenly amicable now that he was paid.

I chugged the rest of my drink, but I didn't order another. Instead, I headed out. I had an ex-boyfriend to track down.

24

Usually when you've lost something, you're supposed to look for it in the last place you remember seeing it. I needed to find Ben, but there was no way in hell I was going back to that dilapidated little house where he kept his stash of drugs and guns and who knew what else. Even if I could remember its exact location, I wasn't stupid or desperate enough to show my face in that neighborhood.

I hopped on the el and dropped by the apartment building that Ben was living in when we were together. His name was still on the registry next to the faded number 308. I buzzed his apartment, but there was no answer. I buzzed again. Still, no answer. I went back out onto the street, which was strangely deserted. Craning my neck, I looked up at his apartment window. It was dark, but that didn't necessarily mean anything. He could be out. He was probably out. He was probably off terrorizing and killing Chicago's residents. If he wasn't in prison, like Sylvain had promised.

I took the bus to the main branch of the public library, which I hadn't visited since my college days. I had no idea what my next steps should be, but I did know that in every TV show or movie I'd ever watched, the amateur detective would make a trip to the library to do research.

The public library was still larger than life, with its giant copper birdlike creatures peering down at me from its towering roof. When I was in high school, I would come here, sit on the restaurant patio across the street, and nurse my coffee, sketching the creatures for hours until the waiter asked me to leave. But now, as I gazed up at my old friends, I could feel their derision and disappointment. I hurried into the building.

"I need help finding information," I said to the cherry-lipped man who stood behind the front desk.

"What kind of information?" he asked in a tone that implied he would rather be plucking his knuckle hair than talking to me.

"Information about . . . how to find someone."

Cherry Lips smacked the gum he was chewing loudly. I scowled and he scowled back. "You're looking for a librarian," he said slowly. "Third floor."

Who the hell was he if he wasn't a librarian? I didn't bother asking. Instead, I hopped on the escalator up to the third floor.

I found myself in an area that had a lot of wood. Wooden walls, wooden pillars, wooden signs. Thankfully, the floor wasn't wooden, or the vertigo would have made me vomit up my whiskey-and-cereal breakfast. I approached a girl who looked like she couldn't have been much older than twenty. She had creamy white skin and beautiful wide-set eyes. She looked like she belonged in a Disney movie, not in the psychological thriller my life was turning out to be. She was standing at a desk behind an "Information" sign.

"Hi. Can I help you?" she said to me, twirling a lock around her index finger. She was infinitely friendlier than the last guy, but I was still hesitant.

"Are you a librarian? The *delightful* gentleman downstairs told me I needed to find a librarian to help me."

"I'm a librarian," she said with a huge grin. She was a little too happy about her job, but I forgave her enthusiasm because she looked like she was barely out of school. She'd lose that passion after a few years on the job. I was sure of it.

"Can you help me find some information?"

"This is the reference desk! I can help you with all your information needs!" It sounded as if everything she said had an implied exclamation point after it.

"I'm looking for information on how to find someone," I said to her.

Suspicion suddenly clouded her hazel eyes. "What do you mean?"

"My ex." I smiled slightly when I realized how that sounded. "It's not what you think. I think he might be in prison? I don't actually know where he is." This did not paint me in the best light.

"Um . . ." Her lips twisted into an exaggerated frown.

I read her name tag. "Listen, Melody. Someone told me that he might be in prison. Is there any way I can find out for sure?"

She nodded, immediately all business. "Do you think he's in jail or prison?"

"What's the difference?"

"Well, if he's just been arrested, he'll be in jail. If he's already been convicted of a crime—not that he will be!" she added hastily. "But in that case, he would be in prison."

I bit my lip as I thought this over. It had been a month since Sylvain had done whatever he'd done to Ben. "I'm not sure. I saw him a few weeks ago."

Melody nodded again, her head bobbing up and down so hard that her bangs flopped against her forehead dramatically. "Okay, well the wheels of justice move slowly here in Chicago! I mean, I've only been here for a few months, but that's been my impression so far. So, he's probably still in jail." She turned to her computer. "Do you have his full name?"

"Benjamin Reynell." I spelled his last name for her.

"All right. I'll see what I can find." Her fingers flew across the keyboard in front of her.

I waited a solid ten seconds before asking her, "Where are you searching?"

She didn't glance up from the screen as she responded, "The local police department's website. This is all publicly available information."

I scowled. "You mean, I could have just googled that?"

She chuckled as she continued to type. "You'd be surprised how many people don't think to check online first. Besides, this database isn't very user friendly." Her grin widened. "But I'm a searching ninja!"

I tapped my fingers on the wooden counter as I watched her navigate the database. Her eyes flicked to my hand in irritation, but she didn't say anything. So, I kept tapping.

"Sorry, no Benjamin Reynell arrested in Chicago in the last month," she said. "Is it possible he was arrested elsewhere?"

I remembered that night when I saw him, only the day before I made that idiotic deal with Sylvain. It was unlikely he'd taken off for a romantic weekend getaway. He wouldn't have left Chicago. He wouldn't have left his job, his crew, his drugs. Me.

I shook my head. "I don't think so. I really need to find him. How can you go about finding a person?"

Again, she became suspicious. "Listen, I can see that you still love him—"

"Whoa, I do *not* love him. I'm just worried about him." It sounded like a lie, even to me. But how could I love someone like that? Someone who could kill another person in cold blood and then carry about their day? Although he hadn't been like that when we were together. He'd been kind. A little zany, but not full-blown psychotic. I liked a little weird, a little peculiar in my men. My mind wandered to Jace, but I shoved away any thought of him.

"I really need to find him," I repeated.

"Are you pregnant?" she asked, wide-eyed.

What the hell? I sighed and cradled my stomach with my prosthesis. "Yes. I'm *pregnant*. With his child. Twins, actually." I saw her eyeing my fake hand, so I couldn't resist adding, "How am I supposed to change diapers with *one hand*?"

At some point during my speech, my voice had carried, and there were more than a few people staring at us. Staring at me with sympathy drenching their expressions.

I turned back to Melody, whose cheeks were stained bright pink. "Um, I can't really help you. I mean, I'm not a PI. I'm a librarian."

"Yeah, I got that," I muttered. The people in the Lifetime movies my mom used to always watch never hit this roadblock. Librarians were supposed to be *helpful*. I started to turn to leave.

She bit her lip. "I know the thought of raising a child on your own is scary, but you can do it. I can give you a list of some amazing resources that helped me when—"

"I'm good." I started to walk away.

"Maybe you should try looking places that you know he likes to go? Like his home, his favorite bar, or his work."

There was no way in hell I was going to his work. "Thanks," I said. "I hadn't thought of that before."

"You're welcome!" she called out after me, completely oblivious to my sarcasm.

I stormed out of the library in a foul mood. I took the bus back to Ben's place. This was my best lead, other than his hideout, but I wasn't going back there. I buzzed apartment 308 again, but again there was no answer.

I was about to leave when a rail-thin guy opened the front door. He stepped out and lit a cigarette.

"What are you doing out here?" he said.

"I'm looking for the guy in 308. Ben. Have you seen him lately?"

He took a long drag of his joint and blew it in my face. I didn't so much as sniffle. I held his eye. He smirked, like I'd passed some kind of stoner test. "The asshole? No I haven't seen him in a while."

"Can you let me in?"

He eyed me. "How do I know you're not a criminal? A thief? A serial killer?" He snickered at the last one.

I froze, thinking of my hand. Thinking of where it might be. I was searching for Ben, in hopes of finding Sylvain, in hopes of finding out who really had my hand, in hopes of finding out if the strange phantom sensations I'd been having in my missing limb were some kind of psychic connection to my hand. To a killer. I shook my head, and these thoughts scattered. Paranoid delusions, nothing more. Regardless of if I was paranoid or just plain crazy, I still needed to find Ben. I still needed answers.

"If I'm a serial killer, my target is Ben. The 'asshole.' Your skinny ass is safe."

He leaned his head back and laughed. His laugh cut off suddenly, and he looked at me with glassy eyes. "Go on in," he said, and he held the door open.

I warily slid past him through the doorway. The apartment building had always been dark and damp, and apparently the burned-out or broken light-bulbs still hadn't been replaced. I slipped into the stairwell and climbed up to the third floor. It was hard to believe that a successful drug dealer would live somewhere like this. Unless he was keeping it as a tax cover, and his real place was a lot nicer? He was always trying to impress me, so I suspected that if he'd had a better place, he definitely would have invited me there.

I jumped as something scuttled out of sight and I quickened my pace up the stairs. I was glad when I was out of the stairwell, but the third-floor landing wasn't much better. I glanced around at the trash on the ground, the black mold, and the dust bunnies that had mated and spawned hundreds more little dust rodents to inhabit this barren wasteland. Now I remembered why I always insisted we stay at the loft, even when Hanna was around. Ben didn't have roommates, but he sure didn't live alone. I shuddered as a cock-roach scurried over my boot.

I all but ran to his apartment and pounded on the door. "Ben! Ben, you fucking asshole, open up!"

A door opened across the hall, and a senior with curlers in her hair peered out at me. "Young lady, if you call him an asshole, he won't open the door."

I set my jaw. "Excellent point," I replied. *Now close your door and mind your own damn business.*

I turned back to 308. Again, I pounded on the door. "Ben! Open up, darling, love of my life!"

There was still no response. I caught myself slumping against the wall in defeat and jerked away. I didn't want to bring any of the local wildlife home with me. Hanna would tolerate a lot from me, but she wouldn't let me get a pet, and I was pretty sure that a roach that size would be the equivalent of a pet.

The senior was still watching me through the crack in her doorway. "He isn't there," she said.

"Have you seen him?"

She shrugged and started to close her door.

"Wait! When was the last time you saw him? I need to speak with him. It's really important."

The senior glanced down at my stomach. Did she think I was pregnant too? I was going to have to lay off the support group brownies.

"I'm pregnant," I said, resigning myself to using this ruse once again.

Her lips formed a thin line and she stared at me for several moments. "I haven't seen him in over a month. Young lady, you shouldn't have given away the milk for free if you wanted him to buy the cow." She closed the door in my face.

She had just called me a cow *and* she thought I was pregnant. I definitely needed to lay off the support group brownies.

My mission was far from complete. I wasn't going to give up this easily. Ben hadn't given me a key, but he hadn't been particularly careful or security conscious either. He probably had a spare, and it was probably hidden somewhere around here.

I glanced back at the senior's door, but it was still closed. I couldn't know for sure if she wasn't hovering by the door, spying on me through its rusted peephole. She was the type to call the cops, but I had to take the risk.

I stood on my tiptoes and felt along the top of the door frame, but there was no key, just a lot of dust and cobwebs and what felt like wadded-up bubble gum. I threw whatever it was across the hall, grimacing, and wiped my fingers on my jeans. These seven-hundred-dollar pants were going in the trash when I got home. The corridor was carpeted, and the fraying rug was curling upward in some places along the wall. I knelt and slipped my fingers underneath, gagging as I thought of what I might be touching. I almost gave up, but then my nail caught on something metallic. My fingers curled around it and pulled it out.

A key!

I prayed that it was Ben's key, and not the senior's key, because then if she was watching, she would definitely be calling the cops. I slid the key into the lock of apartment 308. It turned.

I slipped inside and shut the door behind me with a quiet click. I flipped on the light and glanced around the apartment. It was considerably nicer than the corridor and the exterior to the building. It was well kept, and while the furniture wasn't expensive, it wasn't dirt cheap either. A cockroach scurried across the floor, fleeing the light and informing me that the apartment wasn't that nice. I entered the living room. My eyes roved across the IKEA couch, the coffee tables that were relatively tidy, and the fifty-inch flat-screen TV and video game consoles that were upgraded since the last time I'd been here. These must have been among his first purchases when he became a drug kingpin.

Ben also had his display of ancient-looking samurai swords mounted on the wall. He'd inherited those from his father, who'd been some kind of big-time collector. I studied the arsenal closely. It looked like one of them might be missing, but I couldn't be sure.

I ventured farther into the living room. There was a thin coat of dust on the TV. Was this a month's worth of dust?

I was in the kitchen when I knew. It was cleaner than I remembered it ever being. All the dishes were washed and tucked away. The counter was wiped clean, except for the thin coat of dust that seemed to blanket everything. The ceramic-tile floor was damn near sparkling. Ben had never been particularly clean. I had to bribe him with sexual favors to wash the dishes when he stayed at my place, and I didn't think he even knew the purpose of a mop. This level of cleanliness was not like him. I knelt on the floor and peered at the gap where the linoleum and the cabinet joined. That's when I found it. That's when I knew. A thick line of dried blood had gathered in the crack. Blood had been washed away from the rest of the floor. But this spot had been missed.

Ben was dead. And it was my fault.

25

It happened again in the middle of the night.

I hadn't gone to Group, and I knew that Dr. Lavoie would be pissed, but rather than deal with her quiet fury, I skipped my next session with her. The thick line of blood inhabited my head like an uninvited guest. In bed, I tossed and turned, incapable of releasing my anxiety and fear long enough to fall into even the most restless sleep.

Ben was dead. Or was he? Time had given me the chance to consider other possibilities. What if Ben himself had killed someone in his apartment? It seemed stupid to murder someone in your own home, but rational thought had never been his strong suit. And the last time I saw him, it had seemed as though rational thought—and his impulse control—had left the building.

After hours of sifting through memories of Ben, my phantom limb awoke from its slumber. Instead of tingling or a sharp sensation, which was what I usually felt when the Ryofen was wearing off, I felt a sharp chill, immediately followed by a warm, soft fabric engulfing my hand.

I sat up in bed, staring down at my revolting stump. It was an almost ethereal sight, glowing in the muted glare of the streetlights that oozed through the window. It felt as though my hand was curled into a ball and then stuffed into a coat pocket. Then, it was released into the brisk night air once again.

But it wasn't cold for long.

My fingers suddenly coiled into a tense fist, which struck something hard. It didn't stop there. My fingers curled around something warm and fleshy—firm, yet fragile. They gripped tightly. They squeezed. I could feel a throbbing pulse of a life racing under my fingertips. The pulse quickened, fluttering like a butterfly's wings against my palm. But my hand was strong, overpowering, unrelenting. The beat gradually slowed to a mere trickle, then it stopped. Blood no longer pumped through the veins of my prey.

It was dead.

I ran to the bathroom, but I didn't make it in time, and I was sick all over the floor. When I was finished, I cleaned up with a spare towel from under the sink and returned to bed. I lay there for the rest of the night in a cold, clammy sweat, trying to settle my chaotic thoughts. Trying to convince myself that I was simply losing my mind.

I was now forced to confront the questions and doubts that had been lurking in the shadowy recesses of my mind this past week. Could it be that the Phantom Strangler had my hand? That he was *using* my hand to kill? Logically, I knew that this was impossible, on so many different levels. How could I be feeling the sensations of a killer who was miles away? Unless . . .

I sat bolt upright. What if the Ryofen was somehow giving me a psychic link to my severed limb? That would explain why I could feel what my hand was doing, and why the sensations seemed to coincide with when I had taken a pill.

This was insanity. This was crazy. *I* was crazy. I supposed, come morning, I would have my answer, either way.

I lay in my bed, unable to summon sleep. If the Phantom Strangler was wearing my hand, they would have had it surgically attached. Was the science even there yet? I rolled onto my side and grabbed my cell phone, which had been charging on the floor beside my bed. I opened the internet browser. I made a search: "hand transplants."

Thousands of results filled the screen. I clicked on the first and skimmed the article. By 2022, dozens of successful hand transplants had taken place, all from deceased or brain-dead donors who were carefully screened and deemed to be perfect matches for the recipients. The recipients, if their immune systems didn't reject the new limb, could have functionality and sensation, though it wasn't guaranteed.

I then made the mistake of scrolling through images. I quickly clicked away from the Frankenstein-like monstrosities. My breath hitched as I imagined my hand crudely stitched to someone else's arm. The thought was terrifying.

I looked down at my stump again, a stump that had healed remarkably quickly. Whoever removed my hand had technology or practices that were far more advanced than commonly known science. Who's to say that the person now wearing my hand didn't heal remarkably as well? What if the hand looked like it belonged? What if there wasn't even a scar?

My thoughts and questions whipped through my head like a tornado, destroying any chance of sleep that night. Eventually, I rolled out of bed to put on a pot of coffee. I flipped on the TV long before the six o'clock news began. Hanna obviously never came home, or I would have heard polite yet adorably furious shouts from her corner of the loft. I folded myself into the lawn chair, wrapping my arms around my legs as I anxiously awaited my verdict. I hadn't even bothered to put on my prosthesis. I kept one eye on my phone, but there were no news alerts. No announcements about the serial killer. No updates or bulletins boldly proclaiming that the Phantom Strangler had struck again.

To my intense relief, I made it through the entire morning show without any statement about a new murder. Tension sloughed off me with each news story that had nothing to do with the Phantom Strangler. No one had been killed in the middle of the night. No body had been found. Most importantly, my hand wasn't responsible for any of the murders. I'd hallucinated—or maybe even dreamed—the entire thing.

I sighed with relief once the show had finished. My appetite came back with a vengeance, and I lugged my bone-weary body into the kitchen. I took another Ryofen with a tall glass of cold water and I popped some bread into the brand-new toaster I'd bought online. I was really moving up in the world. I could now afford these finer indulgences, like the ability to toast my stale bread instead of just eating it cold.

My phone chimed just as I was slathering a thick coat of peanut butter on the toast. I glanced down. My stomach dropped at the sight of the news alert.

Breaking: Another Body Found . . ."

I skimmed the article.

The estimated time of death was 3:00 a.m.

26

I had to go to the police. It was the only thing that I could think of that would silence the thunderous guilt that roared through my head.

The phantom killings had happened not once, but twice. Twice I had felt my hand kill. Twice the Phantom Strangler had struck. Twice was far more than a coincidence. Twice was a pattern.

The Phantom Strangler was killing again, and it was all my fault.

Obviously, I had no illusions that I should tell the police the truth. At least, not the full truth. But there were multiple parts of their profile of the killer that were blatantly wrong. The detectives on the news the other day had said that the killer was a white male, in his thirties to forties, and that he came from a poor neighborhood. Well, they'd gotten the color of my skin right, but one out of three was a terrible score, even for the police. The killer must be white, because why would they buy a hand that wasn't the right color? Unless, of course, they planned to spray tan. In that case, all bets were off.

The police thought that the killer was a man. This was their biggest mistake. I needed to tell them the truth. There was no way someone would pay a million dollars to buy a hand to replace their own unless it was a pretty close match. I stared down at my right hand, which was nearly a mirror image of my left. My nails were long with oval nailbeds. My fingers were slender, with a delicate bone structure. My hand didn't look like a man's hand. However, my hands were deceptively strong and dexterous. I had to have strong hands for my art. Is that why I'd been chosen? Is that why they picked me? Because my strong and nimble hands were feminine, yet perfect for squeezing the life out of innocent victims?

The other not-so-minor attribute that the police had gotten wrong was the socioeconomic status of the killer. He—*she*—was definitely not poor. Not if she could afford to buy a hand from Sylvain. He'd paid me a million dollars. I'm sure he'd gotten a commission for his work. The person who'd purchased my hand from him on the black market must have had a lot of money to be able to afford this.

Of course, replacing a limb would be worth draining the savings account for, but to even have that much money in it in the first place was quite telling.

I skipped my rescheduled appointment with Dr. Lavoie that morning, ignoring the phone call from her receptionist. Instead, I lingered outside the Chicago Police Department's Public Safety Headquarters, staring up at its imposing, yet modern facade. I could still turn back. I didn't have to do this. I realized just then that I didn't have to reveal myself to them. I could do the right thing without them ever knowing it was me. Rather than push through the glass doors to the police station, I strode up to the pay phone on the street corner and dialed the toll-free tip hotline number that was conveniently posted on the back of the receiver.

"Chicago Police Department Crime Stoppers. What's your tip?" An almost automated voice greeted me.

"It's about the Phantom Strangler?" It sounded like a question.

"What's your tip?" The voice sounded less automated, more bored.

"The profile on the killer is wrong," I said. "It isn't a man, and he isn't poor. It's a woman, probably a white woman, and she's quite wealthy."

The operator hesitated. "How do you know this?"

"I . . . can't say."

The voice turned sharp. "Ma'am, do you know who the Phantom Strangler is?"

"I can't say. I've already said too much." I hung up, then swallowed, my throat suddenly dry. What had I done?

I remembered the package Sylvain had left for me as a parting gift, which had contained my prosthetic hand and a not-so-veiled warning. *"Tell anyone and the terms are void, and there will be repercussions."* I should have kept my damn mouth shut.

What would happen to me now that I'd gone to the police?

27

"Thanks for fitting me in," I said as I settled into my favorite spot on the couch in Dr. Lavoie's office. Her office was just as warm and cozy as ever, and I was glad to be cocooned by its comforting familiarity, especially after the day I'd had.

Dr. Lavoie observed me with a little smile painted on her lips. "Not a problem," she replied. "I had a cancellation this afternoon." She smoothed a crease in her skirt before continuing. "That was your second missed appointment." She raised a perfectly stenciled brow.

I didn't know what to say. I knew that she could tell when I was lying, even if she didn't always call me out on it. Instead, she would give me that "disappointed" look and make me feel even crappier about my deceit. I wondered if that was a standard psychology trick.

"Sorry about that," I said, without providing an explanation.

Dr. Lavoie's lips curved into an almost undetectable frown, and she made a note in her notebook. I braced myself for a barrage of follow-up questions, but she let it go.

"How are you doing on the Ryofen?"

I should have been grateful for the change in topic, though this was something I didn't want to talk about either. I didn't want to talk about Ryofen, my hand, or any of what had happened to me the last month and a half. But these were the reasons I was coming to a psychiatrist in the first place, so I supposed I would have to suck it up.

"Great," I replied.

"Still no side effects?"

"Not a one."

Dr. Lavoie wrote a lot of notes for the very succinct answers I was giving her. I tried not to read too much into it. "Are you having any headaches?"

"Nope. No side effects, like I said."

"Okay. Just humor me. I have to go through each one so I can report back to the research team. No dizzy spells?"

"Nope."

"No auditory or visual hallucinations?" Her pen scratched in large loops obnoxiously on her paper as she spoke.

"Nope. Although I probably wouldn't know if I was hallucinating, right?"

The writing stopped. Dr. Lavoie looked up at me, a serious expression on her elegant features. "This isn't funny, Roz. If you experience even one of the side effects, I need to know. If you're hallucinating, I need to know. Hallucinations can be dangerous, and this drug is playing with a delicate and vulnerable part of your brain. Anything out of the ordinary needs to be recognized immediately and addressed."

"Hey! Whose brain are you calling delicate?" I joked. Her lip twitched, and she continued to look at me expectantly. I sighed. "No. No hallucinations of any kind."

Despite the lack of change in her facial expressions, I could feel concern emanating from her in waves.

"You know, the possibility of hallucinations would have been something worth telling me *before* I started taking the drug," I deflected.

Dr. Lavoie nodded and turned her gaze back to her notes as she wrote down the insightful words I'd just said. I used her distraction as an opportunity to take a deep breath and plaster on my poker face. I couldn't have her figuring any of this out. Sylvain had killed Ben—or, at the very least, shed a lot of his blood—just because I'd demanded he get rid of him. If Dr. Lavoie started to suspect what had happened to my hand—that I hadn't lost it in an accident and that a serial killer was probably using it to commit her crimes—well, I doubted that Sylvain would just pay her off and buy her silence. Assuming she believed me and didn't just buy me a one-way ticket to the loony bin.

Just then, a wave of dizziness crashed over me. I squeezed my eyes shut, fighting the compulsion to tilt my body along with the spinning room. I wasn't sure if the vertigo was from stress or the two glasses of whiskey that I chugged at O'Malley's just before this appointment.

"How have you been sleeping?"

My eyes snapped back open. Thankfully, the room had stilled. "Like a baby." The bags under my eyes screamed otherwise. I sighed. "Listen, this Ryofen is the best thing that's happened to me—since, well, since I lost my hand. No offense, Doc," I added.

Dr. Lavoie deigned to give me a small smile. "No offense taken. I understand you were hurting quite a bit. And this drug might be the cure for that. I'm really happy for you, Roz." She returned to her notebook and continued writing. The fact that I had no idea what she was writing didn't bother me as much as it usually did. I had a million other things to worry about.

Movement in the corner of my eye drew my attention from her scribbling. My head snapped toward it. It was the portrait that hung above the fireplace. A woman, dressed in a Victorian-era powder-blue dress with a high neckline and lace trim. She wore her hair pulled back in a loose bun under a large hat that was angled fashionably on her head. I'd examined the portrait before, wondering if she was one of Dr. Lavoie's ancestors or just a painting that she'd thought would fit the decor of the room. Something that would soothe her patients. I'd often wondered if that was why the woman wasn't looking out at the viewer, but off to the side. So Dr. Lavoie's patients wouldn't feel studied, watched, judged. I'd thought about that often. But now, the woman in the portrait was looking outward. Looking into the office. Staring right at me.

"Is something the matter?" Dr. Lavoie asked.

I'd gotten up, and I hadn't even realized it. I was hovering a few feet away from the portrait. I couldn't look away. "I-is this new?" I asked. I didn't understand. Had she replaced the painting with a nearly identical one?

"Oh, no. I painted that years ago."

I tore my eyes away from the portrait to glance at her over my shoulder. "You're a painter?"

Dr. Lavoie tucked a wayward strand of hair behind her ear. "I suppose, if we label ourselves by our hobbies. I haven't painted in a long time. That portrait was inspired by an old vintage photograph I found in a box of my grandmother's things when she passed."

I turned back to the portrait. "It's beautiful. But did you replace it? This one's different."

Dr. Lavoie looked at the painting, then at me, her brow furrowed. "Uh—no, I only made one." She chuckled. "One was enough for me to realize that wasn't my style."

"Are you sure?" I should have let this go, but I knew with utmost certainty that the painting had changed.

Dr. Lavoie continued to watch me, concern etched into her forehead. Was this another one of her tests? To see how I would react when she switched out the painting? She must have seen me studying it. Had she wanted to see what I would do? I turned back to the painting. I barely stifled a gasp.

The woman in the portrait wasn't looking at me anymore. She was back to her original position.

28

I didn't have time to worry about whether I was going batshit crazy. All my energy was focused on hiding the fact that I had just had a hallucination. In my psychiatrist's office. While she was watching me. After the portrait incident, Dr. Lavoie continued to interrogate me in her typical quiet yet intense manner. I clamped my mouth tighter than a child being force-fed broccoli. She hadn't switched the paintings. It wasn't a test of my observation skills. Even if she had a secret switch set up, Scooby-Doo style, there was no way she could have silently swapped out the painting in the two seconds I took my eyes away from it. That could only mean one thing.

I was having side effects from the experimental drug. Hallucinations, to be more precise. I paced the loft late that afternoon—after taking a lengthy field trip to O'Malley's—mentally going over my conversation with Dr. Lavoie again and again until I thought I might go insane. Assuming I wasn't already insane. Fortunately, Dr. Lavoie hadn't seemed to suspect a thing. I was confident that I'd managed to throw her off the track. I'd pretended to be jealous that she was able to paint, something that I wouldn't be able to do ever again, now that I didn't have my dominant hand. I'd always preferred sculpture, but I'd been known to grab a sketch pad and draw whatever was around me. I dabbled with watercolor in my teens, and then again in college. I hadn't painted in years, and now the realization was dawning on me that I would never paint again. I didn't have to fake the pain I felt, and by the end of the session, I was emotionally drained. I'd nearly forgotten about the portrait. Nearly. But Dr. Lavoie had been encouraging throughout the whole discussion. She convinced me that the worst part was not knowing. I had to give it a try. I couldn't just ignore this integral part of who I was.

So, on my way home after my appointment, I'd picked up a few art supplies at a hobby store. Everything was overpriced, but God knew I could now afford it. I wasn't sure if I was being masochistic or irrationally optimistic.

Nevertheless, I stood there, in the middle of the loft, for several long moments, staring at a huge block of clay I'd purchased. It wasn't my usual medium, but I thought it would probably be easier to manipulate with only one hand.

But now wasn't the time to test out my abilities. I wasn't ready to get a definitive answer on whether my dreams had been permanently severed along with my hand. I was too distracted, too exhausted, and—quite frankly—too drunk.

I continued my pacing. If I was experiencing side effects—if I was *hallucinating*—could I believe anything that had happened since I started this drug? It felt like that was the first time I'd hallucinated, but I couldn't be sure. It was so subtle, and I'd barely even realized it. Weren't hallucinations supposed to be obvious? If the woman in the painting had turned toward me and grinned, like a cheesy horror-movie jump scare, it would have been obvious. I would have known right away that something was wrong with me.

Right on cue, my phantom limb came to life. It felt like my hand was clasping my other hand, settled on my lap, although there was no sensation at all in my right hand. I frowned down at my prosthesis. Were these sensations nothing but hallucinations too?

The room spun around me, the tall brick walls of the loft tilting, the floor dipping. Unable to continue to hold myself up, my legs collapsed, and I sat heavily on the nearest lawn chair. I squeezed my eyes shut. I took a few deep breaths before cracking open my eyelids. The loft was no longer moving. I sighed, remembering my meeting with the doctors. Dizzy spells were another potential yet "rare" side effect of the Ryofen. It looked like I was getting them in spades.

I had no idea what I should do. I knew I couldn't go to Dr. Lavoie about this, because she would have me taken off the medical trial. As stressed out as I was, this was a million times better than what I'd felt before Ryofen had entered my life. I would take judgmental Victorian portraits over excruciating pain any day of the week.

This begged another question. Was Ben really dead? I believed I'd seen the line of blood on the floor, but that was a stretch. For all I knew, the blood hadn't even been there, and I was just imagining it because that's what I had expected to see.

I shook my head. I needed to calm my paranoia. I'd seen one strange thing and I was assuming that I'd already lost all my marbles. One painting, an optical illusion that may have been simply caused by the angle of the light hitting the canvas. I shouldn't have been already fitting myself for a straitjacket.

It was times like this that I wished I had someone I could turn to. A boyfriend to share the burden with. A roommate I could confide in. A mother who loved me more than vodka. What I wouldn't give to have someone in my corner. What I wouldn't give for someone who cared about me unconditionally.

My cell phone rang, the piercing sound jolting me out of my chair. I checked the call display. An unknown number. Was it Sylvain? Was he calling to make sure I wasn't backing out of our deal? Was it Ben? I realized that I hadn't bothered to sync my new phone or input any numbers into it, other than Dr. Lavoie's and Dr. Hughes's, so it could be anyone. I let voice mail pick up.

As soon as the phone chimed indicating I had a new message, I tapped the little envelope icon.

It turned out that I had more than one message. The first was dated earlier today, though I'd never even heard it ring.

"Hi honey, it's Mom. It feels like I haven't talked to you in forever. Give me a call when you have a chance." It was strange hearing her voice. She sounded different. Sober? I wondered if I should call her back.

The next message began. "I'm looking for a Regan Osbourne? This is Detective Gutierrez with the Chicago Police Department. I'm calling regarding a tip you called in to our hotline. Please give me a call back at your earliest convenience." The woman then produced a string of numbers that I didn't bother trying to remember.

How had they found me? I'd called in that tip from the pay phone outside the police headquarters. Were they monitoring that? If so, that was a sneaky, underhanded thing to do. I groaned. Of course, the police would do that.

I hopped out of my chair and started pacing again. The police were going to want answers. They would want to know how I knew—suspected—that the killer was a woman and that she was rich. If I told them anything about this, I would be breaking my agreement with Sylvain. If he'd killed Ben, I didn't have any doubt about what he could do to me if I broke his rule of silence. I needed to find Sylvain and talk to him. I had to find out what had happened to Ben. Find out where my hand was. Being able to locate Sylvain was a long shot, but I had to try.

During what had to have been my hundredth lap of the loft, something caught my eye. The briefcase that Hanna had found outside our apartment a week ago sat on the floor between the kitchen counter and the bathroom door. It was pressed up against the base cabinet, almost camouflaged, so that I hadn't noticed it sitting there. I picked it up and brought it to the table I'd set up in my work area. The briefcase was light, so it definitely wasn't full of wads of cash, as Hanna had suggested. It also probably didn't have a bomb in it, or I'd be chop suey by now. It was left outside the apartment, like the box with my prosthesis. Was this from Sylvain? I wiped my sweaty palm on my pants.

The briefcase was locked, but that didn't discourage me. I found my welding torch, carefully gripping it with my nondominant hand and bracing it against my left elbow. Once I was fairly certain I wouldn't accidentally scorch myself, I went to town on the lock. It was overkill, but cathartic, and it got the job done in about twelve seconds. I flipped the latch and opened the lid. Inside, there nothing but a single plain envelope.

I picked it up and slid out the folded sheet of paper inside. The message was typed. "Thanks for giving me a hand."

I stared at the words. Had Sylvain sent me a thank-you note? In a brief-case? Why hadn't he just put the note in the box with my prosthesis?

There was something else inside the envelope. I tipped it over, and it slithered out onto the table. It was a gold chain. A necklace. I examined the design of the charm. It was a crown over a heart, with a pair of hands clasped around the heart. A claddagh necklace, and it looked like it was made of real gold.

My heart stuttered as a memory emerged from the back of my mind. I snatched up my phone, my fingers on my right hand fumbling as I drew up a news article from a couple of weeks ago. The first victim of the Phantom Strangler. Tessa Brown. This was her necklace, and it wasn't taken by the killer as a trophy.

It was a gift.

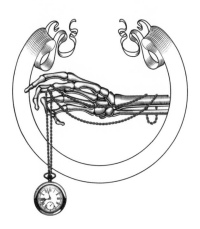

I LINGER.

Tucked into a darkened doorway, I press deeper into the shadows, despite knowing that I wouldn't be seen, even if someone were to look. I gaze upward, peering through the tall windows on the other side of the street. I am unable to look away.

In her apartment, my subject throws her sculpting knife across the room. She kicks a foot outward, nearly toppling herself to the ground. Her frustration is palpable from the street down below. Unable to manipulate wire or a simple paintbrush, she's resorted to carving crude features into a lump of clay. But even that is nearly impossible for her to do with one hand. At even this, she fails.

Of course, had she more talent, she would persevere. But she lacks the skill, the endurance, the drive to succeed as I have. Instead, she throws a tantrum, unaware that she is being observed and judged.

I am sophisticated and demure. Affable and kind. Respected by all, known by few. I am prudent, patient, particular. But on the inside lurks darkness and depravity.

My subject is abrasive—sharp angles and crude edges. Raw. Unseemly. She is impulsive, impatient, imprecise. But on the inside she is soft and vulnerable.

Her imperfection is what makes her perfect. It's what sets her apart from the others. I choose my subjects because of their innocence and innate sweetness, which provides a stark contrast to the cruelty they endure at my nimble hands. But this subject is different. She was chosen by others for her hand, because she was a match. I would not have selected her given the choice. But now I cannot imagine a more satisfying final piece. This subject is tainted an ugly color by tragic circumstance, a gloomy disposition, and a series of poor life choices. Her distress creates a stunning backdrop for what is to come.

I resist the temptation to emerge from the shadows. To get closer to my subject. It isn't time. Not yet. There is still much to do before she is ready. There is still much to do before it is time to put the finishing touches on my masterpiece.

29

The weekend was a complete wash. That gold claddagh necklace that was left on my doorstep told me that the Phantom Strangler knew who I was. This meant that Sylvain must have given her my name. Which meant that he could give me hers.

I'd scoured social media, searching for every Sylvain in the Chicago area, but none of them looked like the James Bond wannabe that I was searching for. Next, I went through the online yellow pages and found every Sylvain, but not a single one of their last names was familiar. I seemed to remember his last name, starting with a *D*, at least, from the business card he'd given me that I'd thrown away. There were fourteen Sylvain D's living in the Chicago area. I'd gone to a few of the addresses, but so far, the three I'd managed to corner definitely weren't my Sylvain. I gave up before heading to the seventh location. I had a sinking suspicion that Sylvain was shady enough and smart enough not to be listed online where any of his victims could easily look him up. "Sylvain" might not even have been his real name. I could have spent an entire day trying to track down a ghost.

I went back to the Ritz-Carlton, but the snooty asshole at the front desk hadn't been much help, even though I wore designer clothes and did my best to look like I belonged. He turned his nose up at me, as if he could smell the poverty and desperation clinging to my fur coat.

I couldn't give up. I needed answers—answers about Ben and the Phantom Strangler. I couldn't just sit around and do nothing. I'd never been what you would call a do-gooder. I'd never snitched on anyone to the cops before. But there's an exception to every rule, and I couldn't just sit by, twiddling my single thumb, letting *my hand* kill innocent people. What would that say about me? If I just let innocent women in Chicago *die* because of my own flesh and blood?

Monday evening, I found myself hurrying to Group, and I actually managed to get there a few minutes early this time. I was exhausted, so I poured myself a huge cup of coffee, caffeine interactions with Ryofen be damned. This time there were cookies, so I grabbed a few. For a recently rich person, I often forgot to eat. I wolfed down a couple of the baked treats. I didn't wander far from the food table, because I couldn't juggle cookies and a coffee with only one hand.

Lowell appeared beside me. "Roz! Nice to see you again. How have you been doing?"

"Great," I mumbled between bites. I noticed his gaze crawling over my designer outfit. He didn't say anything, although I could smell the judgment wafting from him. Or maybe that was simply the effect of his natural deodorant. He always seemed to be wearing the same red flannel shirt and ugly brown wool scarf, both of which were far too warm for the weather, which had only just started to turn. He gave off the vibe that anyone who cared about how they looked was clearly not worth his time. But if that was the case, why wouldn't he let me be? I waited for him to take off, but instead he inched a little closer to me under the pretense of selecting a cookie. Next time I was early for Group I would wait outside and ignore my hunger pangs.

"So how are you doing?" I asked as I casually put some distance between us.

"Good, good. Well, not good. My girlfriend officially broke up with me yesterday." He picked at a lone stray thread on his frayed sleeve. His shiny prosthetic hand reflected the fluorescent lighting. I stared at the chunky monstrosity. It was large—far larger than the hand it was mirroring. What if it wasn't meant to mimic his real hand? What if it was meant to hide one? I shook my head. That made no sense. Why would someone wear a prosthetic to hide their real hand?

I brought my eyes back to meet his. "Well, she wouldn't know a good thing if it smacked her in the face."

He gave me a broad grin, showing off the sliver of a gap between his two front teeth. "Sit beside me tonight?"

I wasn't sure if that was code for something, but I just nodded as I took a bite of my seventh cookie.

He stuffed his hand in his pocket, then wandered off to greet Skunk Hair, who'd just arrived. I watched him as he left. I wasn't entirely sure what his story was. He didn't seem too broken up over his breakup, especially if my promising to sit beside him made him cheer up so dramatically. Maybe he had been hoping that something would happen between us later this evening. I shuddered.

At that moment, Jace meandered in. He didn't look over at me as he poured coffee into a Styrofoam cup. I took a sip of my own coffee—hot and bitter, just the way I liked it—and watched him. During the last Group session that I'd attended, he'd said that he had lost his foot while serving in the Marines. I still wasn't entirely convinced that he was telling the truth and that he wasn't another one of Sylvain's suckers. I mentally snickered at that thought. If I found any of Sylvain's other victims, I would suggest that we start our own support group and name ourselves that.

As I settled down in the chair beside Lowell, I felt Jace's eyes on me. Was he wondering why I'd decided to sit there? It wasn't as if we had assigned seating. *Let him wonder,* I thought as I smirked over at him.

"Welcome everyone!" Lowell greeted us cheerfully. "I see we have a new face. Would you like to introduce yourself?"

Our newest member was a dark-skinned woman around my age who had chosen to sit directly across the circle from me. She was wearing a bulky gray sweater and gray sweatpants that weren't form-fitting at all. Her thick black hair was tied back into a tight ponytail, with a few wisps of hair framing her long face. She had a quiet voice that matched her muted appearance. "I'm Dalia." She jumped when everyone recited, "Hi Dalia." I hid a smile. It was good to know that the group's automatic responses weren't just jarring to me.

Lowell must have noticed how nervous she was, because he didn't ask her to share why she was here. She looked visibly relieved when Lowell moved on, and everyone introduced themselves to her. She looked a little mortified when we all mentioned our missing body parts. It was nice to see that I wasn't the newbie anymore.

"So, who wants to speak first today?" Lowell asked the group. Skunk Hair opened her mouth, but Lowell expertly cut her off. "Other than Sharon? Sharon shared a lot last time, and I want to make sure everyone has a chance to talk. Sharon, if there's still time at the end, you can tell us what's on your mind."

Skunk Hair clamped her lips shut into a thin scowl. She probably had more complaints about her husband and the chores he wouldn't do.

The room was deathly quiet. I studiously dodged eye contact with Lowell as my thoughts crawled to what I'd been avoiding thinking about these past few days as I hunted Sylvain. The other night I'd revisited my art for the first time since my amputation. I'd experimented with the clay, but I hadn't been able to manipulate it the way I'd wanted.

The frustration and despair had been just as tangible as the unyielding block of clay before me. I'd screamed. I'd cried. I'd badly bruised my foot kicking my worktable. Fortunately, Hanna hadn't been home. Fortunately, nobody had been there to witness my complete and utter breakdown. I didn't want to relive that moment, which might have been the lowest moment of my life. I had everything that I thought I wanted, but I'd lost what mattered most.

Jace cleared his throat, and everyone turned to him with relief. "I'd like to talk, if that's okay."

I felt myself involuntarily leaning forward in my seat in anticipation.

"I had a case that brought back a lot of memories."

I stiffened. A case? Was he a cop?

"Can you elaborate?" Lowell prompted.

Jace stared down at his hands, which were clasped loosely on his lap. "Yeah, it was someone from my past. He was on my squad a couple of tours ago. He came back, but he wasn't the same. None of us were, but he was worse off. Not physically, but mentally. He'd had a hard time finding work when he got back. He got into trouble with the cops. Long story short? He was arrested, but he skipped bail. I was hired to bring him back."

So, Jace was a bounty hunter.

"I caught him early this morning. He didn't go down easy. I brought him in and collected my check, but the way he looked at me? I can't shake it. It feels like a betrayal. It feels like I failed him."

The room was so quiet that I could've heard a pin drop. Lowell broke the silence. "You were just doing your job."

Jace scoffed. He still wasn't looking at anyone in the group. His gaze roamed the walls, the ceiling, looking at anything and everything but us. "I didn't have to take this job. There were three others I could have chosen from."

"Then why did you take this one?" I was surprised to hear myself speak.

Jace's hardened gaze landed on me. "Because I knew him. I knew that if I found him, he wouldn't run. He wouldn't use lethal force to get away from me. I used our relationship to catch him."

Skunk Hair inhaled sharply, then covered her mouth. I didn't look at her. I continued to hold Jace's gaze. He didn't break our eye contact.

"If it wasn't you, it would have been someone else. And that someone else might not have been as gentle as you," I said.

Jace cracked a pained smile. "Who said I was gentle?"

We held each other's gaze for far longer than the moment warranted, before Lowell cut in to give a monologue about forgiveness and redemption.

The rest of the night, I kept peeking over at Jace, but he'd basically checked out for the evening. Skunk Hair was saying something about the ladies in the group creating a buddy system, because of the Phantom

Strangler having made this neighborhood his hunting ground. Lowell looked over at me expectantly, his eyes probing. Did he expect me to ask him to walk me home? I'd rather be strangled.

Skunk Hair made a beeline for me after Group, when everyone was mingling. I skillfully dodged her, planting myself in front of Jace.

"So, you're a bounty hunter," I said casually. My ruse to avoid Skunk Hair was really obvious, and she looked offended. But she bounced back quickly and turned her unwanted attention to the latest addition to Group, likely to persuade her into becoming buddies.

"I'm many things. Bounty hunter is one of them," Jace replied, eyes narrowing on me.

"You find people for a living," I said, pretending I couldn't tell that he'd rather be anywhere but here, talking to me.

Jace grunted an affirmative.

"So . . . hypothetically . . . if someone were looking for . . . a person, they could hire you to find them?"

"Why? Who are you looking for?"

I looked up at him with exaggerated shock. "I said hypothetically!"

Jace's eyes flashed. "Fine, then." He turned and strode from the room. Obviously, playing coy didn't work with someone as direct and to the point as Jace.

I caught up to him in the stairwell, where I found him taking the stairs to the ground floor two at a time. I started to follow but was distracted by the view. How could a man with only one foot move like that?

I shook my head. I wouldn't let myself be sidetracked from my goal. "Wait!" I called out as I hurried up the steps behind him.

He stopped at the first-floor landing but didn't turn around. "I am looking for someone," I admitted when I reached the top. "I'm looking for someone . . . and I think you might know him."

Jace turned around and peered at me with his clear-cut brown eyes. "Not everyone in the Marines knows each other."

I shook my head. "Not from the Marines. I'm looking for Sylvain."

I held my breath as I studied his face. His head was angled to the side ever so slightly, and his thick eyebrows were pinched. His brown eyes churned with confusion. But was it all an act?

"Doesn't ring any bells," he replied.

"Are you sure?"

Now Jace looked irritated. "Listen, Roz, I'm not a liar. I don't know who this Sylvain guy is. But if you want to hire me, I charge two fifty a day."

I raised my eyebrows. "Two hundred and fifty dollars a day? I could hire some two-bit PI for a third of that cost."

Jace leaned forward and breathed on me. "Then hire that two-bit PI. Besides, I don't work for liars."

He turned and stalked away.

"Wait!" I called out again. This time, he didn't stop. The door to the rec center slammed shut behind him. He was going to make me chase after him. I grimaced, then hurried out the door. He was already halfway down the block. That prosthetic foot really didn't slow him down at all.

"Wait!" I called out yet again. He didn't stop walking, but he slowed marginally. I jogged to catch up to him.

"Fine. You don't have to play hard to get. I'll pay your astronomical fee," I snapped.

Jace didn't look mad. In fact, he looked amused. His smile faded as he saw my expression. He stopped walking. "Who is this man to you?"

I bit my lip. I didn't respond.

Jace shoved his hands into his jeans pockets. "I know you've been lying through your teeth every night at Group. Does this guy have something to do with what really happened to you?"

Again, I didn't say anything. He must have read the answer in my eyes, because his voice softened. "I'll find him."

From across the room in Group, it had looked like his eyes were a solid brown, but now, up close, I could see that they had swirls of warm copper in their depths. I had a hard time prying my gaze away. I forced a sneer to hide what I was feeling. Not that I understood what I was feeling.

"And for you, I'll drop the fee to two twenty-five a day."

"How *generous*."

Jace shot me a thin smile and started to continue on his way down the street.

"Wait!" I was enjoying myself too much. Jace looked at me over his shoulder. "Aren't you going to walk me home?"

He gave me a look.

"What if I get serial killed?"

Jace sighed and ran a hand over the short black stubble on his head. My hand twitched, and I felt an irrational need to be the one running my hand over his head. Ugh, where had that come from? "Where do you live?" he said finally.

"Five blocks east." The opposite direction from where he was heading.

"Fine." He turned and started in the opposite direction. "But I'm on the clock starting now."

30

The following morning I realized my mistake. I hadn't given Jace my number or asked for his. I'd been so distracted by his broad shoulders and how his T-shirt clung to his six-pack that I simply told him what I could about Sylvain before he dropped me off at the loft. This was so embarrassing. I hadn't felt this way since I was a teenager with a crush on my hostile, erudite math teacher. Was I seriously going to have to wait until our next Group meeting—which was another two whole days away—before I could find out about Sylvain? Before I would see Jace again?

Why was I feeling this way? And why now? My regular sessions with Dr. Lavoie must have been getting to me. Her constant questioning about my family, my friends, had made me realize how lonely I was. I wanted someone to share my time with. But was Jace really the best person to fill that void?

I sat on the lawn chair and ate dry cereal in front of the TV. Of course, the newscaster wouldn't talk about the Phantom Strangler when I actually wanted him to—although I supposed that was a good thing. That meant that she hadn't struck again. I'd been having those strange sensations in my hand off and on since the last killing.

The other night around dinnertime, I'd felt it chopping vegetables—at least I hoped it was vegetables—with a knife. The hand had slipped, nicking a finger with the sharp blade. It was just a scratch—not deep enough to bleed out, though that would have been a convenient resolution to this entire saga. There was a gentle rap on the loft door. I jumped out of my seat and turned off the TV in one swift movement. The room tilted on its axis. I gritted my teeth, mentally willing away my sudden wooziness. After Jace had walked me home last night, I'd immediately gone back out to O'Malley's. I suspected that I was still a little drunk. Humiliation collected in the pit of my stomach at the thought that I was drunk before breakfast.

The knock sounded again.

Suspicion coursed through my veins. This wasn't the hard pounding of the landlord or the assertive hammering of a delivery person. I approached the door, wishing—not for the first time—that there was a peephole. My heart pounded as I debated if I should answer it. What if it was Sylvain? What if it was Ben, furious about whatever it was that Sylvain had done to him? What if it was the Phantom Strangler, here to give me another twisted present or to finish me off?

I swung open the door.

It was my mother.

"Mom?" I couldn't hide the shock from my face.

"Reggie! Honey!" I was suddenly engulfed in a bear hug. When she released me, I barely had the presence of mind to hide my hand—or lack thereof—behind my back.

"W-what are you doing here?"

Mom gave me a stern look. "You haven't been answering my calls. I was getting worried."

"Sorry. I got a new phone." Come to think of it, how had she gotten my new number? Before I could interrogate her about that, she gave me a pointed look.

"Are you going to invite me in?"

"Yeah, sure, come on in." I stepped to the side, letting her pass through the doorway, taking the opportunity to study her. She looked different. Her skin was clear, and there were no bags under her eyes. She looked ten years younger than she had the last time I'd seen her.

She stepped through the doorway, hanging her jacket on the coatrack and depositing her purse onto the floor. She'd been to the loft before, so my embarrassment wasn't as acute as it could have been. Nevertheless, I suddenly realized that I should have spent some of my new money on decent furniture. The apartment I grew up in was a lot smaller than this place, but Mom had kept it tidy—when she was sober. When she wasn't, everything went to hell in a hand basket. At least, that was what she would say when she sobered up long enough to clean up.

Mom thought that living in a loft apartment in downtown Chicago was dreamy, and the first time she'd visited, she hadn't seen much beyond the exposed brick walls and the gorgeous sweeping windows. She hadn't noticed the lack of furniture or the pitiful "kitchen." Although this time she headed straight for it.

"So, what's new with you? How's work? The Horseshoe Hammond, right?" Mom asked.

"Um, yeah, that's the name of the casino," I said vaguely.

Mom released an overstated gasp when she opened the fridge door. "Reggie, where's your food? You're going to *starve!*"

"Mom, why are you here?" I asked. This wasn't like her. Her simply dropping by wasn't normal.

"What, a mother can't check in on her daughter occasionally?" Mom sniffed.

"I haven't seen you in—" I honestly couldn't remember the last time I'd seen her. "Do you need money? Is that it?" I didn't say it in a snide way, but Mom still took offense.

"*I* wouldn't take money from *you*," she said. *Ouch.* I'd stolen from her before, but that was in my teenage years. At the time, my weed-addled brain hadn't been able to discern right from wrong. Yet, I *had* recently stolen from Sylvain. Clearly, I'd never learned that particular lesson.

"Right. Of course not." I moved toward her. "You look different."

"My skin looks fabulous, right?" Mom gloated. "I know! I haven't had a drink in sixty-two days." She produced a coin that I could only assume had come from AA. "The diner hired me back full-time, and I've applied to be manager. The owner says I'm a shoo-in!" Her already rosy cheeks blushed with pride.

"Wow, Mom, that's great!" I said. My words fell flat. I studied her face more closely this time. She looked . . . healthy. Her eyes were less sunken, and her cheeks had a flush that, for once, wasn't related to alcohol consumption. "That's great," I repeated, putting a little more gumption into it this time.

Mom studied me right back. "*You* don't look great, Reggie. What's wrong?"

"Nothing!" I said quickly.

Mom gasped. I realized that I had forgotten to keep my hand behind my back.

She reached out and grabbed my prosthesis. "What is this?"

"Um . . . art?"

Her green eyes stared me down. "Regan Elizabeth Osbourne."

"All right." I sighed. I supposed I would have to deliver her the party line. "I lost my hand while working with some scrap metal."

Mom gasped, then immediately paled. It was depressing how three minutes in my company could undo sixty-two days of good to her complexion. She suddenly looked at my artwork, which was scattered half forgotten around the living area.

"Reggie, you should have been more careful!"

"Well, I know that *now*," I said. "Where were you three months ago?" Mom's face fell, and I realized what I had said. "No, it's in no way your fault. I was trying something . . . different, and it backfired. I suppose I should have been wearing protective gear."

Mom nodded sternly. "You could have put out an *eye*. In a way you're almost lucky."

I wasn't sure how losing an eye was worse than losing a hand, but I laughed, the sound coming out forced. Luck had nothing to do with any of this. Mom gripped me in another bear hug that I patiently endured. She was a lot fuller than she was before. I supposed a steady diet of alcohol and crackers had kept her skinny.

When Mom pulled back, her eyes brimmed with tears. "Reggie, I'm here because it's one of the required twelve steps toward recovery."

I tried not to let that sting. She was only here because she had to be.

Mom shook her head as if she could read my thoughts. "No, Reggie. I'm here because I want to reconcile with you, but I wasn't supposed to do it before I had done some serious soul searching."

She held my good hand between both of hers and apologized. She apologized for the times when I'd had to feed myself because she was passed out drunk. She apologized for forgetting my birthday more times than she'd remembered it. She apologized for neglecting to pay the utilities on more than one occasion, and how I'd had to take money from her purse so I could cover the bills myself to get the lights turned back on. She apologized for everything.

The whole time she was apologizing I couldn't help but focus on the irony that she was pulling her life together just as mine was falling apart.

31

After Mom left, I had yet another surprise visitor. This one wasn't as pleasant or as welcome.

The woman was a little shorter than me, at around five foot three, but her presence nearly filled the entire loft, which was no mean feat. Her pinched face was devoid of makeup. She wore an inexpensive suit, a faded blouse, and loafers I would rather die than be caught wearing. But it wasn't her lack of style that caught my attention. It was the badge clipped to her belt. My blood ran cold.

"Good afternoon," she said in a no-nonsense tone. "I'm Detective Gutierrez of the Chicago PD."

As with everyone I'd met the past month, my eyes were drawn to her hands. Her unpainted nails were bitten down to the quick, a nervous habit I was sure she'd tried to beat, especially as a police officer, where any sign of weakness could be exploited. She didn't wear any rings or bracelets, but a clunky digital watch was strapped to her left wrist. She wore a few plain brown bandages on her right hand and one on her left.

I brought my eyes back to her face. "How can I help you, Detective?" I said as politely as humanly possible given the situation.

"We're following up on a tip that you called in to the hotline regarding the Phantom Strangler."

Trickles of sweat raced each other down my spine. "The Phantom Strangler?" I feigned surprise. "What makes you think *I* was the one to call in that tip?"

Detective Gutierrez raised an eyebrow. "Ma'am, we monitor all the phone booths in the area. You would be surprised by how many people chicken out at the last minute and use pay phones to call in their information."

My lips formed a thin line. "Aren't the hotlines supposed to be anonymous? As in—confidential? As in—you won't show up at my apartment after I make a call?"

"Ordinarily, yes. But you made a unique claim, unlike any of the others that we've received on the hotline. My partner wanted me to check you out." At that, Detective Gutierrez revealed a hint of irritation. *So, she doesn't want to be here.* She probably thought this was a wild goose chase and was just here doing what she was told to do. I hid a sigh of relief.

"I've looked into you," she said. "You have an interesting rap sheet—all from when you were a minor. You're not the type to involve herself in police matters. So, why did you make that call?"

I could have said that it was a prank. I could have said that it was a dare. I could have said I was drunk out of my mind and didn't even remember making the phone call. But what did I say instead? "It was women's intuition."

"Women's intuition? *Women's intuition* told you that the killer is a woman? That she's rich?"

"I took psych at UIC," I said. It wasn't a total lie. I'd taken a few classes in my freshman year before dropping them for a course that was offered in the afternoon instead of bright and early on Monday mornings. "I just thought it was ridiculous how the men on the panel on TV all thought it had to be a man. A woman could do something like that. Women are strong too."

"The crime hotline isn't a place to be making feminist statements, Ms. Osbourne." Her nostrils flared as she looked me up and down. "Are *you* strong enough to do something like this, Ms. Osbourne?"

I smiled and waved my prosthesis in the air. "I might have been, at one point."

She didn't look chastised, but disappointed. "So, you think that the killer is a woman because women are strong too? Listen, I'm all for power to the women—hell, I'm a female police officer—but that just seems a little hard to swallow."

I shrugged. I didn't know what to say. Of course, I wanted her to investigate, but she wouldn't believe me, even if I could tell her the truth. Sylvain might hurt me or someone I cared about if he caught wind of what I was doing. It would be impossible to tell her that I thought the Phantom Strangler had my hand without revealing that I had sold my hand. Now that it seemed like my mother was back in the picture, confessing to the police could put her at risk too. It was time for the performance of a lifetime. "I'm sorry. I don't know what else to tell you." I looked purposefully at the door.

Detective Gutierrez wasn't quite ready to leave yet. "It's funny. For someone who just had to share her thoughts with the police, you sure don't want to share them now."

I smiled tightly. "Well, that was when I thought the sharing part was anonymous."

"So you're not doing it for the attention. What are you doing it for?"

I shrugged.

"Is it possible that you know the killer?"

I shifted my weight from one foot to the other. Realizing what I was doing, I tried to force myself to be still.

"Is it possible that you're protecting him—and trying to throw us off his trail?"

"I don't know what to tell you," I said. "I just had a hunch, and I wanted to share it."

"It sounded like more than a hunch. The way you phrased it during the call. It was like you knew who the killer was."

"Well, I don't. And it's great to see what kind of *exemplary* work my tax dollars are funding." I sneered. "You can see yourself out."

It was only when she left that I realized I was trembling. I had a feeling that this wouldn't be the last I'd see of Detective Gutierrez.

32

The one time I was late to an appointment with Dr. Lavoie was the one time that the receptionist was nowhere to be found. Rather than wait, I pushed open the door to the office and slipped in. Dr. Lavoie was at the window, peering down at the street. She had her cell phone pressed against her ear.

"Harry, I don't want any more excuses," she said in an angry tone I didn't think her capable of.

I shifted uncomfortably, glancing over my shoulder at the door. *Should I leave?*

"I want you gone. Tonight." She sniffled. *Oh God.*

Before I could escape and pretend I hadn't seen or heard anything, Dr. Lavoie ended the call with a shaky hand and turned around. She startled at the sight of me.

"Roz, you're early!" she said. Glancing up at the clock to confirm that I was in fact late, I didn't correct her. She strode toward her desk, dropping her phone into the top drawer. She turned away casually and wiped at the corner of her eye with a sleeve. "Have a seat," she said, gesturing toward the couch.

I averted my eyes and hurried toward my usual spot, basking in the sun of the bay window like a cat. I gave her a few moments before glancing back up at her. She'd pulled herself together remarkably quick. She looked almost normal, though her eyes were still red-rimmed. I couldn't help but notice that her left hand—which gripped her spiral-bound notebook almost desperately—wasn't wearing its usual wedding band.

It was funny. I'd come here half a dozen times to talk about my life, and it hadn't really registered that my psychiatrist had a life of her own beyond these walls.

For once I was at a loss for what to say. Obviously, asking her how she was doing would be awkward. Did she know how much I'd heard? Did she resent me for it?

"What do you do in your free time?" I blurted out.

She blinked at me. She stared. Then, she blinked again. "Pardon me?"

My cheeks burned. "I mean, you know so much about me, and I don't know anything about you." I held my breath, realizing I might have shown my hand, and she might realize that I'd overheard her on the phone.

"I have very little free time. Though, I've been told I'm married to my work, which might be why . . ." She blushed, busying herself with smoothing the crease in her skirt.

"So, no hobbies?" Why was I prolonging this?

Her lip quirked, telling me she wasn't at all annoyed. "Aside from art— which we talked about last time." She looked away thoughtfully. "I suppose I enjoy cooking, the thrill of finding new ingredients and coming up with a road map toward a new discovery. But I do despise baking. It's too prescriptive. And meddling with a tried-and-true recipe too often leads to an inedible combination of flour and sugar."

"That sounds like me with my art," I said, sadness tingeing my tone.

She cocked her head. "How so?"

I shrugged. "I used to love seeking out new pieces, finding focal points or accents to add to an existing or new idea. To build something around nothing. It's . . . It *was* . . . exhilarating."

"You're using the past tense, Roz."

"Am I?" I thought of my tantrum the other night. I'd tried again last night, but the attempt had been half-hearted, so when I'd slipped and gouged the clay too deeply with the knife, I hadn't been devastated. I'd been expecting it.

I didn't want to talk about my art. I supposed I could tell her about other parts of my life, but everything had to be filtered. I obviously couldn't tell her about hiring Jace to find Sylvain. I couldn't tell her that the police had shown up at my apartment. Everything was off-limits. Well, almost everything.

"My mother dropped by yesterday morning." I quickly hid my grimace. I was so relieved that I'd found a topic that wasn't taboo, that I'd forgotten that I really, really didn't want to discuss my childhood, my dysfunctional family, *or* my mother.

Dr. Lavoie's cool blue eyes roved across my face. "Was this a surprise visit?"

I shrugged. "We visit from time to time. She's been to my apartment before, but she never just stops by. Not unless she wants something." I picked at a piece of lint on my five-hundred-dollar jeans.

"How do you feel about her dropping in?"

"Um, I'm not sure." I continued to stare at the piece of lint. For expensive jeans like these, you'd think they wouldn't be such lint catchers. Probably because they wanted to sell fifty-dollar gold-plated lint brushes to go with them.

"Roz, what did you talk about?" As usual, Dr. Lavoie was relentless in demanding my undivided attention.

"Mostly about how she's doing. She's in AA now." I glanced up at Dr. Lavoie. I might have revealed a little more than I'd intended.

"Is that right?"

"Sixty-two days—sixty-three if she didn't booze it up last night."

"That's quite the accomplishment."

"It's two months. It's hardly that impressive," I said sharply. Dr. Lavoie gave me a look that implied that she knew I couldn't go half that long without consuming my body weight in whiskey. "Anyway, she's going through the twelve steps to recovery. She didn't elaborate about the steps, but she said that she needed to reconcile with me. Which was why she came to visit."

"Do you think that's the only reason she came to visit?"

"W-what do you mean?"

"What I mean is that you're very ambivalent about the entire thing. Shouldn't you be happy that your mother has acknowledged that she has a problem, and she's trying to do something about it?"

"Oh, I'm pleased," I said. I caught my tone, and added, "I know I sound sarcastic, but it's the truth. I just want her to be happy."

"Right."

"She's up for a promotion at the diner," I added.

Dr. Lavoie cocked her head.

"Assistant manager, or something like that."

She continued to watch me with her unnerving, unblinking, all-seeing blue eyes.

"I'm happy for her, I am."

"You already said that."

"I guess I did." I wouldn't give her anything else. "I guess I'm just a little . . . jealous." *Shit.*

"Jealous? How so?"

"Well, she's sobered up. She not only has a job, but she's probably getting a pay raise."

"You're envious of your mother's success?" Surprise colored her expression.

"I guess. Why are you so shocked?"

Dr. Lavoie shrugged her shoulders daintily. "From the little you've told me, she wasn't a very good mother. She drank a lot, and you had to raise yourself."

"I . . . It wasn't that bad."

She raised an eyebrow. "Tell me, did she ask about your life?"

I nodded.

"She gave me the third degree about the hand. And she asked about my job." Come to think of it, we hadn't talked a lot about me. "She scolded me about the contents of my refrigerator."

"So, she abandoned you as a child, and now she's finally stepping up to the plate as a mother, and yet you feel *jealous*?"

I stared at Dr. Lavoie. I wasn't sure of what to say.

"Don't you think there are other emotions here at play, underneath?"

"Like what?"

"Dig deep."

I thought about it for a moment. "I suppose I do feel angry, not jealous." There was a little bit of self-loathing thrown in there too, but that was a topic for another day.

Dr. Lavoie smiled. "I think it's perfectly natural to feel resentment. Your loyalty to your mother is quite admirable, Roz. You can be angry with her and still love her."

I mulled that over. "I guess that makes sense."

"Parents bring out the most complex of emotions in us," Dr. Lavoie said. "Sometimes it can be hard to untangle them ourselves."

"Well, that's what you're here for, Doc," I said with a weak smile.

"Glad I can help. Will you see her again soon?"

"Probably not. I mean, she wanted to go to lunch soon, but I told her I'm busy." With a job I didn't have, a boyfriend I didn't have, and friends I didn't have. Although, I was preoccupied with hunting down a serial killer, a black market salesman, and my drug-dealer ex-boyfriend. Did that count?

Dr. Lavoie fixed her gaze on mine. "I think you should go to lunch with her. Tell her how you feel. This process will be just as therapeutic for you as it is for her. It might even bring you two closer together."

I opened my mouth to protest, but there was something in Dr. Lavoie's expression that made me reconsider. "Fine. I'll call her."

Dr. Lavoie produced a rare genuine smile. "Good. I look forward to hearing all about it during our next session."

I strangely did feel better after talking about my mother. Maybe there was something to this therapy thing after all. We spent the rest of the session discussing my prosthesis and how I was gradually growing accustomed to living life with only one hand.

"Now, before we wrap up, I need to ask you: How have you been doing? Any dizzy spells? Hallucinations? Other side effects?"

"None whatsoever," I said, stifling a sigh. I was back to lying through my teeth.

33

"What do you mean, Sylvain doesn't exist?" I spat.

Jace shot me a thin smile from his position leaning against the outside wall of the rec center, his arms crossed over his broad chest. "I looked into him, but he isn't a real person. He's using an alias."

I'd waited all through the Group meeting to hear this revelation, because Jace hadn't shown up early enough for me to interrogate him before the obligatory sharing of feelings started. My heart had raced every time I'd looked at him across the circle. I told myself it was because I hoped that he would have some tangible clue, something that would lead me to Sylvain, not because of the way he looked, slouching in his chair and smoldering in his fleece-lined leather jacket.

"So, he's a dead end," I said.

"I wouldn't say that," Jace said. "Sylvain doesn't exist, but Lenny Stevenson does."

"Who the fuck is Lenny Stevenson?"

At that, Jace smiled, a rare breed of a smile, the lip curling slightly higher on the left. "He's the person who booked that hotel room at the Ritz."

"Now we're getting somewhere. Why didn't you lead with that?"

"Because it's fun to watch you get all riled up," Jace replied, his crooked smile deepening.

My stomach did a little flip at the sight. I made up for it by glaring at him. "So, who's this Lenny Stevenson guy? Did you find him? Where is he?"

His fingers delved into his inner jacket pocket, withdrawing a folded piece of paper. He didn't give it to me. Instead, he said, "He's a lowlife. He doesn't have a job—at least, none that has a paper trail. He has a place in Fuller Park. I have an address for you."

"Well? Where does he live?" I asked, impatience scurrying through me.

"This guy's bad news." I waited for him to elaborate. He didn't.

"Tell me something I don't know. For example—his address."

Jace still didn't hand over the paper. If I'd had more than one hand I would have tried to wrestle it from him, Marine or not.

"Why are you looking for him?" he asked suddenly.

"Who are you, a PI or my therapist?"

"He lives in a dangerous neighborhood. I don't want to send you there unless I know for sure you're not going to get yourself hurt." As usual, I couldn't read his expression. I wondered if it was a PI thing or a Marine thing. I wasn't particularly good at reading my therapist either. Maybe it was a me thing.

"That's sweet," I said. "Really, it is. I'm glad you're worried about me. Now hand over the address," I growled. I felt a twinge of guilt as soon as the words left my mouth. He was just trying to help. He might even have been worried about me. But as usual, I took the kindness of others and shoved it back in their face. It wasn't as if I deserved it.

I sat with that thought for a long moment. Jace was quiet—too quiet—as he scrutinized me with his PI eyes. I wondered if my thoughts showed on my face, but I made no move to hide them.

He wordlessly handed me the sheet of paper. My eyes scanned the page as I quickly memorized the information, in case he changed his mind and tried to pry it out of my one good hand.

"Well?" he said.

"Well, what? Do you want a gold medal?" I snapped, my previous vulnerability burning at my cheeks.

"I already have a few medals. None of them are gold though," he replied, his expression deadpan.

Was he making a joke?

"I don't work for free, you know," he added.

I rolled my eyes. I dug into my wallet and handed him the cash. "That should more than cover it."

Jace didn't count the bills before tucking them into his back pocket. Was that a power play, or did he trust me? "You know, I do protective detail too."

I let out a laugh. "Are you trying to milk me for *all* my money?"

"Not at all," Jace said. "But this Lenny guy—you didn't even know his name. How much do you trust him? Does he even want to be found? What is he willing to do to make sure his identity remains a secret?"

Jace had a point. This guy could be dangerous. Hell, he probably was, especially since he'd somehow managed to get Ben out of the picture.

I sighed. "How much?"

34

I had lunch plans with my mother for the following day at noon, but I told
Jace to meet me at the address in Fuller Park at ten.

My head pounded as I hopped on the el. I'd hit the tables—and the
bar—a little too hard last night. I'd lost, but at least the casino had kept me
lubricated with complimentary drinks, which almost made up for the sting
of being unlucky in every aspect of my life. This morning, I'd been up with
the sun, making a pit stop at O'Malley's for the hair of the dog before heading out to meet Jace.

Feeling woozy—likely from the lack of sleep—I closed my eyes and let
my forehead lean against the cool glass of the windowpane. My body rocked
to the gentle rhythm of the train. Before I could drift off, I felt someone's
presence beside me. Groaning, I opened my eyes one at a time, lifting my
head. The reflection of a man sneering at me filled the window.

"What the fuck are you looking at?" I snarled, spinning around.

No one was there.

A woman across the aisle watched me nervously. Her arms curled pro-
tectively around her toddler. A few other passengers were staring too. None
of them looked at all like the man I'd seen in the reflection.

Heart battering inside my chest, I twisted my features into a smile,
which seemed to frighten the woman and her son even more. *Whatever.* I

was hardly the scariest person they'd come across if they continued to ride public transit in this city.

I hopped off at the next stop, which was just a few blocks away from my destination. I saw Jace up ahead, leaning against a tree, his back to me. I slowed my pace, involuntarily running my eyes up and down his toned body. He had muscles in all the right places, but that was to be expected of an ex-Marine. He also had a swagger about him, one that wasn't at all affected by his limp.

"Hey," I called out. "You came."

Jace turned around slowly and gave me his crooked grin. "Of course. You are paying me after all."

How he had convinced me I needed his services as a bodyguard was beyond me. "Yeah, well. If you fail, and I die, you won't get paid, so wipe that smirk off your face."

Jace's smile broadened. It was distracting, and I didn't have time for distractions. I spun around and strode toward the apartment building that Sylvain—Lenny—lived in.

"Wait a minute," Jace said. A strong hand clamped down on my shoulder, stopping me in my tracks. "What's the game plan?"

"Game plan?"

"Yeah. Who is this guy? What are you planning on doing? What kind of reaction can I expect from him?"

I suddenly realized the fatal flaw in my plan. I couldn't have Jace in there with me when I confronted Lenny. He would find out everything. I would be putting his life in danger as well as my own when Lenny realized I'd broken the "keep quiet" clause of our grisly contract.

"You can't go in there with me," I said firmly.

Jace's grin was replaced with the scowl I was much more comfortable with. "The hell I'm not. How am I supposed to do my job and protect you if I'm not in there with you?"

I considered his words for about a millisecond. There was only one solution. "Well, then you're fired."

Jace growled, "You are incredibly frustrating, Roz. Who the hell is this Lenny person? Does he have something to do with what you've been lying about in Group?"

"Is that why you're here? Because you want to find out all my deep, dark secrets?"

"Well, work has been slow lately, and you're willing to pay premium rates."

I *knew* he'd been ripping me off.

Jace must have seen the murderous expression on my face, because he raised his hands in defeat. "Fine. I'll leave. If you're one hundred percent sure that this guy won't pull a gun on you, or a knife, or some other kind of weapon, then I guess you'll be fine on your own." He cocked an eyebrow.

"I'll be fine," I said, my tone lacking its prior conviction.

"Whatever you say. I'll wait outside." He crossed his arms over his chest.

"I thought I fired you?" I phrased it like a question.

"You can't get rid of me that easily. I'll wait outside free of charge. Just to make sure you're not murdered. Although, by the time I hear your screams, it'll probably be too late."

"Well, whatever eases your conscience." I turned and pressed the button for apartment 612 on the buzzer.

"Yeah?" a guy answered.

Was that Lenny? I didn't recognize the voice.

"I have a delivery for a Mr. Stevenson. It needs a signature."

The line was silent for so long I worried I'd gotten cut off.

"Come on up."

I spared a glance back at Jace as I swung open the door. His expression was nearly blank, save for a hint of scorn. He made a move to follow me. At my glare, he said, "I'll wait in the hall outside the apartment. How else will I be able to get inside when you start screaming?"

"So gentlemanly," I said with a roll of the eyes. I pushed aside the feeling of relief that he'd be there if things got out of hand. I had no idea what to expect.

The elevator moved torturously slowly, crawling the flights to the sixth floor. The tension in the air rose with every creak and shudder of the cables. Just as I wondered if the elevator would give out under our collective weight, that it would dive to the ground with me and Jace in it—it let out a shuddering groan and stopped. The doors screeched open. I all but bolted out of the coffin, my pulse thundering in my ears.

Was this a mistake? I was suddenly glad I wasn't alone. I was happy that Jace had insisted on coming. I considered going back. I considered regrouping, coming up with a plan instead of diving headlong into danger. But I refused to put off the inevitable, no matter how terrified I felt. I was going to get answers from Sylvain—Lenny—or whatever his name was. I was going to get those answers, even if it killed me. I approached his apartment, Jace nipping at my heels like a guard dog.

"Farther back!" I hissed. If Lenny caught sight of him, all bets were off.

Jace grumbled as he slipped around the corner, out of sight. Satisfied he wouldn't be visible from Lenny's doorway, I turned and stared at the apartment door. It was now or never. I took a deep breath, raised my good hand, and pounded on the apartment door.

Lenny took his time answering. I wondered if he was checking me out through the peephole, so I struck a dramatic pose and plastered a fake smile on my face. The door immediately swung open.

It was Sylvain. I recognized him instantly, even though he couldn't have looked more different. Gone was the aspirational James Bond look. In its place were dirty blue joggers and a band T-shirt that was so faded I couldn't even tell what the band's name was.

"What are you doing here?" All trace of his elegant, apparently phony, British accent had vanished with those five words.

"What? Aren't you happy to see me, *Lenny*?"

35

L enny trailed behind me as I strode into his apartment. Despite my nerves, I reveled in the way that the tables had turned. Just two months ago, he'd come into my home and looked around like I was living in squalor, making me feel worse than the dirt under his shoes. Now, I was able to do the same thing, as I took in my surroundings. His home was a giant fall from the sweet digs at the Ritz-Carlton. The apartment was scantily furnished, and the wobbly, abused furniture had seen better days, probably leaning up against a nearby dumpster. There was a lopsided bookshelf on the far wall, which didn't hold even one book. All that decorated its peeling shelves was a potted plant that looked like it had died three winters ago.

"How did you find me?" He didn't seem angry. He seemed worried. That threw me off a little.

"I'll be asking the questions, *Lenny*."

"Ask away," he said in a resigned tone. He collapsed unceremoniously onto the couch.

I blinked. This was a lot easier than I'd thought it would be. "Okay . . . what did you do with my hand?"

He pressed his lips together. He didn't say a word.

"Look. You're clearly broke as fuck. I know you didn't buy it yourself. You're some kind of middleman. I want to know who you sold it to."

He shrugged. "I dunno."

"How can you not know who you sold it to?"

"Like you said, I'm just the 'middleman.' I never met the person I sold it to."

"Fine." I flipped through my mental list of questions to ask. "Why did you pick me?"

"I was told to go after you. I was given your name, a photo, and a place to find you." He counted these items off on his fingers, then shrugged again. "I was told to follow up with one of our donors at the event, and then approach you. I was ordered to offer you this deal." Lenny didn't sound defensive, or even angry. He sounded defeated.

I let his words sink in. He'd come to the art show with the intent of targeting me. He slept with me, fully knowing what he was planning to do. What he was planning to take. I knew this shouldn't be new information—hell, I'd suspected it—but the cold, indifferent way that he said it made the backs of my eyes sting with tears I had no intention of letting him see.

For the first time, I realized what I was. I wasn't responsible for what happened to me. Sure, I'd made the deal, but I doubted that he would have let me go had I continued to refuse him.

I was a victim.

"Why my hand?" My voice cracked.

"It's what they wanted."

"Who's *they*?"

"The people I work for."

The ghost of my tears dried up, replaced with fiery irritation. "Okay, *Lenny*, you're going to have to start giving me answers. Real answers."

He sighed. "I don't have the answers you're looking for."

I started to pace the threadbare carpet, racking my brain. How would I get him to talk? What if he really didn't have the answers I needed? I almost didn't see it. In the next room, which was decidedly less empty than this one. It was on display. In the cabinet.

A samurai sword.

The world tilted on its axis. I suddenly found myself standing in front of it. Lenny had gotten up and was hovering behind me. "Where did you get this?" I asked, my voice even.

Lenny didn't respond. I struck out with my prosthesis and broke the glass. I reached in with my good hand, narrowly avoiding the shards. I gripped the sword's handle with loose fingers.

I spun around, swinging the sword, pointing it at Lenny. "Where. Did. You. Get. This?"

"I—You told me to get rid of him."

"Did you kill Ben?"

Lenny looked like he really didn't want to answer the question, but I could read the answer clearly in his hollow eyes.

"You killed him." I stared down at the blade, which was dull with age but surprisingly lightweight. "Fair enough," I said as sarcastically as I could muster. "I guess I should have been clearer when I explicitly told you to *send him to prison.*"

Lenny blanched, and I was pleased to see that he was starting to sweat like crazy.

"What did these 'they' people do with my hand?" I sounded calm, but I could feel a storm brewing beneath the surface. I was getting whiplash from all the emotions I'd felt in such a short time. First fear, then helplessness, then irritation that was quickly morphing into a red-hot fury.

He bit his chapped lip. "I can't tell you." He sounded like he was in pain.

"Who are you more afraid of? Me or these mysterious 'they' people?" I brandished the sword close to his neck.

"They—I mean them."

I sighed. "Listen, I won't tell anyone you told me. They'll never find out that you're the one who told me about them. I just want to know who is wearing my hand."

Lenny's eyes nearly bugged out of his head. "How did you know?"

My stomach clenched at his slip up. So, someone *was* wearing my hand. Using my hand to wash, to eat . . . to kill.

I knew then and there that it was up to me to put an end to the murders. I had to be the one to find and stop the Phantom Strangler. If I didn't, who would?

I shook my head. "It doesn't matter how I know. What does matter is that they'll think you told me that much. You're screwed, either way. So why not tell me everything else you know?"

There was no denying that Lenny was seriously sweating bullets now. Liquid soaked through his threadbare T-shirt, and the distinct aroma of BO erupted from his sweat-clogged pores.

"Listen. Why are you getting involved in this? They know everything. They're probably watching us right now." Lenny's voice hitched. His panic kick-started my adrenaline.

I couldn't keep myself from glancing around the room, as if we weren't alone. His paranoia was contagious, but instead of shrinking like the coward in front of me, it made me stand taller. "*You* got me involved in this," I said. "*I* am just seeing this through to the end. Now tell me: Who. Are. They?" I pressed, both with my words and with the sword.

"They're a . . . collective. They call themselves the Company."

"How original," I said snidely. I poked at him with the blunt tip of the sword. "Keep talking."

"They're involved in the illegal dealing of organs and other body parts."

"Like the black market?"

"It doesn't get blacker than this," he murmured.

"Someone lost a hand, so they went to the black market for a new one?" I asked. This was confirming my darkest suspicions, but I didn't know if I should be glad that I wasn't going crazy, or if I should be worried that I'd already arrived at that destination.

"Yes." He bit down so hard on his chapped lip that he drew a little blood. He didn't seem to notice as it welled in the cut and started to drip down his chin. I watched it, mesmerized.

I cleared my throat. "Who are you to them? You're some kind of lackey who tricks unsuspecting—"

"Listen—you weren't unsuspecting, and you weren't 'tricked,'" Lenny snapped, his irritation overcoming his fear, if only for an instant. "I told you what you were giving up, and what you would get in return. It's not my fault that you can't live with the consequences."

"Getting your mark drunk isn't exactly ethical bargaining practice."

"It wasn't my fault that you were always drunk. I had to make the deal happen. No matter the cost. The client was willing to pay a lot for your hand. You should be grateful. I saw the shithole you were living in. Your life was worse than mine was before I made my sale—" Lenny's eyes widened, as if he'd realized he'd made a fatal error.

"*Your* sale? What did you sell?"

Lenny sighed. "I made a different kind of deal. One where I get the money up front, but I . . . fulfill my end of the bargain a few years down the road. I blew through my money pretty fast, so I tracked them down because I needed . . . more. They hired me as a negotiator."

"Fulfill your end of the bargain in a few years? What exactly does that mean?"

I dreaded the answer, but I needed to know.

"I sold my heart, lungs, kidneys, and liver to be traded in in 2027."

My hand holding the sword wavered. "That . . . I don't know about the kidneys and liver, but I know that you need your heart and lungs to live."

Lenny's cold blue eyes locked with mine. "That's why I got the money in advance."

"What in the actual fuck is wrong with you?" I almost screamed at him. "Seriously, I was desperate, but not that desperate."

He winced. "I know. And they knew that. Which is why they only wanted your hand. They probably knew that was the most you'd be willing to give up."

My stomach churned, and the alcohol from last night's binge was ready to come back for an after party.

"But they had to have had a buyer in mind. There can't be that many people missing hands."

He nodded. "They would want a match—both in blood type and in appearance. The hand needed to be identical—or almost identical. They have people they hire to do that too. Finding the matches."

My entire body was shaking. I leaned against the wall, lowering the sword. This was a lot bigger than I'd thought. I'd thought it was just Lenny, maybe a couple of other shady guys in black suits wielding scalpels. But this was an entire operation. A *Company*.

"How can I find them?" I finally asked.

Lenny shook his head. "I won't tell you. They probably already know you're here. If I give you any information . . ."

I had a pretty good idea what he was implying, but I didn't care if he got in trouble for what he'd told me. He sure hadn't told me enough.

"I'm going to figure it out," I said. "I managed to find *you*. It's just a matter of time."

"Then you'll figure it out on your own," Lenny said firmly. "I have a few years left, and I don't want them to be cut short."

I took a deep breath as I glared at him. I considered picking up the sword again to threaten him. Instead, I strode toward the front door and swung it open. I hesitated, looking at him over my shoulder. "This isn't over."

"You think that all they want is your hand?" Lenny said. His entire demeanor had shifted, and he looked almost feral. "They know you, Regan. They know who you are deep down. They know your vices. They know you better than you know yourself. They know that you'll blow through the money just as quickly as I did."

The adrenaline must have been wearing off, because my entire body shook with the exertion of simply supporting myself. I braced my body against the door frame as a wall of dizziness slammed into me. I clenched my jaw, pouring venom into my glare.

But he wasn't finished.

"They know that soon you'll be crawling back, just begging them to take more."

36

Even after dodging Jace's questions and being lucky enough to hail a cab, I was still late for lunch with Mom. It might have had something to do with me taking a short trip to a corner store that sold travel-sized liquor bottles. I bought three and had finished them by the time I arrived at the restaurant. It was the liquid courage I needed after everything I'd been through that day, and I hadn't even gone through the worst of it yet. I still had to survive lunch with this new and supposedly improved version of my mother.

I'd made a reservation at a trendy place in Lincoln Square after Skunk Hair mentioned at Group that her husband had broken the bank to take her there for their anniversary. I told myself it was a special treat for my mom, but I realized now that it was just a pathetic attempt to show off. I brushed aside a wave of dizziness as I hurried into the restaurant. I needed to get some solid food into my stomach, since all I'd consumed today was alcohol. I pushed past the hostess, muttering that I was meeting someone. I scanned the room. The place wasn't quite as cutesy as Sharon had described, and more than half of the tables were devoid of customers, despite it being smack in the middle of what should have been lunch hour rush. The place was designed to mimic a retro diner, but the prices were definitely not retro. I supposed the owner of the place realized he could gouge people's wallets in the name of getting an "authentic" experience, when in reality genuine diners with dirt-cheap food were a dime a dozen. I supposed it didn't matter if the restaurant was actually good, just as long as Mom saw the number of zeros on the bill.

I spotted her immediately. She was already seated at a booth by the window, inspecting the little jukebox and tapping her blood-red nails impatiently on the table's laminate finish.

"I'm here, I'm here," I said breathlessly as I hurried over.

"Reggie! I was worried you weren't going to make it!" She jumped out of her seat. She was wearing a too-tight, slinky red dress that had a plunging neckline and was barely long enough to conceal her butt cheeks. I realized that it looked a lot like what I'd worn to Amrita's art show. I couldn't help but wonder if I'd looked that desperate.

Ashamed, I ignored that thought as she wrapped me in one of her notorious bear hugs. As many mixed feelings I had about my mother, I could admit that I'd missed her hugs. I melted into her.

"Yeah, yeah," I grumbled. "I'm only fifteen minutes late. It could have been a lot worse."

The couple at the next table over were staring. Cheeks bright red, I said, "Mom, just sit down."

I followed suit, taking the seat across from her.

"This place is so fancy," Mom said. "There's even a valet!"

"You parked at the valet?"

"Yes."

I sighed. "Where did you get the money?"

She shrugged. "I wanted to order some champagne, but I was worried you'd stood me up."

I didn't miss that she changed the subject. "Mom, it's barely after noon," I protested, fully aware that I was being a hypocrite, even as the empty liquor bottles weighed down my purse. "Wait, what about AA?"

Mom waved her hand in the air nonchalantly. "Going cold turkey is never a good idea. They want you not to drink ever, but this is a special occasion."

I frowned at that. "How is this a special occasion?"

"This is a lovely lunch date with my only and favorite daughter. We haven't seen each other in ages!" She flipped open the menu and began studying the lunch entrees.

"Mom, we saw each other the other day."

"You know what I mean. So, where were you this morning?" she said without looking up from the menu. I didn't like her tone.

"Mom . . ." I sighed.

"Reggie, honey, when you live in a place like Chicago, and then you're late to a lunch date, without a text or a phone call, of course your mother's going to worry!"

I glared at her. She'd always used the argument that we lived in a dangerous city for not letting me do things when I was a child. I couldn't go trick-or-treating with my friends because someone could poison the candy. I was forbidden to go to the park down the street because the play structures were rusted and uncared for and I would undoubtedly fall and break my neck. I couldn't go to the mall after school because that's where child predators hunted. I swear, if she hadn't been passed out drunk half the time, I wouldn't have ever been able to leave the house. I always pointed out to her that it was *her* choice to live in Chicago, not mine. At least, it was her choice when I was a child. These days, I could have moved anywhere I wanted, but I still chose to stay here. I couldn't imagine leaving, not even when I was afraid for my life.

I shook my head. Dr. Lavoie had said I shouldn't dwell on the negative parts of our relationship but instead focus on moving forward. "I had work to do."

"What kind of work?"

"*Private* work," I said through gritted teeth. Three days with my mother back in my life and I was already at my wit's end. I waved the waitress over. "A bottle of your finest champagne. I'll spare no expense for my mother."

Her gaze flicked over to my mother and quickly back to me. I could feel the judgment coming off her. I ignored it and turned to my mom.

"Ah. You have a new boyfriend," Mom said, a knowing twinkle in her eye. I sighed yet again. I didn't bother correcting her, because this assumption was a lot safer. My mother could get a lawyer to confess to a crime he didn't commit. She was extremely skilled at that roundabout way of talking that could make even the most expert liars slip up. I would have to be careful with her. It was one thing for Lenny or Jace to get hurt because of my big mouth. Yet, I was growing attached to a certain former Marine, and I knew that I would be devastated if Jace was targeted by the "Company" because of me. But I honestly didn't know what I would do if I lost my mother.

The waitress arrived with a bottle of champagne. "Are you ready to order?"

"We need another minute with the menu." I impatiently grabbed the bottle from her outstretched hand and poured myself a glass. I stared at it for a long moment, watching the fizzle of the bubbles racing to the surface and licked my lips. I took a deep swallow, emptying the flute in one gulp.

Mom leaned forward eagerly, her breasts nearly spilling out of her dress onto the laminate table. She raised a penciled eyebrow. "Do you want to tell me about him?"

"Well, he's very handsome and wonderful in bed," I said. I snatched up the champagne bottle and poured another glass. "Do you want some stats? I didn't have a ruler at the time, but—"

"That's fine!" Mom said, with a laugh and a roll of her eyes. "I don't need the gory details."

And with that, I'd elegantly handled the situation.

37

Aside from a few hiccups at the beginning of lunch, the rest of the meal went rather smoothly. Mom was drinking again, but I really never believed she would be able to stay on the wagon. Maybe it was better that she was drinking in public and not alone. Drinking alone was something I'd always told myself I wouldn't do, which was why I never kept alcohol in the loft. I didn't have a drinking problem if I never drank in private, right?

I ushered the movers into the loft and directed them to place the new furniture set in the living room. Embarrassed, I hurried to collect my sculpting knife and other tools I'd flung and left discarded on the floor.

I'd picked out a long and sleek black leather couch and a matching love seat, as well as a 4K TV for the wall. I didn't let the movers take away the crappy old TV, though, because if I wanted to watch the local news, I needed it and its antique rabbit ears to stay up to date.

I flipped on the little TV, since I didn't have the energy to try to figure out how to connect the new one to Netflix, and curled up on the couch. A groan of satisfaction escaped my lips. The leather of the couch was a little squeaky, but it engulfed all my curves like it was custom-made for me. It was a definite improvement from the lawn chair that had metal rods that tried to backdoor me every time I shifted my butt. I watched TV for about a half hour, but there was nothing new about the Phantom Strangler. I took this to be a good sign. I'd had more episodes of the peculiar phantom limb sensations, but none had been murderous. Last night I'd felt myself gripping a fork. It was the strangest feeling—the sensation of my hand lifting a fork to my mouth, but I never tasted anything. I supposed that meant I wasn't entirely insane. Just halfway there.

A familiar building appeared on the TV screen, bringing my attention back to the news. "A brutal killing in Fuller Park this morning has the neighborhood in shock. Stay tuned for more information as this story unfolds."

A man wearing a tattered brown suit and a shiny gold detective's badge hanging from his neck appeared on the screen. "The victim appears to have been killed with an elongated knife—or sword—but no weapon fitting this description has been found at the scene."

I sat up abruptly, my eyes locked on the screen. That was Lenny's apartment building.

The camera cut to another guy, someone who was vaguely identified as a neighbor of the victim's. "He was hacked to pieces. He was killed by a madman."

The headline at the bottom of the screen changed to "Madman strikes in Fuller Park."

Was he killed by someone from the Company? I'd just seen him this morning. How could they have gotten to him that quickly? How had they known?

A chill crept up my spine. I'd thought Lenny was paranoid. But maybe he really was being watched. I glanced around, my eyes catching on the ceiling-high windows that made up nearly the entire outer wall of the loft. Maybe I was being watched too.

38

I couldn't shake the feeling that whoever had killed Lenny was going to target me next. The Company had me under surveillance, I just knew it. They weren't visibly following me around in a white sedan, like Ben's thugs had. They were being much subtler about it. I pushed away the niggling guilt that accompanied any thought of Ben. Lenny had murdered him. He'd killed him in cold blood. I supposed it was only fair that the weapon he'd used to kill Ben was used on him. It was karma. At least, that was what I reassured myself.

I spent the next few days holed up in the loft, cocooned in blankets and paranoid thoughts, playing online poker on my brand-new MacBook. But by Tuesday, I realized I couldn't stay cooped up any longer. I'd skipped Group, because it finally dawned on me that because of its anonymous nature, Dr. Lavoie wouldn't be able to check up on my attendance. The only thing standing between me and freedom these nights would be whether I was able to effectively lie to my shrink. Skipping these sessions would mean that I also wouldn't see Jace, but I didn't want to see him. At first, he'd been awfully quiet when we'd left Lenny's apartment, but then, he'd peppered me with questions I diligently ignored before taking off for lunch with Mom. He'd had so many questions, and he would only have more if he happened to have caught the news about Lenny's death.

I put out a fresh bowl of top-shelf tuna for Little Guy. I gave him a little scratch between the ears before heading out. Tonight's destination was a different bar from my usual one, a place a few streets over that was so run-down, they'd never bothered to replace the stolen sign from the front door. To this date, I still don't know what the place is called.

A few drinks in, I was informed that my credit card was maxed out. Again. Sighing, I stumbled out to the street to find an ATM. Night had already fallen. I stood on the sidewalk, swaying slightly, jarred by the sudden change in light. How long had I been in there? Maybe I'd had more than a few drinks. I headed down the street to a bank a couple of blocks over. I'd been to this one a few times, and there was always a line at the ATM. I stuffed my one hand into my oversized heavy coat. It wasn't quite winter yet, but I always seemed to run cold. I was suddenly freezing. I realized that it was my other hand—the one that was no longer attached—that was as cold as a block of ice.

"What the fuck is she doing this time?" I grumbled to myself. "You better not be about to kill someone!"

The person waiting behind me in line watched me warily before deciding that getting money from this particular ATM wasn't worth it. I shot him the finger behind his back as he hurried away.

"Asshole," I slurred.

The man in front of me turned to give me a dirty look.

"Not you," I said. "The other guy."

He tucked his bills into his wallet and looked around. The other guy was long gone. This guy gave me another weird look before taking off at top speed.

It took three tries to get my bank card into the tiny slot. All the while, I muttered about how they were making the holes smaller and smaller these days. When I finally got it in, it was upside down, so I had to start over.

Then, I stood there for thirty seconds trying to remember my pin. When I finally remembered it—my mother's birthday—a wave of confusion washed over me. Something wasn't quite right.

I shook my head, rubbing my bleary eyes so I could read the tiny font on the screen. I checked my account balance. I blinked as some of the fogginess lifted away in shock.

I was down to less than ten grand. Less than ten grand? I'd had a *million* dollars. Where the hell had it all gone?

I'd been playing online poker all weekend, and I'd lost, but I couldn't quite remember how much I'd lost. It definitely wasn't more than a couple grand. *Maybe* it had gone into the five digits. Though, that wasn't the only time I'd lost.

Suddenly more sober than I would have liked, I withdrew a couple of twenties. I couldn't go back to the bar tonight.

As I stumbled back in the direction of home, I tried to do the calculations with my alcohol-addled brain. How had I spent that much money? Where had it all gone? How could I have been such an idiot?

A hulking shape shifted in the shadows outside my building. Someone was waiting to get in. Fear gnawed at me as I slowed my pace. I glanced over my shoulder. It was a lot later than I'd thought, and the streets were nearly empty. Should I turn back? But if I returned to the bar, I would spend money that I didn't have. I was better off dead.

I tried to shake off that dark thought, but it clung to me along with the dread and self-loathing that had become my constant companions. I bit my lip as I shuffled toward the building's entrance. The shadows shifted. I barely held back a shriek as a man emerged from the darkness.

I nearly collapsed with relief as I recognized him. It was Jace.

I laughed, and the sound came out jarring, even to me. Jace's eyes narrowed. He didn't look particularly happy to see me.

"How did you find me?" I asked.

"I'm a PI. I can find anyone," Jace replied, running a hand over the stubble on his head. "Plus, you had me walk you home after Group the other night."

I'd forgotten about that. "Why are you here?" I hated that the words came out slightly slurred. "I don't owe you any money. I fired you."

Jace tucked his hands into his pockets as he took in my appearance. "I saw the news."

"What news?" I asked innocently.

"Like I said, for a liar, you're a terrible one." He was as stoic as ever, but there was something in his voice that told me he was pissed.

"Why are you mad at me? Shouldn't you be worried that I'm next?"

"What did you do in there with Stevenson?"

I stared at him blankly for a few seconds before I remembered that Stevenson was Lenny's last name. "I talked to him. No slicing *or* dicing. Promise."

"Are you sure?"

"Yes. I'm *sure*." I'd put down the sword. I remembered doing it. "Besides, you heard him threatening me as I left. He couldn't have been dead and threatening me, unless you believe in zombies. Or vampires. Or maybe he was a ghost—"

Jace cut me off. "I heard him say something about you begging to sell something."

"Yeah, see? He couldn't have said that while dead." I grinned, feeling triumphant.

"But then you went back in."

"W-what?"

"You went back in," he repeated. He studied my expression. "Don't you remember?"

My stomach was doing acrobatics. I was going to be sick. All I remembered was feeling overcome with dizziness and using the door frame to brace my weight. I had a vague recollection of Lenny leaning over me to close the door, trapping me in his apartment with him. I'd felt faint—from hunger, from the drop in adrenaline, and, quite frankly, from the whiskey I'd drank on an empty stomach. I definitely remembered telling Lenny to fuck off. Everything after that was a blur until Jace and I were leaving the building. "Of course I remember," I lied.

Jace continued to watch me in silence. I tried to keep my expression neutral. Why couldn't I remember more? What had I said? What had I *done*?

"Well, the murder weapon was missing. They said it was a sword," I began. "If I'd left with it, wouldn't you have noticed?"

Jace looked me up and down. "Not with you wearing that bulky coat."

"So you can't say for sure that I didn't leave with the weapon?" I hated that I was asking this. I hated that I didn't know the answer to this question.

Suddenly, everything became crystal clear. "You work for *them*, don't you?" I said.

"Who?"

"Are you framing me? Framing me for murder?" I asked, my voice getting louder with each word. Fury was bubbling beneath the surface, and it was about to overflow.

Jace blinked, like he was genuinely surprised. "No, Roz. I'm not," he said firmly.

"*Pfft*. I know you're one of them. You're working for them. You waited until after I left, and then you killed Lenny. And now you're trying to make me think I did it. Well, you failed."

Jace took a step closer. "Roz, are you on any medication? Anything for the pain?"

I jumped backward. I didn't want to let him get too close. "Pain? How do you know about the pain?"

Jace's voice was soothing, patronizing, maddening. "You mentioned it during the first Group session you came to."

Had I? I couldn't remember. "I won't let you make me think I'm going crazy," I shouted.

Jace's jaw clenched. "I'm leaving," he said. "You need to go inside and get some sleep. Sleep whatever this is off. Tomorrow, you need to go to your doctor. Tell him that you're losing time. Whatever drugs you're on, you need to stop them. Now." Hands in the air, marking his defeat, he turned and started to walk away.

"Don't tell me what to do!" I screamed. Jace didn't look back.

39

My migraine was a killer. I lay in bed, half asleep, questioning if the events from the previous day were even real or if they were just a drunken dream. I settled on them being a little bit of both as I dragged myself and my shame out of bed around eleven.

Hanna was exiting the bathroom. Her ordinarily pale complexion was ghostly, and she was still wearing her blue plaid pjs.

"Why are you here?" I said, brows furrowed. "Did you oversleep?" I hoped she hadn't lost her job, because now that I was on my way back to Brokesville, I needed at least one of us to be able to cover the rent.

Hanna grimaced. "Wow, you look worse than I feel. And I have the flu."

I took an exaggerated step backward as Hanna hacked into a tissue. "Yeah, sorry, but I can't afford to get sick."

Hanna's eyebrows shot into her shock-white hair.

"Save your energy; I know what you're going to say. You have a job, a girlfriend, a life, responsibilities, et cetera, et cetera." I rolled my eyes. "Go back to bed. I'll make you soup."

Hanna slumped back to her sleeping area, head down, looking an awful lot like Eeyore from *Winnie-the-Pooh*. "Not tomato soup!" she called out faintly from under her covers.

I went into the kitchen, popped a Ryofen, grabbed a can of noodle soup—which took far too long to open with a can opener and only one hand—and started to heat it up in a pot over the stove. Last night was a blur, but I was pretty sure I remembered everything accurately. Jace had come to see me. He all but accused me of murdering Lenny. But I *hadn't* killed him. He'd still been alive when I left. I had to admit that I was seeing some things that weren't there. The portrait in Dr. Lavoie's office. The grotesque face on the train. There might have been other things I was imagining too, but I just didn't know it. But was I also losing time? I'd sometimes black out when I was drunk, but I hadn't been that drunk when I'd gone to see Lenny. I felt a touch of unease as I looked down at the bottle of Ryofen. Hallucinations were one potential "rare" side effect, but were there others? This experimental drug had never been tested on humans before. Maybe the doctors didn't know everything about it.

I put the bottle back in the cabinet. I was overreacting. The doctors wouldn't have started human trials unless they were convinced that side effects would be minimal. I ran through the events in my mind for the millionth time. I'd felt faint. Lenny closed the door, likely to keep me out of sight from the prying eyes of his neighbors. I'd told him off, then left. That was it. That was what had happened. I was ninety percent sure.

But I couldn't quite shake away the seed that Jace had planted last night. When I'd first met him, I'd suspected that he might have been one of Sylvain's victims. But now new possibilities were coursing through my mind. What if he was like Lenny, and once he ran out of money from selling his foot, he had started to work for them? What if he'd become a "negotiator," as Lenny had called it? I had to admit that the revelation stung a little. I liked Jace, with his brusque attitude and snide sense of humor. His smooth jawline and piercing brown eyes with copper swirls that seemed to see me—the *real* me. And even more so—I *wanted* him to see the real me. He had a calmness and an intensity about him that was both contradictory and irresistible. But now that I suspected he was one of them . . . I ignored the ache in my chest that accompanied the thought that I couldn't trust him.

I didn't want to analyze what that reaction to his betrayal might mean. Despite my newfound realization that Jace couldn't be trusted, I still had a nagging suspicion that something wasn't right. I'd hallucinated at least twice. Was my judgment impaired?

I sighed, staring at my reflection in the brand-new microwave door. When I'd started the Ryofen, I'd told myself I wouldn't do anything to risk the trial. I'd told myself I would stay away from alcohol. But I hadn't. My mother had only lasted two months sober, and she'd given up so easily. Did I have a problem too? Is that something I was willing to admit? I made a promise to myself then and there that I would stay away from alcohol—for good.

I brought Hanna her bowl of soup, smiling slightly as she moaned her appreciation. All thoughts of Lenny and Jace would have to wait. I had an appointment with Dr. Lavoie, and I could not be late. If she so much as suspected I was experiencing side effects, she would have me pulled from the trial. And I couldn't be removed from it—and not just because it was the only thing that could relieve my pain. I also had a killer to find.

40

"Did you go to lunch with your mother?" Dr. Lavoie asked the moment I settled onto my spot on the couch. Her pen was already poised expectantly over her notebook.

She sure wasn't bothering with casual chitchat anymore. "Yep," I replied.

Dr. Lavoie waited for me to continue. I looked around the room, taking in its cozy warmth. It was a million times homier than the loft, or even my childhood home. I took care to avoid looking at the portrait. I didn't want to know what it was doing at that very moment.

"And?"

"It was fine," I said, finally bringing my gaze back to hers.

"Something is bothering you. Tell me what it is."

What isn't bothering me? "My mom was drinking at lunch."

Dr. Lavoie didn't allow whatever she was feeling to show. She had an impeccable poker face. Though, I was starting to be able to identify her tell. Whenever she was surprised about something, or if I said something concerning, she would grow still. Too still. Not a single muscle on her body would react to what I was saying, which was different from when I usually said something harsh or crass or blunt. Then, she'd allow herself to react as anyone else would. Right now, she was completely immobile. "Is that right?" she replied, her tone perfectly smooth.

"That's right."

"And how did that make you feel?"

I snorted. "Did you seriously just ask me the most clichéd question a psychiatrist could ask?"

Dr. Lavoie looked sheepish. "I try to ask open-ended questions. To give you the opportunity to tell me what you wish to tell me, how you want to tell me." She wrote something in her notebook. She looked back up at me, perfectly sculpted eyebrow raised. "And don't think I didn't notice that you deflected the question."

I produced a pained smile. "I guess I'm just a little disappointed. She said she was sober, she said that she was working again. I just don't know how much of that is true."

"Your mother needs you now more than ever. She's not as strong as you are."

I blinked and stared at her, but she wasn't looking at me. It looked like she was drawing loops in her damned notebook. "What makes you think I'm stronger than her?"

She still didn't look up.

"Oh, Roz, you're as tough as nails. Sure, you have your vices, you lack impulse control, you have a temper and a foul mouth, but I think that if there were a zombie apocalypse next week, you would be one of the survivors."

An authentic grin pulled at my lips. "Yeah, well, Daryl and I would definitely hook up and have little redneck, Harley-riding, crossbow-wielding babies."

Dr. Lavoie finally looked up at me, confusion pulling her brows together. "Who's Daryl?"

I couldn't say I was surprised that she'd never seen *The Walking Dead*. "Never mind."

"You mentioned that you're disappointed in your mother. Does this change what you told me during our last session? About wanting to spend more time with her?"

I thought about this for a moment as I fiddled with the hem of my T-shirt. "No," I said, finally. "You're right. I do think this is a second chance for us, and I don't want to screw it up."

"Good," Dr. Lavoie said with a rare smile. "Now, I want you to know that you will have to divorce your desire to bond with your mother from your belief that you will not be able to overcome your demons. You *will* defeat them. Whether or not your mother can defeat hers is another matter entirely. All you can do is be there for her, but you cannot let her drag you down."

I nodded.

"Now, it might be a good idea for us to start some joint sessions. Would your mother be interested in coming in for therapy?"

I was dreading this part of the conversation. I'd hoped I wouldn't have to bring it up until the end. "Actually . . . I needed to talk to you about this. I don't have health insurance, and my . . . cash flow is running a little dry." I wasn't sure how much these sessions cost, but from the sparkle of the gold-gilt globe sitting on the corner of Dr. Lavoie's desk, I could tell she was raking in the dough. "I won't be able to see you anymore."

Dr. Lavoie looked genuinely surprised at this. "Have you not been looking at your bills?"

"Um . . ." If by "bills" she meant the papers that the receptionist handed me after every session, which went straight into the waste bin, then the answer was no. "I don't think so?" I said diplomatically.

"Because you are a part of the Ryofen drug trial, your psychiatry and the mandated biweekly physical health checkups are covered by their pharmaceutical grant."

"Which means . . ."

"Which means that the Northwestern research scientists have been paying me to see you. I thought you knew this."

"Um, I guess I didn't." Relief enveloped me. I wouldn't have to stop seeing her. In a weird way, I was starting to enjoy our time together. It was nice having someone to talk to, even if they were being paid to listen to my whining without walking out the door when I inevitably offended them.

"Well, it's a requirement. I have to see you two times a week, so I can report on your side effects or lack thereof." Dr. Lavoie gave me a stern look. "Speaking of: have you been having any side effects since our last meeting?"

Unless blackouts and the possible skewering of psychos counted, then the answer was: "Nope."

"No headaches, numbness of the joints, changes in your appetite, dizzy spells, or hallucinations?"

I swallowed. "Nope," I repeated, a little less forcefully this time.

"Good. And Roz? I know that your mother has problems with drinking too much. But if you're drinking on this medication, even just a sip of wine before bed, it can cause serious problems. Not just side effects, but possibly long-term health issues down the line. Particularly with your liver and heart."

My chest squeezed at the thought of potentially damaging my heart. "Not a problem," I said weakly. And it wouldn't be. Not anymore. I'd made a promise to myself that morning. If I couldn't stick to it, then I deserved whatever came next.

41

"All roads seem to lead to you, Ms. Osbourne." Detective Gutierrez stood in the doorway to the loft with her foot lodged in the frame so I couldn't slam it shut on her. I really, really needed to invest in a peephole. At this point, I was ready to crack out the power tools and drill one myself, rental security deposit be damned.

"How can I help you, Detective?" I asked sweetly.

"May I come in for a moment?" It was a question, but it didn't really seem like she was asking. "I just have a few questions regarding a Mr. Leonard Stevenson."

"Leonard Stevenson?" I repeated the name slowly, as if I were trying it out on my tongue. My thoughts were frantically running a mile a minute. The cops had somehow managed to connect me to Lenny's death. But how? This on top of the fact that I was already on the detective's watch list for my anonymous call about the Phantom Strangler, and I was more than a little worried. I realized that I was being silent for too long, so I said, "Come on in."

She strode through the doorway and looked around, absorbing the kitchen and living areas. "It looks like you've recently come into some money."

"Why do you say that?" I asked, but I already knew the answer to my question. The shiny new fridge, the microwave, the massive TV, the deluxe couches still had the price tags on them. They all screamed, "Recently pur-chased!" and "Ask where we came from!"

The detective gave me a small smirk. "Where did the windfall come from?"

"Oh, you know. Here and there. I'm really good at blackjack."

"Right. Blackjack."

"You must have checked me out. I'm a dealer."

"You *were* a dealer. Before you were fired for being rude to customers."

Al must have been running his mouth again. I, however, was done with talking. "Unless it's illegal to tell a customer where she can stick her ace of spades, why are you here?"

"What's going on out there?" Hanna's voice called weakly from her bed.

"Nothing! Go back to sleep!" I called out. Quieter, I said, "My room-mate is sick. Can you try keeping your unfounded accusations to a lower decibel?"

A hint of a sneer appeared on Detective Gutierrez's bow-shaped lips. "I'll do my best." She gestured for me to sit on the couch, which I did, but she remained standing. A power move, I supposed. "Now, how do you know Leonard Stevenson?"

"I don't," I replied. "If that's all you have to ask me, you could have called. It would have saved you the trip and taxpayers' dollars."

"Do you recognize this?" She deposited a photograph on the coffee table in front of me. I picked it up and made a show of studying it, though I recognized it immediately. It was Ben's samurai sword.

"Yes," I said slowly. Now I knew how she'd found me. My fingerprints were probably all over the damn thing. The *murder weapon*. I had to play it cool.

Detective Gutierrez looked shocked at my admission. "Where do you know it from?"

"My ex, Ben Reynell, collects dumb swords like this one. He has them all on display in his apartment. This looks like one of his."

"Do you recognize this specific sword?"

I shrugged. "How many swords like this are there lying around in Chicago? Why? Where did you find it?" I shook my head, laughing. "Did he sell it illegally or something?"

Detective Gutierrez scrutinized my face. I kept my expression questioning yet unassuming while my heart slammed around inside my chest. "It was found at a crime scene."

I allowed my eyes to widen almost comically. "Is that who Leonard Stevenson is? Was he *murdered*? Oh my God, you don't think Ben did it, do you?"

I held my breath, hoping I hadn't tipped my hand.

Detective Gutierrez didn't respond. She continued to study me with narrowed eyes.

"Well, I haven't seen Ben in a couple of months," I said, unable to take the silence. "Besides, Ben loves those stupid swords. He wouldn't use one in a murder and then just throw it away. He would have used something else, like a gun or a run-of-the-mill cleaver." Why couldn't I stop talking?

"Does your ex have a history of violence?"

Why did I feel like this was a trick question? She might have already looked into him. She might have already known exactly who Ben Reynell was. I had to play this carefully. "Well, my ex wasn't exactly Gentle Ben. He had a violent streak, which was one of the reasons why I broke up with him."

"Had?"

"What?"

"You said 'had.' That your ex-boyfriend 'had' a violent streak. Why did you use the past tense, Ms. Osbourne?"

Sweat trickled down my back. "I wasn't aware that I did." *Oh God.*

"So, this sword belongs—or belonged—to your ex-boyfriend."

"Mm-hmm."

"So that would explain why your fingerprints are on it?"

"I guess. I touched at least one of the swords. And I'm sure Ben's fingerprints are all over it too," I said.

"Actually, your prints are the only ones on it."

I caught myself biting my lip and quickly stopped, but not before the detective's eyes flicked down to my mouth, observing one of my more obvious tells. Hopefully, she just thought I was having the general nerves that any innocent person would have about being interrogated. "Okay. He inherited those swords from his dad. He should have paperwork—certificates or something saying that the sword is authentic. You should be able to confirm it's his." My attention was drawn back to the photo. "Are you positive that this is the murder weapon?"

"Absolutely sure."

But the weapon hadn't been found at Lenny's apartment. So where had they found it? I looked up at the detective, but she didn't elaborate, and I didn't want to ask. I didn't want to show that I knew more about the case than the average innocent civilian.

"Where were you Friday morning? And is there anyone who can corroborate your whereabouts?" she asked.

She was asking for my alibi. I'd been with Jace that morning. But given that he was there at the crime scene with me, and that he himself had accused me of killing Lenny, he probably wasn't the best person to name. "I was here. Alone."

"Hmm. That's inconvenient."

"You're telling me," I joked. She gave me a weird look. I was overcompensating for my guilt by being uncharacteristically friendly. I needed to add some of my usual bite. "You don't honestly think I stole my ex-boyfriend's sword, a decidedly *unique* sword, and traveled across town, just to murder someone I've never even met?"

"Across town?"

Shit shit shit. "What?"

"How do you know where the victim lived?"

"It was on the news. It happened in Fuller Park. Unless there were two killings by a sword in Chicago on Friday?" I said that as sarcastically as possible to hide the undercurrents of dread that were coursing through my body.

"Hmm. You don't strike me as someone who pays attention to local news," Detective Gutierrez said.

"Well, I have this lovely new TV to watch it on. And it beats *Wheel of Fortune*."

Detective Gutierrez smiled tightly. "It's funny. I was still trying to figure out why you called in that phony call about the Phantom Strangler. And then your fingerprints show up on this murder weapon. There's some key piece to the puzzle that I haven't found yet."

"Well, I used to be *great* at puzzles when I was a kid. Let me know if you'd like a hand," I said, and I waved my prosthesis in the air for emphasis.

Lightning fast, she reached out and gripped my prosthesis in her small yet deceptively strong hand.

I stared down at the slim, strong fingers that tightly gripped my synthetic wrist. I swallowed back the uneasiness that settled over me as I wrenched my arm back. I half expected her to start a tug-of-war, but she let go with no resistance.

"Oh, don't worry about me." Detective Gutierrez gave me a smile that seemed more like the baring of teeth. "I love a challenge. I haven't met a case yet that I wasn't able to solve."

42

I wanted a drink. I more than wanted it. I needed it. I craved it with the very essence of my being. I yearned for the woodsy scent of whiskey as I cradled an ice-cold glass in my hand. I longed for the burn of it as it glided down my throat, coating my stomach and numbing my senses. There was nothing quite like it. Nothing else could compare.

I threw on my coat and went outside for a brisk walk in the cold. I headed in the opposite direction of O'Malley's because I couldn't trust myself. I saw the nameless bar up ahead. I crossed the street and took another side street to lead myself away from temptation.

I kept my hand tucked in my pocket and thumbed the gold claddagh necklace that I kept on my person at all times. I was glad I wasn't stupid or morbid enough to wear it, otherwise Detective Gutierrez would have arrested me on sight. I simply kept it in my pocket, as reassurance that I wasn't totally insane. It was also a reminder of why I was bothering to look for the killer at all. The girl who owned this necklace—Tessa Brown, and the other victims, Pauline Hobbes and Tillie Simons—were people that I would never forget. They were dead because of me. I might not have been the one to physically strangle them to death, but I might as well have been.

A thought struck me at that moment. The concept of my hand killing innocent women had haunted me since I first realized what was happening.

But what did this say about me? How could my hand kill someone? What did it say about me that my hand could do something so abhorrent, so perverse, so evil as to kill?

And now Lenny was dead, and the murder weapon was linked to me. Had I killed him? Was I a monster, just like the killer who now wears my hand?

I let myself dwell on these dark thoughts before forcing myself to move on. I needed to think about the police and their investigation and what I should do next. Detective Gutierrez was cunning, and she would put the pieces together sooner or later. While I doubted that she would discover how I was truly connected to the Phantom Strangler, she would probably somehow figure out a way to prove that I knew "him." She might even have enough evidence to put me away for Lenny's death. I suspected that the only reason why I wasn't already behind bars was because there was no clear motive tying me to his death.

Who was Lenny to me? Why would I kill him? I could only hope that Detective Gutierrez wouldn't follow the bread crumbs to Jace. He was an ex-Marine, and he likely had a strong sense of right and wrong and justice and all that crap. It was one of the things that I found attractive about him. He wouldn't protect me—not if he thought I was a killer.

The other night, when Jace had shown up outside my building, I'd been drunk and pissed off. I'd accused him of framing me for murder. But all Detective Gutierrez had tying me to the murder were my fingerprints on the weapon. She never mentioned having an eyewitness. Jace didn't strike me as the type to half-ass anything. Even when he was milking me for my money as a bodyguard, he still insisted on doing the job properly. If Jace was trying to frame me for murder, I had no doubt in my mind that I wouldn't be wandering the streets having these realizations. No, I'd be behind bars. Did that mean I'd been wrong about Jace? At this point, it was too late. I'd already scared him off, and I doubted he would be willing to help me—a possible *murderer*—especially after I'd acted like a drunken lunatic.

I needed to think through my next steps.

I ran my thumb and forefinger over the gold chain, my head clearer than it had been in a long time. Lenny had said a lot of things when I visited him. I needed to try to remember everything, to see if there were clues. He'd said that he was given my name and information. So, someone had already identified me as a possible mark. Hardly anyone knew me or how desperate I'd been. There were the people at the Horseshoe Hammond, the people at O'Malley's, a few acquaintances, Ben. Hanna. I couldn't imagine Ben giving up my name. He was overprotective in his own unique and psychotic way. And Hanna wouldn't have done that. I didn't know her well, but she would definitely be living in a nicer building, with nicer things, if she weren't a law student and intern spending all her time paving her way toward a better future. She had a strong sense of right and wrong too, and I couldn't imagine her jeopardizing her principles for quick cash.

Just as I was turning another corner, I remembered something that Lenny had told me. He said that he was sent to Amrita's art show, not just to find me, but to follow up with a donor. I stopped in my tracks, and a fast walker behind me swore in irritation as he swerved to avoid bumping into me. I glared at his back as he resumed his vigorous pace down the street.

Amrita Tejal. My old classmate. I hadn't heard from her for years. Not until her art show. Her first art show ever, which was a whopping success. A success due to her *benefactor*, or so Lenny had told me. At the time, I'd assumed he was implying she had a sugar daddy. But what if it had been something else?

What if she had made a deal, just as I had?

43

I called Amrita then and there and made lunch plans for the following day. She picked a regular restaurant—nothing too fancy—and I was grateful for that. I needed to be careful about how much money I spent. Although the movers would be coming back tomorrow to return all the furniture I'd bought. I was impulsive, but I wasn't a complete idiot. I had to pad my bank account, especially if I needed to hire another PI. I didn't think I'd use Jace again, partly because I didn't trust him and partly because he'd definitely been swindling me.

Mom dropped by that evening with a bottle of rosé to celebrate the re-kindling of our mother-daughter relationship. I suggested we stop drinking together. Just before she dropped by, I'd caved and had a drink at O'Malley's, but I'd limited myself to just one. It would be my last. When I told Mom, she looked surprised, pleased, and maybe even a little proud. We dumped the contents of the seven-dollar bottle down the toilet and pigged out on delivery pizza, canned Coke, and Twizzlers in front of the TV. It was a last party for the furniture and a funeral for the TV, which would all be gone by this time the following day.

I hadn't realized how much I'd missed spending time with Mom. She had her flaws, but didn't we all? The important thing was that she was mak-ing time for me, and that we had a second chance to repair our relationship.

I wasn't going to waste this opportunity.

Early the next morning, I was awakened by loud clattering in the kitchen. I sat bolt upright in my bed, pausing to reorient myself as all the blood rushed out of my head and the room spun around me. I barely registered that this was the first morning I'd woken up without a hangover in the longest time, before snatching up my prosthesis from the nightstand. I gripped it in my right hand like a weapon.

I took several deep, calming breaths before stalking out of my bedroom, ready to fend off a burglar or murderer. A petite woman with curly brown hair was in the kitchen. The sunlight glaring through the loft windows bleached her figure, making her appear overexposed and ethereal, like an old photograph. I rubbed my eyes, sighing as my vision came into focus. It was just my mother. I slipped my prosthetic onto my stump before she realized how close she'd come to being clobbered. I dragged my feet as I crossed the loft.

"Two days in a row. You're going to make me feel like I'm loved," I grumbled.

"Good morning!" Mom said, ignoring my gripe. "I noticed your fridge was empty. Now that you're sober, you're going to have to eat healthier!"

"That doesn't even make sense," I said. "But that might be because I haven't had my coffee yet. Can you put on a pot?"

"Already did!" Mom sang.

I narrowed my eyes suspiciously. "You're still sober, right?"

Mom rolled her eyes. "Of course. It's eight in the morning, Reggie."

The hour of the day had never stopped her before. I pinched my mouth shut, not wanting to say anything to spoil her good mood. "Well, I've been sober for almost twelve hours, and I've never felt better," I told her.

I sat on a stool as she bustled around the kitchen, humming under her breath. It was strange how different she was. There was a skip in her step. Her eyes were wide and bright. She seemed lighter, happier, more alive than ever before.

"Roz?" Hanna called from her 'bedroom'.

I grabbed an extra mug of coffee and brought it to her bedside. Nestled under layers of blankets, she peered up at me.

"Well, you're looking a lot better," I said.

"Yeah, I feel better too, I think. How much NyQuil did you give me last night?"

Enough to put down a horse. "Just the regular amount," I said nonchalantly.

Hanna nodded. "The phlegm is down to a minimum, and I only coughed up one lung when I woke up this morning." Hanna eyed the coffee and I put it on her desk. She pushed the covers off her body and stood up on Bambi legs. "Hey! I'm not dizzy and in danger of toppling over!"

She gingerly took a step, followed by another step, and made her way toward the desk. I found myself reaching out, extending my hand near her back just in case she did crumple and needed me to catch her. She picked up her coffee and took a sip. She turned to me with a solemn expression on her face. "I think I might be ready for solid food."

I nodded. "I think it's time."

At that, she grinned and then followed me out of her bedroom. "So, who were you talking to before?"

"My mom."

"Oh, that's nice," she said. She put her already-drained mug in the sink.

I looked around, but Mom had already taken off.

"Yeah, I talk to my dad sometimes too," she continued.

"Um, that's nice too, I guess," I said, a little confused. "Anyway, my mom brought some groceries. So, if you're hungry, I'm sure I can scrounge up something decent to eat."

Hanna stared at me.

"What?"

"Your mom brought us groceries?"

I rolled my eyes. "Yeah, don't look so shocked. She's sober now. She's doing well. We've been spending time together lately. I don't want to sound pathetic or anything, but it's nice having her in my life again."

I went to the fridge and swung the door open.

"Roz, your mom is dead."

The fridge was empty.

44

My mother was dead.

Awareness slammed into me, ripping the breath from my lungs. I couldn't breathe. Blood thundered in my ears as the room spiraled. Darkness taunted my vision, squeezing in around me as the loft became too tight, too cramped. I sprinted out the door, staggered down the stairs, and burst out onto the street. Harsh sunlight beat down on me. A cutting wind gripped me tight in its embrace. I gasped for breath, all but devouring the dank, polluted air around me.

A horn blared as a car swerved past, jolting me back to my senses. I dove back onto the sidewalk, clutching my stomach as I struggled to continue to inhale and exhale and keep the darkness at bay for a little while longer.

How could I have forgotten that my mother was dead?

I hurried down the street, walking as quickly as I could, my feet almost floating across the pavement. I'd seen my mother multiple times these last few days. In public. We went to lunch. We watched movies last night. I cringed as I remembered the look on the pizza delivery guy's face when I'd told him my mom and I were binge-watching rom coms all night. The same thing had happened at the restaurant, with the customers and waitress. I'd thought they were all giving my mom a strange look because of the way she was dressed. But the whole time they were actually judging me.

They were thinking that I was a raving lunatic.

They weren't wrong.

What was happening to me? My mother had been as real as the air, the trees, the pavement, the necklace I kept in my pocket.

Mom had seemed different, but the changes were all good. She was happier, brighter. Sober. Were these all characteristics that my broken brain had fabricated? She'd died four years ago from liver failure. She'd left me broken in more ways than one. How had I forgotten such an important part of my life? I wasn't just hallucinating about my mother—I'd genuinely forgotten her death. Did Ryofen mess with memory too? Was that another side effect of this experimental drug?

I hesitated outside a bar I'd only been to a handful of times because it was too far from home. I almost went in, but it was closed. I supposed I was lucky. Or unlucky. Depending on how you looked at it.

I shouldn't drink. The Ryofen was messing with my mind enough. Was I having these hallucinations because of the drug interacting with the alcohol? Or was it just the drug itself? Right on cue, my phantom hand began to tingle. I supposed I had to embrace the inevitable. I leaned against the door to the bar and waited. This time, it was nothing too strange. It was writing on paper, in large curlicue letters. I focused on what was being written, but I couldn't decipher it. Maybe it wasn't English. Maybe it was the incoherent ranting of a maniac. Or maybe the killer was just a doodler.

I sat down on the sidewalk, ignoring the side-eye I got from a man who was inserting change in a parking meter. I was probably sitting in pigeon shit, but I didn't care. I needed to make a decision. The Ryofen was doing more than creating mild hallucinations of moving paintings and phantom faces. It was causing me to hallucinate *people*. I had hallucinated entire interactions with another human being. Conversations at restaurants. Cuddles on the couch while watching *Sleepless in Seattle*. A fat tear rolled down my cheek, and I wiped it away harshly with the back of my hand. If I stopped the Ryofen, I wouldn't be able to get to the bottom of who the Phantom Strangler was. But was this worth it?

Another concern was equally daunting. The Ryofen was the only drug that kept me from feeling the phantom limb pain. Dr. Lavoie didn't want to prescribe narcotics because they were highly addictive. Did I want to become addicted to painkillers? Did I want to become an addict and end up like my mother? I looked up at the sign on the bar, which was shut off until noon, when the place would finally open for the day. I already was an addict. I couldn't stop the Ryofen. I couldn't trust myself not to become hooked on pills, desperate for a fix.

The sensation finally faded from my hand, and I realized how cold I was. I was shivering in my spot on the cold pavement, wearing nothing but a sweatshirt and pajama pants.

I didn't know what to do. I didn't have anyone left. I couldn't tell Dr. Lavoie anything, out of the risk of being taken off the Ryofen. I couldn't tell Hanna. She wouldn't be able to help, and it would just put her in danger.

I had only one person left.

45

Exhaustion had nearly overtaken me by the time eight o'clock rolled around. I'd spent the entire day wandering the streets, somehow managing to avoid bars and restaurants that served alcohol. It didn't hurt that I had no money on me, though that had never stopped me in the past. I found myself outside the recreation complex just before Group was scheduled to meet. I supposed this was fate. Or maybe it was my subconscious telling me what I had to do.

I went inside. I got a few strange looks from Skunk Hair and the others. Jace wasn't there.

I sighed, but I wasn't sure if it was with relief or disappointment. I'd come to the conclusion that I had to tell Jace everything. Before, I'd thought he might be involved, but if he was, wouldn't he have gone to the police to tell them that he'd been with me, and he'd seen—or heard—me kill Lenny? That would have been a tidy way to both keep me from finding out more about the Company and frame me for Lenny's death. But he hadn't gone to the police.

I honestly didn't know what to think anymore. But what I did know was that I couldn't do this on my own. I'd managed to convince myself that Jace wasn't trying to frame me for Lenny's murder. If he had, he would have succeeded. If Jace were working for the Company, I had no doubt in my mind that he would have taken that golden opportunity to get me out of the picture.

Besides, who was better to trust than a PI? I was a gambling woman, and I was willing to place my bet on his being an ally, not an enemy.

Lowell strolled up to me wearing a broad grin. He acted as though it was perfectly normal to be coming to Group wearing pajamas that were now filthy from spending hours wandering the streets. "Hey, Roz. I brought brownies tonight. I know they're your favorite."

I suddenly realized I was starving. I hadn't eaten since I'd binged on pizza the night before, if that had even happened. I tried not to think about it. "Thanks," I replied. I stuffed one in my mouth and grinned at him. "I love how your brownies are never stale, not like Sku—I mean, Sharon's lemon squares."

Lowell laughed, but Skunk Hair shot me a dirty look from the other side of the table as she carefully positioned a plate of said lemon squares beside the brownies. I should have kept my voice down.

"Well, I like a girl who loves a good dessert," Lowell replied. He shot me a sidelong look.

Uh-oh.

"Speaking of, there's a new dessert bar a few blocks from here. Have you been to it?" Lowell was speaking extra casually and making a point of not looking at me directly.

I shook my head.

"Well, they specialize in crepes, but they have brownies too. I checked out their menu online."

"Okay . . . a lot of places sell brownies. And crepes."

The tips of Lowell's ears turned pink. "This guy I follow on TikTok gave it a really good review. I'm thinking about checking it out sometime, if—"

"You're here."

I swallowed my mouthful of brownie and turned around. Jace stood inches away, glowering down at me. He radiated irritation and the hint of a woodsy scent I wanted to bury my nose into.

"It would appear so," I said. I nonchalantly took another bite of brownie.

Jace scowled. He took in my pajamas, sweatshirt, and lack of coat, and his frown deepened even further.

"Was there something that you wanted?" I asked him, speaking with my mouth full.

I didn't think it was possible, but Jace's frown deepened even more. He looked like a live version of a grumpy puppet. He didn't respond.

I pushed away my irritation at his stony silence. "If not, you'll have to excuse me. I'm about to be asked out on a date," I said. I spun around and looked at Lowell. "Well?" I said to him.

"Yeah, so, uh . . ." His eyes flickered to Jace, then back to me. "Do you want to go there?"

"Go where?"

"The dessert bar," Lowell's already pink ears were starting to turn red.

"Yeah, I got that part. But what's its name? I have to type something into Uber."

"It's the Dessert Oasis." The words tumbled over each other in his eagerness.

"Hmm. Pithy. When?"

"How's Sunday? Around eight?"

"Mm 'kay," I said between bites of my third brownie.

"Great! I'll meet you there," Lowell said cheerily. He trotted off to greet the other arrivals.

I could feel Jace seething behind me, but I ignored him. I poured myself a cup of coffee, spilling a tad on Skunk Hair's plate of lemon squares. *Whoops.* At least now they wouldn't be so dry.

"He didn't even offer to pick you up?" Jace said.

I widened my eyes dramatically as I looked up at him. "Oh, you're still here? Well, unless he rides a tandem bike, he probably doesn't have a seat for me."

Jace's frown became slightly less pronounced at that.

"Listen, I was hoping to talk to you. After Group."

Jace was staring at my lips. "You have some chocolate," he said, gesturing to his own mouth.

"Oh," I said. I grabbed a napkin and rubbed it off.

"Listen, Roz, I'm sorry for what happened the other day."

I raised an eyebrow. "When you accused me of murder?"

"Keep your voice down," Jace hissed.

I blinked. "Um, okay," I stage whispered. "I'm pretty sure I didn't murder the guy. I mean, I'm pretty sure I would remember if I did." Yeah, I was pretty sure.

"You were right. When you went back into the apartment, there was no way you were in there long enough to find a weapon and kill him. You were gone for maybe a minute. I doubt you could have overcome him so easily. And I didn't hear a thing."

"Lenny was also probably a screamer," I added. "I can't imagine him going down without first letting out a few good shrieks."

"But if you didn't kill him, then who did?"

"Very good question," I said. "How do you feel about skipping Group?"

Jace grunted. "I don't really feel strongly either way."

"Well, I need to eat something a little more substantial than brownies tonight. If you want to take me to dinner, I'll tell you everything."

Jace cocked his head. "Everything?"

"It's because I need your help."

"Well, you know my fees."

"Any chance you can do this one pro bono? I'm almost out of cash, and I don't exactly have a steady income."

"Pro bono doesn't pay the bills." Jace glanced over my outfit again, and I must have looked pathetic, because he said, "But maybe."

Guilt forced me to add, "It's also incredibly dangerous. You might end up getting yourself killed."

Jace's lips spread into a crooked grin. "In that case, count me in."

46

Now that the shock of what had happened this morning had worn off, I realized that I'd skipped my lunch date with Amrita. I texted her a quick apology and asked if she wanted to meet up tomorrow instead. When I finished, I looked up at Jace, who was watching me expectantly. We'd already ordered our food at the little diner across the street from the recreation complex. It looked eerily similar to the place I'd taken my mother—well, the hallucination of my mother—just a few days earlier. But this was the real deal, with the staticky music booming from the overhead speakers, the sticky floors that could use a good scrub down, and the stench of disinfectant overpowering the mingled aromas of kitchen grease and body odor. At least the prices were a fraction of those at its overpriced counterpart. After we settled into a booth, the waiter asked me twice if I wanted anything to drink, and it had pained me both times to say, "Just water."

"So?" Jace asked.

"So," I repeated. I stared down at the table. "I guess I have some stuff to tell you, and it might be a little unbelievable. But I need your help."

I peeked up at him. As expected, he was watching me, his hands folded on the table in front of him.

"Umm . . . I don't know where to start." I tore my eyes away and scanned the restaurant. There were a few families, a handful of single people. There was a man sitting at the counter who'd already glanced our way a couple of times. I couldn't tell if it was because he wanted my number, if he wanted Jace's number, or if it was because he was following me. I memorized his face in case I saw it again.

Maybe it wasn't a good idea to talk about this in public.

"Why don't you start with how you really lost your hand," Jace said.

"How could you tell I was lying?" I asked, stalling for time. "Even my psychiatrist, a woman who's *trained* in detecting lies, couldn't tell."

"I'm trained in detecting lies too."

The waiter came and plopped down my water and Jace's soda.

I waited until the waiter was out of earshot. "I sold it."

Jace looked a little confused. "Sold what?"

"My hand."

Finally, an emotion swept across his face. Was it disgust or disbelief? I wasn't sure which was better. I hurried through my explanation. I told him about how I'd been desperate, and Sylvain—Lenny—had found me and made me this offer. I'd turned him down. But then Ben had come back, and I spared no details in describing how insane he really was. I didn't want Jace's pity, but I wanted—no, needed—him to understand.

My heart was hammering by the time I was finished telling my story. I rubbed my sweaty palm on my bottoms and awaited my verdict. Did he think I was lying? Did he think I was insane? Did he think I deserved whatever came at me next?

He took a torturously long sip of his soda. "Tell me what happened when you found him. When we went to Lenny's apartment."

"I talked to him. I may have threatened him. I saw that he had Ben's sword." Jace startled at this part. "Yeah, he must have killed Ben with the sword and then kept it. I picked it up and threatened him with it—but that was before I went to the door. That was before you heard him talking to me. He was definitely still alive at that point." Jace nodded, so I continued. "So I asked him who he sold my hand to. He said he sold it to a mysterious group called the 'Company' and—"

"Wait, I'm a little confused. How did you know he sold the hand? You told me before that you thought he might have . . . you know . . . wanted it for . . . you know . . ."

"For a late-night, protein-infused snack? Yeah, that's what I thought at first." I bit my lip. "I guess I'm telling the story out of order. I just wanted you to know that I definitely didn't kill him."

"I already knew that, or I wouldn't be here."

I sighed, my attention pinpointed on rearranging the cutlery on the table. "Have you heard of the drug 'Ryofen'?"

"No."

"Well, it's an experimental painkiller that's currently in the human trial phase. You remember that I mentioned having extreme pain in my phantom limb when I first came to Group? Well, I was accepted into the trial testing this new drug. But Ryofen has some terrible side effects."

Jace's expression shifted first to confused, then concerned. "Well, you need to get off it then." He clearly noticed how my entire body went tense at that comment, because he didn't push the issue. "What are the side effects?"

"That's the million-dollar question," I said. "I started feeling my hand. The missing one. But this time it wasn't pain. It wasn't the burning sensation or the pins and needles or the sharp daggers that stabbed me whenever I tried to sleep. It was the feeling that my hand was . . . doing things."

Jace's face was carefully blank. "Doing what kinds of things?"

I inhaled a shaky breath. "Different things. Washing a body, but I could only feel the hand. Drawing. Opening doors." I bit my lip. "Strangling people."

Jace's mouth dropped open. "*Strangling* people?"

I decided to lay it all on him, all at once. "I think that the Phantom Strangler has my hand. Don't say anything," I said as he started to interrupt. "Just listen. Are you familiar with the case?"

Jace blinked slowly. He tipped his head in a subtle nod.

"The Phantom Strangler stopped killing people around a year ago. The police think he wouldn't have stopped killing unless something drastic—

like prison—had taken him off the streets. But what if he—or she—had lost their hand and couldn't strangle victims? The killings started up again right after I lost my hand. My stump healed miraculously over two days, which means that the Company—whoever they are—have advanced technologies that aren't on the market or made public yet. So, the Strangler could have been healed enough to start killing again very quickly. I actually *felt* the Phantom Strangler kill two of the victims. And the times of the murders matched exactly with the times I experienced the odd sensations in my phantom limb. It can't be a coincidence."

Jace wasn't looking at me. He was staring out the window. "That time when you ran out of Group . . ."

"That was the first time. And the time that the second victim got killed also matched up perfectly."

"This drug, Rygen—"

"Ryofen."

"What does it do exactly?"

"It stops—I mean, it prevents pain from being felt in the brain. Or something like that." I blushed. I hadn't paid attention to Dr. Bohmer's science lesson.

"So, the drug is messing with your neurons. It's messing with your brain," Jace said. "What are the potential side effects?"

He didn't believe me. Of course he wouldn't. "Headaches, dizzy spells . . . hallucinations," I admitted with a sigh.

He frowned but didn't say anything.

"I might be hallucinating, but how can you account for the fact that the *only* two times I felt the hand kill someone, a person died? That *cannot* be a coincidence."

"Roz, you're asking me to believe something that sounds an awful lot like science fiction."

"I have some kind of psychic connection to my hand. And it's killing me knowing that the killer has it. That she's using it to kill people. I can't just sit by and let that happen."

Jace leaned forward in his seat. "They say that the Phantom Strangler is a he, not a she."

I nodded. He was engaging with what I was saying. He hadn't called the insane asylum yet to tell them to prepare a cell for me. This was a good sign. "That's what they say. But I have surprisingly strong hands. That might be why they chose me. I am—was—a card dealer, and a sculptor. They would have had other factors to consider, like my blood type being a match, but the other most important thing would be that my hand would have to look the same as the killer's. Which would mean that the killer is most likely a woman."

Jace stared down at my hand. "Well, you do have feminine-looking fingers."

I blinked. "Does this mean that you believe me?"

"Maybe," Jace said. He looked out the window again. "If this kind of operation is going on in the city, it's big. It's going to be dangerous to investigate. Let's revisit the part about the Phantom Strangler having your hand. What did Lenny tell you about the operation?"

I told him as much as I could remember, including what I suspected about Amrita.

Jace nodded. "Okay. I don't want you going to meet her tomorrow."

"What? Why?"

"Because we need to approach this carefully. If she is involved, you don't want her finding out what you know."

"I won't let her know what I know."

Jace gave me a look. "You're a terrible liar."

"Fine. I'll cancel," I lied.

The waiter came with the food, and he all but dropped my burger onto my lap. My stomach let out a huge growl, but I wasn't ready to eat yet. I had one more thing to tell Jace.

"The Phantom Strangler knows who I am. I have proof."

Jace gave me a wary look as he put down his burger, which he'd already taken a huge bite out of.

I reached into my sweatshirt pocket and pulled out the necklace. I set it on the table beside his soda. "I got this along with a note that said, 'Thanks for giving me a hand.'"

Jace picked up the necklace, letting the gold chain trail between his fingers. He swallowed, then his copper-swirl eyes found mine. "All right. I believe you. What do we do next?"

47

I had no intention of canceling my lunch plans with Amrita. It was better to ask forgiveness than permission. Jace would be upset that I'd lied to him, but he would—hopefully understand when I got answers from my old friend. The next morning, I put on a pale-blue blouse and gray pencil skirt that I'd bought and still hadn't had the heart to return. I applied my makeup as the movers came and removed the furniture, a piece of me dying with every item they took.

Hanna watched the movers in dismay. "I thought you came into some kind of windfall," she said accusingly. "You're not taking away the fridge too, are you?"

"No, of course not," I replied. "But the microwave is going."

Hanna groaned and sat on the stool in the kitchen. She put a delicate hand to her head. Ever the drama queen.

"So, I take it you're over the flu?"

"Yes. It really knocked me out. There were a few times I thought I might die. Thanks for taking care of me, by the way," Hanna said with an unbridled grin.

"Yeah, no problem," I replied, brushing her off. I'd barely done anything. I'd just made her soup a few times, and then cleaned up the vomit in the bathroom afterward.

"How are *you* doing?" Hanna asked, suddenly serious.

"I'm fine," I replied. I poured myself a bowl of cereal, dumping the rest of the milk into a separate bowl for Little Guy. I went to the door of the loft and put it in the hallway, making a tsking sound to summon him from the shadows.

Hanna hopped off the stool and approached me. "Seriously?" Her white eyebrows drew together so closely she almost had a unibrow.

"Yeah, seriously," I said, closing the door and returning to the kitchen for my breakfast.

"It's not normal to hallucinate like that. Is that because of the experimental drug trial? The Ryofen?" Hanna asked.

I cast her a sidelong glance. "Maybe."

"Roz, if the drug is having serious side effects like that, you should stop it. What did your doctor say? I can't imagine they thought that you should continue."

"I didn't tell her," I said. I stirred the milk and the cereal with my spoon. I had to wait a bit for the cereal to be the right amount of soggy, the way I liked it.

"Why the hell not?"

"Because it's worth a few fucking hallucinations to not be in pain all the time!" I found myself shouting.

Hanna stared at me like I was a rabid animal. I felt a pang in my chest. I was used to being looked at that way, but not by her.

"Mind your own damn business," I added.

"Fine. Screw up your life. I don't care," Hanna said, though the hurt and worry were painted in Technicolor all over her ivory skin.

I grabbed my bowl of cereal, sloshing some of the milk out onto the counter. I ignored the messy spill and stalked into the living room, leaving her where she stood, shaking her head in disbelief. Of course, I didn't have anywhere to sit. The comfy couches were gone, and I'd tossed the lawn chairs out when I'd thought we wouldn't need them anymore. Sighing, I sat on the cement floor beside one of my wire sculptures that I hadn't had the heart to discard. The one that had been inspired by Rodin's *Danaid*. I stared at it. The tightly coiled copper wire reminded me of Jace's eyes. I bit my lip. The clay had been a bust. But maybe twisting wire wouldn't be too difficult. I sighed. Who was I kidding? Manipulating the fine wire had been challenging with two functioning hands, and even then, I hadn't managed to produce anything that would sell.

I rotated my body to face the little TV, mostly so that my sculptures would no longer be in my line of sight. I didn't bother to turn on the TV. I didn't want to watch the news. Who knew what else fate planned to throw at me? I would rather remain ignorant, at least for the duration of breakfast.

Hanna lingered where I'd left her. "I'm going to work now. Don't wait up for me tonight."

I didn't bother glancing up. "Wasn't planning on it."

The door slammed shut behind her.

48

Amrita was late.

My heart rate quickened with each minute that passed. I was seated at a table in the center of the Italian restaurant, angled so that I could keep an eye on everyone who was coming and going. The sounds of people chattering and utensils clinking against fine china circled me, but I was ensnared inside my own bubble of tension and paranoia.

I checked the time on my phone for what felt like the millionth time. It was possible that Amrita was late as some sort of passive-aggressive revenge for my forgetting about our plans yesterday. But it was also possible that something—or someone—had intercepted her on the way to the restaurant.

The scent of fresh garlic and parmesan tickled the air, reminding me that I hadn't eaten since breakfast. I waved away the waiter for the fourth time, my eyes still glued to the entrance. Every time the door opened, letting in the cool autumn air, I sat up straighter in my seat, only to slouch again when it was someone other than Amrita. By the time twenty minutes had passed, I was a nervous wreck, and I was sure it showed in the flush of my cheeks and the wildness of my eyes.

"Roz! It feels like it's been forever!" Amrita said with her usual level of dramatic flair as she hurried into the restaurant.

"It feels like I've been sitting at this table forever!" The relief I felt at seeing her here, safe and unharmed, overcame my irritation. "But don't worry about being late. I'm so, so sorry for forgetting about our lunch plans yesterday. I've just been so *busy* lately."

"Is that right?" Amrita homed in like a surgeon on a malignant tumor. "Are you finally doing an exhibit?"

I involuntarily flinched at her use of the word *finally*. "Oh, an exhibit? No, I'm not involved in those frivolities anymore," I said, waving my prosthetic hand in the air. I was pretty sure I used the word *frivolities* right.

Amrita stiffened as she took in my prosthesis. "When did that happen?"

I had to be careful when talking to Amrita. Jace had been right. I couldn't let her know that I was investigating the Company. I couldn't know that she wouldn't report back to them, like a loyal lap dog. "Two months ago. Not long after your art show, in fact."

She looked at me with questioning eyes. Eyes that were mismatched. It unnerved me now more than ever.

"What happened to your eyes?" I blurted out.

She didn't look away. "The left one is glass. I lost it in a tragic accident. Not unlike the one you lost your hand to, I imagine. Fortunately, the windfall that came immediately afterward made it worth the while."

I stared at her, at a loss for words. My suspicions had been right. Nevertheless, I couldn't believe she was being so direct with me. I immediately dropped all pretense of being discreet. "When?"

"Six months ago."

"Did you give them my name?"

Amrita's uneven eyes widened in insincere surprise. "Of course not!"

I wanted to scream at her. I wanted to accuse her of ruining my life. I wanted to grab a perfectly polished butter knife and stab out her good eye with it. But I had to keep my cool. I needed answers, and I wouldn't get them by treating her like the traitor she was. "We hadn't talked in a long time anyway. I doubt you would have thought of me, if they were using you to recruit new people."

She seemed satisfied that I believed her. "Well, I for one have never been happier." She picked up a drink menu, and a waiter appeared as if out of thin air. "I'll have a Bloody Mary, please."

"I'll stick with water," I choked out.

The waiter bustled away. Amrita continued to watch me. "Are you dissatisfied with your choice?"

"Was there ever really a choice?"

At that, Amrita broke eye contact. She gazed thoughtfully down at her perfectly manicured nails. "I suppose it depends on what you want out of life."

"Hmm, I *suppose*," I said. The waiter was already back with the drinks. I eyed Amrita's cocktail and chugged my own water, pretending it was vodka. This would get easier. It had to.

"I was recruited at your event," I said, trying to keep my tone nonchalant. "I think by the same person as you. The negotiator they selected was very persuasive."

Amrita nodded. "Christopher is quite good at what he does."

I tried not to let the triumph show on my face. Unless Christopher was another one of Lenny's aliases, I finally had another name. "Hmm, I've never met him. My negotiator was a man named Sylvain," I said.

Amrita nodded. "Ah, yes, right. I forgot for a moment. I met Sylvain the night of the art show. He was there to ensure that the exhibit was to my liking."

I sucked in a breath. "Honestly, this decision has changed my life in ways you cannot imagine."

Amrita smiled thinly. "Mine as well."

"I've been told I can be very persuasive," I said.

"I remember you could convince any professor in college to give you that A," Amrita said with a nostalgic smile. "Even our Intro to Art History professor. What was his name?"

I laughed. "Adelbert. Yeah, he was a tricky one, but my argument was rock solid." I leaned forward conspiratorially, swallowing back the bile that crept up the back of my throat. "I would be interested in becoming a ne-gotiator. Especially considering that I've been through the process. I could probably help to change countless lives if I were to find an in."

Amrita tapped her manicured fingers on the table thoughtfully. "You want to become a Negotiator," she said. It wasn't a question, but a statement. She also said it like it was capitalized, which implied she was more than just a patsy like I was.

I shrugged. "Well, I have more money than I know what to do with now. But I imagine that it will run out eventually. Especially leading the lifestyle I've grown accustomed to." I took a sip of my water. "I think it would be meaningful to help others in the way I've been helped." Saying the words felt like the ultimate betrayal, but I had to do it. I had to say whatever it took for her to believe me.

Amrita was quiet for so long I thought I might have spooked her. She reached under the table and retrieved her Gucci purse. She pulled out a single embossed business card. It looked a lot like the one I remem-bered Sylvain giving me when he first approached me about my hand. The name read, "Christopher Hampton," and there was a phone number with a Chicago area code.

"Reach out to him. He might be able to give you what you're looking for."

Smiling tightly, I took the card and tucked it into my pocket before she could notice the tremble in my hand.

49

"You did *what*?"

I shifted my weight from one foot to the other. Jace looked far angrier than I'd expected. We'd met at his cluttered office, and I'd quickly realized that I'd had to come clean about meeting with Amrita for lunch if I was going to tell him about our new lead. "I met her for lunch." I shrugged as if it wasn't a big deal.

"What part of 'we need to go about this strategically' did you not understand?" he growled.

"I *was* strategic! I pretended to be happy about what I did to myself. She has no idea what my real motive is," I said. "If I hadn't been convincing, she wouldn't have given me this." I dug around in my purse and drew out the business card, presenting it smugly. Jace snatched it out of my hand.

While he studied it, I took the opportunity to look around his office. It was a decidedly cluttered and un-Jace-like office. The reception area was generously sized, with mismatched furniture cobbled together to create a semblance of a waiting area. Something told me that Jace didn't have a need for that much seating.

The place was empty when I arrived. He'd seen me immediately, ushering me past the empty seats and into his office, which was dark and lacked any natural light. It smelled like him in here—of warm leather and a hint

PHANTOM

of pine. I took a deep breath, savoring it, as I circled the room. The book-
shelves that lined all four walls were full of legal boxes, with the edges of
manila folders, spreadsheets, and glossy photographs peeking out haphazardly. His desk was buried under paperwork. A quick glance told me
nothing had anything to do with my case. So, maybe he was getting a lot of
business after all.

I finally took a seat in the chair across from him.

"Who is this man? Christopher Hampton?" Jace asked, the anger fading
from his voice.

"He's the negotiator who recruited Amrita. She knows a lot more than
she's letting on, but I had to be subtle. I think she's little more than a mark,
but she might have needed more information before she gave up her eye.
They might have told her a bit about the business, but she doesn't know
much."

Jace nodded. "I'll look into this guy. It's likely an alias, like Sylvain was."

"I like your office," I said suddenly.

Jace gave me a weird look.

"It seems very lived in."

"My apartment's in the back," Jace said gruffly. "And I know I've told
you this a dozen times, but you're a bad liar."

"Well, I've never been to a PI-slash-bounty hunter-slash-ex-Marine's
digs before, so I have nothing to compare it to." I couldn't contain my broad
grin. My smile must have been contagious, because the corner of Jace's lip
tipped upward. It wasn't quite the unrestrained lopsided grin I'd grown to
crave, but I'd take it. "So, what's our next move?"

Jace cleared his throat, tearing his gaze away from my mouth. He
reached under a pile of papers and grabbed a folder. "I have a contact who's
good at . . . retrieving hard-to-find information online. I can—"

"Do you mean, like, a hacker?"

Jace raised his eyebrows. "Yes, if you want to use layman's terms, Jules
is a hacker. I asked her to look into who deposited that money in your bank
account."

His voice softened when he said her name. I wondered if they were close. Were they sleeping together? Was she able to see his beautiful lop-sided grin any time she wanted? "And?"

He shook his head. "Whoever did it knew how to cover their tracks. She'll need another day to follow the pings."

I nodded as if I had the slightest clue what that meant.

"But if we know that Amrita also received a payment, I'll have her look into that as well. See if there are any commonalities there."

"Whoever bought my hand—the Phantom Strangler—would have paid a large sum too. Is there a way to track that?"

"Yes and no. However much she paid, it won't be the same amount that you were paid. The Company would have taken a commission, distributed some to Lenny and to others who were involved in finding you and identifying you as a victim."

I broke eye contact when he referred to me as a victim. I didn't like how that sounded. It made it sound like what had happened wasn't my fault. But none of this would be happening if I hadn't been stupid enough to take Lenny's deal.

"We might be able to identify her, but not unless we can somehow hack the Company. Which is a long shot when we don't even know where they're based." Jace drummed his fingers on the desk. "I'll give her a call and get her started on that immediately."

I let my eyes wander around the room as Jace pressed her number on his cell.

"Hey Jules, it's me again."

I heard a voice on the other end, but I couldn't quite catch what she was saying.

Jace grinned and let out a laugh, a full belly laugh that was deep and sensual and tickled its way up my spine. I'd never heard him laugh like that before. What was she saying?

"I have another name for you," he said, running his hand over the stub-ble on his head and shooting me a glance. "I don't know how much she got paid, but it would have been between six and eight months ago. An Amrita Tejal. Can you look into her too? She got the money from the same source."

Jules said something else in her husky voice, and Jace laughed again. This time, the sound sent a spark of something ugly shooting through me.

"All right. Give me a ring when it's done." He ended the call and looked over at me. "What?"

"Nothing." I realized I was pursing my lips and quickly schooled my expression into one of indifference. "What about Christopher Hampton?"

"I'll look into him myself. I'll get help if I need it."

I nodded again, feeling like a dashboard Jesus on a rocky back road. "What can I do?"

"Well, assuming that these sensations in your hand aren't just hallucinations—"

"What do you mean, assuming? Haven't I given you enough proof?"

Jace raised his hands, leaning back in his chair. "I need to go into this cautiously. If I took everything at face value, I'd never figure anything out."

"All right. Well then, continue," I said, rolling my eyes. "Assuming . . ."

Jace let out a laugh. It wasn't like the laugh he had when talking to Jules, but it wasn't exactly just a controlled chuckle either. "*Assuming* that those aren't hallucinations, they might provide clues about who the killer is. I want you to keep a record of when you have these sensations. Write down the exact time, as well as the details. What you feel. Not just the sensations, but what you think the hand is doing. Try to do it retroactively. If there are times in the past that you remember having certain feelings, write those down, but make a note that they might not be a hundred percent accurate."

I glared at him. "Okay, so *you're* going to look into these leads, and you want *me* to keep a fucking diary?"

The crooked grin made a reappearance. "So to speak. What you write could be what ends up catching the Phantom Strangler."

"No. I want to do more than that. I'm going to call Christopher Hampton and set up a meeting." I reached out for the business card, but Jace was too fast.

He tucked it into his back pocket as he stood. "Not until I know more about him. It's too dangerous. I don't want you going in there blind."

I clenched my jaw and stood up too. "I'm tired of waiting. Every day that passes, the Phantom Strangler could be tracking down her next victim." I moved closer to him. "I hate feeling helpless," I added in a low, sultry voice. I pushed away any guilt I might have felt at manipulating him. I needed that business card.

Jace's brown eyes swirled with flecks of intoxicating copper as he looked down at me. "I've only been on the case for less than a day. I promise you, I will figure out who she is, Roz."

The sound of my name on his lips sent an involuntary shiver through me. I slid in a little closer. Jace's eyes darkened as his gaze trailed down to my lips. I raised my hand and ran it down his arm, around to his back. Just a little closer and I'd be in his pocket. I was doing this to get the business card, I told myself.

Not because I wanted to be touching him. My breath hitched at the feel of his muscular back flexing against the palm of my hand.

Suddenly, Jace's lips descended on mine, his mouth persistent and warm and surprisingly soft. I clung to his back, the business card temporarily forgotten.

After several minutes, I pulled back. We were both breathing heavily, the tension in the room keeping us from drifting too far apart, and it took all my self-control not to fall back into his arms. "What about, um, finding Christopher Hampton?"

His eyes were heavy lidded as he stared at me for a long moment. "It's late. That can wait until morning."

I nodded, too enthusiastically, and quickly stopped myself. I bit my lip. "Yes, it would be rude to call him at this time of night anyway."

He shot me a smile, as if he knew very well that this was the first time in my entire life that I bothered to pretend to be worried about being rude. He took my hand in his, leading me out of the office, into the back, where his apartment was.

The instant we were in his bedroom, we tore each other's clothes off, Jace helping me with a smirk when, in my eagerness, my shirt caught on my prosthesis. He lifted me by the shoulders and tossed me onto my back on the bed. I lay there, my eyes devouring him for the second he allowed me before diving in. At first, I didn't know what to do with my prosthetic hand, so I kept it at my side, limp, and focused on exploring him with my other hand. My fingers surveyed the rough planes of his body, trailing over the ridges of muscle, dancing over scar tissue that somehow made him even more attractive. He was beautiful and strong and, for tonight, all mine. The thought that I might like to have him for longer—to keep him—flitted through my mind. But then he captured my mouth with his, and all rational thought escaped me.

We were nearing the finish line when it happened. As I clutched his back and our movements became more frantic, more uneven, more desperate, my phantom limb emerged from its slumber. Caught in the throes of passion, I barely noticed when the hand that wasn't there gripped something fleshy and warm and full of life. It squeezed and squeezed and squeezed as a thrumming heartbeat raced, then stuttered, then stopped. I cried out in ecstasy; moments later Jace joined me. He rolled off me and lay on his back, panting and sated. He wrapped his arm around my shoulders, curling me into his strong, unyielding frame. A smile flirted with my lips as I looked up into his heavy-lidded copper swirls.

Then, I realized what had happened. Sobbing, I pulled away from Jace. I sat up, staring at my hand in horror. Hell had infiltrated my heaven.

The Phantom Strangler had impeccable timing.

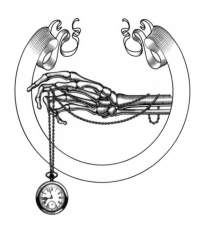

THIS ONE WAS WORTH THE WAIT.

The flashing lights, the shrill of sirens, the bustle of a crowd are foreign to me. This is unlike me, to linger in the crowd, to remain when the police have already arrived.

But I cannot resist.

I study the crowd, searching for my subject, yearning to catch sight of my work in progress. I hope to see how this latest act has painted horror and suffering onto her delicate features.

Typically, I choose subjects that are unmarred, untouched by pain and suffering. But this subject has been all too rewarding. Unlike with my previous subjects, I've had the time and inclination to dig deep. I took the time to delve into her past. I know more about her than she knows about herself, and it's been quite illuminating.

She had a similar upbringing to me. Raised by a single parent who was neglectful—preoccupied with their addictions. We both felt trapped, consumed with a hungering desire to escape through art. But it is from there that we diverged. One took a path through the light, toward darkness. The other, a path through darkness toward light. In the beginning, one could say we were mirror images of each other, yet now we are opposites. Failure vs. success. Visceral vs. refined. Finger painter vs. da Vinci.

Before she crossed paths with me, my subject was already contaminated with a childhood of neglect, an adulthood bursting with vices, loathing, and self-destruction. I have meticulously added to this darkness, which will nicely complement the suffering I have planned for the end.

However, it would be inaccurate to say that my subject and I are completely different. My obsession is chiseling at my patience. I never would have taken a risk such as this one before. To be so close to the police that I could reach out and touch one of them? A brush of the hand, and I would no longer be a ghost, a phantom, but a red-blooded human capable of being locked away behind bars. Torn away from my destiny once again before my masterpiece is complete.

The crowd murmurs. My name lingers on the lips of those I drift past. I am no longer a Phantom, an intangible specter. I am as real as the dead body I left on this doorstep.

I have to admit that the attention brings with it a feeling of validation I claimed not to need. I'm ahead of my time; I don't expect the world to recognize my genius. But now the world is taking notice. I can only imagine their awe once my work is complete.

The city is my gallery, and its denizens are my audience.

I draw back from the magnetic pull of the crowd with a disappointed sigh. I crave just a glimpse of my subject—to see the look on her face—but I cannot discard her anonymity. Not yet.

But there are other ways to satisfy this urge that tickles my darkness. My lips spread into a malicious smile as I pull out my phone. I know that I should be careful. That I shouldn't deviate from the plan. But I cannot resist.

It's time for things to escalate.

50

Jace didn't let me go home that night. He kept me wrapped in his strong, toned arms, where I was swathed in a false sense of security. The Phantom Strangler had killed again. She knew who I was. She knew where I lived. She'd already reached out to me once, and I didn't have any doubt that she would do it again. I would never be safe. I told Jace what had happened in between trips to the bathroom to empty my stomach. The nausea and self-loathing hit me in alternating waves.

I must have fallen asleep eventually, because when I woke, Jace was gone. He'd left a note on the pillow that was almost illegible, but I was able to discern that he was out hunting down a lead on Christopher Hampton. It said that there was coffee in the kitchen, along with some bagels. He also strongly suggested I stop taking the Ryofen. I guiltily tucked the note away before popping another pill.

I didn't bother to check my phone for any news alerts. I knew in my heart that this was no hallucination. The Phantom Strangler had killed again. I threw on my clothes before heading into Jace's office. It took me a few minutes to find it. The business card that Amrita had given me was resting on top of a stack of file folders.

Christopher Hampton didn't say much when I called. He didn't ask who I was or what I wanted. He just told me to meet him at the northwest corner of Harrison Park at noon. He'd given me less than an hour to get there, which was about how long it would take for me to get there from Jace's by public transit if I left immediately. I wondered if he knew not only who I was but also where I was. I made it there with a few minutes to spare and sat on a park bench as instructed. I shivered as the wind picked up. I zipped my coat up all the way to my neck in an attempt to protect myself from the elements and whatever fresh horrors this encounter would bring.

A man in a heavy black overcoat arrived at exactly noon. He took a seat on the opposite end of the park bench. He didn't acknowledge me. I peeked at him through my peripheral vision. He was handsome, with clean-cut features and perfectly styled hair. He was a lot better-looking than Lenny had been.

"Why did you contact me?" His voice was a lot quieter than I'd expected, and more subdued than it had been on the phone.

"Do you know who I am?"

"Yes."

I turned to face him directly. I needed the benefit of being able to read his face, which was, unfortunately, expressionless. "I want to work for your employer."

He didn't provide me with so much as a facial twitch to work with.

"I would be an excellent Negotiator," I continued.

"Is that right?" he said. "Amrita warned me you would be reaching out. How do you know so much? Are you the reason Lenny is dead?"

Was that a hint of fear in his eyes? Was he afraid of me? Or was he afraid of what his employer would do to him if they found out he was talking to me? I noticed how he hadn't accused me of killing Lenny but asked if I was responsible for his death.

I shook my head. "I need more money. I met with Lenny to talk. He told me his story, how he'd come to work for . . . your employer. I want to work for them too."

Christopher's lips spread into a thin smile. "I've already contacted them about you. Apparently, that was your endgame—but you're significantly ahead of schedule."

My stomach did a little flip-flop. They'd always intended for me to work for them? "Well? What are the next steps?" I managed to keep my voice even.

"You need to prove yourself to them."

"And how do I go about doing that?"

Christopher reached into his coat, and I recoiled, bracing for the worst, but he didn't pull out a weapon. He took out an envelope. "You'll find the information you need in here."

I accepted the envelope, fumbled with it single-handedly until I slid out a single paper. There was an address I didn't recognize, a date—next Friday—and a time. There was also a name: Felicia Armstrong.

"I don't understand." I flipped the page over. The other side was blank. This wasn't enough information, though I had a sinking feeling I knew what it meant. What I was expected to do. I looked up to ask for confirmation, but Christopher was gone.

51

I knew something was wrong as soon as I turned down my street. Police cars and news vans littered the pavement outside my loft. I circled the ravenous onlookers who swarmed what looked like a crime scene, from the glimpse I caught of the yellow tape and a scowling policeman. This wasn't anything new; there was a stabbing on this street just last month. I managed to avoid the police officer smoking by the door to my building and slipped through the door.

When I got upstairs, however, I realized that I wasn't in the clear yet. The door to the loft was ajar.

I used my prosthesis to nudge the door open further.

"Ms. Osbourne! So good of you to finally join us." A burly-looking Italian man appeared in my doorway. He looked vaguely familiar, but I couldn't place him. He wore a black suit with a red plaid tie that was slightly askew. Rather than shoes, he was wearing blue booties. I stared down at them.

"I'm Detective Borgnino," he said.

That sparked my memory. "You're the detective working the Phantom Strangler case!"

"That's right. I lead the task force."

"Why are you in my apartment? Is this because of the tip I called in? I already told the other detective, it was a dumb prank."

"Is that right?" Detective Borgnino looked confused, but he hid it quickly.

Detective Gutierrez appeared in the hallway behind me. Her hair was pulled back into a tight ponytail, and the frizzy flyaways framed her face like a lion's mane. She looked fierce. Tessa Brown's necklace weighed heavy in my pocket and a trickle of sweat trailed down the small of my back.

Detective Borgnino's eyes flashed at his partner. "You're late."

She shrugged. "I helped with crowd control."

I glared at the two of them. "You two better have a warrant," I snarled. "What the hell are you doing here?"

"We do have a warrant," Detective Borgnino pulled out a paper and held it in the air. I ignored it and glared at Detective Gutierrez.

"Why don't you come in and sit down?" she said.

"How *kind* of you to invite me into my own home." I brushed past her and stormed into the kitchen.

The two detectives weren't alone. There were half a dozen people in white suits, looking through my things.

"What the hell?" I snapped.

"Please, sit down," Detective Borgnino said.

I plopped down on the kitchen stool. "What the hell?" I repeated.

"When is the last time you saw Hanna Mikkelsen?" Detective Gutierrez asked.

I blinked. They were here looking for *Hanna*? "Yesterday morning. She should be at work now, even though it's Saturday. She's almost always at work."

Detective Gutierrez exchanged a loaded look with Detective Borgnino.

"What is it?" I snapped. "She works at some law firm as an intern or something. Why don't you look for her there? She's obviously not here. The loft may be big, but there aren't a lot of hiding places. If she isn't crouching behind the toilet, then she isn't here." What kind of mess had she gotten herself into?

Detective Borgnino opened his mouth, and then closed it again. He tugged at his tie with a meaty hand, making it even more crooked. "Ms. Osbourne, the Phantom Strangler took another victim last night."

My voice was a whisper. "I . . . Where?"

"On this block," Detective Gutierrez said. "The target was struck just feet away from the entrance to this apartment building. I'm sorry, Ms. Osbourne, but the victim was your roommate, Hanna."

The room shifted around me. I reached out to brace myself on the sink, to keep myself from toppling off the stool. "That's impossible."

The detectives exchanged another look. "I'm sorry, but the body has been identified."

"You're wrong." I jumped off the stool and ran out of the kitchen. I tore past the velvet curtain and into her bedroom, but she wasn't there. Her bed was made, the pillows stacked neatly against the white metal headboard.

I spun around to face Detective Gutierrez, who had followed me across the loft. "You need to look for her at the law firm. I can't remember what it's called. She also might be at school. She's studying to get her law degree. I can't remember where she's studying, though. Also—she has a girlfriend. Elissa. She could be at her place. She—"

"Ms. Osbourne, stop," Detective Gutierrez said, her tone kind but firm. "Hanna's body has been identified. She was killed last night around ten, when she was returning home from work."

My legs couldn't hold me any longer. I all but collapsed onto Hanna's bed. "I . . . this doesn't make sense."

Detective Gutierrez brought me a glass of water, and I chugged the entire thing, wishing it was something stronger. She perched beside me on the edge of the bed. "What is it about you that keeps bringing me to your doorstep?"

I didn't respond.

I couldn't stop staring at the rack of clothes Hanna had pushed up against the curtained wall. The red dress I bought her was missing. Was that what she'd died in?

"First, you make that phone call. If it was a prank, it was a very unfortunate one. Next, your fingerprints are tied to another, seemingly unrelated murder . . . And then your roommate is killed."

"It's a coincidence," I lied half-heartedly, my eyes still glued to the clothes rack. Fog had descended over me, and I could barely think, barely breathe.

"You know, coincidences are funny things. One coincidence, and it could be just that—a coincidence. But once the coincidences start piling up, it becomes implausible, then improbable. Then impossible. These aren't coincidences," Detective Gutierrez said, her tone matter-of-fact. "You're involved. Somehow and in some way. I know this." She rose off the bed and made to leave. She hesitated. "And it won't take much longer before I find out the truth."

52

The police weren't done with me yet. After they'd given me a measly few minutes to process Hanna's death, they hit me from all angles with questions I didn't have the answers to. Who were Hanna's friends? Did she have any bitter exes? Any enemies? What were her plans for last night? Did I have contact information for her next of kin?

Detective Gutierrez heavily implied that I was a terrible roommate, but I'd already known this. I stole Hanna's dress, ate her food, mooched off her . . . I took advantage of her kindness. But those transgressions were all peanuts compared to how I had gotten her killed.

I knew this with utter certainty. The reason she was dead was because she was my roommate. It was like what Detective Gutierrez said. This couldn't be a coincidence. The killer had been to my apartment at least once before—to deliver the note and the necklace. This time, she came to deliver something much more sinister.

If only I'd been here instead of Hanna.

I wished it had been me.

"Where were you last night?" Detective Gutierrez asked.

"Aren't you getting tired of asking me that?" My entire body felt numb.

"You have no idea," she said humorlessly. "Let me guess, you were here, alone all night."

"She was with me." My head snapped up to find Jace standing in the doorway. "I came as soon as I heard."

"And who are you?" Detective Gutierrez asked, seeming annoyed at the interruption.

"I'm her boyfriend."

My eyes widened and some of the weight on my chest lifted the moment that word left his lips. "Boyfriend?" I repeated, eyebrow raised.

Jace ignored me, but I didn't miss the little smile that curved his lips. His eyes found mine and held them.

"Your name?" Detective Gutierrez asked, disrupting our Hallmark moment.

"Jace Moore."

Detective Gutierrez wrote his name on her notepad, but then she hesitated. "The bounty hunter?"

"I see you've heard of me."

Detective Gutierrez grunted and made another note on her pad. "You were with her all night?"

"From dusk till dawn."

I suddenly remembered that I'd felt my hand kill last night. It had been bad enough feeling my hand kill someone and being powerless to stop it. But to know that I'd felt my own hand draining the life out of Hanna? Sweet, innocent, would-never-hurt-a-fly Hanna? "Excuse me," I blurted out. I rushed to the bathroom and threw up what little contents I had left in my stomach.

When I was finished, I came back into the living room to find Jace and Detective Borgnino competing in a staring contest. I wondered what I'd missed, but I was too tired to ask. Weariness had sunk deep into my bones, and all I wanted was to either sleep or scream.

"Is there anything else you need?" I said. I knew I looked terrible, and I bet I smelled even worse.

"Could I have a word with you? In private?" Detective Gutierrez asked me.

"Does she need a lawyer?" Jace asked, sliding a protective arm around my waist. I leaned into his warmth.

"No, I just want to ask her some questions about her roommate," Detective Gutierrez replied. To me, she said, "A place where we can speak privately?"

Unless we wanted to talk in the bathroom, there wasn't a truly private place in the loft, so I led her out into the corridor. A loud meow grabbed my attention. Little Guy weaved between my legs, gazing up at me with his soulful green eyes. I hadn't been home to feed him last night, though I knew he was fine without me. He didn't need me to survive, if the sheer number of dead mice he left on my doorstep was any indication of his self-sufficiency. I bent down and picked him up, holding him against my heart. He was tiny and lean, and he burrowed into my chest. Tears burned at the back of my eyes, but I fought them back.

I faced Detective Gutierrez, not caring if she thought it was weird that I was seeking comfort from a possibly flea-bitten stray.

Her expression didn't hold any judgment, only vague sympathy. "I'll cut to the chase. This isn't public knowledge, so I don't want you telling anyone this."

"Um, okay?" I wasn't sure where she was going with this.

"I need your word."

"You have my word," I replied while imagining that my left hand somewhere, out there, had its fingers crossed.

Detective Gutierrez nodded, as if the word of an alcoholic, hallucinating murder suspect was worth anything. "A woman was seen at the scene of the crime. A witness says that she was the killer."

"A witness? Who?" I squeezed Little Guy so tightly that he growled and launched himself out of my arms. He dashed down the hall, fleeing into the stairwell.

"A CI. Someone that no judge would believe," Detective Gutierrez said. "But I believe him."

"And you think it was *me*?" I asked with a laugh.

"The thought crossed my mind. But you have an alibi, and the witness would have recognized you from the neighborhood. Also, you're missing one of the two required murder weapons."

My stomach churned again at those words. "So, you know it wasn't me."

"I know you aren't the person doing the killing. But you called in that tip a few weeks ago. A tip where you said the killer was a woman. One of means. I need to ask you again how you know this." Intense desperation laced with something else flashed in Detective Gutierrez's eyes.

The sudden urge to tell her the truth collided into me. It could lead the investigation in an entirely new direction. The *right* direction. But I also knew that she wouldn't believe me. And I couldn't risk being thrown in the loony bin. They might cut off my access to the Ryofen. Or, even worse, they wouldn't, and I'd feel my hand murder countless other innocent people like Hanna—and I'd be helpless to stop it.

I swallowed. "I've already told you everything I know."

I returned to the loft without waiting for her response. Jace and I watched as the detectives and their henchmen wrapped things up over the next half hour. Detectives Gutierrez and Borgnino left with an ominous "We'll be back."

Jace didn't reach out for me or embrace me like I'd expected when the door finally closed behind the last officer. Instead, he gave me a thoughtful look. "We need to call Christopher Hampton."

I stared down at the cracked marble countertop. The fissures looked like veins crawling across skin. "I already did."

"What?"

I jumped at his outburst. A sob overcame me, and the tears I'd been fighting back all night gushed down my face. Jace's expression immediately softened as he pulled me close. "We'll stop this bitch."

I let out a half sob, half laugh as I looked up at him. "She doesn't know who she's fucking with."

53

My phone rang, its default ringtone jovial and playful. It grated on my nerves, but I hadn't found the time to change it. I glanced around Dr. Lavoie's waiting room, which was empty except for me, the receptionist, and an older fellow who was rocking back and forth clutching a bundle of blankets that definitely didn't have a baby in it. It looked like a possum. He was probably one of Dr. Lavoie's pro bono patients.

"Yes?" I barked as I answered the phone on the fourth ring.

It was Jace. "I've been thinking."

Just the sound of his voice quieted the storm inside my head. "Uh-oh," I said, a smile tugging at my lips.

"I have one of my guys looking into people with missing limbs—specifically people who are well-off who've spontaneously regrown a limb."

"One of your guys?" I asked, suppressing a spark of irritation.

"Don't worry, he can be trusted. He's got connections in a couple of the local hospitals. No leads yet, but I'm hopeful." His tone sharpened. "I'm still pissed that you met with Christopher Hampton without telling me. I wanted to put a tracer on him, track him, and see where he would go. I wanted to find out who he really is."

"Listen, I already apologized, and I'm not one to grovel for forgiveness." The receptionist called out my name. "I gotta go. Tell me what you find out later." I ended the call without waiting for a response and stuffed my phone in the bottom of my purse.

Sidestepping the blond lady with crutches who had just left Dr. Lavoie's office, I pushed open the door with my good hand and slipped inside.

"Good afternoon, Roz," Dr. Lavoie said, a little smile alighting on her lips.

"Hi, Doc. Thanks for fitting me in," I said.

"Of course. You had to cancel our meeting the other day." She gave me a stern look. "You can't be skipping any more appointments." She faltered when she saw my expression. "Is everything all right?"

"Where to begin?" I mumbled. "Hanna's dead."

Dr. Lavoie's mouth dropped open into an O that would have been comical if I were in the mood for that sort of thing. "Your roommate?"

"Yes. That Hanna. She was killed. By the Phantom Strangler." My eyes started to burn. I hadn't thought I had any tears left. I'd been crying on and off the last three days since Hanna was killed. I blinked, trying to push back the tears. I would not cry, not again. Not now.

"I—that's horrible. Uh—sit down." For once, the eloquent doctor was fumbling for words. She seized a box of tissues and placed them on the coffee table in front of me. She opened her mouth, but she looked like she had no idea what to say. "I'm sorry for your loss." She settled on something that everyone says.

I didn't hold it against her. "Thanks, I guess."

"When did this happen?"

"Friday night. She was killed just outside our apartment. I wasn't home. I wonder if I would have heard anything anyway." I looked around the office, my eyes catching on the portrait. I almost wished it would move. I needed something to distract me from reality.

"When was the last time you spoke with Hanna?"

I returned my gaze back to the doctor. "The morning of the day she died."

"Tell me what happened."

Hanna had been angry that I refused to tell my doctors about the hallucinations. Of course, I couldn't tell Dr. Lavoie that, not without actually informing her about the hallucinations. "We argued. I've been returning the extra furniture I bought." Dr. Lavoie looked at me quizzically. "I may have overspent when I cashed in my severance pay."

Dr. Lavoie nodded. "Right. We'll return to that later. Do you remember the last thing you said to her?"

"She said something about being out late and not to bother waiting up. I told her I wasn't planning on it anyway." I'd been so harsh, when Hanna was just worried about my side effects. Worried about the fact that I was having *hallucinations* about people who weren't there.

"You were getting closer to Hanna, correct?"

"Yeah."

"Roommates fight. It's hard not to when you're forced to live together in close confines."

"Well, our loft apartment is actually quite big—"

Dr. Lavoie raised a hand. "Let me finish. Roommates are like siblings. They fight. They make up. Sometimes they say things they don't mean. It doesn't mean that they don't know how the other really feels about them."

I smirked, despite myself. "Are you saying that Hanna knew I kinda sorta liked her even though I was a bitch to her?"

She smiled. "Yes, I suppose that's what I'm saying."

A tear escaped and rolled down my cheek. I wiped it with my sleeve and stared at the murky black stain on the sleeve of my pale blue sweater.

She nudged the tissue box closer with the tip of her pen. I thought that I might as well just give in, so I grabbed a couple and blotted my face.

I nearly jumped out of my skin when my phone erupted with a cheerful chirp. "Jesus!" I turned to Dr. Lavoie. "Sorry."

She smiled. "For swearing or for forgetting to turn off your phone?"

"Both?"

It chirped again, and this time I only jumped half as high.

"Do you mind if I check?"

Dr. Lavoie pulled her shoulders upward into a dainty shrug. "It's your time. You can spend it how you please."

I grabbed my purse and dug around in it. I'd buried the phone deep, but I managed to find it under a lipstick that somehow managed to uncap itself, painting everything in my purse a blood red.

There were two messages.

Sorry I missed you.

Who was the text from? *Oh shit.* I'd forgotten all about my dessert date with Lowell on Saturday. But how did he get my number? And did this message mean that he thought that *he* stood *me* up?

I checked the second message. It was from the same unknown number.

I was in your neck of the woods and I thought I'd drop by. You weren't there, but your roommate was a nice substitute.

"Fuck," I breathed. "Fuck fuck fuck."

"Is everything all right?" Dr. Lavoie asked, an eyebrow raised. She frowned when her eyes glided across my face. "What is it?"

My heart was racing too fast for me to come up with an adequate lie. "Just some creep," I said. I thought I might be sick. Again.

"A creep?"

"A creep that doesn't know that puns are the lowest form of humor."

Dr. Lavoie's brows creased with worry. "Do you need a minute?"

I nodded. "Maybe a glass of water?"

Dr. Lavoie rose and approached a small bar that I'd somehow never noticed before. Maybe because there was no alcohol, just soda, juice, and sparkling water. What a waste.

Dr. Lavoie brought me a tall glass of ice water, and I took a long sip. I felt marginally better. How did the killer get my number? Had Lenny and the Company given out my personal details to the person who got my hand? Was this a part of some kind of deluxe package?

Did they get to charge the Phantom Strangler more for my hand because of the added incentive of allowing her to torment me afterward? This time, I went into my phone's settings and double-checked it was put on silent before tossing it back in my purse. I wouldn't delete the messages. Maybe Jace could trace the number. Maybe this was the one mistake that would lead to the Phantom Strangler's capture.

Unlikely, but I could dream.

"Do you want to talk about the text message?" Dr. Lavoie asked when I put my purse back on the floor.

"No."

She nodded but didn't press further. "How is your mother?"

Way to kick me when I'm down. I stopped myself before snapping at Dr. Lavoie. She had no way of knowing my mother wasn't alive. I'd avoided talking about her during sessions until after she came back into my life. "She's gone," I said, bitterness soaking my tone.

Dr. Lavoie was quiet for so long I thought she wasn't going to say anything else. "I'm sorry, Roz. Did she start drinking again?"

She had never stopped. At least, the real Cynthia Osbourne never stopped. The one who did was a figment of my desperate and lonely imagination. I hopped out of my seat.

"Listen, Doc. Thanks for seeing me on such short notice. But I really should go deal with that text I got."

Dr. Lavoie stood as well. She went to her desk and retrieved a business card. She uncapped her pen with her teeth and wrote on the back of it. "This is my cell number. You're going through a difficult time that I can only try to understand. If you need someone to talk to, give me a call. Day or night."

I took the card and stared down at her embossed name. "Um, thanks. Do you give out your number to all your patients?"

"No." She didn't elaborate.

"Okay then," I said stupidly. I tucked the card into my jeans pocket and left without looking back. I wouldn't throw out the business card in front of her, because clearly, she meant well, and I didn't want to hurt her feelings. But it would be a cold day in hell when I would call her for her help. Not because I was too proud.

Not because I didn't think I'd ever be desperate enough to need her help. But because there was no way I was going to reach out to her for help when doing so would, without a doubt, put her directly in the crosshairs of a killer.

54

I called Jace as I left Dr. Lavoie's office. He picked up on the fourth ring.

"That was quick," he said. "How much are you paying this lady?"

"About the same amount I'm paying you." I paused. "I got a text from the killer."

A sharp intake of breath was his only response.

"I just forwarded you the number. Can you trace it?"

"I'll see what I can do. What did the text say?"

"That she was looking for me. But I wasn't there, so she killed Hanna instead. She made some joke about being in my *neck* of the woods. It seems like murder isn't her only crime." I let out a strangled laugh.

Jace took a deep breath. "Roz, are you okay?"

"Yeah. Well, no. I just hope you can trace that number."

"I'm already on it." He paused again, a little longer this time. "I know this is hard, but it's a good thing that she's reaching out to you."

I sucked in a breath. "What do you mean?"

"Because her hubris—her need to taunt you, to let you know exactly what she's doing with your hand . . . it's what's going to get her caught."

Jace's assurances washed over me, and I felt marginally better. But I knew what I really needed in order to feel safe again.

"Are you coming to my office?" he asked, oblivious to my realization.

"Soon. I have an errand to run first."

I scanned the path from my perch on the edge of a park bench. Lincoln Park was relatively busy this time of the afternoon. People were out walking their dogs, going for romantic strolls, and picnicking in the middle of the day. It must have been nice not to have a care in the world. I wouldn't have been able to do this even before my life turned upside down.

Trap was once again punctual. It was nice to meet a drug dealer who took his chosen career path seriously. He approached, sizing me up. "You with the cops?"

That was new. I wondered if Kris, my weed guy, had told him about his suspicions since the last time we'd met. Rather than answer his question, I gave him a hard look. "Did you bring it?"

"I thought I told you I didn't want to do business with you," he said.

"Ben is dead."

Trap's eyes nearly bugged out of his bald head. "What?"

"Ben was killed by a guy named Lenny Stevenson. The same guy who took my hand." I gestured to my prosthesis. Trap didn't look impressed, so I continued: "Now, Lenny is dead."

He cocked his head, his soulless eyes sizing me up in a different way this time. "Did you have something to do with that?"

"Maybe," I replied. I hadn't been completely sure, but now I knew that Trap had nothing to do with Lenny's death. Which meant that Lenny was either killed by the Company or by me. I was betting on the former.

"Did you bring it?" I repeated.

Trap cracked his knuckles, drawing my attention to his hands, which were riddled with tattoos and scars. I gulped. "Do you have the money?" he asked, smirking at my expression.

I pursed my lips as I dug into my purse and pulled out the cash I'd just withdrawn from the ATM. "This should cover it."

Trap reached out for the money, but I pulled it away at the last second. "Not until I see it."

He grunted and glanced around before reaching into his jacket, pulling out a sleek black pistol. He held it low, by his hip, expertly keeping it out of the sight of a passing couple. "Do you know how to use it?"

My pride made me consider lying, but lying would only get me killed when it came time to use it. "No."

"You load it like this." He flipped the back, releasing the bottom of the gun. "Put one in the chamber like this. This is the safety—make sure it's on at all times. Well, not at *all* times." He gave me a hard look. "Then point and to shoot, squeeze the trigger."

He handed me the gun, and butterflies hit my stomach as I stared down at it. It was surprisingly heavy. I swallowed, tucking it and a box of rounds into my purse.

When I looked back up, I found him studying me with eyes that were so dark, they were almost black. I suppressed a shudder. To overcompensate for my nerves, I asked, "So, how's the drug business going?"

Trap glared at me. "Not great."

"That's too bad. Missing your kingpin, are you?" Why couldn't I just shut up?

"It's the competition. A lot of other guys in town for little girlies like yourself to choose from."

"Ah," I said, an inkling of an idea forming in the back of my mind. "Well, best of luck to you with your criminal enterprise."

Trap didn't bother to respond before he turned and took off down the path. An elderly man gave me a sunny grin as he rounded the bend. I smiled at him, a genuine smile, as I felt the heaviness in my purse and a lightness in my chest. I was finally taking control of my life.

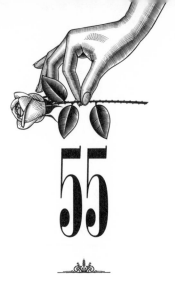

I wasn't sure what was going on between Jace and me. We were both throwing ourselves into the case, trying to uncover information about the Company and hunting down leads for the Phantom Strangler. Every moment that we weren't working on the case, we were together—in his bed, in his office, and twice in his kitchen. The morning after Hanna's death, he'd introduced himself to the detectives as my boyfriend, but he never mentioned the "B-word" again after that, and I'd been too chickenshit to bring it up myself. Was this just a temporary fling? Would it be over once our investigation came to a close, one way or the other? Would Jace be moving on to the next damsel in distress who knocked on his door with an urban legend-esque conspiracy with a science fiction-style twist? Why did the thought of Jace moving on give me this tight feeling in the pit of my stomach?

I'd only ever been in two long-term relationships. I'd met Corey during senior year at UIC, and we'd dated for almost three years, though it was mostly a relationship of convenience that fizzled out when I found him balls deep in his neighbor. Ben and I had been together for a little over a year before I came to my senses and ended things with him. Neither of these relationships had ended well, but I hadn't been particularly heartbroken either time. I'd told myself that I loved Ben, but time and distance helped me to realize that I hadn't, not even when we were at our best. If I'd been honest with myself about how I'd felt, I would have ended things with both of them a lot sooner.

I'd only known Jace a few short weeks, and already the thought of the impending end of what we had made my chest ache. After the hallucination of my mother and reliving her death all over again, and then my budding friendship with Hanna that was cut short, I didn't think I could handle any more heartbreak. This was why I usually didn't form meaningful connections with people. If I wasn't invested in someone—if I didn't let myself care about them—it would be so much easier to handle when they inevitably left.

I was lying in bed with Jace when a phone rang. I tensed even though it wasn't the annoyingly cheerful chirp of my phone. Ever since I'd gotten those texts I'd been on edge—even more so than usual. Even though I was now the proud owner of a shiny black revolver, I still felt naked and exposed. That could have been because I was currently both naked and exposed.

Jace rolled out of bed to answer his cell, and I took the opportunity to hog the covers. I never was good at sharing.

Jace didn't know I'd bought a gun, and I intended to keep it that way. It wasn't that I didn't trust him. I knew deep in the shadowy recesses of my mind that I could trust him with my life. I hadn't told him about the gun because I knew he wouldn't approve. So, the gun was currently tucked away in the bottom of my purse, along with the chunks of red lipstick that I had yet to clean out.

Jace came back into the room a few minutes later. "That was Jules. Get dressed."

I threw on my pants and one of Jace's faded gray T-shirts that I liked and decided to claim as my own and followed him into the office. "What is it? What did she find?"

"She was able to trace the money." He leaned over his laptop and tapped a few keys.

"The money from my . . . transaction?"

"Yeah. Your money and the money that was given to your friend Amrita both came from the same account."

My heart damn near skipped a beat. "Who owns the account?"

The printer roared and started shooting out pages of paper. Jace strode over to it and snatched up the first piece. "A company called Artis Corp."

My heart sank. "Never heard of it."

"There's not much information available online. Apparently, it's a trading company, but they have very little on their website, and it looks like the "Contact us" page is a sham. We do know that Artis Corp is a subsidiary of a huge biotechnology company called Novus Tech. This could be a lot bigger than we thought."

"I always thought it was big," I said.

Jace shot me a lopsided grin.

"Get your mind out of the gutter," I said with a laugh. I was already feeling lighter. "Okay, this is good. Right?"

"It's better than good. That event that Hampton has you going to tomorrow? It's being hosted by Novus Tech."

I stared at him. "That can't be a coincidence."

"I doubt that it is."

I tapped my lip thoughtfully. "So you think that Artis Corp is a shell company used by Novus Tech as a front for their less-than-legal dealings?"

Jace stared at me.

"What?"

His lips spread into a teasing grin. "I like it when you talk business."

I rolled my eyes. "Did Jules have any other information, anything we need to act on immediately?"

His gaze roved over my body. "Nothing that can't wait till morning."

I grinned and started to leave the office. I called over my shoulder, "Well then, why don't you come and show me how big this thing really is?"

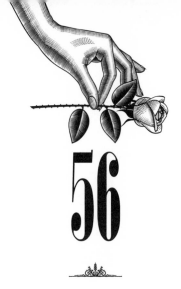

56

I shivered as I gazed up at the brazen giant constructed of brick and mortar. Novus Tech was pulling out all the stops, and like all businesses that wanted to flaunt their wealth and success, tonight's event was being held in one of the waterfront's numerous historic architectural landmarks. Something about tonight—going to an event under false pretenses, pretending that I fit in among the rich upper class—reminded me of that night at Amrita's art show, only a few months ago. The night where it all began. But I was a different person now, and I wasn't here for something as petty as jealousy or as trivial as free drinks.

I was on a mission.

I drew my fur coat tighter around my chest, took a deep breath, and entered the belly of the beast.

"Name?" A man dressed like a butler hovered just inside the front door.

"Pardon me?"

"What is your name?" he enunciated, though not as rudely as he might have had I not dressed the part. "I need to check it against the list," he added.

I glanced down at his clipboard, but he angled it so I couldn't read anything on it.

"Felicia Armstrong." The alias felt weird rolling off my tongue and my heart pounded in my throat as his beady little eyes scanned the page.

"Here you are." With a flourish, he put a tick on the guest list and moved aside to let me through. First obstacle passed without any problems, but I had no doubt there would be many more thrown in my path this evening. I passed through the elegant yet imposing metal detectors at the entrance, relieved that I'd opted not to smuggle in my illegal gun. I deposited my fur coat at the complimentary coat check. Just as I was about to head out onto the floor, my reflection caught my eye. I studied myself in the oval floor-length mirror. I'd decided to wear my two-thousand-dollar little black dress, which I hadn't had the heart to try to return yet. I'd slipped on my genuine Jimmy Choos and curled my hair so that it framed my face in a sexy yet tasteful way. I looked like a completely different person. The only flaw I couldn't hide was the prosthesis. But it was a high-end prosthetic limb, so it effortlessly fit with the role I was trying to play.

Tonight's event was a charity gala for the American Health and Wellness Society. I'd never been to any kind of gala before, but Jace had informed me that a lot of big names were invited. These wealthy patrons were strong-armed into opening their checkbooks and making notable donations to the charity of the month. It sounded like a total waste of time to me. Why couldn't rich people just silently donate money like the rest of us? Not that I'd ever so much as tossed a coin in a "take a penny, leave a penny" jar, but if I'd had the funds, I wouldn't have felt the need to make a big spectacle out of it.

I stepped out onto the main floor, where guests strutted around like peacocks, showing off their colors to everyone in sight. Men radiated power and greed. Women dripped with jewels and greed. Unlike the last time I'd gone to an event where I didn't belong, I didn't feel invisible. In fact, the crowd seemed to part before me. What a difference money—or at least, the appearance of money—makes. The cavernous hall was tastefully decorated with a twenty-foot-tall Christmas tree erected in the center. I stared at it in all its shimmering, decadent glory. Was it already that time of year?

A passing waiter offered me a margarita. I declined. I eyed the drink as he bustled away. I needed a clear head, but one drink couldn't hurt, could it?

I tore my attention away from the glistening glass and forced myself to scan the crowd. I couldn't see Jace anywhere. He'd pulled some strings, managing to snag a job working security.

I had to admit, I liked seeing him in that uniform. I really hoped that later I would see him out of it.

"Excuse me, ma'am?" I turned to see that the waiter was back.

I glared at the tray of drinks he balanced perfectly on the palm of his hand. "What?"

"I was asked to give you this." He handed me a piece of paper, disappearing into the crowd before I could question him.

I unfolded the note. A handwritten, short sentence. "The blond at the bar."

I glanced up and spotted her immediately. She was tall, blond, and in her mid-twenties, wearing a cheap dress that looked like it had been painted onto her. Physically, we looked nothing alike, but I could see myself in her. Particularly when she downed jumbo shrimp after jumbo shrimp like they were going out of style.

I pushed aside my uneasiness and swept toward her. "Hungry?" I asked with a sardonic smile.

Her cheeks flamed crimson. "I just love shrimp," she lied.

"Who doesn't?" I replied, casually picking one up. I'd forgotten to eat dinner, but I obviously couldn't let my starvation show, not when I was trying to impress her. I took a slow bite. "I haven't seen you at these events before," I said, the words unnervingly familiar. I'd taken that line out of Sylvain's book. Hadn't he said something similar when he first approached me? I ignored the knot that realization formed in the pit of my stomach.

"I usually don't bother to come out to these things," she said in a flippant tone.

I hid a smile. She probably wasn't normally invited to events like these. I wondered how they'd tricked her into coming. Had she been "accidentally" sent an invitation in the mail? Had an old friend coaxed her into showing up? "I wouldn't either, but my husband dislikes it when I don't come," I said.

I caught her looking down at my ring finger. She gasped as she took in my prosthesis.

"Who are you here with?" I asked, politely pretending I hadn't noticed.

Her eyes narrowed. "What makes you think I have to be here with someone?"

I shrugged. "You said you don't usually come out to these. I assumed you were dragged here, like I was."

She immediately relaxed. "I'm here alone."

I nodded, taking another bite of shrimp. I wasn't sure what else to ask her. Sylvain hadn't immediately broached the topic of dismemberment. Instead, he'd seduced me first. I wasn't expected to seduce her, was I?

I scanned the crowd, searching for a clue, any hint at what to do next. "Dr. Bohmer?" I said, incredulous. I'd only met the man once, during my interview to get on the Ryofen clinical trial, but I'd recognize that gangly frame and salt-and-pepper hair anywhere.

He turned around. He looked at me, but he seemed confused, like he recognized me but couldn't quite place where he knew me from. "Hello . . ."

Shit. He knew who I really was. He could break my cover. I shouldn't have said anything. For once, I should have kept my damn mouth shut. "Why are you here?" I blurted out.

"I'm sorry, but have we met?" Dr. Bohmer asked. He ran a hand through his hair. The woman he was with gave me a look that could slice through stone.

"From the hospital," I said quickly, relieved that he couldn't place me. "My husband works with you."

"Oh, of course," Dr. Bohmer said politely. "And how are you enjoying the event?"

"I'm looking forward to the speeches, of course," I said. I didn't know for sure, but I assumed there would be speeches.

I must have been right, because Dr. Bohmer nodded emphatically. "Oh yes. They have Dr. Spiretti as keynote speaker and I'm quite looking forward to her words on the future of gastroenterology."

"Yes, gastronomy is quite fascinating," I agreed.

He gave me a funny look.

"So, I wasn't aware that any of my husband's colleagues would be here," I said, hopefully adeptly turning the conversation back to why the hell he was here.

"Oh, I was only invited because of the grant."

"The grant? My husband didn't mention that."

"Novus Tech's most prestigious award. My research team received it for our research into an innovative new drug—"

"Ryofen?" All the blood drained from my face.

"Yes! We're conducting human trials now," Dr. Bohmer said, enthusiasm seeping into his tone. At that moment, his eyes landed on my prosthesis. He tilted his head as he examined my face more closely. "Ms. Osbourne?"

"Who?" I asked sweetly. "Dr. Bohmer, it has been an absolute *pleasure*, but I must be going with my new friend here, Miss . . .?"

"Lauren Southers," she said after nearly choking on another shrimp as she swallowed it whole.

"It was *wonderful* catching up," I told Dr. Bohmer. "Tell my husband to set up a dinner date for us with you and your wife!" I quickly steered Lauren away before my cover was blown. I heard the woman Dr. Bohmer was with hiss, "You have a wife?!" Well, I'd guessed that wrong.

Lauren looked back longingly at the row of shrimp cocktails that adorned the table at the bar. She turned to me. "I'm sorry, I didn't catch your name."

"Felicia Armstrong," I said grandly.

"I've never heard of you," Lauren said with an edge of feigned disdain in her voice. She was a lot more like me than I'd thought.

"My husband is *Doctor* Reginald Armstrong?" I said. I was secretly enjoying this.

Lauren shook her head.

"What rock have you been living under?"

Lauren blushed again. *Okay, maybe she isn't that much like me,* I thought. I looked around. Christopher Hampton was nowhere to be found. I turned back to Lauren, who was picking at a loose thread on her dress. I studied her for a moment. What did they want from her?

A limb? A kidney? A . . . heart?

My mouth suddenly dry, I turned away from her to compose myself. My eyes found Jace, who was watching me like a hawk from the opposite end of the room.

I couldn't do this. I turned back to Lauren. "Well, it was absolutely *fabulous* meeting you."

"And me—you—too," Lauren stammered.

"I'll be in touch," I said, jaw clenched, as I swept away.

I found myself back at the bar, where I wolfed down a fistful of bruschetta.

"That was not bad," a low voice said.

"I didn't spot you earlier," I replied without turning around.

"I'm good at blending in and not being noticed."

"Well, I'm always noticed." I turned and faced Christopher Hampton. "So did I pass your little test?"

"No."

"No?!" My voice was shrill.

"Keep your voice down," Christopher said, still smiling.

I lowered my voice. "Why did I fail?"

"You tell me."

"Well, you neglected to give me any guidance. You didn't bother to tell me who she was until twenty minutes ago. I didn't know what to say to her. I've never sauntered up to a person and asked them for their body parts before. At least, not in this context."

"You failed because you didn't come alone," Christopher said.

I stiffened. "What do you mean?"

"The security guard on the northwest door. He's with you." It wasn't a question.

I shrugged. "You got me. I'm not a total idiot. I had no idea what to expect here. So, I hired someone as protection."

Christopher took a pair of drinks from a passing waiter. He handed me one. I reached out and took it, my hand shaking ever so slightly. I would just hold it. I would not drink it. The smell of temptation wafted from the glass, taunting, seducing me. My mouth filled with saliva.

I realized that Christopher was still talking. "—a PI."

"Sure, he's a PI. He was desperate for cash, so I hired him for something a little out of his wheelhouse. You didn't say anything about me coming alone." I stared down at the margarita. They had even lined the rim of the glass with salt. How classy. How delicious. I licked my lips. I could already imagine the sweet burn as it crossed my lips, caressed my tongue, and glided down my throat.

Christopher laughed. "I didn't give you explicit instructions. They were implied. But I like that you're resourceful."

I sighed, tearing my eyes away from the drink. It took all my willpower, but I put it on the tray of a passing waiter. I'd been sober for eight whole days, and I wouldn't let one stressful evening ruin that.

Christopher looked surprised, but he didn't say anything. He had probably been told that I had a hard time turning away a good drink. Well, any drink.

"So, I couldn't have failed your test if I didn't break any of the rules, then." I tried to make my tone sound bored.

"I suppose you're right," Christopher said, taking a sip of his margarita. He watched me as he licked his lips, and I tried not to let my unbridled envy show on my face.

I wasn't going to let him torture me. "Well, give me a call when your superiors tell you I'm in," I said, making it clear that I knew that hiring me wasn't ultimately his decision. Sashaying toward the dessert table, I glanced back to catch a glimpse of the irritation he finally let break through his ordinarily stoic expression. I grinned.

The tinkling sound of metal chiming against glass caught my attention and the attention of everyone around me. It was time for speeches. I eyed the exit, but I was still too far to make a clean getaway. It wouldn't go unnoticed if I were to leave now. A striking woman appeared at the podium, which was on a stage slightly raised from the rest of the floor. She seemed to command the room with every cell of her being. She gazed out at all of us, wearing an enigmatic smile and a designer evening dress. Her eyes lingered on me, if only for a moment. My breath caught in my throat. I had to have imagined that.

"Welcome to the eighth annual event for the American Health and Wellness Society. It's hard to believe that it's already been *eight* years!" She paused, and a smattering of applause carried across the room. "I see many familiar faces in the crowd, but for those of you who don't know me, I am Katherine Prescott, CEO of Novus Tech."

This earned greater applause. I frowned. Was she looking at me again? There was a room full of people.

It had to be my imagination.

"The American Health and Wellness Society holds a place close to my heart," she continued. "The work that they do is quite remarkable, and their contributions have made significant strides in ensuring equity and access to health care for all Americans, not just for those who can afford it."

I rolled my eyes at that. As if any of the people in this room cared at all about health care for people who weren't in their tax bracket. I plastered a smile on my face.

"Now, I know that speeches aren't the reason why many of you are here. You're here for the night out and the bottomless margaritas"—she paused for the crowd's polite laughter—"so I'll keep this brief. I know many of you have already made your donations, but I implore you to consider contributing even more. Dr. Spiretti is here, and he will be speaking at length later tonight about the incredible work he's doing."

Again, applause. I glared down at my prosthesis. How was a one-handed person supposed to clap?

As Prescott continued to speak, a man standing beside me leaned into my personal space. "It's great to see her out again, isn't it?"

I frowned. "What do you mean?"

"She was out of the public eye for quite some time. There was speculation that maybe she might be stepping down as CEO."

I glanced at the man. He was wearing a suit that had to cost more than my childhood home. "Any idea as to why?"

"It's all gossip, and I don't like to gossip."

I refrained from raising my eyebrows. Something told me that he definitely liked to gossip. I waited expectantly. I didn't have to wait long.

"I heard it was cancer. That she got treatment, and she's in remission. At least, for now. But you didn't hear it from me." He glided away to tell someone else before I could respond.

I returned my attention to the stage.

"So, I'll conclude my brief speech with another invitation to contribute. If there's any way you can give a hand to this wonderful charity, it would be greatly appreciated. Again, that's only for those of you who haven't already given one."

Her eyes locked onto mine.

I couldn't breathe. I couldn't move. I couldn't look away. She held my gaze for what felt like an eternity. She finally broke eye contact. "But for now, enjoy the refreshments, and I hope to connect with each and every one of you sometime tonight!"

She set the microphone down with her beautifully manicured hand and stepped away.

57

My one good hand shook uncontrollably as I took the glass and swallowed its contents in two gulps. Eight days of sobriety down the drain in an instant. The alcohol scorched on its way down. A soothing, familiar sensation that almost calmed my nerves. Almost.

I glanced over at Katherine Prescott. She was less than a dozen feet away, seemingly in deep conversation with a potential donor. My stomach churned. The word *donor* had an entirely different meaning now. Was tonight's charity a front for the illegal organ trade? Was Katherine Prescott involved? And, most important, was that my hand she was wearing?

I moved closer and closer to her, trying not to make it seem obvious that I was eavesdropping. The chatter in the room was loud—too loud—but I caught a word here and there. The man she was speaking with was talking about his charity work in Uganda, and that he wouldn't be able to contribute to this *particular* charity because he'd already contributed to so many others. Then why was he here at this *particular* event? The phoniness of it all would have bothered me if I weren't more bothered by the fact that I was convinced I was standing mere feet away from a serial killer.

I licked my lips, and yet another drink appeared in my hands. I glanced down at it in surprise before chugging it.

"I should wear designer more often," I said to myself.

"What?" the waiter who took my glass asked.

"Nothing," I replied, baring my teeth. "I'll have another."

The corner of his lip took a downward turn, but he presented me with another glass without objection.

I was taking a slower sip of this new drink when she noticed me.

"A new face in the crowd." Her mellow voice sounded honey-smooth to my ears.

I stared up into her frosty green eyes. "Mrs. Prescott, it's a pleasure to meet you."

"Ms.," she corrected me with a smile. "And the pleasure is mutual."

She might have had everyone else in this room fooled, but not me. I knew who she was. I knew what she was.

I focused on relaxing my tense fingers, which strangled the margarita glass. Liquid courage coursed through my veins. I opened my mouth, but someone stepped in. A man in a black suit leaned forward to whisper in Katherine's ear. I caught the words "breach" and "immediately."

The skin around her mouth tightened almost imperceptibly. "If you'll excuse me, Miss Osbourne, I'm afraid there is an important matter that must be dealt with." Her green eyes bored into mine. "I do hope we can continue this conversation at a later time?"

She disappeared into the crowd. My heart hammered in my chest as I stared after her. Whatever her security guard had said must have rattled her, otherwise she wouldn't have slipped up so easily. She'd called me by my name, but I'd never told it to her.

58

The instant I was back at the loft, I popped a Ryofen. I'd waited a little too long between doses, and the pain had returned with a vengeance. I drank half a glass of water while standing over the kitchen sink. I was still more than a little drunk, and I hoped that the water would help dilute the alcohol, at least a little bit. The room spun around me, and I clutched at the counter, combating the sudden dizziness. I realized I should have eaten more at the gala. No, what I really should have done was refrain from drinking.

Shame shrouded me as I stared down at the rusted sink, willing myself not to glance toward Hanna's bedroom. I didn't want to think of her and how I'd failed her, even as I drank out of a glass that she had bought in an apartment full of reminders of her.

I'd spotted Jace before I left the gala, assuring myself that whatever breach Katherine Prescott had been summoned to handle hadn't had to do with him. The plan was for him to follow Christopher from the event, to see if he led to any clues in the case. I sent Jace a vague text warning him that they knew he was working with me. I would wait until we met in person before telling him about what had happened with Katherine. I didn't know much about the Company, but it stood to reason that they could easily be hacking my texts and phone calls. I probably should have gone to his place when I left, but I didn't want him to see me like this. I was better off alone in my self-loathing and regret, at least until all evidence of tonight's binge had passed through my system.

I tried to ignore the worry that gnawed at my gut. Jace could handle himself. My stomach let out a low growl, and I laughed at the sheer volume of it. It wasn't just worry that was bothering my stomach. I was starving. I should have tucked some hors d'oeuvres into my purse, even though I knew from experience that loose shrimp did not travel well. I opened the fridge, but it was still empty, save for a bottle of spicy Dijon mustard. I sighed and pulled my cell out of my purse to order a Franco's Pizzeria special.

I'd just changed into sweatpants and a hoodie when there was a knock at the door. I stared at it warily. Franco's never delivered that quickly. I retrieved my gun from my nightstand and tucked it into the small of my back.

The cold steel emboldened me as I strode toward the door. I swung it open.

It was Lowell. "Hi, Roz."

My brows knit together, as my alcohol-infused brain tried to make sense of his presence here. "Lowell, what are you doing here?"

"'Hi Lowell, it's nice to see you,'" he said in a singsong voice, a smile dancing across his lips.

"What?"

His smile faded and he shifted his weight from one foot to the other. "I waited for you at the Dessert Oasis the other night, but you never showed." He glanced past me into the loft.

"Yeah, um, I got busy." I stared at him, willing him to leave. "Do you want to come in?" I'd ordered a pizza with no way of paying for it. Maybe Lowell would cover it, especially if he thought this was a date. My chest tightened as my thoughts strayed to Jace, wondering how he'd feel if he knew Lowell was with me.

Before I could tell him that I'd changed my mind, Lowell moved past me, entering the loft. I was hyper-alert to his body language, but he didn't look disgusted or turned off by his surroundings. I wasn't sure if that improved or worsened my opinion of him.

"It's dark in here," he commented.

"Yeah, electricity is expensive," I replied. Now that I would be covering the rent and utilities myself, I had to be more frugal. "I get enough light from the street."

"Yeah, those are really nice windows. Big," he said. "Don't you ever worry that you're being watched?"

My stomach twisted. "Sometimes," I admitted.

He took off his coat and scarf and handed them to me. I scowled and tossed them on the floor beside the coatrack. Lowell didn't even seem to notice.

"How did you find out where I live?" I blurted out.

"I asked around."

A chill washed through the room. "Are you stalking me?"

"No, of course not," Lowell said. He answered a little too quickly. It was almost as if he'd been expecting that question.

My eyes darted toward the closed door. "Why are you here?" I asked again.

He shrugged, wandering farther into the loft. I followed him. "Well, you stood me up. And you haven't been to Group at all this week. I wanted to check on you and see if you were all right. I was worried, so I figured I'd see if you were home. Maybe we can go out somewhere a little closer."

I was getting a bad feeling about this. "I don't think so."

His eyebrows went up. "You don't think so?"

"Yes, that's a polite way of saying 'fuck off.'"

Lowell's cheeks flushed. "You didn't have to accept my dinner date in the first place."

"It was a *dessert* date."

His eyes flashed. "Same thing."

"Maybe you should go." I gave a pointed look toward the door.

He didn't take the hint. Instead, he shifted closer to me. He was wearing the same red flannel shirt and blue jeans that he always wore. I wondered if that was all he had in his closet. But then I realized that he'd taken the scarf off for the first time since I'd known him. His neck was bare, and my heart jumped into my throat.

I licked my lips and pried my eyes away from the intricate set of tattoos that crawled up his neck. Coiled vipers creeping around a skull with blood-red eyes. I swallowed. "W-why are you really here?"

He cocked his head. "I just want to get to know you better."

I was feeling lightheaded, although I couldn't tell if it was from the alcohol, Ryofen, or fear. Maybe it was a mix of all three. "What is there to know?"

He shrugged.

My mind was racing. The tattoos meant he worked for Ben. Did he think that I was responsible for Ben's disappearance, like Trap had? "H-have you been spying on me?" I sounded breathless.

Lowell laughed, a different laugh from his usual. It was almost like his normal sporadic, nasal laugh, but it had an edge to it. It seemed less spontaneous, more calculated. "Why would I be spying on you?"

"You searched out where I live. You say you trekked all the way out here to check on me because you were worried." I scoffed. "I find that hard to believe. Who do you work for, Lowell?"

"I work in sales for a winter sports equipment company. I've mentioned it before in Group." He didn't meet my eye.

"You're lying."

Ben was a drug dealer and had been moving up in the crime world. Ben had been a lot of things, but he hadn't been unambitious. He'd been dealing drugs and illegal weapons, and it made sense that he would have moved on to bigger and better things. Like the organ trade. Had Ben been the one who initially put me on the Company's radar? Was Ben the reason why I was targeted? Was Ben the reason why I'd lost my hand?

The moonlight reflected on the shiny surface of his prosthetic hand. A hand that was far too bulky to be of any real use. It could only have one purpose. To hide something. To hide a real hand.

My hand.

The Phantom Strangler had been closer than I ever could have thought.

Watching me. Waiting for his chance. And now, he had me alone, trapped with him in my apartment.

Unadulterated fear laced with rage coursed through me. "It's all connected."

Lowell frowned but didn't say anything.

"You work for the Company, don't you?"

"What co—"

"I know who you are. I know *what* you are."

His eyes darted toward the door. "You know what? I should go."

I pulled out my gun. "Already? But you're in my *neck* of the woods. And I thought you wanted to get to know me better."

He raised his hand. "Put down the gun, Roz."

I began to pace. "You've been taunting me this entire time. You sent me the necklace, the texts, and you wanted to watch me suffer, so you've been going to the amputee support group." I paused. "But you didn't want the others at Group to realize that you had a new hand. No, so you've been wearing that prosthesis to hide the truth!"

"Listen, I don't know what you're talking—"

"SHUT UP!" I pointed the gun at his face, and he cringed. "This makes sense. It all finally makes sense. You worked for Ben. You got involved with the Company, and when you lost your hand, they gave you the chance to get a new one. You made a deal, like Lenny did. After all, you needed two functioning hands for your sick, fucked-up hobby!"

I sized him up. "I thought that my hand would go to a woman, but you're scrawny. My bone structure wouldn't be out of place on you."

"Listen, you—"

"Was it Ben? Was it Ben who told them about me? Is that how they found me?"

"I—I don't know what—"

I shook my head. "Of course, you wouldn't be given that kind of information. You're just a lackey. A minion, just like Lenny and Christopher." I laughed.

"Please, I'm innocent, I have no idea—"

"You're not innocent," I spat. "You have the tattoos. I know who you are. You're the Phantom Strangler."

"Listen, I just want to leave." He again shot a longing look at the door.

"You're not going anywhere until I have answers." My hand wobbled. "Why Hanna? Why . . ." I trailed off as hot tears streamed down my cheeks. I clenched my teeth, cocking the gun.

A strange expression crossed his face. One I couldn't read, though I didn't have much time to decipher it. With his right hand, he gripped his prosthesis, wrenching it off his arm, sending it flying in my direction. I shrieked, jerking backward. I pulled the trigger. Once. Twice. Three times.

Two bullets went wide, but the third hit the bull's-eye. He fell to the floor.

My heart pounded so hard that I couldn't hear anything but the rhythmic pulsing of blood coursing through my skull. Lowell lay on the floor facedown, motionless. I inched closer to him. He didn't move. I used the corner of my shoe to nudge him. Nothing.

He could be faking it, waiting for me to let down my guard, like the bad guys in B-horror movies. I tightened my hold on the gun, crouched, and used my prosthesis to roll him over. There was a hole in the middle of his chest, right where his heart would be. Blood had completely saturated the red flannel.

I took in a ragged breath, then another. My eyes were glued to his left wrist, which ended in a smooth stump.

I'd been wrong. He wasn't the Phantom Strangler. He wasn't wearing my hand. He hadn't come to my loft tonight to taunt me. To kill me.

But he wasn't completely innocent. He'd been working for Ben. Maybe he'd come to get revenge for whatever Lenny had done to Ben. Maybe . . . My thoughts trailed off as dread infiltrated my defenses. My eyes slowly crept upward toward his neck. My right hand, holding the gun, began to shake so badly I lost my grip and it fell to the floor.

The tattoos were gone.

59

"Chicago PD! We're coming in! Put down your weapon!" The front door whipped open, striking the coatrack and sending it flying. Detective Gutierrez stood framed by the doorway. Her eyes rapidly scanned the room, taking in the body, the blood. Me.

"Put down the gun," she ordered. Her own gun was pointed at my forehead.

I looked down at my hand. I thought I'd dropped the gun, but I must have picked it up again.

I forced my fingers to loosen their grip, and the gun fell to the ground with a loud clatter. I stared down at Lowell's body. At his smooth, bare neck.

There was a dark and bitter feeling stirring in the pit of my stomach that I couldn't ignore. Lowell hadn't admitted anything to me. He'd looked confused when I confronted him. I'd thought he was the Phantom Strangler because of the convenience of his prosthesis. I'd assumed he was one of Ben's men because of the tattoos. But he was missing his hand and I'd been imagining the tattoos. Did that mean he was innocent?

Had I just murdered an innocent man?

I started to shake, convulsions racking my body so badly that I could barely feel the rough hands of the police officer as he twisted my arms behind my back and handcuffed me. I could barely hear the distant words of the detective as she read me my rights. I blinked and found myself in an interrogation room. Everything was metal. Gray. Cold. I looked around, disorientation clutching me. I had no memory of leaving the loft, of getting into the police car, of being driven to the station. Detective Gutierrez sat across from me, her emotionless eyes studying me. Her lips dipped into a frown.

"You're in shock," she said unsympathetically.

I pressed my lips together, inhaling slowly through my nose. I looked down, relieved to note that at some point, they'd removed my handcuffs. A video camera was mounted in the corner; the little red light informed me that it was recording. I licked my lips. "H-he attacked me. I had no choice."

"What was his name?"

"Lowell . . . I don't know his last name. He showed up at my apartment and attacked me, I—I had no choice."

"You're repeating yourself, Osbourne."

I clamped my mouth shut. She didn't believe me. Of course she didn't. Because he was innocent. He wouldn't have flung his prosthetic hand at me if I hadn't been pointing a gun at him. He tore off his prosthesis to show me that he wasn't wearing my hand underneath. He probably thought it was the best way to prevent me from shooting him. But it didn't save him. I still shot him. I still killed him.

I was a killer.

A murderer.

No better than the Phantom Strangler.

Nausea roiled in my stomach.

"How many drinks did you have tonight?" Detective Gutierrez was asking.

"One," I lied.

"Tell me what happened."

I clenched my jaw.

"It's in your best interest to be forthcoming with me, Osbourne."

As I studied her, her face seemed to soften. I wondered what I looked like. Lowell had been close enough to me when I shot him that there was blood spatter on my hoodie. I picked at the crust of blood with my thumbnail.

I told her a version of the truth. He'd shown up shortly after I'd gotten home. He was upset that I'd missed our date. He charged at me, so I shot him.

She tapped her pen on her notepad. "You're leaving things out." Her tone wasn't questioning or accusatory. It was matter-of-fact.

I didn't answer.

"Why do you have an unregistered gun?"

"To protect myself."

"You could have gotten a legal gun for that."

"Not fast enough."

Her eyes flashed at that admission.

Irritation rankled at me. "In case you haven't heard, my roommate was just *brutally* murdered by a *serial killer*. This isn't exactly the safest neighborhood. It makes sense I'd want to protect myself."

She gave me a long, hard look. She sighed and stood up.

"Where are you going?"

"I'm going to give you a little time to think about where you are. What position you're in. Give you some time to realize that it is in your best interest to *tell me everything*." She glared at me.

I glared right back at her. "Fine. Sit down."

She took her time settling back into her seat. At that moment, the door swung open, and Detective Borgnino stalked into the room.

"Look who's decided to join us," I said. The shock was wearing off, and I was starting to feel like myself again. That meant that I was going to have to pray that my mouth didn't get me into even more trouble.

He ignored my sarcasm as he claimed the chair next to his partner. He placed a Styrofoam coffee cup in front of Detective Gutierrez and took a sip out of his own. His entire demeanor was closed off and disinterested. While Detective Gutierrez held her pen poised and watched me expectantly, her partner leaned back, arms folded across his chest, and an unwavering scowl marked his pudgy face. I supposed this was their version of good cop, bad cop.

I was suddenly getting cold feet. "Are you sure you want to know everything? This knowledge seems to be getting everyone involved killed."

Detective Gutierrez didn't look deterred. "Tell. Us. Everything."

My mind raced. At this point, what did I have to lose? I was under arrest for killing Lowell. I was a suspect in Lenny's murder. My idiotic phone call to the tip line had put me on the police's radar, and Hanna's murder had only made the target on my back bigger. Once the Company found out that I'd been arrested, they might consider me too much of a liability. They might revoke their offer of employment. They might even take me out, just to be sure that I wouldn't jeopardize their business.

I didn't know if I could trust the police, but it was very possible that they were the only ones who could protect me—both from the Company and from the Phantom Strangler.

I told them everything. Well, almost everything. I told them about Lenny Stevenson, and how he had approached me with a deal. I talked about meeting with Lenny and losing my hand. Instead of telling them about the Ryofen, and the hallucinations, and the fact that I was somehow connected to my severed hand, I told them about the note and the texts that I had received from the killer, and how I put two and two together that way.

"Lowell worked for the Company too," I said. The lie ate at me, but I had to tell it. It was the only way to stay out of prison for the rest of my life.

"Rewind back to what you said about Stevenson. You said he sold his organs to this 'Company'?" Detective Gutierrez asked.

"Yes, his heart, liver, kidneys, and lungs. To be acquired in 2027." I shuddered.

Detective Gutierrez had been tapping her pen on her pad impatiently, but at my words, she froze.

"What is it?"

She faced Detective Borgnino. "The initial examination of Stevenson's body. He was missing internal organs."

"See?" I said. "That's *proof* that what I'm saying is true!"

"Maybe," Detective Borgnino said slowly. "There was a mix-up at the morgue and the body was sent to be cremated before it could go through a full autopsy."

"A *mix-up*? That sounds like more than a mix-up to me!"

He shrugged. His indifference really grated on my nerves.

Could the Company have a mole in the police? That thought was sobering. Could I even trust these two detectives? I supposed that Detective Gutierrez wouldn't have told me this if she was dirty. But that didn't prove that Detective Borgnino wasn't.

I stared at them. "That doesn't make sense. Why would they leave Lenny's body in his apartment to be found in the first place?" Realization dawned on me. It was to frame me for his murder. To neatly get me out of the way.

Detective Borgnino's eyes didn't leave me as he addressed his partner. "She could know about the missing organs because she's the one who did the cutting."

"*She* is right here," I said, irritable. "And I've never even held a scalpel, let alone performed a surgery. And I'm willing to wager that the organs were expertly removed? Like, by a *professional* surgeon, not just some hack who learned a thing or two off TikTok?"

Detective Gutierrez didn't answer, but the look on her face told me I was right on the mark.

"And I'm also willing to bet that Lenny's body wasn't dissected in his apartment, right? They took him somewhere else, carved out his organs, then brought him back and left him there to be found. Does this really sound like something a woman with *one hand* can do?"

Detective Borgnino smirked. "You seem resourceful." He leaned forward. "You also seem to know an awful lot about the crime scene of a murder you claim not to have committed."

Detective Gutierrez shot her partner an indiscernible look. She turned to me. "What about the notes? The ones you claim are from the Phantom Strangler. Can I see them?"

"The first one went in the trash. The second one was a text." I pulled out my phone. I hesitated. "But the first note came with a . . . present." I slipped my hand into my hoodie pocket and pulled out the necklace. Fortunately, the rookie who'd booked me had missed it while processing me. The gold chain glimmered in the fluorescent lighting.

Detective Gutierrez inhaled sharply. She reached out and grasped the necklace gingerly. Her eyes hardened as she glared at me, then turned to Detective Borgnino. "Just when I was starting to believe her."

"Fuck." He frowned. "I guess she isn't our girl after all."

"She's just a liar."

"What?" I asked, my gaze ping-ponging back and forth between them.

Detective Gutierrez all but threw the necklace back to me. "Ms. Osbourne, the first victim didn't have a necklace stolen. That was a clue planted by the police to weed out the crazies and the fame seekers who always call in with tips, looking for their fifteen minutes."

My stomach sank. "You mean there was no necklace? Then what is this?"

"You tell me."

I opened my mouth, then closed it again. "I want my phone call."

60

"Where have you been? Are you okay? There are police at your building, and they won't let me up—"

"I've been arrested." I gripped the phone's receiver tightly as I glanced around the room I'd been brought to for privacy for my one phone call. It didn't seem like anyone was eavesdropping, but that didn't mean they weren't.

Jace was quiet for so long that I worried that the call had been disconnected. "What happened?"

I gave him the altered version of events, the one where I killed an employee of the Company, not an innocent, harmless man with a crush that had turned deadly—for him. The thought of what had happened still churned my stomach. But I couldn't risk falling apart. I couldn't afford to think about what I had done. I tried to push the truth far back into the dark recesses of my mind. But the guilt wouldn't be so easily quelled.

"I told them everything," I continued.

There was a pause. "Everything?"

"About the Company. About Lenny. My hand." I lowered my voice. "Obviously, I didn't tell them about the Ryofen—"

"Stop," Jace said. "They could be listening in."

I swallowed. "Right."

"Do they believe you?"

"I think they were starting to." I could feel the necklace weighing heavily in my sweatpants pocket. "But apparently, Tessa Brown—the first victim of the Strangler—didn't have a necklace. It was a plant to weed out the crazy people." I let out a sob. "But then why did the killer send it to me?"

"Because you didn't know there was no necklace," Jace said. "It served the same purpose, regardless of where the killer actually got it."

"Yep. It still scared me shitless." I wiped away the tears that streamed down my face, glad that Jace couldn't see me. "Did you learn anything from Christopher Hampton?"

"This call could be being monitored, Roz," Jace reminded me. "I'll tell you later. I will tell you that Jules found something . . . promising. Are the cops dropping the charges?"

I sighed. "I don't know. I doubt it. They don't seem to like me very much."

"Must be your winning personality," he said. "Roz, please don't antagonize them."

"I can't promise that."

"Osbourne." A uniformed officer who reeked of garlic appeared in front of me.

"Yes? Can't you see I'm in the middle of something?" I gestured toward the phone.

He crossed his arms over his chest. "Your lawyer is here." He turned and left the room before I could tell him I didn't have a lawyer.

"What's that, Roz? What did he say?"

I sighed. "I have to go. I'll talk to you later."

"Wait—are they going to set bail for you? I'll post it."

"I don't know." I hesitated. I felt like I didn't know anything. "You'll post my bail? Aren't you worried I'll run?"

I could hear the smile in his voice. "I'm a bounty hunter, Roz. Wherever you go, I'll find you."

I kind of liked the sound of that.

A smile lingered on my lips as I ended the call and let the police officer lead me down the hall to yet another room. This police station was like an assembly line, one efficient path straight to the big house.

The room was empty except for a few chairs, a table, and a beautiful red-haired woman who stood at the far end of the room. She wore a simple black pencil skirt and a plain white silk blouse, but I could tell they were expensive. She nodded to the police officer as he shut the door firmly behind me.

"Funny, I don't remember calling a lawyer."

"I'm Ms. Woods. Have a seat."

I gave her the once-over as I took my seat across from her. "You don't look court appointed."

She sniffed. "That's because I'm not. What have you told the police?"

I froze. "Who do you work for?"

"You."

"Who told you I'm here?"

"You have friends in high places."

It didn't escape my notice that she expertly avoided answering my question. "Are you here to get me off or to make sure I don't tell the police what I know?"

She gave me a tight-lipped smile. "I'm good at multitasking."

I made a noncommittal sound.

"Well, the detectives have a pretty sound case. They found you standing over the body, holding the murder weapon. You even confessed to killing him." She shot me a disdainful look. "You didn't think to ask for a lawyer sooner?"

I frowned. Something didn't quite add up. "Why are you here?"

She looked at me. "Are you slow? I suppose brain damage could be a good defense." She said the last part almost to herself.

"No, I know why you *said* you're here, but it doesn't make sense. Why would the Company frame me for Lenny's murder, but then send a lawyer to get me off for another murder? It doesn't make sense." I was repeating myself, but I didn't care.

Ms. Woods looked amused. "I have no idea what you're talking about."

I gritted my teeth. "Of course you don't."

"Why don't you tell me why you killed Lowell Honeycutt?"

I clenched my teeth. "It was self-defense."

She inclined her head. "Self-defense. Did you know Honeycutt before . . . tonight?"

"Yes, he's from my amputee support group."

Her eyes latched on to my prosthesis. She grinned. "Good. You're missing a hand. That makes you look even more like a victim."

"Excuse me? I *am* a victim."

"If this goes to court, you'll need every little thing that you can get going for you. But this won't go to court. I'm *that* good." Despite the fact that she claimed to be on my side, the smile she gave me still sent a shiver down my spine. "Now, tell me what you know about Lowell."

"Well, he led the amputee support group. He had a girlfriend, but when she broke up with him, he asked me out. He came to my apartment tonight because he couldn't take the hint when I ghosted him."

I'd told the detectives that he was working for the Company. Had they mentioned the Company to my lawyer? Did she know that I ratted them out? If she did, it was only a matter of time before I was next on their hit list. I clamped my mouth shut.

"That's perfect. He was obsessed with you. Followed you home. Attacked you on your property and you defended yourself, as any law-abiding American would."

My stomach sank, even though getting away with this was what I wanted. "He was unarmed."

She shook her head. "You had no way of knowing that. You were frightened for your *life*." She paused. "Wait here." She left the room.

The seconds climbed into minutes, until I couldn't sit idle any longer. Just as I neared the door, it swung open, and Detective Gutierrez entered. She closed the door behind her.

I felt a touch of unease. "Isn't my lawyer out there talking to you?"

"She's talking to my partner." She hesitated. "Lana Woods is a pricey lawyer. One of the best. How are you affording her?"

"I've been told not to answer your questions without my lawyer present," I said in a saccharine voice.

Her eyes narrowed. "I'm here to help you."

"Could've fooled me," I replied. Why did I always have to be so caustic? I tried again. "What do you want?"

"I know you can't afford a lawyer like that."

I shrugged.

"Who's paying for her?"

I gave her a look.

"You can't honestly expect me to believe that everything you said was true. It's too far-fetched, Osbourne."

"You don't know the half of it," I muttered. I had intentionally left out the sci-fi elements of my story and she still didn't believe me.

Detective Gutierrez looked like she was choosing her next words very carefully. "We're going to be letting you leave. It doesn't mean that you aren't still our prime suspect for Stevenson's murder, and we're definitely not forgetting about what happened tonight. You're still in deep shit."

I frowned. "Why are you changing your tune? What happened in the last"—I made a show of checking my watchless wrist—"ten minutes to change your mind?"

She gritted her teeth. "Lana Woods is what happened."

"She's that good, huh?" I grinned. Not only was I not being charged with Lowell's death, but she must have convinced the cops to overlook my possession of an illegal gun. "Imagine what she'll do when she finds out you came in here to talk to me without her being present."

Detective Gutierrez looked like she was going to say something and then thought better of it. She spun on her heel and left. My shit-eating grin disappeared the moment she did. I really was in deep shit.

61

Ms. Woods flipped me a business card as I was leaving the precinct. "Next time, give me a call *before* confessing." I gave her a deathly sweet smile before tossing the card into the trash. There was no way I was getting myself even more mixed up with the Company.

Something told me that prison time was preferable over being even more indebted to them. It was late by the time I got on the el, but as exhausted as I felt, I wasn't going home. I wasn't even sure if I could, since it was an active crime scene.

Instead, I headed straight for Jace's.

"Turn on the coffeemaker," I said the second he swung open the door.

"You're here," he said. His eyes wore a mixture of worry and relief. "Come in," he added. He glanced out onto the street after me, and closed the door, sliding the lock.

"The Company sent a fancy lawyer," I said. "Took her ten minutes to convince them to let me go."

Jace ran a hand over the stubble on his chin. "Are they dropping the charges?"

"For now. What about last night? Did you follow Christopher from the gala?"

"Yeah. He stayed for the entire thing. When he left, he went straight home. I staked out the place for a couple hours before coming back here. When you weren't here, I went straight to your loft."

I bit my lip at his unaired question, remembering the shame I'd felt last night when I fell off the wagon.

"Forget about Christopher Hampton," I said quickly. "I met Katherine Prescott at the gala. Did you listen to her speech?"

"Vaguely. I was focusing on the crowd."

"Did you hear what she said about giving a hand to the charity?"

He shook his head. He crossed his arms over his broad chest and leaned against the wall.

"She was looking at me when she said that."

"And?"

I waved my prosthesis in his face.

He frowned. "That's a coincidence."

I scowled at him. "Haven't you learned? There are no coincidences. Besides, after the speech, I found her. I talked to her for two seconds before one of her security guards pulled her away. And guess what, Jace? She knew my name. My real name, not the name I used to get in there."

Jace didn't react. Why didn't he look more excited about this discovery?

"This is another connection between the Company and Novus Tech," I prompted.

He nodded slowly.

"Do you not believe me?"

He wouldn't meet my eye. "It's not that I don't believe you. But why would the CEO of Novus Tech know your name? You're nobody."

"Ouch," I said, moving away from him.

"No, I mean, you're just a single donor. Sure, they're thinking about recruiting you as a Negotiator. But that has to be way lower in rank than whatever her position is. She's CEO of Novus Tech, so it stands to reason that she would be high up in the Company as well."

I was reluctant to admit that he had a point.

"She made that comment about a hand," I said. "What if she's the person who got my hand? What if she's the Phantom Strangler?"

He didn't look convinced. "Maybe. Or maybe the CEO is just taking an interest in you for other reasons."

"Like what?"

Jace gave me a slow grin. "Because you're trouble."

"Because I'm investigating the Company, I hired a PI, I got not one, but two of their Negotiators killed, and I just told the police everything," I said. "Hmm, maybe I am trouble."

I brushed past him as I headed into the kitchenette to turn on the coffeemaker myself. Turned out, there was already a pot waiting for me. I grabbed a mug from the drying rack and poured myself a cup. I was so tired. I was tired of all of this. I was tired of everything.

The little round kitchen table was laden with files on the case. Printouts from PI databases on Novus Tech, the board, its CEO. I swallowed as I stared down at Katherine Prescott's headshot. Could she be the Phantom Strangler?

I sighed and looked away, rubbing my temple with my one hand as exhaustion set in. I couldn't afford to make another rash assumption about who the Phantom Strangler was. The last person I pointed my finger at was innocent. And now he was dead. Because of me.

All this time, I'd been so worried about what the Phantom Strangler was doing with my hand. Killing with my hand. I'd even wondered how my own hand could be complicit in such a horrific act. But just last night I did something like that myself. I killed a man. I was a killer. A murderer. A monster.

Pink and gold light streamed in through the little window over the sink. I stared at it. I couldn't remember the last time I'd seen a sunrise. I imagined mixing these colors on a palette, trying to replicate the sight on a blank canvas. Capture this moment in time forever. The calm before the storm.

"I can't believe that Lowell was working for the Company," Jace said suddenly.

I tensed.

"He's been running Group for a while now. Really solid guy. He helped me a lot when I first got back." He leaned against the counter. Grief was etched across his features. "I just can't believe it."

Guilt pressed heavily against my chest.

Jace reached out and grazed my cheek with his hand. "Are you okay?"

I shook my head. Searing pain shot through my phantom hand. I winced, dropping my mug. Coffee and ceramic shards shot across the room. Shaking, I opened the kitchen cupboard, retrieving the bottle of pills that I had left here for an emergency. There was a single Ryofen left. The rest of my prescription was in the loft, which was now a crime scene. I glared down at the little white pill. It was both my salvation and my destruction. I'd killed Lowell because of this pill. An innocent man. I dry-swallowed it. The relief was almost immediate.

I caught Jace watching me with a strange expression on his face. "Do you have the necklace? Maybe I can find out where the killer bought it. If we're lucky, maybe she slipped up and used her credit card."

I relaxed. He thought I was upset because of the serial killer, not because I had killed an innocent man in a paranoid frenzy. I drew the gold chain from my pocket and placed it in the palm of his hand. He tucked it into his own pocket.

I bit my lip. "Listen," I said, stepping closer to him.

"Wait!" he said. "You'll hurt yourself." He gestured toward the mess I'd made. He reached under the sink and pulled out a worn-looking rag.

"Sorry," I mumbled.

"It's okay."

"I've been having more hallucinations," I said before I could stop myself.

His hand stopped sweeping up the ceramic fragments. He didn't look up at me. He didn't move. "About what?" he asked quietly.

"I thought . . . I thought I saw tattoos on Lowell. Gang tats. I thought . . ." I swallowed. "That's why I shot him."

Jace's brows furrowed as he angled his head. "I thought you shot him because he attacked you."

I chose my next words very carefully. "He ran at me, so I shot him."

He stood, the mess at our feet forgotten. "I've told you before that you're a terrible liar," he said in a quiet voice.

"He—I thought I saw—"

He cut me off. "Was he working for the Company?"

"I—I don't—"

"Was he?"

"No. He wore a bulky prosthetic. I guess I panicked. I thought that maybe . . . that maybe he was using it to hide what was underneath. A hand. My hand. I thought he might be the Phantom Strangler."

Jace stared at me. "Not everyone can afford a fancy prosthesis, Roz."

I swallowed. "I—I know that. But I also thought I saw gang tattoos on his neck. He came to my apartment when I hadn't told him where I lived. What was I supposed to believe?"

I didn't like the look on Jace's face. "He *liked* you, Roz."

"He liked everyone—"

"And that's an excuse?" Jace's voice was getting louder. "You killed him because you were hallucinating on Ryofen, and I *just* saw you take another pill."

I cleared my throat. "Yes, but—"

"But what? You're not worried that you might take another innocent life?"

It felt like he'd punched me in the stomach. "The pain is excruciating, Jace. I can't just stop taking the Ryofen."

He pulled even farther away from me, his hulking frame hovering in the doorway. "And who will it be next time, Roz? Me?"

"No, I would never—"

"Lowell was one of the most compassionate people I've ever met. Possibly the best person I've ever met. He poured his heart and soul into helping others. And now he's gone. All the goodness he brings into this shitty world is gone. Because of you." His entire body was rigid, radiating fury, disappointment, disgust. He couldn't even bear to look at me. "You should go."

Panic surged through me. "No, I can't go—I need help. I don't know what to do. The Company—"

Jace laughed.

I bit my lip, taken aback by his unexpected reaction. "What's so funny?"

"That you think I can believe anything you say. All of this—the Company, the murders, the Phantom Strangler having your hand?" He shook his head. "It's all insane. And now I know why. Because you're insane, Roz."

"I—I'm not insane."

He laughed, this time humorlessly. "You just killed someone while hallucinating, Roz. Doesn't get much more insane than that."

"It's not my—"

"It's not what? It's not your fault?" Jace finally looked me in the eye, but I didn't see compassion, love. Even the anger and revulsion were now overpowered by one emotion: hatred. "You knew that there are side effects, you knew what they were, and you *still* took the drug. It is one hundred percent your fault, Roz. You are a *murderer*."

His words cut through me. I could barely breathe. "Fuck you," I spat. I couldn't spend another minute in there, drowning in his resentment and my own guilt and self-loathing. I grabbed the stack of files that Jace had printed out about Novus Tech and tore out of there, not looking back.

He didn't follow.

62

One of the benefits of confessing to a murder is that the crime scene investigation wraps up quicker than most. The loft was devoid of any forensic scientists or cops when I showed up not long after leaving Jace's. I ripped the yellow tape off the front door and went in. I made sure to slide the deadbolt behind me.

A sizable blood stain decorated the cement floor in the center of the loft. I stared at it for a few long minutes before giving it a wide berth and heading to my bedroom. I barely made it to my bed before the sobbing started. It was only when I'd finished crying that I was finally able to sleep.

I awoke long after the sun had set. I stared at the half-empty bottle of whiskey on the floor beside my bed. I'd picked it up at the corner store after I'd left Jace's. Sobriety was the last thing on my mind, and that little rule of never drinking at home that I'd once had? I'd been fooling myself. I'd thought I wasn't as bad as my mother, when in fact, I was worse than her. At least she'd never killed anyone.

I took a swig of the lukewarm liquor and peered around my bedroom. Everything was blurry and out of focus. My eyes were bleary from the hours of crying. I didn't think I had any more tears left in me.

Jace was furious—as he should have been. I was a murderer. He was right about that. But he also no longer believed that a serial killer had my hand, or that the Company even existed. I lay back down in bed, staring up at the ceiling. What if it was all inside my head? What if I really was imagining everything? It would make a lot more sense that I'd lost my hand in a welding accident, and that the drugs had addled my brain beyond repair. They had, after all, convinced me that my mother was alive and well when in fact she'd been dead for years. I'd had complete conversations with a figment of my imagination, and I hadn't even noticed anything out of the ordinary.

I sat up, suddenly starving. I went into the kitchen and found a Franco's pizza box sitting on the counter. They must have delivered after the police had taken me away. I absently wondered who'd paid for it, but I wasn't going to look a gift horse in the mouth. The pizza was cold and a little stiff, but it soaked up some of the alcohol and took away the aching in my stomach. If only there was something I could do for the aching in my chest.

That familiar and vile burning sensation began to creep into my phantom hand. I found myself wavering as I reached for the Ryofen bottle. Maybe a few days off the Ryofen would give me the clarity I needed to figure out what to do next.

I barely lasted two hours before I gave in, popping another pill and chasing it with a glass of water. Ashamed, I slumped down onto the kitchen stool. I was a murderer. I was addicted to a pill that was supposed to not be addictive. The police didn't believe me when I told them about the Company. Hell, my boyfriend didn't even believe me. Ex-boyfriend. He thought I was a murderer and a junkie, and while he hadn't officially broken it off, I would have to be an idiot on top of everything else not to read between the lines.

I eyed the empty bottle of whiskey, and a fresh bout of shame washed over me as I considered heading to O'Malley's or maybe picking up another bottle from the corner store. There was only one thing in my life that I could control now, and that was following the simple—yet unbearable—rule of not drinking alcohol while on Ryofen.

I was debating what my next move should be when the sensation in my phantom hand started up again. I stared down at it in horror as it wrapped around yet another throat. Wrenched the life out of it. Let the body drop to the ground.

I jumped to my feet. I would not let her get away with this.

When I'd left Jace's, I'd grabbed a handful of the files that had been strewn on the kitchen table. One of them was a detailed background check on Ms. Katherine Prescott. But I wasn't interested in reading about how she'd had a rough childhood or that she'd gotten her MBA at Yale. No, I was interested in where she was currently living, and the address was there, written in black and white.

I had barely any money to my name, so I hopped on a train, which ended up taking a lot longer to get to her neighborhood than I'd thought it would. It was well after midnight by the time I arrived, but I knew that she would be awake. There was no way she could sleep after taking a life.

I would know.

Katherine Prescott lived in a mansion guarded by a tall iron gate. I could see the driveway continue on past the gate, cutting through a precisely trimmed lawn. The entire property was bordered by a plain brown brick wall. The gate was impenetrable, but the wall was easy to scale, even with only one hand. Within minutes I was on the other side. No sirens blared, which I took to be a good sign. I didn't see any guards, which struck me as odd, considering the size of the property, and the fact that Katherine was clearly swimming in money.

I kept my body hunched over as I jogged toward the building. Made almost entirely of glass, the large and intimidating structure seemed to sparkle in the moonlight. The lights were on in a few rooms, and I swore I could see almost all the way through the house, but for a few strategically placed opaque walls. Katherine must have been convinced of the security that brick wall provided, otherwise she didn't particularly care about privacy. At the front door, I wrapped my hand around the handle. It turned. It was unlocked.

Swallowing, I pushed it open, craning my neck to peek inside. An expansive foyer greeted me. I glanced around, taking in the simple glass vase of white lilies sitting on a table, the sweeping chrome staircase that led to the upper floors. The gentle chords of a piano trickled in from another room. I hesitated. What was I doing? What was I planning? If Katherine was the Phantom Strangler, she could easily subdue me. If she wasn't, then was I about to attack another innocent person? I glanced back toward the front door. I should leave.

"What are you waiting for?" a honey-smooth voice called out from the other room.

I froze.

"I've put on a pot of tea, though I suspect you'd prefer something stronger. Won't you join me, Miss Osbourne?"

I wiped my sweaty palm on my pants and followed the sound of the music.

63

The music led me to a large area that I supposed was intended to be a living room, though it hardly looked lived in. The sofas were all sharp angles, with pillows perfectly positioned at severe angles. The artwork on the walls was a little too abstract, a little too avant-garde, even for me. My eyes landed on the source of the music, an old-fashioned phonograph.

Unsteadiness coursed through me as I took in its worn wood and faded brass horn; the antique was so at odds with the rest of the ultra-modern architecture and décor.

Katherine stood at a small bar with her back to me, pouring from a glass decanter into a tumbler. "Would you like some?"

"Um, no."

She turned to face me, and I was surprised to see a pleasant smile on her face. She shrugged. "Suit yourself."

"How did you know I was here?"

"I have security cameras all over the property. I knew you were here before you even hopped over the wall." She raised a stenciled brow. "I left the door unlocked for you, though I doubt a locked door would have stopped you."

I was at a loss for words. I'd rehearsed what I would say the entire forty-five-minute ride here, but now my mind was a blank slate.

"Won't you have a seat?" she asked, gesturing to the couch that didn't look like it had ever been sat on. She placed the tumbler on a coaster in front of where I was to sit, and then took a seat opposite it.

She picked up her teacup and took a sip while watching me. I made no move to sit down, eyeing the tumbler suspiciously. Why ask me if I wanted a drink if she was already pouring one for me? Did she know that I was trying to avoid alcohol? Was this some kind of sick ploy at distracting me from my mission?

I did my best to ignore the glass of pure temptation, even as a bead of sweat trickled down my spine.

"A little late for a social call, don't you think?" she asked pleasantly.

"I want answers."

She laughed, an elegant laugh, one that sounded practiced and fake. "And I thought you were here to negotiate your starting salary."

That gave me a start. "Come again?"

"Generally speaking, I don't deal with low-level Negotiators, but your being here shows that you are quite resourceful. I can see you moving up the ranks quite quickly."

"Framing me for murder didn't work, so instead you decided to recruit me?" I spat.

Her eyebrows nearly met her hairline. "*Framing* you for *murder*?"

"Yes. Lenny Stevenson. Or maybe you don't know him, since he was just a low-level Negotiator."

At that, she laughed. "You weren't being framed for anything."

I rolled my eyes. "Right. I found Lenny after you took my hand. It didn't take much to get him to talk. He told me all about the Company, about the illegal organ trade, everything he knew. And you punished him for it and framed me. You somehow made sure only my fingerprints were on the sword. Clever plan, really. But it didn't work."

She laughed again, and this time it sent chills racing up the back of my neck. "Miss Osbourne, you don't understand. That was a part of the plan."

"What?"

Again, she gestured for me to sit, then took another sip of tea. When it became clear that she wouldn't continue to talk until I'd accepted her hospitality, I dropped down onto the couch gracelessly.

She looked amused. "As I said, I'm not involved in those low-level dealings, but I do know how they work. I took part in the design of this system that works quite flawlessly. Generally speaking, if a Donor is resourceful, cunning, or desperate enough to track down their Negotiator, they're let in on the secret. It's how we keep a steady number of new Negotiators in the mix."

I opened my mouth, then closed it again.

"If you hadn't reached out to . . . Stevenson, was it? If you hadn't found him and asked him your little questions—you wouldn't have been recruited at all. It's as simple as that."

"That's not the whole story, there's something missing. *You* killed Lenny. *You* framed—"

"Nobody framed you, Miss Osbourne," Katherine said, her tone suddenly sharp. "We didn't have Mr. Stevenson killed. He wasn't due to fulfill the terms of his contract until 2027. After he was stabbed, he called his handler for help. But when she arrived, she was clearly too late. Mr. Stevenson was unconscious from blood loss. He was dying. But more importantly, his organs were dying." Katherine shook her head and took another sip of tea. "Drastic measures had to be taken to keep him alive long enough so that his organs would still be viable. Unfortunately, not everything he'd sold to us was able to be . . . procured. They'd been damaged from the stabbing. Such a waste."

I stared at her. A man had died and all she cared about was losing income. "You're a monster."

Her lips twitched into a frown. "I'm not a monster. I'm pragmatic. We are not in the business of simply killing people, Miss Osbourne. You of all people should know that."

I scoffed.

"What I'm saying is that he was already dying when my people arrived. He was already essentially dead."

"Essentially dead and actually dead are two very different things," I said. "But if your people hadn't stabbed him, then—" I cut off, seeing her expression. "No, that's impossible."

"We have video surveillance of the areas around the homes of all our employees. We saw you leaving his apartment building with an unknown male companion mere minutes before he called for help. It was *you*, Miss Osbourne, who stabbed Leonard Stevenson. It was *you* who killed him."

"No, I didn't." I felt like I was going to be sick all over this showroom couch. I'd murdered Lenny, and I didn't even remember doing it? What else had I done that I didn't remember doing?

She inclined her head. "If it wasn't you, then was it your male companion? I believe his name is Jace Moore?"

I flinched. "He has nothing to do with this," I said in a low voice.

Something in my expression made her smile. "Don't you see, Miss Osbourne, if we wanted you to go to prison for that murder, all we would have had to do was hand the video surveillance over to the police."

"This still doesn't make sense. You put the body back. You could have just cleaned up the crime scene."

"We could have, but we needed the police to know about the murder. To find the evidence you undoubtedly left behind. That way, if you ever turn on us . . ." she trailed off and gave me a pointed look.

Understanding dawned on me. "I see. So, if I decide to turn on the Company, you'll release the evidence that can get his murder case reopened."

"Opened and closed in a matter of minutes." She chuckled. "See, I knew there was a reason I liked you, Miss Osbourne. You catch on quickly." She took another sip of her tea. "Mr. Hampton reported that you passed his test with flying colors. We could use someone like you on our team." A frown crossed her face. "Though it would be appreciated if you would stop killing our employees."

My breath caught in my throat. "Employees? As in, plural?"

"Mr. Honeycutt should not have shown up at your apartment. He was to observe from afar, as he did with other Donors who have found their way to that support group." She waved a hand in the air. "As far as I'm concerned, he got himself killed."

"Lowell worked for you?"

She gave me a funny look. "As if you didn't already know that."

"Right," I said quickly. The relief was almost palpable. Sure, I'd found out that I'd killed not one, but two people, but neither of them was innocent. *Lowell* wasn't innocent.

My thoughts went back to Jace. I had to tell him the truth. He had to know that I hadn't killed an innocent man, that his friend hadn't been who he'd thought he was.

Katherine continued, "He was a Donor turned Keeper."

"Keeper?"

"A position for those who have a different skill set from Negotiators. They are placed in such a way to ensure that Donors don't spread the truth about the Company."

How many employees did they have?

She smiled as if she knew what I was thinking. "Our reach is a lot further than you've likely imagined."

"If there are that many Donors, aren't you worried that someone might slip through the cracks? That one of us will end up telling someone who matters, even if you have all these Keepers in place to prevent that from happening?" I thought of Jace, but I pushed him from my mind out of fear that just thinking his name would put an even bigger target on his back.

Katherine gave me a look akin to pity. "Regan—Do you mind if I call you Regan?"

I didn't respond.

"We receive donations from a variety of sources, not just the deals that we make with Donors. The City of Chicago has thousands of souls that nobody would miss should they . . . disappear."

Her implication sent a wave of nausea over me.

She continued, "Those we select to be Donors carry very specific . . . qualifications. There are those who move up the ranks, to become Keepers and Handlers, like Mr. Stevenson and Mr. Honeycutt. You. And then there are those who are repeat Donors." Her cold, hard eyes latched onto mine.

I recalled Lenny's words from the last time I saw him: "*They know that soon you'll be crawling back, just begging them to take more.*"

"I think you won't be surprised to learn that the compensation we provide can be quite . . . irresistible." Her gaze flitted down to the tumbler before me, then back to my face. She gave me a knowing look. The Company knew about my weaknesses and exploited them. It was why I was chosen.

She glanced up at the large steel clock that was mounted on the wall over the bar. "I have an early morning tomorrow, so I'm afraid that your negotiations will have to wait. And while I applaud your gumption, I'm going to have to ask that this goes through the proper channels. Mr. Hampton has been promoted from Negotiator to Handler. All your future dealings are to be with him."

I blinked at her. Was she dismissing me? "Listen, I'm not here to negotiate."

She set her teacup on a tray in front of her. "Then why are you here, Regan?"

"I know that you've been killing people. I know that you're the Phantom Strangler, and that you're using my hand as your murder weapon. I received the note, the text . . . the necklace." My voice broke.

"The person who has your hand is the Phantom Strangler?" She looked genuinely surprised. A smile curled upon her lips. "Interesting . . ." she said thoughtfully. She gazed out the window.

"Are you denying that you're the Strangler?" All my previous conviction had drained from me like a sieve. She'd been so forthcoming about everything else. It just didn't make sense that she'd also be the killer. The Strangler had been toying with me, and she was not doing that at all. If she were the Strangler, wouldn't she have been baiting me this entire time?

Her eyes swiveled back and locked on mine. "I promise you I am not the Strangler. Nor am I the recipient of your beautiful hand." She waved her left hand in the air as she rose. "I can assure you that your hand is in good hands." She didn't chuckle at her pun, and I wondered if she was even aware that she'd made it. "Now, if you don't mind, I will have to see you out."

I stood, suddenly overwhelmed by uncertainty and helplessness. Tonight had not gone as I'd hoped, though I finally had some answers. But these answers brought about new questions, more than I could keep track of.

"I'll call you a car to take you back to the city," she continued as she herded me toward the front door. "But Regan? If you do decide to pay me another unscheduled visit, I will not be so hospitable."

She opened the door and turned to me expectantly. I stepped out, the chilly night air a shock to my senses. I turned back. It was now or never.

"If you don't have my hand, then who does?" I hated how small I sounded in that moment.

Her icy green eyes cut into me. "It went to one of our best employees." Her lips curled into a smile that was not unkind. "If you choose to serve us well, move up the ranks and make a significant contribution to the Company, then in the future we just might return the favor." Her eyes lingered on my prosthesis. I sucked in a breath when I realized what she meant.

With that, she shut the door.

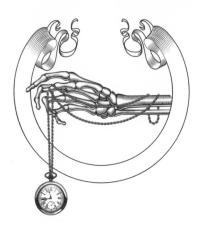

I T'S ALMOST TIME.

Watching her has become an addiction. Other aspects of life have lost all color. Music is devoid of emotion. Food tastes bland. The world feels stagnant. But there is a constant itch under my skin that I just cannot scratch, and the only time the yearning settles—the only time I feel like I can breathe—is when I'm watching Roz.

I spend hours shadowing her. I am not so foolish that I cannot recognize that there have been consequences to my loss of self-control. Where before I was little more than a fleeting whisper on the wind, my fixation has made her corporeal. There was a witness who'd caught a glimpse of me with the roommate. But I just cannot bring myself to care. Everything I do is for the sole purpose of bringing me closer to my masterpiece. All I can do is fantasize about how it will feel when it's finally time to wrap my fingers around that slender neck.

But now? Anxiety worms its way through my confidence.

I hover outside the house made of glass. I'd only left Roz for an hour as I disappeared to finish another work. I'd returned just in time to follow her here.

I'd wanted to keep Roz isolated. Separated from the Company and all that they do. After her donation, she should have fallen off their radar. But

Roz has proven to be more resourceful than anticipated. As before, I fluctuate between frustration at yet another obstacle and the thrill of the unknown. But I've discovered that molding Roz into the perfect piece has kept me on my toes. And I like it.

This wouldn't be the first time Roz has forced me to do something unplanned and impulsive. Two weeks ago, I slipped into that dank little apartment. I retrieved the sword. I sliced into the weak man's pudgy stomach with it. This dead end was supposed to crush Roz's quest for answers, not fuel her on.

But it had been a happy consequence that Roz thought herself to be a murderer. A generous heap of guilt was added to my palette, which I then blended into the beautiful backdrop of pain and suffering, against which her final anguish will be the pièce de résistance.

Inside the glass house, Roz seeks to learn more about the Company. I find this curious. I know that she has no intention of joining. But Roz has changed these past months. Her selfishness has given way to compassion and morality, both of which had long been dormant, nearly snuffed out. I suppose that this is in part my doing. Stealing her hand and using it to destroy was the tipping point, pushing Roz toward light instead of darkness. Roz is in that glass house right now learning about the Company in hopes of destroying it. Of destroying me.

I'm not worried about the Company I have poured seven years of my life into. The Company has been in place for decades and will continue decades after Roz is gone. It will continue for as long as the powerful are in need of something more, and the desperate have something to give.

I'm not worried about myself either. I have been observing Roz for weeks. I have researched her past. I know her better than she knows herself. I know her weaknesses. I know how to exploit them.

All this new development means is that my plans must once again be altered. Once again, I must expedite my timeline. With the roommate gone, Roz's pain and suffering has been brought to intoxicating heights. She'll further detach until there's no one left. It's only a matter of time before she's drawn into my snare. It's only a matter of time before she's desperate for the end to come, and she runs to me, begging for release from her suffering.

And I will be waiting with open arms and extended hands.

64

I woke the following morning to a voice mail on my phone from Jace. I scarfed down cold pizza over the sink while trying to scrounge up the courage to listen to it. When I finally did, I wasn't satisfied. He said he needed to talk to me. That it was important. That was it. I listened to the message a second time, then a third. I couldn't glean anything from his tone. It was businesslike and formal. Though, I supposed that fact itself was telling. But was he still mad? Could he find it in himself to forgive me? I stared down at the phone, willing it to answer my questions.

Tired of torturing myself, I snatched up the phone and tapped on Jace's name. He answered after the first ring.

"Roz, are you okay?"

"Uh, yeah . . ." Those weren't the words of someone who hated my guts. I tried not to feel too hopeful.

"I went to your place last night, but you weren't there."

I'd probably already been on my way to Katherine's. "I was out. Probably doing what insane people do when they're not murdering." My tone was bitter.

He was quiet. I wished I could see his face. "Roz, I shouldn't have said those things."

I held back a sigh. "Well, you were right. I *am* insane. I *am* a murderer."

"Roz, I'm not angry because you've hallucinated. I'm angry because you keep taking that damn drug—"

I cut him off. "Is there a reason you called?" My stomach clenched. He wasn't wrong. Not at all. I was the one in the wrong. He was trying to apologize, and my master skill at self-sabotage was working in overdrive.

"Don't go anywhere. I'll be there in twenty minutes." He ended the call before I could respond.

I stared down at my phone screen. Something soft rubbed against my leg, and I looked down into Little Guy's clear green eyes.

Last night he'd darted into the apartment when I'd come back from Katherine's. He'd never tried to come inside before, and I'd wondered if he could somehow sense how lonely I was. Or maybe it was Hanna's prolonged absence that made him bolder. Either way, Little Guy's warm presence last night had kept me from having a complete breakdown.

I spent the next twenty minutes freshening up—brushing my teeth, my hair. I put on mascara and changed into a pair of jeans I hadn't worn in a while. They were moderately clean. I wanted to look presentable on the off chance that Jace might consider taking me back. Even if he didn't, I thought I should at least show him what he would be missing, although a guy like Jace could easily find someone who wasn't carrying half my baggage and remembered to floss regularly.

He barely looked at me when he entered the loft. I closed the door behind him.

"I heard from Jules."

I supposed I should have expected he'd want to get straight to business. "And?"

"She's been looking into Artis Corp, which is the subsidiary of Novus Tech that both you and Amrita received your payments through. She's been following the money that's been funneled through them."

I stared at him. "Does this mean you're back to believing me?"

"She managed to trace payments received by multiple accounts. We can't figure out who they were received from, at least not directly, but we can trace who received them. Guess they weren't as cautious about protecting the donors as they were the recipients."

"So, you believe me?" I repeated, my heart hammering in my throat. I needed to hear the words from him.

He stuffed his hands into his pockets. "I was upset yesterday. I said some shit that I shouldn't have said. But I stand by some of it. Roz, you need to stop taking the Ryofen."

I averted my eyes.

"Roz, there are other painkillers out there, other therapies, I doubt you tried *everything* in the two weeks you were handless before starting this experimental drug."

"*Two weeks* feels like an eternity when you're in pain." I released a shaky breath. "But okay."

He blinked. "Okay?"

"The whole reason for not taking other painkillers was because they're addictive. Newsflash—Ryofen is just as addictive—at least, it is to me. If only because it stops the pain."

Jace's expression softened, and he took a step closer to me. "We'll find another way."

My heart hiccupped at his use of the word *we*. "Listen, I have something to tell you."

His guarded expression morphed into fury, then shock as I told him about going to Katherine's last night, about what I found out about the Company and Lowell. I left out the part where I learned that I'd been the one who stabbed Lenny. There were some things that he just didn't need to know, and the fact that the Company had something on me, that they were blackmailing me into keeping silent, was something he didn't need to know. Not if I wanted him to help me take them down.

"Lowell really was working for the Company," I said again as I studied Jace's face. I couldn't tell what he was thinking.

Jace rubbed the back of his neck. "You should have told me you were going to her house. Anything could have happened to you."

"I'm fine."

"You might not have been. I should have been there."

I shook my head adamantly. "Don't blame yourself for my stupidity. Maybe once I quit the Ryofen I'll stop acting like an idiot all the time."

Jace's lip tugged upward into an almost smile. "Don't be hoping for miracles."

"Hey!" I said with a laugh, swatting at him. I was about to lean forward to try to draw him into a kiss when a loud meow broke our eye contact.

Jace blinked down at Little Guy. "Who's this?" He crouched and extended a hand for the cat to sniff.

"That's Little Guy." I glared at the little cockblocker, who appeared oblivious that he'd interrupted anything.

Jace scooped him up and held him against his chest, rubbing him between the ears with his fingers. I braced myself, worried that Little Guy would sink his teeth and claws into Jace's flesh, but instead he nuzzled against Jace's chin and began to purr.

Seeing Jace standing there, holding the tiny feline in his broad, muscular arms did something to me. I thought my ovaries might have exploded.

"*Little Guy?*" Jace asked, his lips quirking.

I shrugged. "He's little. He's a guy. Seemed to fit." I grinned. "Look, it's my little guy and my big guy."

At that, Jace gifted me with his full, crooked grin. I closed the distance between us and stood on my tiptoes, pressing my lips against his. His eyes searched mine for a fleeting moment before they fluttered shut and he kissed me back. Little Guy let out a little grumble in protest before leaping from Jace's arms, leaving his hands free for more important things. I felt Jace's chuckle against my lips before he sank deeper into the kiss.

So many emotions were coursing through me that it was hard to keep track of them, but most of all, I felt relieved.

Relieved that while I'd killed a man in cold blood, at least it turned out that he was far from innocent. Relieved that we had a break in the case. Relieved that Jace didn't hate me.

Relieved that I hadn't blown the best thing to have happened to me in, well, ever.

I pulled away first. "So, you said that Jules looked into the money?"

His eyes were unfocused. "What? Yeah. Right, yes, she did."

I smirked at his flustered, one-track mind. "Does this mean you can locate the victims? Other people like me?"

He cleared his throat. "Yeah. She's found about twenty already." Jace suddenly looked somber. "And she's started looking into them. Roz, at least half of them are dead."

"If I give that list of names to Detective Gutierrez, she might be able to find their autopsy reports. When they find critical parts . . . missing . . . then she'll have to believe me. Even if all those bodies are missing, that's evidence in my favor too!" I couldn't quite contain my excitement. "She'll *have* to believe me."

"It's not a smoking gun," Jace warned. "But it's pretty damn close." He tugged me closer for another kiss.

65

That afternoon I went to the police station for a surprise visit with my favorite detectives. I came bearing the list of victims and the money trail that Jules had given Jace. I was disappointed that I hadn't had a chance to meet her. I needed to size up the competition. But I supposed that could wait until after I took down a black market organ-smuggling ring and caught a serial killer. My priorities were in the right place.

The building was bustling with officers, victims, and the occasional criminal doing the perp walk across the floor, handcuffed and unruly. I watched a drugged-up lunatic shrieking at the top of his lungs. He wasn't wearing pants. I was suddenly glad that Trap had refused to sell narcotics to me a month ago, or that could have been me.

"Can I help you, miss?" an officer asked. He didn't look at all perturbed by the pants-less man wearing discolored tighty-whities that revealed far too much.

"I hope so. I'm looking for Detective Gutierrez."

"Right over there. She has one of the enclosed offices." The officer shot an envious look in the direction of her vicinity as he returned to his cubicle. How anyone got any work done in this animal house was beyond me.

I hurried over to her office and pounded on the door.

"Come in!"

I swung open the door to find Detective Gutierrez sitting behind a desk. I'd expected a scowl, but strangely, her expression lit up when she saw me. Detective Borgnino sat at a desk beside hers.

His hand went to his holster.

"Oh, don't get your panties in a bunch," I said, rolling my eyes.

"Here to confess?" Detective Borgnino asked dryly.

"You wish. Lovely office, by the way. Could use some ventilation, though. It smells like lasagna and piss." Before I could infuriate him into drawing his gun, I pulled out the envelope. "I know you two are homicide detectives, but how do you feel about taking down a corrupt organization that deals in the illegal trade of body parts?"

"This again?" Detective Borgnino muttered.

"Don, could you give us a moment?" Detective Gutierrez said.

He gave her an unreadable look but didn't argue as he slowly rose and left the room.

"Could you close the door?" she said.

I complied without so much as a snarky retort.

"One of our officers ran a background check on Honeycutt," she said.

"Who?"

"Lowell."

I took the seat across from her without invitation. "And?"

"And it looks like he didn't work for a winter sporting company. Well, he used to. Before he lost his hand."

"In a zip-lining accident," I said.

"Is that what he told you?" Detective Gutierrez said. "There's no record of how he lost his hand. Just that one day he had it, and the next, it was gone."

"Okay, maybe he went to an underground zip-lining place. The odds are that it wasn't up to code. I mean, he lost his hand on it, for Christ's sake." I leaned forward. "*Or* maybe he sold his hand to the same Company that took mine."

"There isn't a single hospital record documenting his stay." She gave me her signature impenetrable stare. "Just like with you."

I gulped. "You've been looking into me?"

She gave me a look like I was certifiably insane. "You've been a person of interest in several murder cases. Of course I've been looking into you." She pulled a file out of the top drawer of her desk before continuing: "He didn't just work for a winter sports company. He owned one. But it turned out that Mr. Honeycutt didn't have a very good business acumen. He went bankrupt, then into debt. He owed a lot of money to the bank, and I'm willing to bet that he owed a lot of money to other people too. But then, one day the debt was miraculously paid off. All at once."

"By who?"

She shrugged. "Still looking into it. But the timing of the debt being paid off and him losing his arm—"

"So, you believe me."

She raised her hand. "I wouldn't go that far. I'm saying that there's some evidence in your favor." She hesitated.

"What else is there? What aren't you telling me?"

"I received a call from the medical examiner's office. Honeycutt's body never showed up at the morgue."

"What?"

"It's missing."

My stomach churned. "And Lenny was prematurely cremated."

"Right now, all this is circumstantial."

"But you believe me."

She didn't respond.

"You'll be hopping on the bandwagon soon enough," I said. "I have enough evidence to get you started in this envelope." I waved it in the air.

She extended a hand, but I held it out of reach. Her eyes narrowed.

"In exchange for this envelope, I would like immunity."

Her eyes narrowed even further. "For what?"

"For any murder I may or may not have committed."

Her eyebrows shot through the roof. Before she could respond, I continued: "I have a feeling that the Company has framed me, in case I turn on them. They said if I told people about them that there would be consequences. I want to . . . avoid those consequences at all costs."

Detective Gutierrez gave me a look that indicated she didn't quite believe me.

"So, what do you say, Detective? Do we have a deal?"

"I'll take a look at that, then get back to you on that one."

I scowled.

"You don't have much bargaining power, given that I don't believe you."

"This here envelope contains the names of twenty people like me. Twenty people who were paid off by Artis Corp shortly after losing a body part or organ. I don't watch basketball, but it seems like a slam dunk to me."

She snatched the envelope from my hand, slipped it open, and flipped through the first few pages. "It might not be."

I frowned. "Well, our hack—um—associate is looking into tracking the payments the other way. Seeing who was doing the actual paying."

She dropped the file onto the desk, then tapped it with a long, slender finger. She was lost in thought for a long moment. "Contact me when you have something."

"Do I have immunity?"

"If—and that's a big if—this proves to be lucrative, then yes." She locked eyes with mine. "I'll protect you, Regan."

A weight was lifted from my chest. Detective Gutierrez had given me no reason not to trust her. And I did trust her. I just had to hope that this trust wasn't misplaced.

"Let me know when you have the other names." She was back to business, but I still felt relieved knowing that she was in my corner. "But don't tell anyone else. Including Detective Borgnino."

At that, I froze. "You don't trust your partner?"

She sighed and turned away, effectively dismissing me. "Just let me know when it's done."

66

Back at Jace's office, I quickly realized that I wasn't alone. There was a slender African American woman sitting at Jace's desk. She was dressed conservatively in a black pantsuit, but her red-bottomed heels added a streak of color and style to the ensemble.

She didn't look up when I came in. She was inspecting her fingernails. "You must be Roz," she said to them.

Heart in my throat, I glanced toward the exit. Where was Jace?

"I'm Jules," she continued in a bored tone, still not looking up.

Jules? I stifled a sigh of relief. I'd thought she worked for the Company.

I laughed. "Nice to finally meet you. I've heard only good things."

At that, Jules looked up at me. "I should hope so." She nodded toward her laptop, a large clunky thing that she had set up on Jace's desk. "I'm running some code now."

"Oh, okay," I said. I glanced around again.

"Jace is in his apartment in the back," Jules said. "He's taking a shower."

Why had he needed to take a shower? I just now noticed the wrinkle in Jules's blouse. How had she gotten that? *I will not punch her. I will not punch her.* "So, how do you know Jace?"

Jules looked up again. She smirked but didn't answer. "I think what you meant to ask was: Where are you in the case, Jules?"

I will not punch her. "You don't look like a hacker."

"'Hacker' is not my job title. It's just a side hustle." She sighed and stabbed a few keys on the keyboard with her perfectly sculpted nails. "I have a hunch about where the money's coming from. How they're receiving the payments for the trading of body parts."

I was seeing red. "How much did Jace tell you?"

"Everything. He trusts me."

"Well, I don't know you from Eve," I snapped.

Jace chose that moment to walk in. He smelled of the evergreen soap he kept in his shower. "I see you two have met. Have you got anything?" he asked Jules.

I will not punch him.

Jules smirked again. "Not yet. It should be another ten minutes."

"You told her *everything*?" I hissed.

Jace looked surprised. "Jules is one hundred percent trustworthy. I trust her with my life."

"I saved his life once," Jules said, drawing my attention back to her. "I'm not exaggerating. He fell out of a tree. Dumbass climbed it to the top, without realizing that he might not be able to make it down. He broke his leg in three places. If I hadn't been there to see it happen, run home, and call an ambulance, he'd still be there, rotting right now."

Jace grinned at my expression. "I was eight."

I looked between them again, confusion painted across my face.

"I'm his sister," Jules said. To Jace she said, "She thinks I'm your side piece. As soon as I'm done here, I'm going to go vomit." She returned her attention to the laptop screen.

Jace looked at me, a grin tugging at his lips. "Jealous?" he whispered.

"No," I lied. "Well, not anymore."

"Done!" Jules said. She grinned, a crooked grin, and I realized in the moment that she looked a lot like Jace. "The payments are being wired through anonymous donations to Novus Tech's largest charity, the American Health and Wellness Society. The payments are split up into separate installments, rewired through multiple routes, but the amounts add up." She looked up at Jace. "There have been at least hundreds of separate transactions in the last few years."

"They're funneling money through their charity?" Jace said, running a hand over his chin.

"Yep."

"That's another white-collar crime we can get them for," Jace said. "Assuming, of course, that we can't tag them for what they're actually doing." He looked at me. "That's how they caught Al Capone, you know. For tax evasion."

I rolled my eyes. "Yes, we live in Chicago. I'm fully aware of that story, but thank you for mansplaining it for me." I glanced over at Jules and caught her looking between me and Jace with a little smile on her face.

"This should go to the police too," I said.

"The police?" Jules seemed skeptical. "You do realize they're probably in on it, right?"

"No, not these police," I said. My voice lacked conviction. I realized how naïve I sounded. I didn't know why I trusted Detective Gutierrez, but I felt like I could.

"This should go to the FBI. There's marginally less corruption with them. At the very least, they have more accountability," Jules said. "And they actually have the resources to take down a company like Novus Tech."

"Yeah, but how will I get them to believe me?" I said. "I could barely get a two-bit cop to listen." I couldn't very well tell her that I had a deal for immunity through said two-bit cop, and the FBI likely wouldn't extend that same favor.

"You have enough to make them interested," Jules said. "Well, I'm off." Jules closed her laptop and slid it into a sleek leather shoulder bag. She handed Jace a flash drive. "Everything you need is on here. You might have to do some more digging. I'm sure you can track down whose organs and body parts came from where. It's like a twisted game of Operation," she added thoughtfully.

She shook her head. "After you do that, then you should have enough for the FBI." She swung her laptop bag over her shoulder and glided over to the door in her Louboutins. She turned back. "If you get stuck, just give me a ring. My fees are double now that this is dangerous." She winked at me, and then she was gone.

67

It was a quarter past eleven at night, and my eyes were fuzzy from staring at the laptop screen. My phantom hand was throbbing, which I supposed was a blissful break from the searing pain I'd managed to survive earlier. It had felt like I'd shoved my hand in a deep fryer, and that no matter what I did, I couldn't pull it out. It took everything in my power not to self-medicate. I was on my third glass of Jace's single-malt scotch, however, so I couldn't say that I was completely sober.

I glanced over at Jace who was sprawled out on the couch, asleep. I wished I could sleep. I'd been up for forty-eight hours straight. Jace was snoring, and despite my jealousy at his ability to sleep, it didn't bother me in the slightest. It was almost cute. *Ugh.*

I returned my attention to the laptop. I had a theory about one of the transactions. Large donations were made by a man named Jaya Chaudhary, an Indian diplomat who resided in Chicago. He'd been on the organ transplant list, desperate for a new heart. There was no record of a surgery, but he should have died two years ago.

He was still alive. Last summer, pictures had been taken of him on a Caribbean vacation, and he'd looked better than ever. I was willing to bet my good hand that he was a client. I just wasn't sure who would have received the Donor's payout. Would it have been the Donor, like with Lenny, but years ago? Or would it have been someone else, like a family member? Until Detective Gutierrez looked into the list I'd given her, I wouldn't be able to make the connection between recipient and donor.

My phone rang. I fumbled to answer it quickly, glancing over at Jace, who was still sleeping, unperturbed.

"This is Gutierrez. We need to talk."

"Wow, just cut out the pleasantries entirely, why don't you?"

"I looked into those names."

"And?"

"We need to meet. I'll be at your place in a half hour."

She hung up before I could tell her I wasn't there. I groaned.

I unplugged the flash drive from the laptop and slipped it into my pocket. I threw on my coat and fetched my purse from the hook by the door. I hesitated, glancing back at Jace. I felt a tug on my heart, and I wasn't sure what to do about it. I did know that I wasn't going to wake him, and not just because he needed the rest. If this deal with Detective Gutierrez fell through, I needed Jace to be as far away from it as possible. I didn't want the Company knowing that he was involved. All they knew at this point was that I'd hired him for protection. I didn't want them to know that he knew as much as I did.

By the time I made it to the loft, my hand was being shredded by an invisible chainsaw. I wanted nothing more than to cut it off to stop the pain, but it was already gone. There was nothing *to* cut off. But I did have one option.

There was only one thing that could stop the pain.

I stumbled into the kitchen and grabbed my prescription bottle, working by the beam from the streetlights coming in through the windows. I needed the Ryofen. I couldn't live without it. I was going to die.

I stared down at the little white pill that trembled in my unsteady palm. The sight reminded me of a time when I'd gone to a palm reader, back when I was in freshman year of college. The woman had feigned enthusiasm when I'd asked her about my career. She'd said my money line told her I'd come into quite a bit of wealth in a few years. Then, she'd let go of my hand and taken my money and shooed me out the door. Now, the milky-white capsule rested just between my heart line and my life line, both of which were looking a little too thin, a little too ragged. A little too short.

I threw the pill in my mouth and swallowed. I took several deep breaths until the pain finally subsided, but it was immediately replaced with guilt. That had to be my last pill. I held the bottle of Ryofen over the sink, my hand shaking from the effort of this tiny act. If I poured the pills down the sink, then the choice to be clean would be taken away from me. But could I do that?

Trembling, I returned the bottle to the counter and fastened the lid. I just needed a clear head for the deal with Gutierrez and whatever came after it. Then, I would have all the time in the world to focus on getting clean.

Detective Gutierrez showed up a few minutes later, pushing past me and striding into the loft. "Welcome. Come on in," I said.

"Where did you get the names?"

"Did you look them up?"

"Yes," she said. She ran a hand through her frizzy brown hair, pushing down the unruly stray hairs that framed her, for once, frazzled face. "The names on that list—the ten deceased—their bodies all went missing from the morgue."

"*All* of them?" Hope tinged my voice. Now she had to believe me.

"Every single one of them. The problem is, they weren't reported missing," Detective Gutierrez continued. "There's just no record of it."

"Then how do you know they went missing?"

"Because there's no record of them leaving the morgue. It isn't piled high with unclaimed bodies, so they must have gone somewhere. And a couple of them had families that reported the bodies missing. It just wasn't followed up on by anyone."

"So, you're starting to believe me."

Detective Gutierrez stared at me. "An organ-smuggling ring? Like kidney thieves? This is the stuff of urban legends. This can't be real."

"Oh, they're smuggling far more than just kidneys," I said, waving my prosthesis in the air. "They have an impressive business going on. I got paid a million dollars for this hand. I can only imagine how much someone would be willing to pay for a more vital body part. Like a heart." I took a deep breath. "Is this enough for the immunity you promised me?"

Detective Gutierrez made a noncommittal sound. She looked around the loft. "You didn't have a chance to clean up, did you?"

I just now realized that Lowell's blood had become the focal point of the space. From an artist's perspective, it was quite striking. I tore my eyes away from the crusted brown stain.

"I've been busy," I snapped. "I have the list of names. The names of the people who made the payments. I'm hoping you can do some of the work yourself to put two and two together?" I pulled out the USB. "So what about my immunity?"

She frowned. "And who got you these names?"

"I'm not naming any names."

She didn't even crack a smile. My humor was vastly underappreciated by Chicago's finest. "All right." She sighed. "Who else knows about this?"

A shiver crept down my spine. It didn't escape my notice that she was avoiding my question about the immunity. Had she lied? Did she even have the authority to offer it to me? "Just me and my heretofore unnamed associate."

"The PI, is it? Moore?" There was a darkness in her eyes that wasn't there before.

I licked my lips, unease settling over me. "No, it's not him," I said quickly.

She took a step forward. Despite the fact that she was petite and shorter than me by a few good inches, I still found myself recoiling. "You're lying to me. Why are you lying to me?"

All the little hairs on my arms stood to attention as I observed her change in demeanor. Jules had been right. I shouldn't have trusted Gutierrez. I shouldn't have trusted any of the police. And now I was here, unarmed and one-armed and about to be taken out by a dirty cop.

Before I could come up with a response, the door slammed open. Detective Gutierrez's hand went to her holster, but she was too late. One shot, two shots, and she dropped.

I stared down at her body. I watched, transfixed, as the pool of blood grew around her, spreading from where she fell, yearning to merge with Lowell's. This apartment had seen so much blood.

And this wouldn't be the last of it.

My eyes crawled upward. It couldn't be.

Ben stood in the doorway. "Surprised to see me?"

68

"Ben?" Blood rushed in my ears, and I could barely hear his response as he closed and locked the door behind him.

"Bet you didn't think you were going to see me again," he said with a smirk.

I blinked rapidly several times, but the sight before me never changed. My eyes darted toward the exit. He was between me and the door. Which was locked. It would take me several seconds to unlatch it; the fucking thing was finicky, and I only had one hand. Plus, Ben had a gun and an itchy trigger finger that he'd demonstrated to me more than once now. I was trapped. I was locked inside with a madman.

"What, no sarcastic words for your long-lost lover?" he asked, cocking his head.

"Ben, where have you been? I thought you were dead."

"Of course you did," he replied. He moved farther into the loft, and I backed away from him, trying to maintain a considerable distance between us. "You sent that asshole—what was his name?"

I wouldn't fall for that trick. "Who?"

A sporadic, chaotic imitation of a laugh erupted from him. He drew even closer, stepping into a patch of light that shone in from the street. I gasped.

A thick band of gauze was wrapped around his head, sweeping across his forehead and covering his left eye. The gauze was filthy, and blood had seeped through the material and dried to become a murky brown. "Y-your eye," I whispered. I took in the rest of him. My stomach turned. "Your skin . . ."

"It's yellow, isn't it? Ask me why that is, Roz."

He moved toward me. Not waiting for my answer, he lifted his shirt. A jagged wound sliced across his stomach, blood oozing from between the stitches. "I ripped the stitches making my escape. I tried sewing them shut again, but they keep popping open." He let out a hysterical laugh at that, like what he'd said was the funniest thing in the world and not nightmare fuel.

"Escape?" I whispered.

"Don't play coy, Roz. It doesn't suit you. The guy you sent told me your deal before he knocked me out."

I shook my head in disbelief, but he didn't seem to notice.

"I woke up in a cold room. Naked. Strapped to a bed. At first I thought I was in a hospital, that I was safe. That that man who had attacked me hadn't been able to finish the job. Turned out, he wasn't sent to kill me, and I was far from safe. The only reason why I wasn't dead yet was because they hadn't planned for me. They needed time to auction off my body parts."

He took another step closer. "The only reason why I'm not long dead is because they wanted to get the best price for my heart."

Dizziness washed over me as I remembered Katherine Prescott's words. *"We're not in the business of simply killing people . . ."*

I'd believed that Lenny had killed Ben. But the truth was far worse.

The horror must have shown on my face, because Ben hesitated. Then he shook his head. "Unfortunately for you, the drug they used to put me under was the weak shit. They didn't take into account that I had built up a tolerance. I escaped a few nights ago. I've been laying low. Biding my time."

A few nights ago . . . was that the breach that Katherine Prescott's bodyguard had been talking about at the gala?

"I had nothing to do with—"

"Don't you *dare* pretend you weren't the one who sent him." He pointed the gun at me.

"I didn't!" I said quickly. I fumbled over my next words. "I was a victim too!" I showed him my prosthesis. "They took my hand."

"You sold it to them. Just like you sold me to them."

I shook my head back and forth, stopping suddenly when vertigo slammed into me. I took a few deep breaths.

I was out of options. I shouldn't have come here alone. I should have woken Jace and brought him with me. He would have protected me. I squeezed my eyes shut, both to fight the dizziness and to not have Ben's horrifying face be the last thing I saw. Instead, I pictured Jace's copper swirls as I waited for Ben to finish me off.

The slam of the front door opening had my eyes whipping open. It was Jace. "Put down the gun," he shouted, aiming his own weapon at Ben.

Jace surveyed the room. He saw me, then he saw Gutierrez's body, and his mouth popped open in shock. He hesitated a split second too long. Ben swung his gun around. One, two, three shots fired. Jace collapsed onto the ground.

"No!" I screamed. I lunged for Ben.

He hadn't been expecting that. He fell under my weight, and together we collapsed to the floor. I tried to pry the gun from his hand, but his grip was too strong, my nondominant hand too weak, so I kneed him in the stomach, right in the vicinity of his wound. He wailed, swinging around, slamming the gun against my head.

I fell off him with a grunt. My head hurt, but the Ryofen must have curbed the pain. I scrambled to my feet.

"You fucking bitch!" Ben screamed. He clutched his side as blood seeped through his shirt.

I ran toward Jace, who lay on the ground, an alarmingly substantial pool of blood collecting around him. He'd been shot in the chest. He was still. Too still. I fell to my knees, pressing my hand against the wound. But the blood had slowed to a trickle. His eyes were open. Unseeing.

Dead.

A sob erupted from me. Jace was dead. And it was my fault.

A voice tore me from my thoughts. "All I did was love you."

Ben had risen, but he was swaying in place, one hand clutching his abdomen, the other holding the gun.

He was strangely calm. Resigned. Lethal. "Why couldn't you just love me the way I love you?"

He didn't wait for an answer. He raised his weapon and pointed it at me, his hand shaking uncontrollably as he cocked the gun. I raced out of the open door as a torrent of bullets chased after me.

69

I didn't stop running until I was half a dozen blocks away. I must have kept walking long after that, because when I snapped out of my stupor, I had no idea where I was or what time it was. It was still night. That much I could tell. I looked down at my hand, which was red and glistening like a candy apple. That was Jace's blood. I threw up behind a dumpster and leaned against it heavily. I didn't know where to go. Detective Gutierrez was dead. Ben was after me. I didn't want to think about Jace. I didn't want to picture his handsome face completely slack and lifeless. His warm brown eyes glazed over. I would never see his lopsided grin again.

Tears cascaded down my face, as pain squeezed my heart. I could call the police. But Detective Gutierrez had told me that she didn't trust the others. I wasn't sure if she had been planning on betraying me. Running through those last moments of her life, it could have gone either way. She was upset that I'd been lying to her, that I was keeping things from her, but that was a reasonable response. She might not have been dirty. She didn't trust her partner, and that meant that I couldn't either. I needed to think. I needed time to come up with a plan.

I started to shiver uncontrollably. I continued to walk, if only so I wouldn't freeze. I hesitated outside a bar as the urge to drown in warm whiskey came over me. But I had no money on me. I supposed that was a good thing. I couldn't afford to get drunk now anyway. If I started drinking, I was as good as dead.

I couldn't go to Jace's either. I wouldn't anyway, even if we'd gotten to the point in our relationship where we'd exchanged keys. I didn't want to be surrounded by his things, his scent, his memory. My guilt.

I felt around in my jeans pockets, looking for loose change. The sharp edge of a piece of cardstock pricked my finger. I pulled it out, holding it under a streetlamp to read it. It was Dr. Lavoie's business card.

"Can I borrow your cell phone?" I asked a tipsy co-ed who was leaving the bar.

"Fuck off," she said. Then she handed me her phone.

I eyed her as I dialed Dr. Lavoie's number. It rang ten times before she finally answered. "Hello?" her voice sounded muffled. She yawned.

"Hi, Doc. It's me, Roz."

"Is everything all right?" She was suddenly alert.

"No."

"Roz, whatever you're thinking of doing, it's not worth it. Everything will be clearer in the morning—"

"Don't worry, I'm not going to do anything like that. I'm in trouble. I need someplace to go."

"You can come to my place. Just for tonight. I have a spare bedroom you can use," she said.

"Are you sure? I don't want to get you in trouble."

She insisted I come to her place. She gave me her address, and since she lived on the other side of town, she said she'd pay for my taxi too.

Dr. Lavoie lived in a well-kept three-story home in Forest Glen. I couldn't stay there long. I didn't want to put her at risk. I thought I'd be fine for one night, but after that I'd have to come up with another plan to keep myself safe. Ben didn't know Dr. Lavoie, so he wouldn't think to look for me there.

She hurried down the walkway, holding her winter coat closed with one hand and a credit card in the other. She looked like she'd gotten dressed in a hurry. Her blouse was untucked, and her shoes were mismatched. She paid the cab driver.

"Where's your coat?" she asked. Without waiting for my answer, she shook her head and said, "Hurry, let's get in from the cold."

Inside, I noticed that the immaculate tidiness and cozy warmth of her office extended to her home as well. She ushered me into the living room, where with the flick of a switch, the fireplace was roaring.

"Would you like something hot to drink?"

"God yes," I said, taking a seat in front of the fire. "I like my coffee black."

Dr. Lavoie smiled, but it didn't reach her eyes, which were lit with concern. "I thought you might." She disappeared down the hall.

I tried to warm up, but my toes were like ice blocks. I stood and crept closer to the fire. My gaze wandered across the picture frames on the mantel. A photo of her and a ten-year-old girl. Did she have a daughter I hadn't known about?

I noticed there were no pictures of her husband. Although, if they were separated, it made sense that she would remove his photos. Perhaps she'd even burned them in this fireplace.

There was an award granted by the American Psychiatric Association for excellence of practice. There was a plaque commending her as a major donor for a charity.

The room went cold.

The American Health and Wellness Society.

She'd donated to the charity that had connections to the Company. Was it a coincidence? Or—

"Admiring my accomplishments?" Dr. Lavoie asked.

I jolted, spinning around, plastering a smile on my face. "Oh yes. The American Psychiatric Association. What an achievement."

Dr. Lavoie gave me a half smile. "Hardly. They were just commending me for doing my job. Have a seat."

I chewed on my lower lip as I refrained from glancing back at the certificate. It might mean nothing. It could just be a coincidence. But was I willing to bet my life on that? "I really can't stay," I began.

"Sit."

I swallowed, nodded, and then sat on the edge of the armchair by the fire. Dr. Lavoie angled her head as she took me in. Too late, I realized that, like with her office, my choice in seating might have given away what I was feeling. There were multiple options. There was a sofa. A love seat. A rocking chair angled beside the loveseat. And then, there was the lone armchair by the fire. The armchair I had chosen was set apart from the rest. According to what she'd said during that first session with her so long ago, this choice indicated that I was reluctant to be here. That I didn't trust her.

That I suspected she wasn't who she said she was.

Dr. Lavoie didn't say a thing as she handed me the mug.

"Thank you," I said. I made a show of cooling it with my breath.

"Do you want to tell me why you're here?" Dr. Lavoie asked as she settled onto the sofa. Her eyebrows creased together. "Is that blood?"

Jace's blood was still on me. My breathing hitched. "Oh, no it's just—it's nothing."

My eyes were glued to her hands. She held her own mug of steaming hot coffee in her left hand. Her delicate yet muscular hand. A hand with slender fingers, and long, oval nails, with round nailbeds. A hand that she told me had painted long ago, and that she had stopped for no apparent reason. A hand that now suddenly looked like it could be mine.

Dr. Lavoie was watching me silently. "It doesn't look like nothing."

"What?" I couldn't focus on the conversation. Everything was falling into place. I'd felt the killer chopping vegetables, and Dr. Lavoie told me she loved to cook. She wrote with large curlicue writing, which I'd felt my hand do on multiple occasions. The Phantom Strangler had taunted me, but she hadn't reached out to me often. Was it because she was seeing me twice a week? But the killer had sent me a text message during one of our sessions! It couldn't have been Dr. Lavoie. I sighed with relief.

"Have you been drinking, Roz?" she asked.

"No."

"Still on the Ryofen?"

"Yes."

"No dizzy spells or hallucinations?"

The way she worded it seized my attention. I had been having dizzy spells and hallucinations, always in quick succession. The portrait that had moved in her office had been preceded by the first time I'd had a dizzy spell. With my mom, I'd had dizzy spells just before each time I interacted with her. The grotesque face on the bus, the tattoos on Lowell's neck. Every time I'd hallucinated, I'd had a dizzy spell not long beforehand. And earlier tonight? Just after Ben tore into my apartment and killed Detective Gutierrez? I'd had a dizzy spell. But what after that could I have imagined? Jace's death? I didn't dare to hope.

Dr. Lavoie was still waiting for my answer. "Nope," I said quickly.

"That's good to hear," she said with a smile. She sipped her coffee, watching me expectantly.

I didn't have time to dwell on my realization about the Ryofen and its side effects. I needed to focus on the present. I hadn't had a dizzy spell in over an hour. It was safe to assume what I was experiencing now was real.

My gaze crawled back to the mantel, confirming that the certificate was there, in black and white. Proof that she was involved with the phony charity that was a front for the Company.

I quickly looked away, hoping that Dr. Lavoie hadn't noticed my attention linger. I mimed taking a sip from my mug. "Mmm."

The Phantom Strangler had contacted me while I was in Dr. Lavoie's office. But there were ways to schedule texts, I was sure of it. You could schedule tweets and emails, so why couldn't you schedule texts? There must have been an app for it. The fact that I was texted while in Dr. Lavoie's office wasn't proof of her innocence.

"Have you heard from your mother lately?"

"No." I glanced up at her face, which gave away nothing.

She couldn't have known my mother was dead, could she? A sudden chill infiltrated the warmth of the room. I'd filled out detailed paperwork at Dr. Bohmer's office for the research team. I'd lied about some things and omitted others in the paperwork. But had I mentioned that my mother died from liver failure? If I had, as my psychiatrist, Dr. Lavoie would have undoubtedly received a copy. Had she known that my mother was dead all along?

"How are you dealing with Hanna's death?" she asked.

I froze. There was something in her tone that I just couldn't place. Then, I understood. I'd been spending more time with my roommate. I had even canceled an appointment with Dr. Lavoie. She had probably taken care of my roommate, hoping I'd come running to her for comfort. And I had.

"I—I'm all right," I managed to get out. "We weren't that close anyway." Dr. Lavoie watched me with unreadable eyes. I could try to overpower her and escape, but if she was the Phantom Strangler, she could easily take me. If she wasn't, I would be rudely tossing aside the only person I had left.

I gestured toward the far wall, which was adorned with several landscape oil paintings. "Those are beautiful."

"Thank you." She looked at them appraisingly. "Those were from my Impressionist stage."

"You painted them? I totally forgot that you're an artist," I lied.

"Yes, well, I work mostly in oils, but occasionally I sketch. Though lately I have been inspired to try my hand at sculpture. That was your art form of choice, correct?"

"I—Yes."

"I tried molding something out of clay. Turned out that I don't have a knack for it." She shrugged daintily. "Turns out that my talents lie elsewhere."

My stomach dropped as I thought of those nights I'd attempted to mold clay myself. I'd thrown the sculpting knife across the room. I'd never told her about it, not once during our sessions together. Had she been watching me? Was she taunting me? Or was I overreacting from lack of sleep and the stress of everything that had happened tonight?

I casually placed the coffee mug on a little wooden table at my side.

"Please use a coaster," she said. "And you should drink that. It will warm you up."

"I shouldn't be drinking coffee, but thank you," I said. "I'm on Ryofen, remember?"

"Right. Caffeine or alcohol can interact with the drug, causing dizzy spells and hallucinations."

I nodded, sharply. "I should be going."

Her brows were furrowed with concern. "I have a room you can stay in. It's always set up in case of an unexpected visitor."

"That's smart," I said. I couldn't think of an excuse. "I—thank you." I followed her up the stairs, down the hall, and into a guest room. The walls were a lemon yellow. The furniture seemed Victorian. Everything was in its place. A line of twelve porcelain dolls sat on a chest below the window.

"Cute," I said, gesturing to the dolls. *Cute* wasn't the right word. *Creepy* was more like it.

"Thank you," Dr. Lavoie said. "I made them myself. It's just a little hobby to pass the time." She shrugged. "There are some spare clothes in the drawers. There should be something suitable that you can sleep in."

"Great, thank you," I replied. I didn't turn around. There was no way I was letting her out of my sight.

"Please do let me know if you need anything." She hovered in the doorway.

I made a show of yawning wide. "I will, thank you."

As soon as she left down the hall, I closed the door. There was no lock. I looked around the room, but I couldn't find anything close enough to push in front of the door. I ran to the window. Of course, there was no tree, no trellis to climb down. Just a long, two-story drop to the cold, hard ground.

The porcelain dolls watched me with lifelike glass eyes. A blond doll, second on the far right, caught my attention. I inched closer to it. With ice-blond hair and cool blue eyes, it wore a slinky red dress and an innocent smile. My breath caught.

It looked just like Hanna.

My eyes roved over the others. Tessa. Pauline. Tillie. All victims of the Phantom Strangler.

Any trace of doubt in my mind was gone.

Dr. Lavoie was the Phantom Strangler. And I'd fallen into her trap.

I ran to the dresser and flung open the drawers. They were empty except for a few folded items of clothing. There was nothing in this damn room that I could use as a weapon. I would have to run. I tiptoed to the bedroom door and pulled it open.

Dr. Lavoie stood inches away from me. I shrieked, jumping backward.

"I noticed there's something off about you tonight, Roz," she said, her tone and expression pleasant. "Ordinarily, you're not exactly the picture of politeness and etiquette, yet you said thank you to me almost a dozen times tonight."

"Um, that's because I'm grateful," I said. I cut myself off before I could thank her yet again.

Intent eyes watched me with a hint of curiosity mixed with anticipation. "Oh, Roz. I too am grateful. I'm grateful for the time I've spent with you this past month and a half. But, most of all, I'm grateful for your sacrifice." She flexed her left hand—my hand—and gazed upon it admiringly. "Without it, I would not have been reborn. The world would have been deprived of my renaissance."

I wasn't sure what she meant by that, but it looked like all pretense was off. "Why did you reach out to me afterward? Why couldn't you just leave me the fuck alone?"

She looked taken aback. "I'm a Keeper. It's my job, you see. I've been watching over Donors for almost a decade, making sure they stayed quiet, doing my part. Then, when I was in need after a particularly feisty subject of mine slammed a car door on my hand, damaging the nerves beyond the repair of even their most advanced healing technology . . . well, they delivered." She cocked her head. "I wanted to be close to you. To get to know you. Had you not suffered phantom limb pain, I still would have found a way.

Perhaps I would have moved into your building. Or maybe I would have impersonated a collector and feigned interest in your pathetic excuse for art." Her chuckle grated on my heart. "Honestly, you should be thanking me. Your passion for art never could make up for your lack of talent. But now? Now you will be a part of something greater. First, by providing me with the tool I needed to create my brilliance. And now? You're the final piece."

"I trusted you," I spat.

She smirked. "I suppose if you hadn't, success wouldn't have tasted so sweet. Your trust made my work so much more . . . inspired."

"You're messed up." I took a step backward. She was blocking the hall. The window was looking like a better choice.

Her mouth flickered into the semblance of a frown. "If anyone should understand, it's you, Roz."

She took another step closer.

I needed to distract her. "Understand? You're psychotic. You killed Hanna," I said, my voice cracking.

She shrugged. "That was not a hardship. She fit my preferred artistic medium quite brilliantly. Besides, Hanna was not the only person I killed for you."

"W-what?"

"Call me selfish, but I wanted to keep you all to myself. After you made your sacrifice, I watched you. I followed you. I planned how my artwork would unfold. Then, I found out that you were about to be brought into the Company. That they wanted to bring you into the fold as a Negotiator. I didn't want to lose you. I . . . panicked." She looked thoughtful for a moment. "I've never killed on instinct like that before. It was invigorating."

I blinked rapidly, staring up at her. "Lenny?" I breathed.

She cocked her head. "The Negotiator. I thought that dead end would stop you from digging around the Company and halt your quest for answers. Keep you isolated and alone and all mine. I suppose I hadn't realized just how relentless you are." She leaned forward, the hint of a manic smile on her lips. "But I'm relentless too."

She took another step closer to me, and I realized she was quickly cornering me. "I stabbed him. It was different from my usual work. Messy. I liked it. It almost made me consider changing mediums, but I'm a creature of habit, even if this little cat-and-mouse game we've been playing has put me on edge. Made me escalate things. Improvise. Your impatience and recklessness are contagious. The anticipation became impossible to resist. I had to move up my timeline. Yet still, you're pushing me to my limits. I hadn't intended to finish this tonight, but you've left me with no choice." She grinned down at me. "I don't mind."

I swallowed. "I'm pretty scrappy in a fight. You really don't want to mess with me." I glanced around. I needed a weapon. Anything to ward her off.

Dr. Lavoie inclined her head. "The police were wrong about so many things. Do you truly think I would attack my victims from behind? No. I want their faces painted with shock as I grip my hands tightly around their lives. I mold their expressions into ones of pain and horror, emotions that last for an eternity, far beyond the deaths of their mortal bodies. It is this startling and cruel honesty that sets my art apart from the rest."

This wasn't the first time she'd mentioned her "art," but her words finally sank in. "So, what? This is all some kind of performance art? You're batshit crazy."

She smiled. "I knew you'd understand." Her eyes developed a faraway look, as though she was gazing past me. "When you first came to me, you were in so much pain. I knew in that moment that you would be one of mine. That I would carve anguish and destruction into your delicate features. I knew you would become the most exquisite piece. My finest yet. A true masterpiece," she added softly. She closed the space between us, reaching out with my hand. Frozen in fear, I let her place the hand that had once been mine loosely at the base of my neck. The palm was cradled by my collarbone, with the fingers and thumb on opposite sides of my neck. "Your heart is racing," she murmured. She tightened my fingers around my throat.

The realization struck me. I had a weapon. I'd just forgotten about it. It had become a part of me.

I faked moving backward, instead leaning forward and swinging my left arm around with all the strength I could muster. The crack when my prosthetic hand hit her head was deafening. She stumbled backward, hitting the wall, knocking down a framed landscape painting.

I gasped for breath as I dashed out the doorway. Footsteps resounded behind me. Fear nipped at my heels as I sped along the hallway and down the stairs. I reached the front door, unlocked it with fumbling fingers, and swung it open. I launched forward, slamming into something large and warm.

I shrieked, jumping backward.

It was Jace.

"Where is she?" he asked, his expression tense, yet alert.

Wordlessly, I pointed up the stairs. Dr. Lavoie stood at the top, her eyes wild with frustration and desperation. In an instant, she wiped all emotion from her face, replacing it with a cold and calculating intensity. Her lips dipped into a frown. "This isn't over."

She disappeared down the hall, like a phantom. Jace chased after her before I could yell at him to stop.

I reeled with shock. Jace had been shot. Three times, in the chest. I'd cried over his lifeless eyes, eyes that would haunt me for the rest of my days. He was *dead*. How could he be here?

He reappeared at the top of the stairs.

"Where is she?" Two uniformed police officers appeared in the doorway behind me.

"She got away," Jace told them. "She climbed out a window where she deployed an emergency ladder. She's heading east. Hurry, before she vanishes."

The two police officers peeled out of there, barely giving me a second glance.

Jace descended the stairs and pulled me into his arms. "She won't make it far," he murmured.

Tears rolled down my cheeks. "I thought you were dead."

He cupped my chin in his hand. "I thought *you* were dead."

I pulled backward, my eyes and hand roaming across his chest. His shirt wasn't bloody. There were no holes, no signs that he'd been near fatally wounded. "I don't understand. You were shot. There was so much blood. How—"

"Are you still on the Ryofen?"

I blinked up at him.

His jaw clenched. "I guess that's my answer," he said quietly. "I woke up on the couch, and you were gone. I checked your apartment, and I found the detectives, dead—"

"Wait, detectives? More than one?"

"Gutierrez and Borgnino," he replied.

It hadn't been Jace that I'd seen get shot, but Borgnino. I'd known I'd had the dizzy spell beforehand. I'd had another hallucination. It made sense. I'd been missing my mother before I had a dizzy spell and hallucinated her back into my life. I'd been looking for answers before I'd felt woozy, then hallucinated Lowell's tattoos. I'd been wishing for Jace to be there with me when I'd had a dizzy spell, so when Borgnino showed, my Ryofen-addled brain took care of the rest.

"The place was swimming with cops. They'd arrested someone—some maniac who confessed to killing the detectives, said he wanted to kill you." His voice broke on the last word as his eyes searched my face.

"My ex," I said.

He nodded. "You sure know how to pick 'em."

I let out a bark of laughter. I'd never felt so happy to see anyone in my entire life. I'd believed wholeheartedly that he was dead, but now he was here, alive, cracking jokes and indulging me with his beautiful, crooked grin. I had a second chance. I would not fuck it up this time.

"It had felt so real," I said to him. "I thought I lost you." A realization niggled at me. I'd been drinking alcohol tonight before taking the Ryofen. The time before that, I'd drank alcohol at the gala before taking a pill and seeing Lowell. I'd been drinking nonstop when I conjured up my mother, until the end, when I'd sobered up and I'd started to see cracks in her shiny veneer, even before Hanna pulled the wool from my eyes. "It was the alcohol and the Ryofen together. It was an interaction." I remembered how Dr. Bohmer had told me not to take Ryofen with caffeine or alcohol. That it could raise the likelihood of the rarer side effects, which were dizzy spells and hallucinations.

Jace angled his head. "Causing the hallucinations?"

I nodded, then bit my lip. I couldn't be one hundred percent sure, but I did know one thing for certain. Jace's death was going to be my last hallucination. When I got home, I would dump the Ryofen down the toilet. I would chain myself to a radiator like a werewolf during a full moon before I'd let myself touch that drug ever again.

"How did you know where to find me? How did you know I was in danger here?" I asked, already feeling lighter after making this decision.

"While I was asleep, I got a text from Jules. She found someone who'd bought that same gold claddagh necklace at a jewelry store downtown. It fit the time frame perfectly. She'd used her credit card. I recognized her name as your shrink." Jace pulled me closer. "Jules texted me an address, and I drove here faster than I'd ever thought possible. The police had a hard time keeping up."

I smiled up at him. "Sounds like you have a lead foot."

Jace gave me his crooked grin. "Actually, it's carbon fiber."

I rolled my eyes, then glanced out the window as more police cars pulled up to the curb, their flashing red and blue lights filling the room. I had the flash drive, and with it the evidence that would take down the Company. The Phantom Strangler had been identified, and it was just a matter of time before she was caught and arrested. My eyes found their way back to Jace. Everything was coming to an end. Well, not everything.

"You're still on the Ryofen," he said with a frown.

"Tonight was my last dose. I swear it." This time I meant it with every fiber of my being, but I knew that my resolve would only last so long. I couldn't do this on my own. "I'm also quitting drinking." My cheeks flamed red. This was the first time I'd admitted out loud that I had a problem. "But I think I might need help," I added in a small voice. Dr. Lavoie might have been a psychopath and a serial killer, but I'd learned a few things from my sessions with her. First and foremost was that I would need a support network if I was going to overcome my demons. I couldn't do it alone. And, for the first time in a long time, I wasn't alone anymore.

His eyes searched mine, and he nodded slowly.

The two policemen reappeared in the doorway, wrenching us from our heartfelt moment. "We lost her."

My heart plummeted. "No!"

Jace cupped my chin gently, drawing my attention back to him. "She'll be caught," he said with such conviction I barely had the nerve to question him.

"How can you be so sure?"

"Because she won't be able to stop killing. And she won't be able to stay away from you."

She'd called me her masterpiece. I kept that to myself as I shuddered.

"You're her weakness, Roz. She'll reach out to you; she won't be able to help herself. And when she does? The FBI will be waiting in the wings with handcuffs and a lifetime supply of prison soap."

I basked in the warmth of his confidence, but he must not have been convinced of my trust in him.

"We'll get through this. Together."

"Together," I repeated, warmth filling my chest as I lost myself in his copper swirls. A smile flirted across my lips.

He leaned in and kissed me.

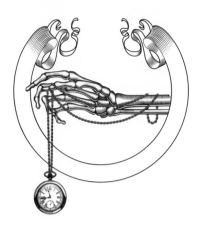

I LOUNGE ON THE BEACH CHAIR, martini in hand, watching the sun set over the Atlantic Ocean. The sky explodes in pinks and reds over the foamy blue water that crashes onto the sandy beach that I have all to myself. When the vibrant colors begin to fade into darkness, I shake the sand off my towel and wrap it around my body. I languorously stroll back up to the resort.

"Senora, how was the sunset?" a bellhop asks as I pass.

"Perfection," I say with a small smile. I tip him, even though he's done nothing more than greet me pleasantly every evening.

Back in my luxury suite, I find a stack of stationery in the desk drawer. I pen a short note. It is to the point, with no puns, because I've been told that puns are the lowest form of humor.

Newspapers lie on the desk beside my letter. *The New York Times* headline tells of an international organ-trafficking operation that has been exposed, thanks to the work of one of their victims and a private investigator. Beside it, there is a local newspaper. It's open to an article about a young woman who was found washed ashore on a private beach in Varadero. The cause of death was strangulation.

I carefully cut out this article and include it with the note. I seal it with a kiss.

This is the first of many letters I plan to send to that shabby loft apartment in Chicago. I smile as I imagine the reaction this letter will get from its recipient. The expression of horror and guilt that will forever be chiseled into those beautiful features. My finest work. A masterpiece.

I may be gone, but I will not be forgotten. I am the Phantom.

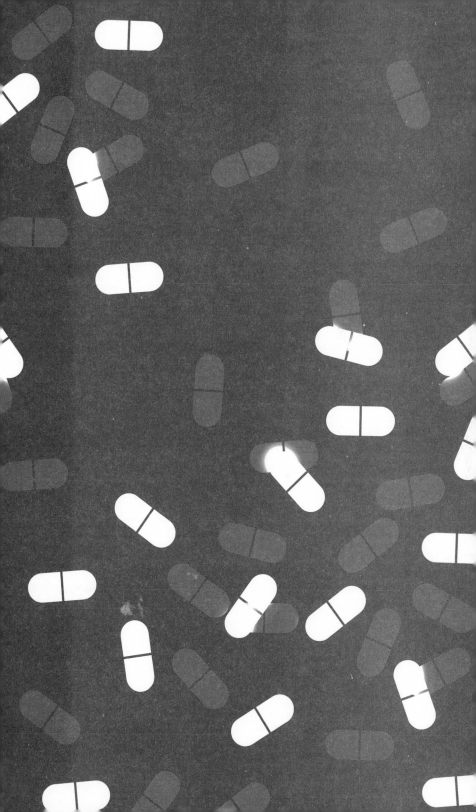

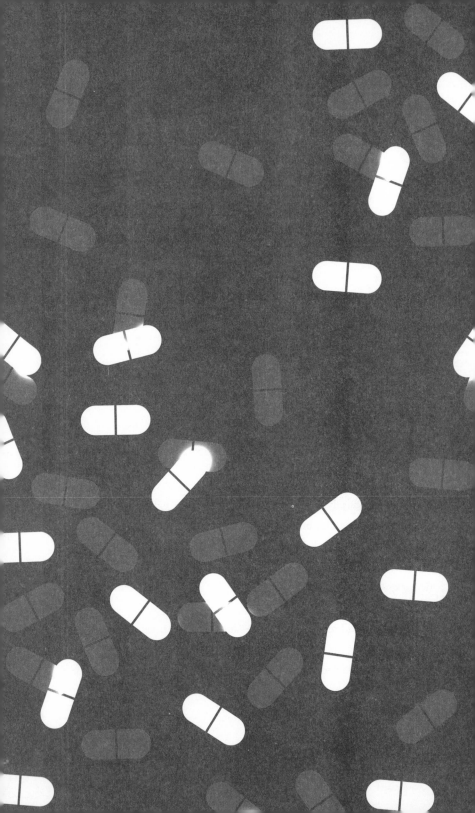

ABOUT THE AUTHOR

Helen Power's very first story featured a vampire that liked to stab unsuspecting princesses with needles, despite having a perfectly functional set of fangs. Even though she was only seven when she wrote this story, this massive plot hole has haunted her to this day. Since then, she has had several short story publications, including ones in *Suspense Magazine* and Dark Helix Press's Canada 150 anthology, "Futuristic Canada." Her stories range from comedy to horror, with just a hint of dystopia in between. Her debut novel, *The Ghosts of Thorwald Place*, won gold in the IBPA's Benjamin Franklin Awards for Best New Voice: Fiction. *Phantom* is her second novel.

She's an academic librarian living in Saskatoon, Canada. Her education is all over the map. She has degrees in forensic science, environmental studies, and library science collecting dust in the corner of her closet. This eclectic background has helped with both her job and with her writing, though she rarely has to conduct criminal investigations in her role at the library.

She is an avid reader of all genres and publishes book reviews weekly. In her spare time, she haunts deserted cemeteries, loses her heart to dashing thieves, and cracks tough cases, all from the comfort of her reading nook.

ACKNOWLEDGMENTS

I stumbled across the idea for *Phantom* during my day job. I'm a librarian at a university. At the time, I was working as a liaison for the School of Nursing, which meant that I taught classes on research skills, managed the collection in this subject area, and helped students find resources for their assignments. Typically, undergraduate students in nursing pick topics that are all variations of the same research question. After a while, it gets tedious, and the consultations all bleed into one another. But then one rainy day, a student dropped by my office. She was researching something unique. She was interested in phantom limb pain and the use of mirror therapy to treat it. I was immediately fascinated by the concept. After she was gone (I'm pretty sure I remembered to help her), I read a few journal articles on this topic—about the elasticity of the brain, and how neurons can essentially be rewired to the intact limb. Almost immediately the idea of Roz and her predicament took form. What if you didn't lose your limb in an accident, but you sold it? What if it was being used by someone else? What if you could feel what they were doing with your hand? What if they were using it to *kill*?

Shortly afterward, I whipped up a first draft of *Phantom* during National Novel Writing Month. (I reached 72,000 words in one month!) This is the second NaNoWriMo novel that I've published, and I'm hopeful it won't be the last. Thank you to this incredible non-profit organization for providing a forum for people like me to write our weird and disturbed little hearts out!

I'd also like to thank my family. My mom, who's always the very first person to read my work and is always the first person to worry about the darkness of my stories and what that says about her as a mother. When I'm visiting home, she gives me the side eye at the dinner table before hiding the steak knives. Thank you to my dad for being an accidental reader of an early draft of this book. He'd gone onto my mom's computer after I asked him to read my first book, *The Ghosts of Thorwald Place*, and instead he read this one. I was mortified, because I did not want him to meet the broken and caustic Roz. But he loved her and the story and finished the book before I could inform him that he was reading the wrong one. Thank you to my sister, Alexandra, for giving me tons of feedback and for being the one to suggest I give Roz a cat. Thank you also to Uncle Alek and Aunt Antoinette for always being staunch supporters.

Thanks to all my friends—both in-person and online buddies—for saying they loved the premise of my book before I even found a home for it. Thank you to my writing friends—Amanda, Tori, and Jill—for listening to me ramble on and on about God only knows what. I wrote this book while I was living in Windsor, Ontario, so I'd like to thank my writing friends from there—Alison, Lexie, Sebastien, Cindy, Susan, and Celia. I miss y'all right now just as much as I missed you when writing this part of the acknowledgments for *Ghosts*!

Thank you to the Saskatchewan Writers Guild for their great programming, including the virtual write-ins where I worked on edits for *Phantom*, wrote these acknowledgments, and met some fantastic local writers!

To all my friends, family members, and coworkers who read *Ghosts* and gave me kind words: I hear you. Thank you so much for your support and I promise I won't kill you off in my next novel, even if you do something to irritate me in the meantime.

I'd like to thank the CamCat team who made this book the shiny, polished gem you're holding in your hands, including, but not limited to Kayla,

Helga, and Bill. Thank you for tolerating Roz and bringing her story into the world. A special shout out to Maryann Appel who designed the chilling, yet elegant cover. Because of her design, I decided to make the Ryofen pill a milky white.

To Rachel Fulginiti: Thank you for your dynamic audiobook performance of *The Ghosts of Thorwald Place*! I can't wait to hear your interpretation of my cantankerous heroine. To Eunice Wong: I'm looking forward to feeling chills chase each other down my spine as I listen to you bring my arrogant serial killer to life!

And last but not least, thank you to you, the intrepid reader! If you enjoyed this dark and twisty thriller, please consider leaving a review on social media, your blog, or carved into my front door.

ALSO BY
HELEN POWER

The Ghosts of Thorwald Place

If you liked Helen Power's *Phantom*,
consider leaving a review to help our authors.

And check out
Brendon K. Vayo's *Girl Among Crows*.

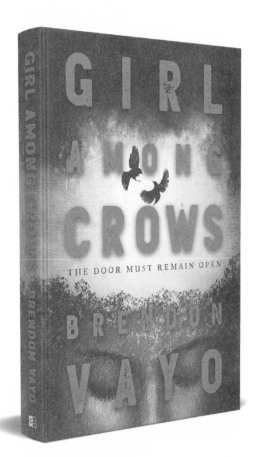

CHAPTER ONE
April 22, 2021

My husband Karl shakes hands with other doctors, a carousel of orthopedic surgeons in cummerbunds. I read his lips over the brass band: *How's the champagne, Ed?* Since he grayed, Karl wears a light beard that, for the convention, he trimmed to nothing.

The ballroom they rented has long windows that run along Boston's waterfront. Sapphire table settings burn in their reflections.

The food looks delicious. Rainbows of heirloom carrots. Vermont white cheddar in the macaroni. Some compliment the main course, baked cod drizzled with olive oil. My eyes are on the chocolate cherries. Unless Karl is right, and they're soaked in brandy.

At some dramatic point in the evening, balloons will drop from nets. A banner sags, prematurely revealing its last line.

Celebrating Thirty Years!

Thirty years. How nice, though I try not to think that far back.

I miss something, another joke. Everyone's covering merlot-soaked teeth, and I wonder if they're laughing at me. Is it my dress? I didn't know if I should wear white like the other wives.

I redirect the conversation from my choice of a navy-blue one-shoulder, which I now see leaves me exposed, and ask so many questions about the latest in joint repair that I get lightheaded.

The chandelier spins. Double zeroes hit the roulette table. A break watching the ocean, then I'm back, resuming my duties as a spouse, suppressing a yawn for an older man my husband desperately wants to impress. A board member who could recommend Karl as the next director of clinical apps.

I'm thinking about moving up, our careers. I'm not thinking dark thoughts like people are laughing or staring at me. Not even when someone taps me on the shoulder.

"Are you Daphne?" asks a young man. A member of the wait staff.

No one should know me here; I'm an ornament. Yet something's familiar about the young man's blue eyes. Heat trickles down my neck as I try to name the sensation in my stomach.

"And you are?" I say.

"Gerard," he says. The glasses on his platter sway with caffeinated amber. "Gerard Gedney. You remember?"

I gag on my ginger ale.

"My gosh, I *do*," I say. "*Gerard*. Wow."

Thirty years ago, when this convention was still in its planning stages, Gerard Gedney was the little boy who had to stay in his room for almost his entire childhood. Beginning of every school year, each class made Get Well Soon cards and mailed them to his house.

We moved before I knew what happened to Gerard, but with everything else, I never thought of him until now. All the growing up he must've done, despite the odds, and now at least he got out, got away.

"I beat the leukemia," he says.

"I'm so glad for you, Gerard."

If that's the appropriate response. The awkwardness that defined my childhood creeps over me. Of all the people to bump into, it has to be David Gedney's brother. David, the Boy Never Found.

My eyes jump from Gerard to the other wait staff. They wear pleated dress pants. Gerard's in a T-shirt, bowtie, and black jeans.

"I don't really work here, Daphne," says Gerard, sliding the platter onto a table. "I've been looking for you for a while."

The centerpiece topples. Glass shatters. An old woman holds her throat.

"Gerard," I say, my knees weak, "I understand you're upset about David. Can we please not do this here?"

Gerard wouldn't be the first to unload on what awful people we were. But to hear family gossip aired tonight, in front of my husband and his colleagues? I can't even imagine what Karl would think.

"I'm not here about my brother," says Gerard. "I'm here about yours." His words twist.

"Paul," I say. "What about him?"

"I'm so sorry," says a waiter, bumping me. Another kneels to pick up green chunks of the vase. When I find Gerard again, he's at the service exit, waiting for me to follow.

Before I do, I take one last look at the distinguished men and a few women. The shoulder claps. The dancing. Karl wants to be in that clique—I mean, I want that too. For him, I want it.

But I realize something else. They're having a good time in a way I never could, even if I were able to let go of the memory of my brother, Paul.

The catering service has two vans in the alleyway. It's a tunnel that feeds into the Boston skyline, the Prudential Center its shining peak. Gerard beckons me to duck behind a stinky dumpster. Rain drizzles on cardboard boxes.

I never knew Gerard as a man. Maybe he has a knife or wants to strangle me, and all this news about my brother was bait to lure me out here. I'm vulnerable in high heels. But Gerard doesn't pull a weapon.

He pulls out a postcard, its edges dusty with a white powder I can't identify. The image is of three black crows inscribed on a glowing full moon.

"I found it in Dad's things," says Gerard. "Please take it. Look, David is gone. We've got to live with the messes our parents made. Mine sacrificed a lot for my treatment, but had they moved to Boston, I probably would've beaten the cancer in months instead of years."

"And this is about Paul?" I say.

"When the chemo was at its worst," says Gerard, "I dreamed about a boy, my older self, telling me I would survive."

I take my eyes off Gerard long enough to read the back of the postcard: *$ from Crusher. Keep yourself pure, Brother. For the sake of our children, the Door must remain open.*

Crusher. Brother. Door. No salutation or signature, no return address. Other than Crusher, no names of any kind. The words run together with Gerard's take on how treatment changed his perspective.

Something presses my stomach again. Dread. Soon as I saw this young man, I knew he was an omen of something. And when is an omen good?

"Your dad had this," I say. "Did he say why? Or who sent it?"

An angry look crosses Gerard's face. "My dad's dead," he says. "So's Brother Dominic. Liver cancer stage 4B on Christmas Day. What'd they do to deserve that, huh?"

"They both died on Christmas? Gerard, I'm so sorry." First David, now his dad and Dominic? He stiffens when I reach for him, and, of course, I'm the last person he wants to comfort him. "I know how hard it is. I lost my mom, as you know, and my dad ten years ago."

The day Dad died, I thought I'd never get off the floor. I cried so hard I threw up, right in the kitchen. Karl was there, my future husband, visiting on the weekend from his residency. I didn't even think we were serious, but there he was, talking me through it, the words lost now, but not the comfort of his voice. I looked in his eyes, daring to hope that with this man I wouldn't pass on to my children what Mom passed down to me.

"Mom's half-there most days," says Gerard. "But one thing."

The rear entrance bangs open, spewing orange light. Two men dump oily garbage, chatting in Spanish.

"Check the postmark, Daphne," says Gerard at the end of the alleyway. He was right beside me. Now it's a black bird sidestepping on the dumpster, its talons clacking, wanting me to feed it. I flinch and catch Gerard shrugging under the icy rain before he disappears.

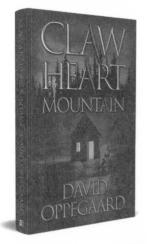
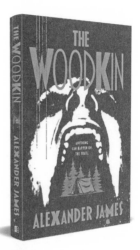